THE ALBATROSS

Dorothy Field

First Edition - December 2011

ISBN 978 0 9570957 0 0

© 2011 M & D Field , ALLOA, FK10 1TF

Produced by Banbury Litho Ltd.,
Banbury, OX16 9UX

List of Illustrations

Cover - Figurehead of sailing ship Glenlee, The Clyde Maritime Trust. Photograph © M. J. Field 2011

Special thanks to :
Roni McGrath and Barbara Halliburton for reading and commenting on early drafts,
and to
Dr Christopher Mason, Chairman of Clyde Maritime Trust,
for encouragement and advice

LYDIA

Chapter One

Poole January 1874

The quayside at Poole was its usual hive of activity on the Thursday morning that I ran away. Two ships near to the Harbour Office were carrying loads of timbers for the saw mills. The covers to the large holds were open, and huge lengths of timber were being levered up, roped together and hauled out of the holds of the brig Lady Anne and the brig Saucy Jane. Further down two other ships were tied up, laden with coals for the gasworks and Lewin's foundry. Huge circular rope baskets were being lowered deep into the darkness of the holds of these coal ships from the quayside derricks, where teams of dockers, deep in the ships were sweating and shovelling coal into the baskets for hauling up and disgorgement into the waiting horse drawn wagons which together with hand carts, constantly criss-crossed the busy harbour front.

Poole in 1874 was in economic depression; the Newfoundland salt cod trade having relocated its business to larger ships and the deeper harbours of the Bristol area. Poole was virtually bankrupt. Many of the mighty ships of Poole's former Newfoundland trade lay rotting in Holes bay, and Poole, with its large but shallow harbour was eking out a living on the transportation of stone from the famous Purbeck quarries, and the carriage of clay, pottery, coal, grain and timber cargoes. The once powerful and proud firm of Spurrier had been made bankrupt, and the mighty families of Joliffe, Rolles, Slade, Jeffrey, Lester and Garland found themselves facing hard times. Many of Poole's local ship owners were almost entirely reliant on the coal trade. In previous years, the town's feuding council, through ridiculous internal squabbles and foolish litigation had brought the town to its knees, and the failure of the Poole Town and County Bank in the early 1860's had ruined the town's economy, so that many Poole residents lived in dreary hardship and squalor, particularly in the narrow alleys and lanes close to the harbour front.

Against this depressing background, the entrepreneurship of some individuals was remarkable. The Lovejoys were enjoying better times. Captain William Lovejoy, late of his majesty King William 4th's navy, served during the Slave Wars of 1840-45, and made prize money, which his son Captain James Lovejoy invested into the purchase of a schooner, which he named the Daphne, and often referred to as his wooden goddess, and himself as her Apollo. He used the Daphne to ply for trade around Britain, Europe and North America, wherever profit was to be found, generally channelling his cargoes through the town of Poole. His home, which he referred to as 'the Poop Deck', was in a thin narrow building on the quayside, distinguished by an odd, bulbous shaped bay window on the first floor. When in port, he was often visible sitting at a little table in his window, writing in his ledgers, or gazing across the harbour with his telescope.

Visibility from the watery, January sun was good that day, and the slight early frost was clearing. Across the water, Captain Lovejoy's 'Daphne' lay moored, gently rising and falling in the placid harbour waters, its paint a cracked and peeling memoir of its adventures in the sun and seas of the southern oceans and the cold, swamping fury of the Atlantic seas. There was an epidemic of activity aboard, renewing rigging, replacing a whole mast, caulking decks, shouting and whistling.

Years later, I can still clearly remember the men's and horses' breath clouded white like pipe smoke in the chill air as I stepped across the rail lines and past the impatient horses, through the taut mooring ropes tied to the iron bollards and through the stinking rotting sludge on the boards at the quay's edge. The tide was high, and a fascinating carved woman at the prow of the Saucy Jane had attracted me. The figurehead's grotesque full breasts were hardly covered by a red dress, and on inspection, I was surprised to note that besides being crudely carved, she was only the top part of a person. Definitely a woman rather than a lady, I thought, as I looked past the timber edging of the quay into the slippy, sloppy water, which was its usual deep, opaque green, turbid with abundant filth. In the noise, I suddenly heard a man shouting, 'Come away from the water!' in a great voice developed to thunder orders and ensure obedience through darkness and tempest, and was terrified as he ran over to me.

'What you'm doing my maid?' he asked, only a little more quietly, gazing closely into my face, 'you aren't even dressed properly.' I was perplexed, not at all sure of how to reply. 'Silence is golden' mother often said, so I made no answer, but assessed from the form of his address and the fact that he was relatively clean and well dressed, that he must be someone who is in charge, who gives orders. Noticing blood on me, he asked 'What has happened to your face and hands my maid?' There were too many questions, too loud, too fast and too gruff. I started to cry, but as was usual for me, this was only part in fear, part expediency to give myself time to think. 'Wait a minute', he said 'aren't you Missis Teague's granddaughter?' I nodded. 'Haven't you a tongue in your head' he asked. I opened my mouth and poked my tongue out to show him -to test if he had an even temper. He laughed. By then I was beyond freezing, and actually very frightened. He quickly realized how very cold and frightened I was, despite what mother would have described as 'Lydia's nauseating self posses-sion'. Perhaps Captain Lovejoy was worried that he might have frightened me, as he was certainly very big, and at the age of four and a bit, I was small for my age. He unbuttoned his great thick navy jacket, picked me up, and held me against his chest, inside the coat. Taking a large hard thumb, he rasped the tears away from under my lower eyelids, and said 'If you aren't going to speak, I'd best take you to Missis Teague to get you warmed up and made shipshape'. He smiled, and feeling less afraid, I remembered seeing him before. He was my Grandfather's friend, Captain Lovejoy, and I was able to get a close look at his long black and grey hair, tied at the back of his neck, his beard and a waxed moustache as wide as the yardarm of his ship. I was very fright-ened of being taken back to mother, of what she might do, what grandmother might say and think and so I decided not speak, not to tell anyone why I had run away.

It had all started whilst I was in my bedroom. My brother Michael had taken himself to school, Eddie my baby brother was asleep and Ellen was rattling around downstairs in the scullery. Mother was arranging my long, curly chestnut hair. She seemed to be having problems keeping her balance and her breath smelt strongly of those violet breath lozenges she'd been using lately. She was so rough with the brush, scouring my head, yanking the tangles impatiently and shouting at me to keep still. My nose and eyes were running with the pain from my head. Mother bent down to fasten my shoes and was sick all over them and the hem of my white, starched pinafore. I felt that this was beyond disgusting, as being a small person at the time, I was very frightened of sick and its implications of loss of self control. I ran away. I ran into the garden, past St James's church, and tripped when my legs got mixed up in my long pinafore, and I grazed my face and hands. I went down to the waterfront where I was not allowed to go and resolved never to go back home again.

But Captain Lovejoy caught me. He smelled salty, and of clean air, and his jacket was hard. His arms kept the cold air off me, and I felt safe. I was glad to be going to Grandmother's shop. Grandmother was always gentle with me, and I loved her. Even so, I was very well aware that Grandmother would make me go home, because I wouldn't be able to tell her the truth.

Teague's grocery shop was one of the largest retail business-es in Poole, with a double frontage to the High Street and extensive premises at the rear. Very strangely, for those days, the names of both my grandparents were painted outside, E and C. Teague, High Class Provisions, Tea Merchant and Ships' Provisions. Even more unusually Grandfather Ethelred always gave Grandmother Lottie (Charlotte) full credit for her part in their purchase and the building of the business and its clientele. Outside in the street, there was always a delicious smell of fresh roasting coffee beans, and through the window, where jars of 'Military Pickle', tins of cocoa and 'Punch Sauce' were displayed, could clearly be seen the giant red painted wheel of a hand-operated coffee-mill. Inside the shop was bright, with a good light from the central gas mantles, and either side of the shop was flanked by cold, marble topped counters. There were always small displays of tins, bottles and jars carefully arranged on a central table to tempt discerning shoppers. Just in front of the serving counters, there were modern, fashionable bentwood chairs positioned sideways on, where customers might dictate their weekly orders to the assistants. Bessie, the senior 'girl' in the shop, aged about 50, was sitting on her stool behind the counter carefully transcribing an order from an extravagantly hatted lady into an order book, which had the top two sheets interleaved with deep blue carbon paper. Paraphernalia for cutting, weighing and wrapping cheese, butter covered by muslin, and a large hand cranked bacon slicing machine was arranged on the marble topped counters round the three sides of the shop. There were three male and one female assistant. Behind them, wooden shelves from floor to ceiling were stacked with large containers of useful ingredients - loose teas, flour, rice, sago, dried peas, and lentils and so on, ready to be weighed into little bags to suit customers' needs. At the bottom left hand corner of the shop was a small glass cubicle with a latching door where a bespectacled man was sitting on a wooden stool behind a hatch, ready to take money from any customers paying their bills or cash from those to whom no credit was extended. As credit payments were normally requested weekly or monthly, there was rarely much of a queue. Paid bills were put on to a bill hook at his right hand side, once they had been entered into the ledger. Bills for daily purchases were totted up, and accounts submitted to customers at agreed intervals.

Years later Grandmother said she was very concerned when James Lovejoy appeared in the shop that morning with me looking like a little frightened ghost in his arms, face and hands covered with dried blood and dirt, cold and without a coat or hat. This was her first presentiment that something was far from right in our family. The Captain, with me still in his coat, disturbed her at the back of the shop as she weighed up sultanas into the lovely purple blue bags she used, folding the tops in just so, to make tight, secure packages for customers' orders. 'Poor little cherub!' she said on seeing me 'Thank goodness you recognized her and brought her home to me, Captain James. Her mother must have been going wild with worry about her.' He replied 'I caught this maid at the harbour side of all places, looking into the water if you please! No coat on her. Can't get a word out of her – she is yours isn't she?' Obviously preoccupied, he rushed away closely followed by the large dog he called Cerberus, dog of Hades or something. Grandmother never allowed dogs in the shop, and felt the dog to be aptly named, nothing but a pack of trouble on shore. Captain James called out that he had business to do at the Harbour Office and the Shipping Office and was gone.

Grandmother took me through the back preparation area where Grandfather Ethelred cut the cheeses and boned the bacon. We walked through her own room and into the scullery, where the range was warm. Liza, her latest workhouse acquisition was learning household ironing under the tutelage of Lucy, the senior servant. She sat me on the draining board, whilst Lucy found warm water and clean rags for Grandmother to clean me up. By the time she'd finished – Lucy never needed telling, the tea tray was ready, and she took me, her precious darling little girl back into her room. Lucy knew that Mistress Teague always found a good cup of tea very calming. Just the ritual of laying a teaspoon into the saucer and poising the spout of the teapot over the cup seemed to relax her. Grandmother left me at the table, with one of her woollen shawls round me, warming my hands round my cup. She found Wesley, the delivery boy, who was still loading his handcart, and wrote a quick note to my mother, telling her not to worry, that Lydia was safe with her. I heard her telling Wesley that Mother had enough to do looking after young Eddie, the baby.

I refused to be drawn on why I ran away from home. Grandmother sighed. She seemed to understand that I had intelligence and awareness beyond my chronological years. 'I suppose Lydia' she said 'that in this instance I must just put what had happened down to some kind of jealousy of your new baby brother, but all the same, this behaviour just doesn't seem like you dear.' Years later, she admitted that when she went to visit Mary, my mother,the previous week she was white, seemed sleepy and her speech was slurred. At the time she had believed Mother's excuse that her condition was as a result of being kept awake most nights by young Eddie, with colic, plus the fact that she herself was suffering from a sick headache. Grandmother later confessed to me that she did not exactly regard herself as an authority on rearing children, having only ever had the one child, Mary, and that she had supposed Mother's behaviour to be reasonable.

I told Grandmother that I had eaten breakfast, and with a cup of tea and several biscuits in me, I felt fine and well, but denied being sick over my shoes! I cannot tell a lie. Grandmother said she supposed that little people like me do get distressed over things like this, and she tried to explain that things like this can happen to all of us sometimes, usually as a result of something we've eaten disagreeing with us. 'Could it happen from something a person drank?' I asked very seriously. 'Yes chick-a-biddy, of course it could' Grandmother replied. She decided to keep me home from school, on account of me having no coat, and being rather busy herself. She always said I was a really easy child, and very bright, as I had taught myself to read and write before school, so she gave me her copy of 'The Water Babies', which I was already familiar with, and looked very surprised when I said 'Grandmother, if you are like Mrs Doasyouwouldbedoneby, why does mother act like Mrs Bedonebyasyoudid towards me when I try so hard to be a good girl?'

References

Poole's economic status
Hillier J., 1985. Ebb tide at Poole, 1815-1851. Pub. Poole Historical Trust
Conditions on the Quay
Bristowe E., 1998. Poole was my Oyster

Chapter 2

I was five when it happened. Under Grandmother's instructions I was collected by Wesley, to walk straight home from Miss Squires's School, to the shop, but on that evening we had been naughty and made a deviation, using a route expressly forbidden to me by Mother. We went to the bottom of Market Street, and down to the harbour. It was a clear, very cold day, with no wind, and I and the fourteen year old Wesley observed the setting sun across the harbour, bright red, slowly bleeding into the sky and sea. That particular November afternoon was much like most other days in my early childhood in that I spent the time with Grandmother. I had been sitting on a very high wooden stool in the preparation room, a tiny booth at the back of the shop, at the opposite side to the stove, working with Grandmother and a set of scales. A huge wooden box had been delivered, and when Grandmother had prised it open with a crowbar, it had a great package inside, wrapped in greaseproof paper. She was very strong, and turned the heavy contents out on to the counter and unwrapped a huge, solid glistening lump of white lard. She had some squares of greaseproof paper in her drawer with 'E and C Teague, finest lard' printed on them. Grandmother positioned the paper on the weighing plate of the scales, cut neat slabs of lard, weighed them carefully, by watching how the beam of the scales tilted, gently adding and subtracting from the pieces to make an accurate pound, and showed me how to pull and fold the paper tight around each piece. These would later be put into customers' orders for delivery, or displayed on the marble counter tops for immediate sale. 'Always remember the importance of accurate weight' she said 'Too little robs the customer, and too much robs us of our living.'

I had been going to Miss Squires' school for a quite a while by then, rather young to have started at four, but I often heard mother describing me as 'a trial' and she told me privately that she was glad to 'get me off her hands'. I had read about trials in the newspaper, but didn't understand how I could be a trial myself, so

I asked Mother and had my head smacked, but when I asked Grandmother, what mother could have meant, she had replied 'your mother is beyond the wit of a woman such as I', so I was left with the impression that Grandmother didn't understand either. However, after this conversation, Grandmother had started sending Wesley the errand boy to fetch me back to the shop after school, to 'keep Lydia occupied' as she said to Mother. This followed my running away across the quay that January morning. Mother had boxed my ears for that after Grandmother had gone back home.

I lived with my family in a rented terraced house in Market Street. It had a kitchen and scullery, dining room, parlour and three bedrooms. My Mother was discontented with this perfectly respectable, large, comfortable house, and was always commenting to father that we must 'rise up the social ladder.' I was listening in as usual, and asked what the social ladder was, as it sounded most exciting, but was slapped by mother for impertinence. Grandmother later tried to explained this fascinating concept as 'rising from one's station in life', but I didn't really understand this either. In time however, I became very aware that mother was fairly well obsessed with 'social ladders', as the daughter of a shopkeeper on Poole High Street. This was despite the fact that many of her fellow citizens in Poole lived in abject poverty. In the poorer streets, often more than one family were packed into a single putrid room. Children lived day after day in the same stinking rags that passed as clothes, actually sewn on to their bodies in the winter. In these vile surroundings, young women with lank hair and rotting teeth sat on doorsteps (for lack of any furniture), smoking their pipes or plying gin bottles whilst breastfeeding their latest arrivals. The street air was fouled further by curses and the vilest language.

In contrast, my grandparents had progressed by sheer hard work, thrift and studying at Sunday School and in all of their spare time from being semi illiterate vegetable sellers located under the arches of the town cellars. Grandfather had even admitted that whilst he was a boy he had used the light in the church porch to study by on dark evenings, as he was too poor to buy a candle. Ethelred Teague had first rented, and then purchased a small shop. Eventually the family business of Ethelred and Charlotte Teague moved to larger premises and established one of the most exceptional shops on the High Street as family grocer and tea dealer, purveyors of rare foods, specialities plum jam three shillings and threepence per seven pound jar, mildly cured hams seven pence, seven pence ha'penny and eight pence. The shop supplied all the best houses in Poole and some in the surrounding area. My mother could have felt justifiably proud of her parents' achievements. Instead, Mother often remarked 'I agreed to marry your father as he was a man likely to become a gentleman'. She was telling the truth there. Doubtless she perceived marriage to father as a suitable escape from a life of helping in the shop, making jam with Grandmother and working with her on 'social projects'. Whatever her motives, it wasn't a marriage made in heaven, given that she and my father had, probably before the time of my arrival on the scene, developed opposite priorities within their marriage, which led to absolutely cringing embarrassments on many sides.

As an example, my father Daniel Curtis's family lived in the village of Longfleet, and his father was the verger at St Mary's Church. It was due to the good offices of the vicar that my father, who was apparently a most exceptional scholar, became articled to Charles Inkpen, who had an accountancy business on Poole High Street. His financial acumen, excellent manners and general amiability led to him being made a partner in the business by the age of 24. Father's surviving brother Mark, was simply delighted at his immense success and fine house in Market Street, as he and his wife lived in two rooms up at Longfleet village. Unfortunately, my Mother, Mary Curtis, was not similarly delighted with Father's family, and would pass his brother on the street, quickening her pace and looking into the sky. I can remember hearing my uncle say to my aunt, 'Oh dear, she never saw us', even though I was tugging at Mother's skirt and saying loudly 'Look Mother, its Uncle Mark!' On one occasion when our family were invited to

Sunday lunch with Uncle Mark, my mother engineered a headache, and the necessity of staying in bed. I felt particularly upset about this, as I was aware that Aunt Sally had been shopping expensively at Teague's shop, buying luxuries that even I didn't think she could afford, like coffee, dried fruit and cheese. In the end, Father bravely decided to go without Mother, and left Ellen, the 'cook general' in charge at home. In fact, Michael and I both liked going to Uncle Mark and Aunt Sal's, as they were so cheerful and happy. On his return home, Father was very angry with Mother behind the closed doors of their bedroom -Michael said I was a spy, and we both heard her scream 'but I had a headache. You can't condemn a person for having a headache.' Anyway, that's the way things were between them. There was no reason to think they were happy together, despite their favourable circumstances.

So, it was that particular winter of 1874 that the catastrophe occurred. Our evening meal was poached eggs and spinach, cold ham and sago pudding. I had taken my regular stand in terms of refusal to eat a milk pudding. This usually heralded violent warfare on Mother's part, the situation typically escalating something like this:

'If I say you'll eat it, you'll eat it.'

You know I can't stand milk.

'Starving people would be glad to have it.'

Give it to them then.

'Don't you be rude to me.'

I just don't like it.

'You will have to go to your room.'

I don't care.

(Increasingly threatening) 'Don't care was made to care, he was put in a pot and boiled till he was done.'

I still don't care.

Mother would then give me a big open handed slap.

I would lose my temper and rail against the injustice of it all and be sent to my room in opprobrium with no meals until official forgiveness was granted following a grovelling apology from me. On this occasion, unusually, hostilities were terminated at the 'I can't stand milk' stage, and I left my pudding.

I had two brothers, Michael, two years older than me, and little Edward. It was exceptionally cold that year, and Michael and I were finding it difficult to keep warm. I at least had a good covering of flannelette petticoats, skirt and pinafore but Michael was making do with short trousers, and his knees were red and chapped at the sides and already in November, when winter still had months to run, he was covering his chapped legs nightly with lanolin ointment. Father was home from business, and following the family evening meal, we all retired to the parlour where a good fire was established in the hearth. Mother was acting distantly, and didn't seem interested in Edward at all. Little Eddie was a lumpish child, with little natural co-ordination, and was carried by father to the side of the fire, still in the high chair which was used in the dining room. It was just a tiny chair on stilts really, with no guards on it to keep a child in. Michael and I had obviously preceded little Eddie as previous users of the same chair, and come to positively no harm at all. Probably father left him in the chair to keep clean, as no matter how well Mrs Kitkat, the daily woman cleaned, the dust from the coal made the hearthrug a potentially messy place for a tiny child to play.

It was ferociously cold that evening. We were able to warm our fronts, but our backs were progressively chilling as the frost established itself outside. Eddie had developed little hot red cheeks, and may have squirmed in the high chair as like the rest of us, his front must have been hot, and his back cold. No one remembered it actually happening, as Michael and I were playing draughts on the floor, but there was sudden screaming from Mother, and for a moment we were all transfixed by the sight of little Eddie, there, face down amongst those flaming coals, and then everything seemed to slow down. Father appeared to drop his newspaper intolerably slowly, and to appraise the situation and inexorably slowly extend both his hands deep into the flames and pull Eddie out onto the floor. In the gaslight, Eddie looked like raw meat, blackened with streaks of cooling ash. Father, Mother and Michael were paralysed with horror. Then I ran, tripping through the blackness of the pitch-dark hall to the kitchen, my feet, my arms, my body seeming to move so slowly despite my every physical urge, to fetch Ellen, the family's Cook General in the sure and certain knowledge that my mother had never even noticed that Ellen was wise. Ellen could help. Ellen would make it better. Ellen would stop the screaming. 'Lydia, dear whatever is it?' she said in alarm, grabbing me with arms wet up to the elbows from the washing up in the sink. 'Lydia, speak to me.'

Precocious child that I was, I couldn't articulate a single syllable. I pulled Ellen, and she, drying her hands and arms on her apron allowed herself to be dragged into the inky blackness of the hall and on into the parlour of the now awesomely silent house. The scene resembled some awful tableau, my parents and brother gazing down at the silent little Eddie, resting on the hearthrug where father had placed him. Taking in the scene rapidly, Ellen grabbed father by the shoulders, and yelled 'Run Sir, run for the doctor', then, noticing the state of his hands, seized Michael instead, hissing urgently, 'You must go Master Michael.' Out he went, coatless into the November darkness, out on the cobbles, where the puddles were turning into treacherous sheets of ice, away to Holmdale, the mansion in the High Street, where Doctor Edwards lived. 'Oh Please God,' my soul prayed within me, 'let the Doctor be home.'

'Let me take him, Ma'am' Ellen said firmly to Mother as she carefully gathered up Eddie from the rug, and bore the floppy child down to the kitchen, where she laid him on the scrubbed deal table in the full glow of the gas lamp above. The bright light in the kitchen now revealed the extent of the damage to little Eddie. Ellen snatched clean towels from the airing rack above the kitchen range, positioned the silent Eddie on one, and covered his little body with another. The images were frozen into my mind. Ellen gave Mother the butter dish from the dresser, and bid her cover Father's burns with some of the fat. Time stood still as we watched Eddie's laboured breathing, and the towels soak through with amber liquid draining from his little body.

Doctor Edwards arrived, wearing his black frock coat and a white scarf, breathing asthmatically, carrying a small leather bag with the instruments of his trade, with a panting blue cold Michael in tow. He clumped the bag on the table, and unwrapped the still and silent child and stood looking, stroking his white beard. He muttered to himself, 'sturdy strong child, only just breathing.' He took a tiny bottle from his bag, and dropped two drops of brown liquid on Eddie's tongue. 'Warm water, rags and a bowl' he instructed Ellen, and taking a pair of sharp scissors from his bag he set to work gently slitting the remnants of Eddie's clothes away from his body, and soaking off the charred remnants from the front of his body with clean wet rags. When all was done, he uncorked a large bottle of tannic acid and began to liberally cover Eddie's body. 'Infection Ma'am' he said to Mother, 'mustn't get any into the burns if the child is to survive.' 'Now Mistress Ellen' he said kindly, having suddenly registered our presence, 'is there a cup of hot milk and a biscuit for these good children? It must be time for their bed.'

Still feeling shocked, we sat on stools over by the range, with biscuits and milk. My 'milk' was Ellen's invention to avoid trouble for me with Mother. Actually it was hot water, tinged vaguely with milk, flavoured with vanilla and coloured pink with cochineal. Ellen always sneaked some sugar into our 'milk.' Our mother never permitted us to have biscuits at bedtime, so this was a treat. My biscuit tasted like sawdust in my throat, but I knew I had to eat it. I knew the adults wanted to get rid of us, and the slow drinking and eating was a means of prolonging our fringe involvement in the drama. Michael complained quietly to me that he was getting 'hot ache' in his hands and feet as they began to warm. Doctor Edwards was putting lint over our father's hands and fingers now, and Ellen was tearing strips from an old sheet for the bandages, but suddenly I didn't want to stay. Normally I was very inquisitive, but I felt very cold, very frightened and unbelievably tired. Michael and I took our candles, and went up to bed. Ellen soon followed and undressed me, as it was hard for me to be able to do myself, with all the layers and rubber buttons. She arranged my clothes over the back of a chair and let me get into bed without washing or brushing my hair. She was very gentle. The bed was already warm with my precious round, brown, hard earthenware hot water bottle, which I slid gratefully down to my feet. I drifted into deep sleep.

In the morning I woke early, lying in the darkness, on my hard, hair mattress, listening to the hall clock chime six, but I wasn't alone, Ellen was lying in bed with me, and I jumped with surprise. Ellen normally slept in the attic. 'I was worried about you little Lydia', she said, stroking my hair.

'Eddie', I said urgently, sitting up in bed in shock.

'The little lamb died. He was nearly gone anyway before the doctor got his hands on him' Ellen said haltingly. 'He has gone to live in Heaven with the Little Lord Jesus and all the other little lambs.' She wiped her eyes and her nose with the back of her hand. I was glad Ellen had told me, as I couldn't stand my mother's hysterical emotions at the best of times, especially when she and father had what Ellen called 'a bust up'. Eddie was a stolid child, never made a fuss about anything, and I would have wished his going to be calmer. I already knew about going to heaven and all that anyway, as the Miles girls from down the road were already there after getting the diphtheria last autumn. Doctor Edwards hadn't been able to save them either. Ellen had a little brother and two sisters who were in Heaven too. I went to tell Michael about Eddie. Ellen raced downstairs, anxious not to get caught, having slept in my room, on the well known grounds that Missis Curtis seemed to suffer waking nightmares about cleanliness, particularly where servants' bodies and their idiosyncratic habits were concerned.

I had an extreme struggle getting dressed on my own, putting on my wool vest, flannelette chemise, bodice, two pairs of knickers that had loops to attach them to the bottom of my bodice, two petticoats, then my dress and pinafore. By the time I reached the kitchen, Ellen was washed and tidy, and was already doing technical things with the range, and Michael was doing everything he could to help her with her tasks. I fervently hoped Mother wouldn't find out Ellen had slept with me in my bed. I had quite a shock when Grandmother emerged fully dressed from the parlour, having she said, spent a few hours on the chesterfield. Her hair was still in a long plait, as she had been called urgently from her bed the previous evening.

The next few days were a blur of pictorial memories. Mr Negus the undertaker and cabinetmaker from the High Street, a small very young man, sombrely dressed, with immaculately white linen, and an exquisite frock coat and well brushed beaver top hat was called in, and arrived with a similarly exquisite small black pony and trap. He took a plain wooden box from the back of the trap, and came in through the front door. Michael and I were of course, banished upstairs, but spied on proceedings from his bedroom window. Mr Negus stayed about an hour, and left, carrying his box as if it contained something precious, hid it under a black cloth at the back of the trap, and left as smartly as he had arrived. The Vicar of St James's Church came and left. Meals were scrappy and infrequent, our mother stayed in her room, our father stopped shaving because of the state of his hands, and Ellen had to feed him. Eventually Michael and I were happily banished to the premises of E and C. Teague, High Class Provisions.

Note
The death of the child from a fall into the fire was an historical event from the author's oral family history.

Chapter 3
Late November 1874

It was whilst Michael and I were in exile at 'E and C Teague's High Class Provisions', that we came to know and like Captain Lovejoy better through our grandparents. I found myself quite surprised. Anyone on first acquaintance might have thought this man, often talked about, but seldom seen due to his absences at sea, to be a rather crusty seafarer, well focused on his ship, cargo and crew, probably in that order. I had long been aware that when on land, he delighted in my grandparents' company, but was surprised to hear him joking that Grandfather Ethelred had 'stolen Lottie' (Grandmother Charlotte) from him. He was a good few years younger than my grandparents. 'My loss, your gain' he said jokingly to Grandfather. Sometimes Grandfather replied smugly, 'My boss, my gain'. Michael and I spoke to Grandmother on her own to check whether it was true that Captain Lovejoy was really her first love. 'No, indeed!' she said laughing – 'I've known him for years, but he's much younger than me. I'd not have married that salty old seadog for all the tea in China. He married Charity, a lovely girl, but sadly she died when Harry was born, and he never looked at another woman, much to Caroline Baskett's chagrin'. 'Hmm.....' I thought to myself, 'I must find out more about Mistress Baskett.'

Captain Lovejoy was about the town for a few weeks around the time of Eddie's funeral, from which Michael and I, unusually for the time, were excluded on Grandmother's insistence. Captain Lovejoy, having discharged a cargo of grain during the previous three weeks, was in the process of loading a cargo of ball clay from the clay mines near Wareham, which was being moved across the harbour by barges, having been loaded from the wooden piers off Goathorn at the 'back of Brownsea' where only shallow rowing boats and dinghies could go. When it arrived in Poole, the dockers had to dig the clay out of the barges and shovel it into large baskets to be hand winched to the deck of the Daphne, so that the clay could be dumped in her hold. Such loading when carried out efficiently took 2-3 weeks according to the weather. This was because if it rained, the work had to be stopped, and all the clay had to be covered up to protect it.

This period in our lives was, as Mr Charles Dickens would have put it 'The best of times, and the worst of times.' It was the best of times because our grandparents spoiled us, and it was the worst of times because we had lost our little brother, father had been horribly burned, and we both felt worried about what exactly things would be like when we got home again. However, a written invitation from Captain Lovejoy for the four of us, Mr and Mrs Teague, Master Michael and Miss Lydia Curtis to join him for an early supper on Thursday, at 'The Poop Deck' on the quay, and please to come at 5pm produced much excitement for the four of us. Grandmother, following a discussion with Grandfather on the propriety of accepting this social invitation whilst the family was in deep mourning agreed that their dear friend had probably devised this for the children. She smiled at us both, and quickly went to her work table to write a letter of acceptance.

Our Teague grandparents ran their shop and home at 61 High Street, on the corner of Weston Lane. They had developed themselves and their excellent business by sheer hard work, self-denial and business acumen. Whilst quite young, Grandfather had come across a little book called 'Self Help', by one Samuel Smiles, who described how many great men had come from very humble, often impoverished backgrounds. 'Heaven helps those who help themselves' was one of Mr Smiles' axioms that Grandfather quoted frequently. Once the business began to be established, he and Grandmother set out to help others to help themselves. The two initial staff they employed were drawn from 'the respectable poor' of Poole. They took trouble to ensure that all staff came to work as clean as possible, and they were each greeted and inspected on arrival. A short bible reading and prayer followed, before the shop door was unlocked and the staff prepared for the business of the day. The shop was always shut for one hour at noon so that 'the family' could sit with the whole staff, (and in our childhood, there were four counter staff, one messenger boy and four house servants) in Grandmother's large, comfortable room at the back of the shop. A good lunch was provided, so that, as they said 'the staff can look healthy and keep well.'

In addition, all members of the family and staff had to learn the golden rules of 61 High Street:

> Put others first, think about yourself last.
> Learn to be gentle and patient with other people.
> Control your temper, and never speak or act in anger.
> Remember that silence is sometimes golden.
> Say kind things to other people, encourage and help them when they are in difficulties.
> Never leave anything undone, particularly anything that could affect the safety or comfort of others.
> Never start or pass on gossip.
> In the event of hearing a nasty comment about someone else, balance the conversation by mentioning their good points.

Grandmother carefully explained to us that every member of the staff had to work hard to 'improve themselves'. She said that staff who lived in the poorer areas of town had to work particularly hard to remember 'the golden rules' as they might live in 'mean, violent, careless, dirty and drunken streets and alleys.' In addition to this massive undertaking of staff education, there was Grandmother's personal project. She went up to Poole Union Workhouse every once in a while to find a suitable girl or boy to train for 'a useful occupation', either as a shop assistant or in domestic service. Indeed, Ellen, our excellent cook and general help had been trained in Grandmother's home and kitchen and had been helped to further develop her reading and writing. As a result of this, the business and home were always deliberately overstaffed and the income from the shop and ship provisioning trade only just covered the family and business expenses. Customers regularly asked Grandmother if she had a girl who would be suitable to work for them. She was quite strict about this, and would only allow 'her girls' to be placed with decent families, and she charged the new employer a 'premium' which she regarded as a small contribution to the overall costs of the training. Some girls took longer to be 'ready' than others. However, on taking up their new position as a household servant, each girl would have mastered 'the Golden Rules', be able to read and write tolerably well, be competent in household washing and ironing, cleaning and simple cookery. On leaving 61 High Street, each girl would be given her very own copy of Mrs Beeton's Cookery book, with a little personal message written by Grandmother on the fly leaf. Boys were given Samuel Smiles' Self Help book.

E and C Teague's Family Grocers, was the happiest, most comfortable place to be shoe-horned into. Whilst downstairs spread into a single storey addition, upstairs was relatively small. The two most recent trainees, Liza and Susie shared the pull out bed in the kitchen and Ann the Cook Housekeeper had a room in the attic to herself, as did Lucy, Grandmother's 'Senior Girl.' Wesley the errand and delivery boy, another of her 'rescues' from the workhouse also lived in an attic room. Grandfather said that during our stay Michael would have to 'bunk in with Wesley in the crow's nest', and a spare straw mattress was found for him. I had the privilege of staying on the middle floor, in mother's old room, next to the parlour. Grandmother and Grandfather had their own bedroom on this floor, and their family dining room. They seemed to be rather noisy sleepers, and sometimes I could hear from across the landing, their bed creaking and there were odd grunts and squeals which worried me. When I spoke to Grandmother about it, she explained, saying ' Because we are older, we do have a lot of happy, magic dreams, and you mustn't worry. If you come to wake us, it would break the magic, and we might never have such beautiful dreams again. ' They always seemed so very happy together, and when they didn't think anyone was looking, Grandfather would often surreptitiously pat Grandmother's bottom, which made me giggle. One day I went down into the basement area where Grandfather stripped the cheesecloth off and cut the great round cheddar cheeses and I saw them both kissing! I was very happy living in this busy, real house, where everyone tried to be kind and helpful to each other, and didn't shout. Michael and I felt relaxed, not having to constantly worry about innocently saying or doing the wrong thing and getting into trouble.

Captain Lovejoy's son Harry had been in a lot of trouble recently. I didn't like him anyway, as I'd seen him spitting in the High Street, and he'd been before Poole Police Court in September. I had read in the Poole and Dorset Herald that Harry Lovejoy, Henry Budden and Charles Barnes were fined ten shillings each for obstructing the passage of the highway and for throwing stones at Jeremiah Rigler, whilst he had been engaged in his work. I read this story out loud to Grandmother, and she had tutt tutted in her most censorious manner, saying Harry was known to be a 'handful', probably as a result of never knowing his mother, and having a father often away at sea. Caroline Baskett, who had been entrusted with his care over the years was what Grandmother described as 'one of a kind.' On my request for an explanation, she said, obviously feeling that she had imparted too much information, replied 'Mind your own business' Further enquiries from Bessie in the shop, elicited the fact that Caroline Baskett owned Blake Hill Farm, was a little younger than Captain Lovejoy and had in Bessie's words 'saved herself for him all these years.' Furthermore, she had brought Harry up 'by hand', having made it her life's work to 'set young Harry in order'. I knew what she meant, having read in 'Great Expectations', how Mrs Jo Gargery slapped young Pip about the head frequently, and having often experienced it myself from Mother. I sincerely hoped that Harry Lovejoy would be spending the evening at Blake Hill Farm, where he lived most of the time and not at the Poop Deck when I visited with my family.

Michael and I were very excited about the visit to the Poop Deck, as we had always been in love with the idea of having a room that looked directly across the harbour, particularly with a telescope on a stand! Mr Belben, the senior man in the shop, was given the honour and responsibility of checking and closing down the shop at the usual hour of 6pm, and had been given the keys and all his instructions by Grandfather. The four of us walked down the cobbled High Street, before the lamps were all lit, and had to proceed with care around any detritus, Grandmother rattling along in her metal patens, clutching Grandfather's arm to avoid tripping. The route, although longer, was chosen to avoid the darker, dirtier route via Weston Lane that we would otherwise have had to use. We reached the quayside, that area which filled mother with such loathing, and no wonder. It was filthy. In the daytime, a massive coal hopper was used on the quay when unloading coal ships. The practice of filling it from the top and allowing the coal to drop down from a great height through various meshes to sort the large coal from the small caused an immense dusty filth right across the whole town when it was windy, and a smutty, stinking coal train, used to carry cargoes from the docks to the railway station evenly disseminated 'blacks' all across its route round the West Shore, as far as Poole Pottery, polluting most of the town. Mr Rigler, was employed to keep the rails clear from fallen coal and other debris. He was allowed to keep the coal that he gathered from between the rails as a 'perkquisite' of his job, and was still out pushing the strange rig employed for this purpose. 'Good evening Mr Teague', he said, courteously raising his cap. 'Good evening Mr Rigler', said Grandfather raising his top hat, 'I am pleased to note that the weather is dry for your work today. Are your family all well?' 'Yes sir!' came his cheery reply.

We arrived at last at the Poop Deck, Grandmother having already mentioned that the Captain kept an eccentric house, was generally slightly intolerant of the female sex, and only employed men. The house was crammed between the Seamen's Institute and a rather noisy inn. A paraffin lamp was lit outside the front door, and by this light, Grandfather and Michael and I made vigorous use of the iron foot-scraper. A large ship's bell had been screwed to the outside wall, and Grandfather grabbed the rope dangling from the clapper, and caused it to ring loudly. Captain Lovejoy himself appeared at the door holding a barking, growling Cerberus by his collar. 'It's a wonder my friend, that people from the mission next door don't mistakenly appear at the sound of this bell, thinking you're having a church service here', said Grandfather.

'Come in, come in, come in,' said the Captain, putting out his free arm to take Grandmother's arm and practically dragging her across the threshold. She sat on the hall chair and in the light of the paraffin lamp in the hall, unstrapped her patens, and then made me use the chair to remove my boots and put on my house shoes.

Oh dear! Just at that moment, Harry Lovejoy, the Captain's eleven-year-old son bounced through the door, looking like a small sailor, wearing a peaked cap and a pea jacket. The Captain, to my terror, released his hold on Cerberus's collar, who, with a clacking of his giant claws on the tiled floor walked meekly over to Harry, and wagged his tail, as Harry scratched his head firmly. 'Hello', he said to us, 'my name's Harry', stretched his hand out, and shook first Michael's hand, and then mine. 'Cerberus only pretends to be fierce, and would like to be your friend too,' he said. 'First you must be very brave, and put your face down to his, to show you're not afraid, and get quite close to him. Then let your nose breathe into his nose, and he will breathe into your nose.' Michael, being the bravest, went first, and was rewarded by the dark, monstrous mongrel offering him his right paw. 'Me next,' I said nervously, and I too was rewarded by the offer of a giant paw. 'Cerberus guards those he loves', said Harry positively, 'but hates strangers. He will love you now'. He clearly had an amazing power over animals.

The Captain thundered 'steward!' whereupon a strange, very dark skinned silver haired man wearing white pyjamas issued silently from the nether regions of the house and graciously received our outdoor clothing. 'Come up to the poop deck' ordered the Captain. We nervously ascended the steep, polished stairs, holding the fixed rope that did for a banister rail, and reached the glistening, polished wooden landing. Harry took Michael and me to the darkened room at the front of the house, so that we could see the harbour view. Over by the wonderful window glinted the Captain's beautiful brass telescope. He used this to watch over activities on and around his ship when it was in port, to watch for other large ships entering the navigation channel and to watch the stars. 'This room has a wonderful view' explained Harry enthusiastically. You can see through the telescope three masted barquentines lowering their t'gallants and topsails off old Harry rocks and waiting for the steam tug to bring them in. You can watch timber from the Baltic, coal from Newcastle, oil cake from Liverpool being unloaded. Our Poole ships sail out carrying local clay, stone and pottery. Here,' he said, lifting me by the waist, 'Have a look.'

'Put me down' I shrieked. I admitted to myself that Harry had been perfectly well behaved thus far, but sadly as far as I was concerned, his reputation preceded him. He lit the paraffin lamp, and I was able to appraise my surroundings. There was a large globe in the corner, and over by the far wall was a strange narrow bed, with drawers underneath it. 'Oh, that's Father's berth' said Harry. 'He likes to keep his house as shipshape as possible' and giggled.

I felt relieved to be called to the dining table at that moment. The food served was exceptionally good - tasty, but very fishy. The meal began with fried sprats and bread and butter, followed by haddock fishcakes and peas. Captain Lovejoy pronounced loudly that 'nothing that is produced ashore is ever as good as food pulled out of the sea!' At this stage I was getting slightly sweaty with the fear that a milk pudding would appear. I hadn't exactly won the last encounter with mother. Mother had chosen a tactical withdrawal on grounds that even she had to concede. For some odd reason, milk puddings made me sick. It was therefore with great relief that I noted the arrival on the table of apple compote. The man who did the serving was a slight, nervous young Englishman, called Edward. This was disappointing as I was hoping to see the dark man again, as I thought he might be a lascar, an exciting person from a hot country.

When everyone had finished eating, Edward served tea from the tea trolley, in the Captain's blue spode cups, and all traces of food and serving were rapidly removed from the table. Edward placed a small, rather battered cardboard box in front of the Captain, which bore the words 'Tiddly-winks.' As only four could play, Grandfather and Grandmother sat back and cheered. Michael apparently won, but I felt secretly sure that he had in fact been outplayed by Captain Lovejoy. Harry looked unimpressed at all the proceedings. As we left the 'Poop Deck' to go home to the shop, I felt really amazed that such an important man would have made time and fun for two children, as after the tiddly-winks he had made everyone play Prussian Exercises (with Harry acting as 'the Corporal') and the Dumb Orator. As for Harry, I thought, he's an enigma (my new word for the day). I wondered if I should like him, or continue to dislike him. His father obviously cherished him, kissing and hugging him in a most affectionate manner. Michael remarked later that he'd never seen a man behave like that before.

References

'Stone throwing incident' taken from Poole and Dorset Herald of the 1880s
Conditions on the Quay
Bristowe E., Oliver J., 1998. Poole was my oyster: my life in Poole 1903-1964. Pp 22-24

Chapter 4

Our last years in Poole were memorable in terms of the mourning period for Eddie. According to the customs of the time, adults were supposed to publically mourn a lost child for a year. My Mother insisted on having a very special black dress made for 'going out' into the town. It was made of paramatter, a very expensive fabric made with a silk warp and a woollen weft, trimmed with crepe and looked strikingly beautiful. She was as proud as a peacock. Her jewellery was made from jet, and even with her light black net veil covering her face, many male heads turned to admire her beauty. Social activities for the family were out of the question during 'deep mourning', so mother made do with plenty of (essential) shopping and displaying her black finery in church. Within the house, she wore a black bombazine dress. As the inveterate eavesdropper, I heard father saying 'The trouble with you Mary is that your public display of congealed grief merely marks your inner insincerity.' Michael and I were glad to escape from these public dress displays, and were only required to wear a little 'light mourning' for six months, just grey or white clothes for me, and for Michael a black tie with his Eton collar.

I was eleven the summer the Curtis family moved to Parkstone. There had been a particularly warm spring, and two suspected cases of typhoid fever occurring in the Boar Lane area were sent to the new isolation hospital at Baiter. Grandmother and Grandfather commented darkly that given the highly unsanitary conditions down there, with no privies at all in Boar Lane, and just two for the houses round the corner, it was no wonder that disease was prevalent. There had been very little rainfall all spring even to wash the gutters out, and some areas of town were literally 'stinking to high Heaven' as Bessie, in the shop remarked paradoxically. Captain Lovejoy, who overheard the remark suggested a mariner's alternative – 'stinks like a net full of dead mackerel.'

Anyway, mixed metaphors notwithstanding, the town was in a low state by the end of May. At home, Mother had produced another baby referred to in the family as 'Babs', but actually christened Barbara. In retrospect, I concluded that it had a lot to do with mother not even wanting to consider a proper Christian name for poor Babs. Mother's temper had not improved during her confinement, and she was frequently heard from behind closed doors, berating poor father regarding her 'happy' condition. 'It was you, you fool, your entire fault. You had taken too much wine to be cautious.' Generally he ignored her, but one day when I was listening, I suspected that Mother had thrown a perfume bottle at him, as I heard a loud smash. I heard Father reply 'On that occasion Mary, you were so drunk that I finally had the opportunity to get anywhere near you!' My sympathies were always with father, who was a gentle, clever, thoughtful man, and I had by this time ferreted out the answer to my mother's waspish temper and frequent sick headaches. She had fallen deeply in love with another, but that 'other' was a gin bottle. It made life increasingly difficult at home in Market Street, as the family only kept one live-in servant, Ellen, who was described as a 'cook-general' which meant that she was responsible for most things in the house. It was therefore incumbent on Mother to do a certain amount of hard work in the kitchen, particularly in the making of jams and fruit bottling and the more complex cookery, but the load on Ellen and Mrs Kitkat who cleaned floors, windows, and grates and helped on washday grew heavier and heavier. Unsurprisingly, I had to help a lot too.

Father's strength was in his tolerance and kindness. Friends and neighbours attributed Mother's poor behaviour to our appalling family tragedy, but father may have suffered more deeply, both physically and emotionally. His hands were very burned, and he was never able to use his razor to shave again. His beard grew from the morning of Eddie's death, and was trimmed regularly at the barber's. His left hand was deeply scarred into a clawed shape, and once healed, he wore a specially made silk glove to cover it, and frequently tucked it self-consciously into his waistcoat. His right hand was fortunately less severely affected, and he was still able to manage to do his accountancy work, but employed a Miss Dacombe as an amanuesis in his office. Some years previously Mr Inkpen had offered him a partnership in the growing firm, and this had the effect of increasing Mother's demands to 'get this family out of this stinking town.' By the time I was ten years old, I began to have a sneaking sympathy for her demands. It was difficult to continue sitting at that same fireside in the evenings, with all those memories, and there was no doubt that domestically, a lot was required of Mother as our family grew. I didn't sympathize with her love of gin, but many people, grandmother included, seemed to think that it was a reaction to the loss of little Eddie.

Always a cautious man, father had been able to accumulate a tidy sum towards his purchase of 'Otterwood', in Sandringham Road, Parkstone, which Mrs John Kemp Welch, a widow had put up for sale. As I later realized, father's partnership with Mr Inkpen, his obstinate refusal to listen to mother's pleas to move earlier on and some very shrewd investments had quickly placed him in a favourable financial situation. Given that the advertisement in the Poole and Dorset Herald had described Otterwood as 'a gentleman's residence', Mother's general temperament improved by the day as negotiations proceeded. She even made arrangements for iced buns to be available for consumption on the afternoon of the day father took her to look at the house for the first time.

Mother described our new home to us in glowing terms - its beautiful setting, the morning room, parlour and dining room, four bedrooms and dressing room, BATHROOM, kitchen , scullery and pantry. The WC upstairs was newly fitted, and was a George Jennings 'symphonic closet of the century.' She became even more animated when she mentioned the two-stalled stable and coach house, although Father said very quickly that these would not be used as such, as he would not be able to afford it. He would very easily be able to catch the railway train at Parkstone at 8.07 to get into Poole to work. Father was, amazingly, lauded for his foresight and thrift at embarrassing length, and his former parsimoniousness was not mentioned that day.

Mother spent a lot of time with her dressmaker, arranging for new gowns, and ordered calling cards from Mr Snook the stationer. We finally moved on a Saturday in the middle of August, leaving our comfortable rented home in Market Street for the luxury of Sandringham Road. Ellen had been sent ahead a week before, and Grandmother had supplied us with Liza Loader, whom she had 'trained' herself to be a second servant to help run the much larger home. I heard her giving Mother a good talking to, explaining that although she'd had Liza with her for some years, she was very inexperienced and vulnerable, and would need careful supervision and looking after, even though she was twenty. Together with our household goods and chattels, Mother, Liza, Michael, Babs and I took the London and South Western railway train from Poole to Parkstone Station. Michael and I confided to each other that we were feeling sick with excitement. Father was already at the house, waiting to welcome his family, and Ellen was at the station, ready to help Mother. A 'fly', a two-passenger cab had been hired to take mother and Ellen, who was to hold 'Babs', up the hill. Liza was to walk up the hill with Michael and me.

It was a slightly dreary August afternoon, with misling rain, and a light breeze, which did nothing to dampen our spirits. As soon as mother was out of sight, the three of us moved sharply down the platform to inspect the great black leviathan that had brought us up from Poole. Unfortunately, as we reached it, there was an almightily loud hiss of steam, followed by a great chuff of smoke, which caused Liza and me to take hasty refuge in the Ladies' Waiting Room where Michael found us, with his white shirt and Eton collar spotted with black. He and I continued with our new adventure, running noisily across the floorboards of the booking hall to see the cart being heavily laden with some of our household effects which had been brought from Poole in the goods van, and I shouted to Michael 'Look, our beds!' as I spotted the brass heads of our beds being loaded on to the cart.

'Mind your shoes young master and miss' cautioned Liza. She had already said to Michael when she saw the state of his shirt,

'You'll cop it when your mother sees you'. Without doubt, she was very worried about delivering two grubby children to her new mistress. The station yard was indeed slightly mucky, despite the generous covering of gravel, as the continuous turning and manoeuvrings of the horse-drawn carts kept the surface well stirred. We walked very carefully around the edges, and turning out of the yard, we passed the Station Hotel, and kept to the side of the road, to keep our shoes as clean as possible, to turn across Parkstone Bridge. It had wonderful little cut outs in its concrete structure, and Michael immediately climbed up on to the parapet a little as he had heard a train coming down the line from the Bournemouth direction. 'Get down Master Michael' shouted Liza ineffectually; she was labouring behind us, carrying a bundle containing everything that she owned, which wasn't much. Michael did not respond quickly, and a great cloud of smoke belched back into his face as the express train rushed under the bridge. 'You look like a chimney sweep' said Liza desperately.

The few houses we passed were all quite new, and on the left side, just past the bridge was the most beautiful garden we had ever seen in our lives. Its sloping sides, flower covered, made it look like a fairy dell. On either side of us were many trees and bushes, and at the bottom of the road, opposite a large house called 'Pinehurst' there appeared to be a little wood. 'Fairy land' I whispered to Michael, as we looked across to the woods, but he retorted 'Sherwood Forest.' The furniture cart, just ahead of us now, made heavy labour of mounting the gravel hill that was Sandringham Road, the driver dismounting and leading his horses. The horses' metal shoes were striking sparks from the flint stones in the gravel. We three walkers reached the house first. Father was there at to greet us, and we admired the carved wooden name plate on the green painted gates with the name 'Otterwood' picked out in white. Liza was sent up the road a little to enter at the smaller, green gate, reserved for servants and tradesmen, which father took us along to admire too, and it had a much smaller cast iron sign which said 'No hawkers or circulars'. I began to feel sensible of and awed by my family's 'change in station.' Father was completely oblivious of Michael's grubby condition, and ruffled his hair with great affection, saying 'Good journey young man?' The three of us passed up our very own short driveway, and father ushered us through the conservatory and into a large hall.

The rest of the day passed in a further whirl of stomach-churning excitement. Michael was quickly pronounced by father to be so dirty that he would be required to take the Curtis family's first bath in their new bathroom. We watched father giving Liza a lesson on how to light the gas hot water geyser that had been fitted – a large copper contraption in the bathroom, capable of providing instant hot water to the bath. Father leaned his long arms around Liza, putting her hand on the gas tap, and helping her to light the gas which made a loud 'boff!', and she would have fallen back through terror had he not caught her. The gas made a constant roar as the steaming water cascaded into the bath, and all the females went downstairs as father and Michael prepared to sample the delights of the new bath.

Supper that first evening was a makeshift affair, served in the morning room on a lovely round table, a recent purchase. This was the room where the Curtis family would come every day for breakfast, and there was even a gas fire for comfort on cold mornings. Over the collation of cold meats, bread and blancmange, biscuit on a plate served to me- victory! Father made it very clear that now that family had a modern home with all its attendant comforts, baths could be taken as frequently as once a week, and the hot bath water shared by Michael and then himself on Fridays, and by me, followed by Mother on Saturdays. Little Babs would continue to have her baby bath every other day.

Michael settled into his new life with gusto, making a pal called Robert from 'Eaglehurst', the house up the road, and playing happily amongst the woods and bushes accompanied by Bruno, Robert's boxer dog. There was nothing I would have liked better than to be Maid Marion to their Robin Hood, but I was stuck in long pastel coloured dresses, long petticoats and a white starched pinafore, and from mother the menacing decree was 'Get dirty at your peril, Lydia.' August 14th, the anniversary of the Queen's Coronation was one of the few happy family days I remember. We went on the tram to Bournemouth, for the ceremony of opening the new pier with a golden key. Excitement at the new home however soon turned into deep boredom for me, and a return to reading, embroidery and helping in the kitchen. It was slightly enlivened when father occasionally asked me to 'take a letter' for him.

On our second summer at Otterwood, on dry, breezy days, I had several times suffered from dirt actually lodging under my upper eyelids and grazing my eyeballs. Dr Stone had attended each time. As a result Father sent this letter to the Parkstone Reminder, entitled 'The Dust'.

Sir, In our present state of comfort, we shall soon forget the horrible discomfort and annoyance to which we are all subject in this place on account of the clouds of dust which obscure every-thing and penetrate everywhere, if a day or two passes without rain. Last year, of course, the annoyance was reduced to a mini-mum, because we had a wet season; but this year we have already had a stiffish dose, and we know what to expect in the Autumn. Parkstone is pretty heavily rated; perhaps it would not be too much to ask for the very homely luxury of a water cart to prevent our roads from being blown into our eyes, noses, ears, mouths and houses during the dry weather. If the proper authorities were approached, who knows but what proper remedy might be forth-coming? With a capacious water cart, efficiently horsed and discreetly driven, even Parkstone might defy the dust.
Signed, Habitans in sicco.

I continued to go to Miss Squires' School in Poole, as although St Peter's School in Parkstone cost parents only three pence a week to send their children, it had over 200 pupils, and just a master for the boys and a mistress for the girls. I went with Father on the early train, he took me to Grandmother's and I continued to be taken to school and fetched by Wesley. It was on my return from school one day in the late afternoon that I saw Harry Lovejoy again. He was only a young man, but was clearly very drunk, and in the company of three other young men. I saw him vomiting in the street, too incapable with drink even to reach the gutter, and actually fouling his own clothing. He was clearly an absolutely repellent person.

References and notes

Hillier J. 1990. Victorian Poole. Poole: Poole Historic Trust. (Conditions in Boar Lane)

'Habitans in sicco' had his letter published in a contemporary issue of 'The Parkstone Reminder'.

The houses mentioned in Sandringham Road are mostly still standing, but many are now flats. They were not quite built by the time frame in this chapter, and the plumbing and water heating would not have been as fully developed as this chapter suggests. It was many more years before Parkstone had a telephone exchange.

Chapter 5

Mother was initially very happy at Otterwood. She enjoyed wearing her new gowns, and eagerly awaited the arrival of calling cards from her neighbours in Sandringham Road, Mrs Haynes at Eaglehurst, Mrs Bance at Ivanhoe, Mrs Pardoe at the Manor, Mrs Fawkes at The White Lodge and the Misses Greenish at Trefloyne. Within a week, calling cards were delivered from the ladies at all the neighbouring houses. These were left in the polished brass tray, with the pie crust edges, which stood on a table just inside our front door. The cards each had their bottom corner turned down to denote that they had been delivered personally. Etiquette dictated that the back of each visiting card denoted when each lady would be 'at home' to receive visitors. Mother then returned the calls. She was in a high state of excitement, and prepared to return these calls within one week, to fit in with the formal requirements. She thus met all her immediate neighbours, who then began to make return visits.

Mother's 'At Home' day at Otterwood was to be Thursday afternoon. I was quite fascinated with a social world of which we had all, until this time, been quite ignorant. The room formerly referred to as 'the parlour' became 'the drawing room', and Thursday afternoons were eagerly awaited. She would sit there in her 'tea gown' and wait for the front door bell to ring. Liza would answer, wearing her 'best' uniform, newly purchased for the purpose, and receive the visitor's card on a small silver tray, which she would convey to mother, whilst the caller waited in the hall. Mother would then say 'Yes, I am at home to Mrs Pardoe' and ask Liza to show the lady in. Customarily three cards were presented, one from the lady, and two of her husband's cards. This would give father a potentially useful means of introduction to his male neighbours.

I was definitely a little less happy in those early Parkstone years than my mother or brother. Outside of school, Michael was able to escape from the house and do more or less what he liked provided that he didn't rip his clothes or get just too dirty. As for me, anchored in and around the house, I had nowhere to turn. Mother was continuously going on about the necessity of 'training' me, which seemed to be conferring upon me some kind of lower servant status. Outside school, life became one constant round of baking, cleaning, laundry, sewing and mending, which became more onerous as Mother was less and less able to do her share due to increasing social engagements. Apart from school friends in Poole, I had few friends of my own age, and within Sandringham Road, because of my home duties, little opportunity for socializing with other young people. St Peter's Church offered some chances for getting out and about. I helped with the annual 'Penny Party' in the church hall, to raise money for the 'Additional Curates Fund,' and was occasionally able to go to a magic lantern show, pantomime or an annual event such as the pre Christmas Bazaar or the summer Garden Party, held in the grounds of St Peter's House, hosted by Canon Dugmore and his wife, Lady Elizabeth.

Father seemed happier than I had seen him for years, and really enjoyed his journeys from Poole to Parkstone on the train. One frosty late December Monday, when I was at home with a cold, he hurried off for the train on his own loaded with an umbrella, a travelling bag of papers, a parcel and letters for the post, and a brace of pheasants he'd shot over the weekend. During our evening meal he told the story of his arrival in Poole. 'I found my way blocked by a small boy, with a gigantic pin, begging

'Please sir, would you pin my jacket?'

Pin his jacket! The cunning little street arab, he was chaffing me for having my hands so full! No, he was not though. I looked at that pinched face, grayish white, too poor and bloodless even to redden in the keen wind of this December morning. I looked at the baby brother he was carrying, all ragged, on one ragged arm, with a small wan face of less than two years old, cuddled close asleep near the wan face of six years. I put down all my belongings on the flags and pinned on the jacket, just because I couldn't help it.

'Thank ye sir!' said the small boy all in a chirp. I picked up the travelling bag of papers, the umbrella, the big parcel, the letters and the pheasants. 'Please sir' said the very small boy in the same pleading tone, producing another gigantic growth of a pin, 'would you just put a pin in the baby?' I groaned aloud at this shocking request, not that it mattered in the least to me how many pins were put in the baby, but what was to become of my early start in the office, my bag, my umbrella, my long tailed pheasants – 'Oh, tut and nonsense' I said, losing patience. 'I'm in a hurry my lad, get your mother to manage the pins.'

'My mother is dead!' the weak low voice cracked with a sob and went up into a little cry saying the word. He was turning away without looking up any more, trying to pin the baby brother's cloak with his left hand. Either I should fling down my possessions instantly and stop him, or see myself for the whole of Christmas, to use the mildest expression – as an unmitigated monster.'

'You see,' he said looking at Michael and me, 'One does not like to feel oneself an unmitigated monster at Christmastime; sympathies are stirred by sharing one's joy, and indifference looks like cruelty, and even a little bit of selfishness worries one's heart like a crime.'

The happy, dream time at Otterwood had to end. The great improvement in Mother only lasted about eighteen months, before she returned to her greatest love, the gin bottle. Calls were not returned, she was never 'at home' to her neighbours – Liza was sent to the front door to say that Mrs Curtis was indisposed, and therefore not 'at home.' This further isolated me, and indeed, the rest of the family. Mother was unable to help father by entertaining his colleagues and friends, to advance his business standing in Poole. Driven to desperation Father confided his concerns to me one evening, as we sat together in the railway carriage, coming up from Poole, and said 'I am going to consult the new Doctor, who has set up practice in Osborne Road, the house facing the bottom of our road'. He fetched Doctor Stone one Thursday morning, when Mother was lying in bed, just beginning one of her 'bad' days, very intoxicated, and I acted as a chaperone whilst he examined her. In summary, his advice to mother was a measured dose of Laudanum regularly, four times a day. I waited outside the Morning Room door, eavesdropping the conversation he had downstairs with Father, which went something like this:

'My dear chap, you have to face facts. Your wife is an invalid, and needs to avoid any unnecessary stresses, living a quiet life, mainly at home. The regular doses of Laudanum that I have prescribed must be fully supervised, and never exceeded. If her illness has an acute exacerbation, please send for me, and if necessary I will inject her with diamorphine. Meantime, every fluid ounce of alcohol within the house must be immediately destroyed, and not replaced, and the Laudanum kept under lock and key.'

This new, regular arrangement generally suited us all. Mother took to her new role as an invalid with equanimity, thus removing any vestige of expectation members of the household might have had of her in terms of general organization, and removing nearly completely any interference from her in terms of cleaning and cooking. Her responsibilities thus fell almost entirely upon me, assisted by Ellen. This was a very heavy load, on top of going to school in Poole. Grandmother became very concerned about the domestic stresses in Sandringham Road, but unable to help because of her responsibilities in the grocery business. I really needed Grandmother's emotional support at this time, but we rarely had more than a few minutes to speak to each other. My first problem hinged around Arthur, the male servant. Arthur was employed by father for a variety of tasks. His principal function, as mother became less capable, was to help father dress and undress, and generally help him with managing his clothes and other personal matters. He lived in the two small rooms over the stable, and had overall management of the garden (Father also employed a lad). I derived great pleasure from the garden initially, as there was an espalier peach tree against one wall of the house, apple and pear trees and a vegetable garden. During my second summer at Otterwood, it was my supreme pleasure to go into the garden with a colander, in the very early morning and pick fresh peas and beans. Arthur sidling up and saying 'morning missy', in an almost insolent tone, frequently marred this innocent little pleasure. Very early one morning, before school, I was walking around the stables seeking distraction after a particularly unpleasant engagement with mother, when Arthur appeared from around the side of the building with his trousers open at the front, and a most enormous amount of flesh sticking out, that he was fondling tenderly. I was frozen to the spot, trying to avoid swooning, when further sickening developments erupted over his hands. I then ran away, and managed to get into the scullery door, in a state of mild collapse. Liza obviously saw me approaching from her station at the sink, and shouted 'Ellen, Ellen, come quick, It's Miss Lydia.' The two of them dragged me into an armchair in the back kitchen. 'Get my box from the pantry, Liza' I heard Ellen say through the rushing and roaring in my ears. Ellen gave me two teaspoons of sal volatile and then held a McKenzie's smelling bottle under my nose. I dimly remember hearing Liza say to Ellen 'I wonder if she's working up to - you know.......' Anyway, Father was informed that I wasn't well, and came wandering gently into the back kitchen, full of concern, saying 'I hear you have a bad case of the colly wobbles, Lydia dear. No school for you today. You must take a rest.'

My second problem was around the 'you know' that Mary and Ellen had mentioned obtusely, and happened a few weeks after the first. Actually I didn't know anything at all, and everything was a complete shock to me when it happened, following quickly after the unpleasantness with Arthur. I woke up one morning with a tummy ache and feeling rather sticky down below, looked under the bedclothes, and saw BLOOD. I quickly realized that I was bleeding to death, and started screaming for Mother, as I couldn't think what else to do. Mother arrived wearing a wrapper over her nightgown, looking very irritable, with black rings around her eyes and a great swathe of bad breath. 'Whatever is it?' she asked crossly.

'I'm bleeding to death' I said in a little voice, throwing back the bed covers.

'Oh, that,' she said dismissively. 'I only hope you haven't spoiled a good pair of sheets. I'll get Ellen', and rang the bell beside my fireplace.

Ellen arrived looking hot and sweaty, as it was the busiest time of her day, said 'Poor lamb,' and gave me a kiss. She returned quickly with some rags, and said 'have a wash, and make do with these. I suppose I'll have to talk to you about it later, but don't worry, it happens to all of us' and dashed back downstairs.

Father was kind at this second occasion of me being 'indisposed', and I felt that he might have understood a bit. Probably Mother had the same, and he could remember from when they used to share a room. I stayed at home for a few days, and had a slight rest, and felt the better for it. I was at least able to speak to Grandmother on my father's newly installed electric telephone, number Parkstone 05. I asked for Poole 16, and when Grandmother came to the telephone, I tried to code my comments to her as 'I am away from school today, as a result of having a mild indisposition. It is the first time I have suffered from this' as it was widely believed that Miss Yates, the Parkstone telephone operator listened in. I never did get a satisfactory explanation of what was happening to my body.

Ellen said 'It is the way of all women, Lydia. I can only understand it from the Bible. Eve was responsible for giving Adam the forbidden fruit, and God cursed her, saying that he would greatly multiply her sorrow and that in sorrow she would bring forth her children. It is clearly linked to having children, and is a strong sign that you are becoming a woman. Many people call it the curse, and it comes about every twenty-eight days, and generally lasts for four or five, sometimes seven. The New Testament speaks of a 'woman with an issue of blood', and I think it means that hers never really went away. I think probably the doctors understand it a little, but who would want to ask a medical man!' Ever the practical, she then said 'I've got time now to show you how to fix your rags, and how we deal with soaking and washing them. I've stirred some laudanum from my own bottle into your tea to help with the pain.'

During these few days off school, I particularly missed dear Michael, who (lucky for him) had eventually been sent away to school in Winchester, so I spent my time amusing little Babs, who didn't get much of a life either. She had a nursery in the attics so that Ellen and Liza could get up to her if she cried at night. In the daytime she had a specially-made low baby chair in the back kitchen with a tray arrangement fixed at the front to keep her in, where Ellen and Liza would spoon feed her whilst they took their own meals, and then she went into a playpen for most of the day, as no one had much time for her. As Babs was starting to walk, the servants were grateful for my help.

Arthur got an instant dismissal, as he and Liza were found by father, at the back of the stable one evening, Arthur having quite shockingly been caught red-handed with his hand inside Liza's top clothing, his trousers open and his mouth clamped over hers. Liza fainted on rescue, and was carried indoors by father, with both her top and lower clothing much disarranged. I was very sympathetic to her, and said to father that Arthur's appalling behaviour had caused me to stop using the back garden, but that I had felt too embarrassed to tell.

Father was becoming much attached to Liza, and always gave her a little reading and writing lesson every evening in the Morning Room, which he also used as a home office. I supposed it helped to pass his time a little, but Ellen commented darkly one day, after seeing him patting Liza's bottom 'She'll be thinking she's something she isn't if she's not careful. We must ALL remember our stations in life, your father included.' One evening, sitting close beside Liza at the table, with his hand on her knee, he asked her to read aloud a particularly funny article from his newspaper, which she managed faultlessly. It was from a local paper that had a reputation of meticulously recording squalor, and was titled 'When may a baby drink beer?' It stated that: 'At a

London Police Court the other day, a man was fined five shillings for giving beer to a two year old infant without the order of a doctor or in case of sickness or other urgent cause. We should have thought that the cause must have been considerably urgent that would excuse people for giving beer to a two year old. In the case in question, the offender explained that he gave his child a sip outside a public house to stop its crying! We have heard of inexperienced papas doing funny things to achieve that object, even to hanging baby up by a belt to an old fashioned turn spit, when such a thing could be obtained, and letting him slowly be turned round and round; but after giving him beer we shall expect him to be offered a cigarette next, to soothe his nerves.' We all laughed.

Ellen wasn't the only one to be concerned about Liza. On clear evenings, I had twice noticed her skulking in the half light in the front garden, actually inside the large canopy of a huge bush by the front gate that Michael and I had formerly used in our 'hide and seek games'. In the dusky light, I could see Liza in there with a man. The man had her up against the massive trunk of the bush, her skirts were rucked up, and they were kissing in a most extraordinary manner, and had their hands all over each other. The spectacle gave me very strange, new feelings all over, which I didn't understand, but quite liked. A couple of months later, when Liza was supposed to be in the kitchen, I saw her in the bush again, this time it could have been with Harry Lovejoy, but I was surprised, as I had heard he was at sea following his latest transgression, reported in detail in the Poole and Dorset Herald:

POOLE POLICE COURT
Monday- before the Mayor (Mr W. Mate) and Mr H. Farmer.
DISTURBING THE SALVATION ARMY

Harry Lovejoy was charged with being drunk and disorderly in Fish Street on July 26, and with refusing to leave when requested by the police; also with assaulting Robert Persey and Charles

Amey, members of the Salvation Army. P.C. Real said that on Friday evening he was sent for to go to the Salvation Army Barracks. On getting there he found the defendant, who was the worse for drink, holding on to the Barrack gates. There was a crowd of people around him, and as the defendant would not go away, he took him into custody. Gideon Patten, a member of the Salvation Army, gave evidence as to the violent behaviour of the defendant, who kicked Amey and Persey, who prevented his going into the building.

Robert Persey also gave evidence, stating that while the Army were in Market Street, the defendant came into the ring and disturbed them. He followed right round the town to the Barracks. He was refused admission, and thereupon kicked Amey and the witness. Someone, whom he did not see, also struck him with a heavy blow on the head, breaking his hat and nearly stunning him. Charles Amey, hall-keeper, said the defendant and another came to the hall the worse for drink. He would not allow them in on that account, and the defendant struck him several times and kicked him. Someone went for a policeman, and he was then given into custody. They had had to keep him out on several occasions, because when he got in he made rude noises and made the other young men laugh.

Defendant admitted that he had had a little drop of drink, but he would try to keep away from it in the future. The Mayor told the defendant that it was very wrong to go and disturb the Salvationists. He had no more right to go and disturb them than to go and make a disturbance in a church or chapel; but a lot of young men seemed to think that they had a right to go to the Salvation Army Barracks and do just as they liked. If they were, therefore, to let defendants go, and not impose a fine, some other young men might go and do as they liked there. There were three charges, one of being drunk and causing a disturbance, another of assaulting Amey, another of assaulting Persey. The magistrates could not fine him less than two shillings and sixpence and costs for being drunk, and for each of the assaults, he would have to pay a fine of five shillings and costs, a total of one pound and six shillings.

A few months later, a veritable storm blew up one Saturday morning. Mother was having a very restless time. Her doses of Laudanum were failing to keep her calm, and she was in an angry and disruptive mood, and was commencing a savage invasion of domestic demands downstairs, insisting that I would ensure that the hall floor be polished again, although the oilcloth was glistening (clearly there was only a ten to one risk of breaking a leg on the hall floor, instead of a hundred to one risk). I had left Liza in the drawing room, doing her usual carpet cleaning with damp tea leaves and a brush. As Mother and I entered the room, she climbed on to a box and started cleaning the windows using a handful of newspaper and a mixture of vinegar and water. Liza's silhouette was revealed in the sunshine, showing a clearly defined, very swollen belly. Mother started screaming 'You hussy. You dirty little whore,' and yanked her off the box and slapped her full in the face. Father and Ellen appeared, and I saw the colour drain from his face as he saw what had been hidden from them. I didn't really understand what the fuss could be about at the time. He gave out orders 'Lydia, take your mother upstairs. Ellen, go for Doctor Stone, and ask him to attend Mrs Curtis at his earliest convenience. Liza, go and wait in the back kitchen.'

By the end of what proved to be a very long day, mother had received her first injection of diamorphine and enjoyed both the attention and the drug. She was also given a bromide mixture to take at night. Liza, whom I had last seen looking like a broken doll, sobbing on the drawing room carpet, had gone, not to be seen again. Ellen had withdrawn into total silence, in her armchair in the back kitchen, and father had gone to the Parkstone Hotel to partake of a few glasses of whisky with the publican, Mr Hayball and Mr Wills the Station Master, and Babs was a happy little girl, playing with her dolly.

Notes and References

The residents named in Victorian Sandringham Road all actually existed, (with the exception of the Curtis family). Canon Dugmore, his wife Lady Elizabeth, Mr Hayball and Mr Wills are Parkstone characters too.

Father's story about the brace of pheasants and the article about the baby being given beer to drink were taken from the Parkstone Reminder.

The story about Harry Lovejoy attacking members of the Salvation Army was adapted from a report in the Poole and Dorset Herald of the time. The Salvation Army suffered a lot of intimidation in its early days, as similar reports were noted in the Stirling Observer in Scotland. Young men seemed to see the Salvationists as 'fair game' at the time, and did not usually receive severe punishments.

PHEMIE

Chapter Six
Alloa, Clackmananshire, Scotland

My full name is Euphemia, but in the family I was always Phemie. I was born in Alloa in 1859. My pa worked at the Paton's woollen mill driving a cart up and down from the quay. You probably already know Paton's knitting wool, but may not have known that it is processed and spun into the yarn you use in the town of Alloa, where I was born. One morning, at Paton's Kilncraig mill, whilst struggling to get a very wilful Clydesdale horse into harness, the horse crushed my pa against the stable wall. The injuries to his head were very severe, and he was brought home in a cart and laid on his bed. Dr Christie was sent for, but he was dead within hours. I was just twelve years old, and my big sister Isabel, (always known in the family as Isa) was thirteen. The manager at the mill was kind, but our cottage soon had to be returned for another company workman and his family to use. Unemployment in Alloa at that time was very serious. Generally help was only given to the sick. We did get a little help from Patons to begin with, as far as managing to pay for a simple funeral, and some money to help us with food and coals for a few weeks, as my pa had died suddenly from a work accident. At that time able-bodied men without work got no help at all to keep their families until they became sick, from slow starvation. Widows and children had precious little. We were more fortunate than others, because although we'd lost pa's wage and our lodging, my ma was a 'howdie wife', working as a midwife and maternity nurse. We were able to share a hoose on the Main Street with Mrs Mack, an older, widowed friend of ma's. I speak of the hoose in the Scottish sense, you climbed an outside stair on a long row of cottages, and each side, top and bottom were two hooses, just a room and a kitchen each. We did all the cooking on the coal-fired kitchen range, and Missis Mack slept in the bed in the kitchen alcove, which was the warmest place in the hoose. The three of us Maudes shared the room, and our lighting in the evenings was with an oil lamp, which gave a good, soft light for sewing by, as of course, we made all our own clothes. Our neighbours were small traders, labourers and workers from the woollen mills, glassworks and breweries. The streets outside were cobbled, and people threw their minging rubbish and excrement into the gutter in the middle to wash away. It wasn't nice, but it was what we'd all grown up with and got used to. On fine days washed clothes hung literally everywhere, on every wall and fence, and in good weather, women stood outside their doors, gossiping and watching their weans play. The men stood in groups, looking at the women and the goings on in the street and smoking. Fish cadgers went up and down hawking their wares. We were grateful for the shelter, but it was not as good as our previous lodging.

My ma's work meant that she kept odd hours, and was frequently away from home for weeks at a time. She worked very closely with Dr Christie, and when he had wealthy women expecting, she would go and live in the house with them, so that she could help to prepare for the wean, and be there when the pains started. When the woman started her pains, the doctor would be informed, and sent for in time for the birth, normally delivering the wean himself, with ma providing expert support and help with the mither and all the birthing requirements, and often providing an extra 'hand' if the delivery was complicated. Sometimes the doctor didnae get there in time, and she would have to deliver the wean hersel, but he'd told and shown her everything she needed to know over the years, she'd watched and helped many times, and the doctor never minded if she had to deliver in an emergency. The one thing she didnae dae for the doctor's patients was to cut the wean's cord. That just wasnae allowed. Then she often stayed in the hoose for some weeks. She made sure that the mither was able to put the wean to the breast, and was generally managing to look after the wean and hersel. Dr Christie insisted that all these private patients stayed in their beds for a full two weeks after the birth, sometimes longer, which we found a little strange as our neighbours would be back at their work in a day or so, if they had work.

This 'lying in' made a lot of welcome work for us, washing the mither and the wean and generally managing the room, visitors, laundry, instructing the servants and so on. Many of these richer women needed a lot of explaining and encouragement, as they had led very protected lives, and wernae as strong as us. Pa had never minded her doing this work, so long as it was not too often, and as we had precious little to live on, she was happy doing it, and it bought our family a few extra bawbees.

When my pa James Maude died, things changed a wee bit, as Dr Christie began to prefer ma to the other howdie wifies that he used, particularly if he thought there might be a complicated birth, and so she got more work. She would also attend any local poor wifies without charge if she were available when the call came to 'send for Mistress Maude'. Our neighbours paid her if they could, and gave her a lot of respect, and many weans in the streets around us had been birthed by her. By the time I was fourteen, and had learned my reading, writing and arithmetic at the church school, my sister Isa was fifteen and already becoming very skilled at Paton's mill. I always preferred my ma's work, and she began to take me out with her to train me. This was because sometimes the women who she was booked in with went over their time, and she wisnae done with the nursing side before she had to go to the next woman. She would leave me behind to help with the breast-feeding and general care, or send me ahead to her next booking, to get the mother and the house ready for the birth.

By the time I was eighteen, I was working as a howdie in my own right, and had plenty of experience, a lot of it from helping our poor neighbours, who although I was young were glad to see me when ma was busy. My ma was glad to see my progress, as up till then, she had been ower busy. Often she had to travel some distance to important peoples' homes in surrounding villages, such was her reputation, and with my help she appreciated doing a little less. By this time, the other doctor from the town was giving us work as well, but we booked Dr Christie's patients by preference, and were never short of work.

It was as a 'howdie wife' that I first met the man I later came to call Alec, in his parents' house at Claremont. I remember it all so clearly, as it changed my life dramatically. He had another name by birth, but I decided to call him Alec when I got to know and love him, as he so strongly disliked his given name. I remember walking up to the Claremont side of town for the first time in the spring. There were trees planted up there with pink and white blossoms, and there were birds singing in the trees and flitting about. There were squirrels chasing their tails and each other, and I even saw two rabbits run across my path. It was such a change from the town. I breathed in the clean air, and my heart was singing in the sunshine, as I went looking for the house called 'Aberlour.'

Alec's sister, Margaret Paterson, was not long married, and had come home to have her baby in the larger house, with the bigger staff, as it would be easier to manage that way. Mr Ross was a solicitor with a practice on Mar's Hill, and he and Mrs Ross had the massive, new, large pink sandstone house, Aberlour, that had been built for them on the hill. It had five good big bedrooms, and four rooms downstairs for the family, kitchens and so on. Besides this there were four attic rooms for female staff, and a hoose over the stables for the cook and head gardener/ groom, a married couple. The family's rooms were all lit by gas, and Mrs Ross had even had a gas fire put in her bedroom for the cold winter mornings!

On the Monday in late April, when I arrived, Mrs Ross greeted me pleasantly. 'Good morning Mrs Maude' she said. I was actually known locally as 'young Mrs Maude', as, although I wasn't married, it was considered by my mother to be better professionally for me to be a respectable 'Mrs'. I believe that I was very well educated and well mannered for my background, and my work had made me act very grown up. Mrs Ross seemed very intelligent, and interested in what I would have thought then to be 'lofty pursuits', but I think now, in the light of my own experiences, that she had a rather 'shut in', empty life. Mr and Mrs Ross were great ones for the kirk, and she was aye dressed in sober, dark clothes, with a little peplum at the back. She was very slim and neat in her appearance. During my stay I sometimes heard her playing the cello or the piano in the drawing room, and she gave 'musical soirees' together with married friends who also played and sang. This group of friends also gave benefit performances at St Mungo's Kirk.

She was always pleasant but firm in her instructions to me and the other servants. She said, in her well-polished accent, 'you will take all your meals on your own in the morning room, and will observe normal house rules during your stay with us.' She was putting me a tiny bit above the servants, but keeping me in my place. I settled in and began helping young Mrs Paterson to prepare everything needed for the birth of her baby. I say young, she was actually older than me, but I'd a deal more life experience than her.

To me, that house was as far as the east is from the west in terms of the education the folks had and the money and power they possessed. It's beautiful, still clean pink sandstone made it look like a huge piece of sugar candy perched on the hill. The air was fresher and cleaner up there, and standing in its own landscaped grounds, the house was quiet and private behind its own grey stone walls. It was the complete opposite of the bustling, noisy smelly area where I lived. At Aberlour no factory whistles were heard, no carts clattered over cobbled streets and there was no coarse shouting. I thought of the hymn 'All things bright and beautiful' this was 'the rich man's castle', and I was the 'poor woman at the gate'. Even though I was very well dressed and shod for a person of my class, I felt like a fish out or water, cheap and mean by comparison, even with their well-uniformed and drilled servants. There were four sons, Abraham, David, Charles and 'Alec'. Mrs Paterson doted on her younger brother, and was simply delighted to see Alec, who was four years older than me, when he returned unexpectedly from Edinburgh. He was supposed to be studying at the university to be a doctor. I also quickly learned that there were some problems between Alec and his father, who was not at all pleased that Alec was not studying law, as he wished Alec to follow him into the family legal practice. I heard Mr Ross giving Alec a right good telling off in the study when he arrived home. 'What're ye doing coming back from Edinburgh so soon, without finishing the year? I can't believe that an intelligent person like you could fail these medical examinations.' I wasn't listening deliberately, but his father had a very quick temper, and tended to shout. There was a long silence, and then he roared 'Answer me boy!' I saw Alec later hanging about in the garden and he seemed to be in a very low mood, probably perturbed about his father's displeasure, or the problems with his future prospects.

I didn't see any more of him for about a week, and Mrs Wilson the cook, said he was staying in his room, and not eating. His father went in to shout at him periodically, but it had no effect. One evening Mrs Ross sent for me very urgently, to tell me that her son had accidentally severely cut himself with his razor, and I hitched my skirts and went bounding upstairs after her, having grabbed some of the clean old linen that I'd prepared for the expected birth. Alec was lying in sweaty sheets, with a growing crimson tide flowing from the upper part of his left arm. I grabbed the arm and raised it, clamping a clean cloth over the cut, and pressing firmly. Accident my eye! I don't think so! He looked awful – disordered in himself, and she looked very, very frightened. I have to say at this stage, young as I was, my heart didn't even go pitty pat. Delivering close to home, I'd dealt with drunken husbands, feckless women, death and haemorrhage in childbirth, and was well able to keep my nerve. This was a nothing compared with the fire and brimstone I'd already been through. I said something mild like 'No cause for alarm at all Mrs Ross. As you say, just a wee accident. Best call Dr Christie.'

Dr Christie came and patched Alec up, and was most concerned about him. Before he left, I could hear something of what he was saying outside the bedroom door, speaking to Alec's parents.......'very serious self harm.........remember his uncle in Bellsdyke......stress and strain....keep him quiet....lower expectations....' as I washed away the blood, generally cleaned him up and sorted out his bed. From that day, I had a double responsibility, and the opportunity to know Alec better, in the way of being a nurse rather than a howdie wife. He let things go bit by bit. He told me he had been a successful scholar at Dollar Academy, always pushing himself to be the best, and liked challenges, as he generally achieved all that he set himself to do. However, he was continually taunted about his baptismal name, became a loner and really took the teasing to heart. He felt so very inferior in comparison to his three elder brothers. He had been struggling at Edinburgh University. He never reached his personal standards of perfection and as he got angry with himself about this, it ate away at his powers of concentration, creating a continuing downward drift to pathetically low exam results. He battled to hide how desperate he felt most of the time and to act normally. His family had no idea of his personal agonies, which he hid through his ability to look cheerful and help other people with their problems. Secretly, he was cutting himself, as he so much hated his continual failure to reach his own high standards.

'Alec' as I referred to him as he so hated his given name, slowly became more confident with me. We developed a great feeling of mutual warmth. I did not ask any questions, and tried to be positively encouraging to him. Fortunately his sister, Mrs Paterson, went two weeks past her time, and I was at Aberlour longer than planned. Apparently Alec's uncle Euan had been confined to Bellsdyke hospital for many years, having 'gone mad' at a similar age to Alec. At the bottom of Alec's worries was the grave concern that he might have developed a similar illness. Fortunately, frightened by the drama surrounding Alec, and having taken Dr Christie's advice to heart, his father put no further pressure on him to return to the university. Instead, he had got him a short period (in view of his medical training) of being articled to the ageing Mr Malcolm who ran the local pharmaceutical chemist's shop in the town. The plan was that on successful completion of his Pharmaceutical Society examinations, he would succeed Mr

Malcolm as the local pharmaceutical chemist and druggist. Young Mrs Paterson was, in due course, happily delivered of a fine daughter, and when my work was finally done, I returned home to gather myself together ready for the next job. Alec had seemingly recovered well, was studying for his pharmacy examinations and was taking to his work in Mr Malcolm's pharmacy with gusto.

Chapter Seven

Life continued for me much the same as ever. The four of us, with three of us working and old Mrs Mack in charge of the hoose, were soon able to move into a better hoose in Bank Street, with an inside, shared stair. For ma and me, the better jobs, which were 'live in' were the best, as all our meals and laundry were provided. When I wasn't working, life in the poorer parts of town continued interesting and challenging. Many desperately poor people lived within the town, and Mr and Mrs Barr who stayed up the stair nearly got into trouble with the law when they were accused of sending their children out to beg on the streets. Indeed, the road around the railway station was quite infested with child beggars at night. The police were always bringing the Barr boys home, to find out whether the begging 'for ha'pennies to buy scones' was the boys' own adopted profession, or whether the parents had sent them out to do this. The parents were scolded and warned, but as Mr Barr said to me, his eldest son was beyond his control, and would have been far better if he could have gone to the Industrial School to learn how to make a better living. The Barrs, like many others, were hard put to clothe their family properly and feed them.

Drunkenness in Alloa was rife, which made the widespread poverty even worse. As neighbours, we always tried to help each other out as we could. A woman around the corner, Agnes Lowie, lived in a room with her family. Neighbours were already caring for two of her children, and I had helped a third, a girl aged about fourteen to find work as a servant. I had not seen the Lowie family for a couple of days, and I persuaded Jock Barr to come with me and see what was going on. When we got into the filthy, stinking room, there was no furniture except a sort of a bed. There was a 'shake down' on it, but no bedclothes. Two young children were lying on the bed, wearing just their everyday rags, and an old coat was flung over them. The weans, when I roused them, were so weak and thin that they could hardly stand, and the youngest so reduced to skin and bone that she died a week later. I know that

Mrs Lowie was at one time getting seven shillings a week from the parish authorities, but when they discovered that she was spending the money on drink, it was stopped. Food and coal was supplied to the family instead, but Agnes Lowie was a right besom and had been secretly selling these for drink. I sent for the constable, and when Agnes Lowie turned up, both she and the children were taken in charge by the polis and sent to the poorhouse.

By way of a contrast to this, the Ross family lived I felt, like princes and princesses. Alec's oldest brother, Dr Abraham Ross got married to Miss Ann Reid of Woodville, one Wednesday, in spring 1881, at the West Church. I was between booked jobs at the time, and decided to attend the service to watch. The local newspaper described the event something like this:

'Well before the appointed time of eleven o'clock, crowds were wending their way towards the church to watch. The church was completely filled, even the aisles, and there was still a considerable crowd outside. The marriage party was late, by a full quarter hour, and the congregation were restless, there having been several 'false alarms' regarding the appearance of the bride. At last, the organist, Mr Charles Allum, struck up Weber's 'Wedding March'. Four bridesmaids, her cousins, attended the bride. She was dressed in ivory satin, trimmed with lace and orange blossoms. Her jewellery was gold, and she had a tulle veil. The bridesmaids carried baskets of snowdrops, and wore blue cashmere dresses and cream straw hats, trimmed with cream lace and blue velvet. His brother David accompanied Dr Ross, and Charles and Alec Ross were ushers. The marriage party all sat within the rails. The choir and congregation sang 'The voice that breathed oe'r Eden'. The marriage ceremony proceeded, the bride being given away by her uncle. The choir chanted the 67th psalm 'Be merciful to us and bless us', and eventually, when all was done, the marriage party left the church to Mendelssohn's wedding march, and departed to 'Woodville' for the wedding breakfast.'

Meantime, I got to know Alec quite well in the pharmacy, as I sometimes had to go there on messages to fetch things for Dr

Christie or to buy items needed for my own work, and to be honest, we were strongly attracted to each other. He asked me to walk out with him, but I always said no. It would have been impossible to consider, due to the obvious great social and wealth gap between us. He did confide to me one day when we were in the shop alone together, that although his father had arranged his pharmaceutical training, he remained fairly disgusted that he would never be as good as his brothers, Abraham a wealthy doctor, David in account-ancy, and Charles a senior manager at Patons. Mr Ross had openly stated over dinner one day, that being a pharmacist was barely a step above being a shopkeeper, and to expect no inheritance.

Anyway, one day in the autumn of the same year, I was in the pharmacy waiting for Alec to dispense some colic mixture for a new born wean where I was lodging with a maternity patient in Grange Place. I was out on an excuse really, as they could easily have sent a servant, but to be honest, the entire Galbraith clan in that hoose were unbearable, particularly the new mither. 'Take your time, Mr Ross', I said, relaxing in the customer's chair beside the counter, enjoying a rest from the wind outside, which was enough to fair eat the face off a body. I was resolving to ask for some face cream for myself. He re-appeared from behind his stained glass partition at the back of the shop, with a tiny, corked glass bottle, with an equally tiny label fixed. 'This should soothe the child' he said confidently. 'It's one of Mr Malcolm's own recipes, and there is none better.'

'I'll be needing some cream for my face. Can you recom-mend a brand at all?' 'Naturally, I recommend my own mixture' he said smiling. 'It goes under the name of 'J.E. Malcolm's Alloa facial cream.' It is more expensive than the proprietary brands we also stock, but has more costly ingredients, and provides our Alloa ladies with better protection. Please be kind enough to accept a professional sample with my compliments.' I accepted his gift graciously, and little by little our relationship began to develop despite my earlier, sensible reservations. I made more excuses to visit Malcolm's Pharmacy, and generally got to see Alec, as Mr

Malcolm did not keep too well, particularly in the cold weather, and was progressively leaving things to Alec. Unfortunately, this did mean that they had taken on Miss Davie to provide the counter service, but I quickly learned that it was possible to get to see Alec himself by requesting professional advice from the pharmacist. He had arranged a large display in the middle of the counter, and Miss Davie tended to stay busy at the other end by the till. She was unable to see the way we always smiled, and how he held my eyes with his, and touched my outstretched hands as he carefully put my little parcels into them.

In spring the following year he asked if I would accompany him to a concert in the schoolroom of the Alloa Church School -the new pink sandstone building at the town end of Bedford Place, with the pretty tower on it- in aid of Miss Catherine Forrester-Paton's Womens' Missionary Home in Glasgow. I was extremely nervous about accepting, as I was completely unsure whether I wanted our relationship to progress, and very frightened about the possible consequences with his father if it did. He was very pressing, but kind, and in the end I gave way, as more than half of me really, really wanted to know him better. He called for me at home in Bank Street, and was very sweet and polite with ma and Isa, whom he referred to as Miss Isabel. I got myself into a complete tizzy about what to wear, as I had very little choice of clothes, but Isa lent me her 'Sunday coat' - ma and I had no such luxurious garment, and I borrowed ma's best skirt and wore a blouse and cardigan I'd made myself. Walking down the street together for the first time, he told me shyly that he thought I looked 'a right wee stotter,' and I could feel myself blushing. The acts at the concert included a comic singer from Glasgow, an amusing short play and St Mungo's church choir singing some popular songs.

Throughout the performance, I kept wondering about how the evening would end, and whether he would want to see me again socially, and how I would deal with it. It was actually quite easy. As we turned into Bank Street, a Mr McKay that I knew from the High Street ran up and grabbed me, and said 'Thank goodness! It's oor Mary. It's her first, and it seems to be coming awfy quick.'

'Perfect!' I thought to myself. I said 'I'm so very sorry, Alec' and dashed off up the street after Mr McKay.

In the end, I was even more glad that Mr McKay had caught me when he did, as without my help the wean would clearly have died. It was in a rush to come, and I scarce had time to take off Isa's good coat and my cardigan and roll up my sleeves before my hands were needed. Bridie McKay was lying on her back, and I could already see the hair on the wean's head. Fortunately, having been caught unexpected before, I always carry a reasonable sized bag with me wherever I go, with basics such as my special scissors, clips, ties and bandage for binding, as this was by no means the first time I'd got called when in the middle of trying to have a social life. I unwrapped the clean cloth my instruments were in, and laid it close at hand. I put my right hand on the wean's emerging head to prevent it being propelled dangerously quickly into the world, and told Bridie to pant with the contraction. She did exactly as she was told, but the wean was making no progress. I wondered if a shoulder was stuck, or the cord was around the neck. I swapped my hands round, put my right hand well inside, and located the wean's neck. Within a second or two, my fingers felt the cord tight round the neck, threatening a delayed delivery and a dead wean. I grabbed my first long, curved clip with my free hand, and struggled to clamp it on the cord. Cold sweat was lashing off me as I secured the second. I grabbed my long curved scissors, and bravely inserted them to cut the cord between the two clips, with only the fingers of my other hand to guide me and protect the wean's neck. The wee laddie came out quickly then, very blue looking, and then going grey whilst I held him down, trying to get the mucous out of his mouth, smacking his back and wiping his mouth out with my cloth. I thought all my efforts to save him had come to nothing, but eventually he took a little breath, and then another till at last he had some colour, but it seemed like an age passed before he cried. I put him into a clean cloth, and put him on to her breast straight away, to help prevent her from bleeding, and to encourage delivery of the afterbirth.

I was so glad that Bridie McKay kept a clean house, and was all ready for the birth. I hadn't even had time to wash my hands, but had delivered the wean straight from the street so as to speak. My instruments were clean, but I was worried about childbed fever, which takes away many mothers, especially if a birth was complicated, like this one. Two women from up the street, having got wind of what was happening appeared to help, and Mrs McKay, and the wean were soon washed, and I put the binder firmly around the wee lad's tummy to support his umbilicus. The neighbours sorted the room and tea was made. Mr McKay, having witnessed exactly what had happened, insisted on giving me two shillings, which I accepted, as it was their first wean. I refused the wee swally whisky that was being passed round. The poor were never able to pay much, if at all, especially if it was a long family. When Dr Christie got to hear my tale, he clapped my back, and said I'd been a good apprentice, as it was from watching him I'd learned my skills.

The situation with Alec took a new turn the next time I saw him in the Pharmacy, when he asked me if I would be interested in joining an amateur theatrical group. He was all excited, and said he had it in his head to produce an American drama called 'The Unknown: a river mystery' if he could find sufficient people in the town to help him. In fact, I was very glad that I wasn't able to commit to it, as the actors and actresses all came from privileged positions – 'the better people' in town, and I was pretty certain that I would be left feeling foolish and inept. Because he thought a lot of me, he wasn't able to see that at all. I made the excuse that it was because of my work, but agreed to help with sewing and fitting some of the costumes. Alec got fully involved in the production, making great use of his vast imagination, and ability to look at things through different perspectives. He was exhilarated, riding the challenge of being creative, and doing something he had never done before.

You might have expected his apprenticeship at the pharmacy to suffer from the amount of energy he was putting into the play, and also taking the leading role, but oh no! Every time I went into the shop, I noticed the changes in him. He went up, and up and up, acting so full of life, and power. His parents found out that we had taken up with each other seriously, but he told me he didn't give a silver sixpence for what his mother or his father thought about our walking out together. I learned from other sources in the town that the difficulties within the family were unendurable, and he was flying into great rages at home. When I dared to say that I was concerned about our situation he answered 'I don't care. I know I have it all, the talent, the energy, the gift for running a great business and the brilliance to develop new medicines as yet unheard of. In the future, I will be great, rich, and admired, and you will be at my side.'

I have to say, that the play, 'The Unknown', was a resounding success, and played for three nights in the Union Hall. It was reported in the local newspaper, which showed considerable insight in the summary published.

'The play is highly sensational, consisting of a series of striking 'situations'. The plot is interesting, but loosely worked up, and unnecessarily drawn out. Of the style in which the drama is put on the stage, it is impossible to speak too highly. Mr Ross as 'The Unknown' has a difficult part to sustain, requiring as it does, the assumption of madness with occasional gleams of reason. His performance is one of great merit, revealing at times a capacity for interpreting higher tragedy than a work of this kind pretends to. The heroine, 'Bessie Merrybright' finds a fitting representation in Miss Grace Balmaine, whose fascinating style of acting admirably suits the character of the heroine. The 'Unknown' was warmly received, the principal actors being called for at the end of each act.'

Notes and References

Phemie's 'hoose in Bank Street' is in fact a tenement, a large building with access to the individual dwellings via a communal staircase. People would have lived in one or two rooms, with shared sanitation accessed via the staircase.

The stories of the Barr boys begging and Agnes Lowie and the child neglect were taken from the Stirling Observer of the 1880s.

The wedding described and the report on the play 'The Unknown' are also based on reports published in the Stirling Observer of the 1880s.

Chapter Eight

As we moved into summer, everything finally seemed to be getting too much for Alec. He told me that he wasn't sleeping from the pure excitement of living, he felt like God, he felt golden inside and out. I noted that he was drinking quantities of alcohol and taking drugs to try and stifle his racing thoughts. I blame myself. I should have broken it off with him then, I suppose, but he said that I was the centre of all this turmoil, that he was so, so, in love with me, intoxicated with my beauty, natural intelligence, charm and character. And he was sincere in saying this. I didn't know which way to turn, as I felt that something was far wrong with him.

It happened the first night of the Summer Fair in August, which was held at the Candleriggs. I was free from booked confinements, and ma said she'd cover for me if there were any unexpected calls. Alec and I had arranged to meet up outside Campbell's Drapers on the corner at 7pm, but there was no sign of him. I wasn't exactly sure of the time, so I hung about the place for a while, and got pestered by a few drunks, but I waited on. Eventually he appeared, from Cram's Bar, next door to the drapers. I could see that he was as fou as a puggie, but of course, love is blind. We went round the fair, met friends, and were having a pretty good time, although I'd told him exactly what I thought of him for getting into such a condition. 'We both have a position in town to keep up you know, and you've let yourself down, and let me down.'

Eventually we wandered off up Mar Street to the West End Park, and he had a wee, and appeared to have sobered considerably, and I felt less concerned about what his ma would say to him when he got home. 'Come here,' he said, and took me in his arms, and stroked my hair and started kissing me very passionately. It must have been the heat of the evening and the sweetness of the drink on his lips, but I felt myself returning his passion, melting to him, and getting a thrilling, pumping feeling deep down inside my body that I'd never felt before. After a while, I pulled away, because I of all people knew exactly what goings on like this led to wi lassies, and I had always strongly resolved to take no risks myself outside of the marriage bed. I was firm and straight with him. 'No further' I said clearly. But he, he would not take no for an answer. He forced me to the ground, and was pulling and ripping at my petticoats and drawers, and he would have his way with me, no matter that I cried out with pain and fear, he forced his way in, and pinioned my arms whilst he had his hard, hurtful way with me. He wasn't sorry either, not a word of apology did I get, as he helped me home.

I got into the house, and ma on seeing me said 'darlin' are ye no weel?' I was sobbing, and she saw the disordered state of dress that I was in, and guessed immediately. There is little privacy in a two-roomed house. I had to ask Mrs Mack to go into the other room whilst I washed him off me with the coal tar soap in the kitchen. Ma handed a clean nightdress through the door, and took me into bed with her, though I normally shared with Isa. Isa was at home and ma, with slitty eyes hissed to her 'not a word from you now.' Later, in bed together, she whispered 'was it him?' 'Yes' I said through my gritted teeth.

I just got on with my life. I ignored him, as far as possible, and he seemed to be taking a sulk anyway, as he was skulking around in the back dispensary. Mr Malcolm appeared back in the shop a lot more. When it came to my monthlies, nothing showed up, and I realized what had happened, and felt myself to be the most unfortunate of women. I knew right away there was a change on me. Tea and coffee started to taste disgusting, and then I started with the morning sickness. 'That this could happen to me,' I said to ma. 'We're both finished in the town now. Both our reputations are completely shot. How can we start again elsewhere?'

'Haud yer wheesht' she replied, 'you know as well as I that things don't always work out so bad. You may lose the wean yet. Tell no-one, and try to hide your belly if things progress. We'll think of something.'

Well, I thought of something. I didn't see why I should be the only one to suffer. I went right up to the house one evening, up in Claremont, determined to see Alec and demand that he made an honest woman of me. I went to the front door, asked to see him, and the housekeeper fetched Mrs Ross, whilst I waited, standing on the front porch, with its beautiful tiled floor. I had to be very brave confronting the Ross family across the big social gap which separated us. 'He is unable to see you, as he is lying in his bed, very sick' said Mrs Ross. I wasn't going to take no for an answer, and got very loudly persistent. 'I am telling you for the final time,' she insisted, 'he is indisposed, and too ill to see you or anyone else.'

'It is for shame he is sick', I replied. 'He forced himself on me, and has put me in the family way, and I am at risk of losing my livelihood through his selfish behaviour.' 'Keep your voice down' she replied in her firmest, deadliest tone. 'It is you, throwing yourself at him, which has caused his illness and the damage you claim is your own responsibility. Now get off my doorstep. If you come again I will get the sergeant to have you taken away.'

My temper reached white heat. And I suddenly had an inspiration of how to deal with her. On the way through town, I had seen children chalking a game of hopscotch on the pavement. 'Very well, Mrs Ross, but if that is your answer, I will chalk on the pavements of every street in this town, what your son has done to me, and to my family.' She shut the door in my face.

Well, I didn't carry out my threat immediately, as I knew it would do our family as much harm as theirs. I still had to consider making my own living, and the possible results for our little family group. A month passed, and something of a miracle occurred. Mrs Ross sent a note round to our house, asking me to come to Aberlour 'at my earliest convenience.' I went right away, that very afternoon, and she invited me into her drawing room, and rang for afternoon tea. I was very surprised, and very mistrustful. 'You do know that I regard any possibility of your marriage to my son completely insufferable' she said, as we sat drinking our tea from her fine delft.

'Yes, you did give that impression' I returned.

'However', she continued, 'things are not that simple. I find myself obliged to make an urgent submission to you for help. When you have finished your tea, I would like you to come upstairs with me, and see him for yourself. '

I went upstairs with her, and that was when I discovered that Alec's 'high' had finally come to an end. He had reached a full stop. He just couldn't do anything anymore, couldn't take the responsibility of his actions or the shop. He had been lying on his bed day after day, dirty and smelly. He wasn't eating or sleeping, simply regarding the cracks on the ceiling. I sat with him until the light faded, and he made no movement, and gave no acknowledgement of me.

When I finally went back downstairs, both Mr and Mrs Ross were there waiting for me. His father, speaking quietly in his carefully manicured tones, made it very clear that this was a repetition of his own brother Euan's behaviour. Euan had been committed to Bellsdyke Hospital and had remained there for years, without improvement. If he had not been carefully supervised during this time, there was little doubt that he would have killed himself.

'So, what do you expect me to do?' I said angrily. 'Despite anything you tell me, it's clear that I am not the cause of this, but he is definitely the cause of my own condition.' He answered 'We have discussed this matter in the family, and remember your kindness and help to him when he was ill before. We wish to come to an arrangement with you. You come and stay in the house, and work as his nurse. If he recovers sufficiently to marry you, we would not stand in his way. Hopefully he will be able to resume his training with old Mr Malcolm and take his examination. It was always our plan to buy out the pharmacy business for our son, so that he will have the means of supporting himself.'

I went home, and discussed the matter with ma, Isa and Mrs Mack, as they were all aware of my condition. Despite the great wrong done to me, I was ready to acknowledge that it was due to

Alec's illness. I felt unconvinced about marrying him, the way things had turned out, but he and his family owed me for the damage done, and I saw becoming Alec's nurse for a little while at least would give his father the opportunity to devise a suitable settlement for me and my child.

As far as 'nursing' Alec was concerned, I adopted a strict no nonsense timetable, and poured away the doses of sedatives Dr Christie prescribed, in the hope of improving Alec's awareness. I started early with him in the mornings, washing him when he wouldn't do this for himself, got him shaved regularly – without previous experience of a cut throat razor, which lived up to its name. I eventually got the hang of it, but he quickly took on this task himself - I wonder why! - so that was a little triumph. I got his hair sorted out, washed and cut, and in short, gave the poor lad little rest in the daytime from my pestering ministrations. I was determined that he wouldn't succeed in making day into night for himself any more. The curtains were opened, gas lamps lit on dull days, windows opened as much as possible, and I asked the servants to be as noisy as possible. I spoke to the cook, and we got as much nourishment into him as we could, making porridge with milk, and I made him take Cadbury's drinking chocolate instead of tea or coffee.

Then I lost the wean. Ma had been right, not all weans get to birth. I had been feeling a bit achey and out of sorts all day, but was putting it to the back of my mind, as the rain had eased off that Thursday, and I had finally got Alec out for a walk in the garden. I felt something give, and there was a sudden wetness around the tops of my legs, and I guessed. I left him outside, and went into the kitchen and explained to Mrs Brodie the cook, what was happening. She sent one of the maids to tell Mrs Ross, so that she could attend to Alec in the garden. I was brought to bed in one of the best bedrooms on the first floor, and Dr Christie was summoned. I lost the wean at seven months, and that is all there is to say about it. I lost a lot of blood. Alec had been unaware that I was even expecting, but I was told that he was asking for me, and being very insistent to see me. My inability to care for him for about three weeks seemed to bring him back to his senses considerably. Mrs Ross and I agreed that it was unwise to tell him about the wean. He did come and visit me often, and we both felt more secure and comforted, me lying in bed a lot as I was still faint and dizzy from all the blood I'd lost, and he sitting beside me, holding my hand. In the end, he made me tell him what ailed me.

He cried. I cried. I felt very sad for myself and the loss of the wean, but little sorrow for him over this. He went and fetched ma. I was staggered that he had found the strength to do this, given his mental and physical debility, but apparently he walked down to fetch her, and arrived at the door, nearly fainting. He then took her arm, and brought her up to Aberlour, but as for taking her arm, ma said it was he who leaned on her, but none the less, this was great progress. I hardly need to say that ill or not, when ma was gone, Mrs Ross was simply furious with me, saying 'I don't doubt Alec will be in his bed again by the end of the week.' She was wrong. The loss of our child finally united us in grief, and he, and I both began to get better.

Alec asked me to marry him. I had to think long and hard about this. For myself, I knew that I could always earn a living, and the marriage would not lead to an estrangement with my little family, even though they might consider me foolish to take on Alec. The greatest consideration was whether I could manage Alec's problems, and weather the possibility that he might end up like his uncle Euan, confined to Bellsdyke Lunatic Asylum. Life is full of chances of course. Perhaps we would never get out of bed in the morning if we considered the unknowable possibilities of each day. I said 'yes' to him in the spring of 1884 simply because I love him, and I felt that with God's help, we might be able to manage a day at a time.

Note
Chalking on the pavements or walls was a common way for poor people to leave messages for each other.

Chapter Nine

I stayed at Aberlour House through into the early Spring of 1884. They gave me the attic room I'd had during my first stay, and I kept company with Alec as much as possible during the day. His mother, who had found the very notion of a possible marriage with Alec 'repugnant', was not aware of the fact that we were still considering this in spite of his illness. With my encouragement, he resumed his apprenticeship with Mr Malcolm, and was finally going slow but steady. I insisted early on that he would for the time being, drink nothing stronger than tea, and stay off the Laudanum that Dr Christie had prescribed throughout his illness. This had led to an angry tirade by the good Doctor against me. 'I am the doctor here, whatever airs and graces you are giving yourself these days young lady. I diagnose, and I prescribe.' He was that angry he went as far as to tell Mrs Ross to dispense with my services 'immediately'. To give her credit, she did not do this, but looked him in the eye, and said 'And you Doctor Christie do not decide the ordering of my servants. Mistress Maude, get back to your work immediately.'

One good spring Sunday afternoon, Alec took me walking out of the town, away from the docks, woollen mills, breweries, glassworks and into the fields towards Cambus village. We passed through a flock of ewes, with red stains up their rumps and necks. One particularly satisfied looking beast with a large splodge over its back from the attentions of the ram paused from chewing to look at me, with a long strand of seeded grass poking from its mouth. Alec put his hand on my shoulder, and said, 'Shall we make arrangements now to get married Phemie?'

'Let us bide a while as we are now,' I said.

I knew what it would be with his parents. I had a strong suspicion that his mother would not stand in our way. She wanted so very much to see him settled, and keeping at least reasonably well, that she would probably by now swallow her social objections, provided everything was done quietly and discreetly. His father was more difficult to read. Clearly he cared about his son, but this seemed to be concentrated on 'seeing him make his way in the world', and obviously, in his father's opinion, I would always be a social block to this. The other matter was of course, Alec's position with regard to his apprenticeship with Mr Malcolm. It was much shortened, due to his medical studies, but must have been affected by his illness. In the end, his father called Alec into his study one evening and decided the matter for us. Apparently he thought, not surprisingly, that it was not seemly for Alec to be seen out walking with a person who was not his wife, and was in fact employed within the household, ostensibly to manage the linen. He suggested that we had a church marriage without proclamation. He and Mrs Ross would not attend, and Alec and I would remove to the vacant premises above Mr Malcolm's shop and live there until Alec's articles were fulfilled and he had passed his examinations. Alec's father had already purchased the shop and stock for him. Mr Malcolm, who continued to have a presence in the shop, would take on another apprentice and continue a little longer, so that should Alec be seriously unwell again, the business would be safeguarded.

Alec discussed the matter with me, and the plan seemed the best possible under the circumstances. I agreed to getting married sooner than planned, but I had something very important that I needed to ask Alec to do first. Many people in Alloa at that time wore 'The Blue Ribbon of Temperance.' Although the ministers of most of the churches in Alloa tried to persuade their parishioners to abstain from drinking alcohol to excess, the Greenside Mission where I attended had been well influenced by the Francis Murphy campaign in Dundee in 1882 and took a stronger approach. I signed the pledge 'With malice toward none, and with charity for all; I the undersigned, do pledge my word and honour (God helping me) to abstain from all intoxicating liquors as a beverage, and I will by all honourable means, encourage others to abstain.'

Even William McGonagall who wrote that awful Tay Bridge poem in 1879 wore the blue ribbon, and had a rambling incoherent poem published in the newspaper which includes the lines:

What is strong drink? Let me think.

I answer tis a thing,

From whence the majority of evils spring,

And causes many a fireside with boisterous talk to ring,

And leaves behind it a deadly sting.

I made it very clear to Alec that I would under no circumstances marry him unless he signed the pledge himself and wore the blue ribbon. Our marriage was going to be hard enough for ourselves to bear if his bad times returned, but if he took alcohol when he felt his moods begin to change up or down I could foresee disaster. He was very rational about my suggestion, and agreed that this would be for the best and said he would wear the blue ribbon on our wedding day at the West Church.

Our wedding day was a huge contrast to his brother's wedding. 'Without proclamation' meant that there were no prior announcements, and the arrangements were known only to the close families and ourselves. On the appointed Thursday, all my family, ma, Mrs Mack and Isa -who forfeited a day's pay at the mill- attended, wearing their best clothes, but on Alec's side, there was just his mother and sister. Mrs Ross and Mrs Paterson walked to the kirk to be inconspicuous, as Mr Ross was against them coming at all, and they wore their everyday clothes. I wore a deep blue bombazine dress, and my mother's cameo brooch at the neck, and Alec wore a dark worsted suit.

When the minister had pronounced us man and wife, and I had Alec's gold band on my finger, Mrs Ross and Mrs Paterson went to back Aberlour for their lunch, and our little family went back to the rooms above Mr Malcolm's pharmacy, which Alec and I had furnished from a little money his mother gave him. Ma, Mrs Mack and Isa had prepared a wonderful lunch. We had lentil soup, cold ham, tatties and carrots, followed by a total luxury – Ecclefeccan Tart which even had tiny crunchy pieces of crushed butterscotch in it. They stayed long enough to do the dishes, and then went away home.

What a rare afternoon and evening we enjoyed! For Alec, our little rooms were doubtless a come down from the space and comfort of Aberlour, but I felt myself transported into a little heaven, the reason being that this was all ours! We had money only to do three of the amazing six rooms available to us, so had left the attics untouched. We had stained boards on the floor of our main room, and the walls were painted in a bright peacock blue. A square of bright blue Brussels carpet occupied the middle space, on which sat, facing the fireplace, a leather covered Chesterfield, with turned legs, and two matching chairs. We sat together and held hands, and later turned to a little gentle, sweet kissing, which led on and on into full embraces and more and more.

So began our marriage, in gentleness and in joy. However, it proved as I expected, a commitment that was sometimes very difficult to bear. From the very beginning, I resolved to help Alec as much as possible in his pharmacy work, so that in the bad times I could give every help, both personal and professional. There was no possibility of an apprenticeship for me at that time, as I didn't have the knowledge of latin and the sciences to be able to take the examinations. I believe a woman was practising medicine in London, but Alec said she'd had to train in Paris. We didn't know of any female pharmacists. He had a lot to teach me in the evenings, regarding calculations and the Latin in which prescriptions were written by the physicians so that patients couldn't understand them. I was fascinated to discover that rx at the beginning of the prescription meaning 'recipe' or 'take' originated from the astrological sign for Jupiter. The sign of Jupiter was used by ancient Roman physicians to invoke the blessing of Jupiter on the medicine to help the patient to get well. From the planet Jupiter, the ancients believed that all good things came. Alec was such an interesting teacher, and it was a pleasure to learn from him. Mr Malcolm and Mr Roberts, the new apprentice, kindly allowed me to help with making the pills when I could find spare time in the day. They weighed the precise ingredients on their apothecary's scales, and allowed me to mix them with the syrup of glucose, a drop at a time, using a large pestle and mortar. Using the pill machine was not easy, as it was essential to make the pills as equal in size as possible so that the doses were standardized. I became highly skilled at using the pill rounder to roll the pills into regular little spheres that were coated with talcum powder so that each looked like a pearl. I learned about elixirs, emulsions, syrups, suspensions and tinctures for our patients to swallow. Most surprising were the preparations that went into various unmentionable orifices. I started to ask Alec about the illnesses each medicine was used for, and developed a great appetite for knowledge.

Of the times that weren't easy, there were plenty. To survive at all, Alec had to involve and rely on me a lot. Sometimes his temper would flair like a fire cracker, and he would be blind to reason. The best thing was to leave him to himself. I can at least say he had the sense to leave the shop and go off on his own when this happened. From that point of view, we were well supported by the staff, but often, I didn't know where he'd gone, or if he would ever come back. In the bad times when he was very down, I felt drawn into his illness myself, and together we passed many dark days, dark nights and black weeks. As a couple, it became a daily struggle to keep our marriage and the business afloat. Even talking to folks during his bad times was so hard for Alec that he had to withdraw completely behind the dispensary screen. Going out alone or with me whilst he felt like this was very demanding on him, and he wasn't regular at the West Kirk, so I started back at the Mission. I arranged for us to take a day off and go on the train to Edinburgh to walk along Princes Street, and see how the Edinburgh folks arranged their pharmacies. Come the day, he felt it was too much to bear, going to a crowded station, and sharing a compartment with other folks. However, for my sake, I felt, he never cut himself again after we married.

When he was 'up', he scarcely slept, and neither did I. To give him his due, he never ever resorted to alcohol, and still wore his blue ribbon. In spite of all that I'd said to Doctor Christie in the early days, I did occasionally pour a good slug of Laudanum into his tea to calm him a bit. It was however as these 'up' episodes were coming on that he had some of his best ideas for changing things in the business. I felt that I had little opportunity to manage my own feelings, and on really bad evenings with him, was often out walking the streets, or sitting in with my ma at her hoose.

Alec and I always tried to speak our problems to each other. We wondered about the possibility of making a complete change, selling the business and setting up again somewhere else. When he felt well, we often went down to the waterfront, to see which ships and cargoes were in, and fantasized about a new life together, where the past with his family, and the town he never felt that he had really fitted into were left behind us. When the chance to make a complete change came, we both jumped at it.

HARRY

Chapter Ten

My start in life wasn't good, but in comparison with many other children of my time, it wasn't all that bad either. I just felt unnecessarily grouchy about it in my early years! My father did what he felt best for me. From what he and Miss Caroline tell me, Charity, my mother died two days after my birth, from bleeding following my birth. I was initially put out to a 'wet nurse,' in Parkstone, and when I was weaned, Caroline Baskett, my late mother's best friend, who was also my godmother, took me to live with her and her father at Blake Hill Farm because my father was at sea. With my father being captain of a ship, there was no shortage of money for me, just the shortage of a father, sometimes for years at a time.

Blake Hill Farm was well run, and very busy, and there was little time available for the amount of care and attention needed by a small boy who lacked a father figure. I ran pretty wild, but it was a place of safety and Miss Caroline showed me unfailing motherly love. She never married, and some said that it was all to do with hoping that Captain James Lovejoy would eventually ask her. She was a bit younger than my own mother would have been. Myself, I think during those years, she liked helping to run the family farm, and there was nothing to prevent her inheriting it as she had no brothers. When her father died, she really enjoyed being the boss, known as Mistress Baskett and having to deal with men on equal terms. In 1884, when I was eighteen, men owning property with an annual value of ten pounds were given the vote, but women owning property in their own right were excluded. She ferociously resented her lack of a vote, often pointing out to others that she was always able to hold her own with fellow farmers, male workers, dealers and businessmen. Her fierce independence wasn't something I saw as unusual as a child, but now I realise that like Mrs Teague, she was unusual for the age she lived in. Most men considered women to be completely useless at running anything except a household.

As a child, I was content to play with the cowman's children, and generally help out with milking, calving, mucking out, sowing, and harvesting, but that wasn't what I wanted to do as an adult. I felt generally discontented because I was not on the sea, and because my father was a respected sea captain, and I wanted to imitate him. He was a very busy man, managing his own books and cargoes, as his ship was his own, and didn't belong to any company, so he didn't find much time for me. He brought me interesting presents when I saw him, a whale's tooth intricately carved and polished, with the figure work all in black – scrimshaw he called it. Another time it was a ship in a bottle. There was never any shortage of genuine affection from either him or Miss Caroline.

Miss Caroline was a big blue-eyed brown haired, suntanned woman, rotund but never flabby. She was strong, and could and did work as hard physically as any man about the place. She smiled a lot, laughed a lot and put more store on practicality than book learning, although she saw what she called 'reckoning' as one of the most important jobs in running the farm effectively. I got better arithmetic lessons from her and later from my father than I ever had at school. Very unusually for the times, she was highly demonstrative in her affections towards me, with plenty of hugs and kisses, as she saw me as her own son. Strangely too, my father gave me plenty of hugs and kisses, even when we were both grown men. Of course, I stayed with him at the Poop Deck whenever he was ashore, together with his steward Edward, who always went to sea with him, and Vasistha his lascar, who now 'kept house' for him.

I remember one wonderful summer, after he had been away around the world for a couple of years, and was discharging goods and then having a clay cargo loaded, that he took me to Salterns, and taught me to swim. We went out several times on a drifter with a fisherman, and he showed me how to use a ship's sextant. When he had time for me, it felt like Heaven on earth. As time passed I became more and more restless at the farm. 'What irks you boy?'

Miss Caroline would ask me fondly. It wasn't true, the gossip about her. She rarely struck me, and never hard. She just pretended to everybody else that she was severe with me, but she never was. I wasn't brought up by hand at all! Why did she pretend to be hard? Well, I think it's just the way she had to be seen to be because of the men she had to deal with. She needed to keep up an appearance as being 'hard' in a man's world, but at the same time, she found she had precious little in common with other women, and was much misunderstood. She had a strange relationship with my father too, as she could not let any man 'best' her. As they were both used to being obeyed, their encounters whilst loving, were frequently stormy.

Thanks to Miss Caroline, I was able to help with difficult calving, and do all the other jobs on the farm, so she always gave me a calf or two for my own, which I was free to sell, and I was rarely without a few shillings in my pocket. Yes, I was naughty, and liked being with the lads in the town after my day's work. I know they had worse lives than me, and their behaviour was often crude and common, but I was desperate to become part of a group, the next best thing in my mind to being a member of the Daphne's crew. I started to drink a lot by the time I was sixteen, and I certainly developed a taste for it. By the time I was seventeen, blind drunk many a time, I would frequently spew over my clothes and sometimes in my bed. I was often shaking in the mornings for the need of a drink, and Caroline started to get desperate with me. I shamed her, and the good upbringing she'd tried to give me. 'Without help, my boy, you're going to Hell in a handcart', she said. In January, she called in the help of Canon Dugmore, from St. Peter's Church, Parkstone. 'Join the Church Temperance Society, my son' he said gently. 'You're young yet, and can reform. There is no need to pursue this path to self-destruction.' Well, I drew the line at joining the Temperance Society! I did agree to go regularly to church again, and as a sign of goodwill agreed to attend a church meeting, and enjoyed some magic lantern slides of the Zulu War. To be fair, I was drinking less as a result of their kind efforts. I just wanted to DO more. The prayers one Sunday were for 'The protection of British troops, and those associated with them in Afghanistan – (the British had learned nothing from their costly mistakes in Crimea); that in dealing with that country, the counsels of our rulers may be guided by the principles of Justice, Mercy and Charity. That good order may be restored ere long in the goodness of God, to the sister kingdom of Ireland – (Parnell was beginning the Land League Campaign) and the merciful relief of it's present distress.......' Fine, I thought, all this praying, but let me DO something exciting too!!

One Sunday in early Spring, I was outside St Peter's Church in the sunshine, shaking Canon Dugmore's hand at the end of the service when my eyes lit upon a goddess disguised in a straw bonnet, leaving with Lydia Curtis; clearly she was a servant in the Curtis household. Things inside my trousers began to stiffen up in a most delightful way. 'Bathsheba.....' I said under my breath. 'Pardon?' said the Canon sharply. 'Beautiful day I muttered'.

I did a fair amount of lurking around the Curtis home morning, noon and night to try and catch a further glimpse of their beautiful servant. I finally got lucky, catching her one evening inside the garden walls, by the domestic rubbish dump. I gave her a fearful start. 'I saw you at church, and have been trying to meet with you to find out if you would be able to walk out with me one evening' I explained. 'Do you have family locally' I asked? 'No, I am alone in the world, having been born in the Workhouse', she answered. 'I have my monthly half day next Saturday.' 'In that case,' I answered, may I invite you to tea at Blake Hill Farm on that day.' I think the mention of Blake Hill Farm, together with Miss Caroline's unimpeachable respectability convinced her that I was a genuine admirer. 'Yes', she said, 'and my name is Liza, but I can't meet you until about two o'clock, and if you could wait in the trees at the bottom of the road, as I don't want the Curtis family knowing my business. Now please do get out of the garden, as you will get me into all sorts of trouble for encouraging followers here. I could be sacked for it.'

We met as arranged. I asked her permission to hold her hand the day we walked round to the farm. Her lips were beautiful, and I could scarcely take my eyes off her. Miss Caroline was accommodating about supplying a plentiful afternoon tea, but did make a quiet aside that Liza looked at least a couple of years older than me, and best not to get too serious with the first pretty girl I met. I couldn't help it. I just needed to get my hands on her. Though it was dusk, and rather cool, I took her out 'to see the rest of the farm', but actually took her into the barn, and touched her beautiful tawny hair, which was gathered together into a firm 'bun' at the back of her head, and kissed her, which she was very ready for, and very responsive.

I took her home, but didn't want to leave her, and developed a great ache for more than the further kisses we exchanged furtively in the woods at the bottom of Sandringham Road. I became a perfect pest, and hung around in the Curtis's gardens at night, hoping to catch her with the intoxication of my open mouthed kisses and to handle through her clothes, her well stayed breasts. We could hardly wait for her next half-day. I arranged a 'secret picnic,' as I had no more desire for Miss Caroline's respectability. I wanted Liza. All that I wished for happened. She felt as strongly as I did, and we were leaning against a tree, and one thing led to another, and she was pulling me to her, and moaning, and I was finally in her skirts, and with appalling rapidity, it was all over. After a short while lying together on my coat, we were able to do it all over again, with her jumping and groaning in my arms.

Well, as you can tell, I was sort of trying to lead the quiet, sober and upright (sometimes!) life that Miss Caroline and the Canon were encouraging me into, but one Sunday, after lunch I decided to walk into Poole. The rest is a matter of court record. Yes, I had drunk a spectacular amount of rum, and was larking about with my friends by the Guildhall, when the Salvation Army band formed a circle and started to play. Things are still hazy in my mind, but I did bother them rather a lot, and we did follow them back to the Citadel, and I was arrested. As a result I was quite knocked about myself, apparently having resisted arrest.

At the time, I didn't know whether to feel glad or sorry that the Daphne was about to dock after an absence of ten months. The constable had already allowed Miss Caroline into the cells, and she remained very cross but practical, and demanded that more drinking water be made available to me, and had brought me ham and eggs 'to line my stomach.' My father turned up unexpectedly at the Police court, straight off the Daphne, looking positively apopleptic with anger, and then publicly wept with shame as judgement was passed. Only after paying a very substantial fine were he and Miss Caroline allowed to march me straight back to the Poop Deck, where I was fed and put to bed.

That evening, we spoke together after dinner. Miss Caroline, not a small woman, had fitted herself into Father's biggest armchair, which looked as if it had been built around her, and was looking very displeased. 'I need an account of your behaviour, Harry,' Father said severely, 'and of why you have put dear Miss Baskett through such terrible trials. She has told me everything.'

'Dear Father, and dear Miss Caroline,' I said. 'I am most overwhelmingly sorry for my selfishness and stupidity. I have been so grateful for such an excellent home and all the care and attention I've been given every day of my life. I have no excuse. However, I'll never make a farmer, hate being out of sight of the sea and need to be with you now, father, and share your learning. I've been sad inside, and instead of speaking to either of you about it, I've been selfish and stupid.'

'You, Harry, have destroyed my good name and standing both within the village of Parkstone and the town of Poole' said Miss Caroline. 'You are of my family too, by my adoption if not by your birth, and I have been greatly pained at your behaviour.' Tears of weakness and contrition were running down my face.

'I'm so sorry,' I blubbered.

Father answered gently, 'I am sorry too, as I had left things too long before deciding that you were ready to make decisions for yourself. Your mother was so precious to me, and you are all I have left of her. The life at sea is so hard and dangerous, that I had sincerely hoped that you might take to farming instead. I can offer you only a life of boredom, contrary winds and currents, dysentery, drowning, fever, fear, frostbite, hurricanes, icebergs, leaks, mutiny and desertion, pirates, rocks, seasickness, shortages of food and water, treacherous waters and plenty of vermin. Miss Caroline and I have come to a decision. You will be coming to sea with me. We sail in about six weeks with a mixed cargo for Luanda on the west coast of Africa, where we are hoping to pick up further cargo. I will arrange for you to sign your articles as an apprentice seaman. You are clearly unable to control your appetite for alcohol, so I will personally make sure you behave yourself aboard Daphne.'

'It's a new beginning for you' said Miss Caroline. 'Now make the best of it.'

A couple of days later, I was aching to have further time with Liza. The weather was very wet, and I got soaked through waiting have a few moments with her by the kitchen refuse dump, so I took her inside the tree just inside the gate, and I had my way with her. 'How long will you be?' she asked. 'At least two years' I replied, feeling that this could well be a permanent goodbye.

Note
Blake Hill Farm was really the property of the Viney family who later ran a large business in lower Parkstone.

The prayers for the British troops in Afghanistan were taken from the Parkstone Reminder of 1880.

Chapter Eleven

It was my first voyage. My dear father was now Captain Lovejoy to me – the Cap'n. He gave me notice of requiring a premium of thirty pounds. Of course, I had been spending wildly. The reasonable income that Miss Caroline had provided me with as a working member of her family through my farming activities, I had largely wasted. Nonetheless, without me even asking, she discreetly stumped up the cash for me, muttering aggressively 'I know youm put to vor money'. On paying the money over and signing my apprenticeship articles, I became 'bound' to father as my Master whilst undertaking my training for my Certificate of Competency as a mariner. I thus became 'a brassbounder', bound by my premium to see out my apprenticeship. The Cap'n told me that if I was to learn well, he could show me no favours. Apprentices were normally aged from fourteen to twenty one, so at eighteen, I was truly a late starter, working for my Certificate as a mate. I would start out as an apprentice, and if successful, progress in my seamanship skills and through the Board of Trade Examinations to my Mate's tickets. When I qualified and worked satisfactorily as a First Mate, I would then become eligible through further examination, to Captain a vessel in my own right.

We took on a 'general' cargo from Poole, which included domestic sanitary fittings from local potteries, tiles, ropes, nets, brushes and ironwork. It was the longer trips which the Cap'n always preferred, describing them as a way to 'earn a better living'. Trade from sailing vessels such as ours was less threatened by steamers which were less reliant on favourable winds and could often offer shorter delivery dates of speciality perishable items to prospective customers. With no requirement to carry coals to fuel heavy engines, we could fill our holds with larger, heavier cargoes. We were expecting to be away for about two years, possibly longer. I was very surprised to find that more than forty percent of a trading vessel's time was taken up loading and unloading cargo or moving in ballast between ports. The Capn's incoming cargo of wheat took twenty one days to discharge in Poole, and her cargo for West Africa was loaded in twenty days, so this granted me time to gather together the meagre kit of an apprentice mariner. I bought a massive amount of gear (using a further generous loan from Miss Caroline) mostly from Piplers on Poole quay. Just to show you how much preparation I had to make, here is just a part of my long list of purchases:

Felt cap with small peak
Black leather belt with a brass buckle and a sheathed knife hanging from it
Seaman's weskits (2)
Unbleached canvas trousers (3)
Blue flannel shirts (3)
Knitted Guernsey
Watch coat
Kerchiefs
Buckled shoes
Boots
Oilcoat and trousers
Journal books
Travelling ink stand, black ink, letter sealing wax, pencils, paper
Soap, razor, sewing kit
Pewter eating vessels, knife, fork and spoon in a canvas pouch
Flint and steel

I moved on board the Daphne with my kit, within that first week of her docking. Apart from my one visit to Liza, I was on the ship, or with my father and the other apprentices as there was much work to be done, preparing the Daphne (and me) for sea. I had to make my own mattress called 'a donkey's breakfast' by filling a mattress ticking with clean straw which I placed on my berth in the spartan deckhouse located between the main and mizzen masts, allocated to the apprentices. There were two senior apprentices, Mr Downton and Mr Hardy who had been given shore leave, to visit their families. When I met them, I got on better with them as they were closer to my own age. Given that the Cap'n was expecting me to progress faster due to my education, age and previous life experiences, I spent time learning as much as they could teach me. The two junior apprentices were Bertie Snell, a local boy and Peter Le Lacheur from Guernsey.

Captain Lovejoy was assisted by his First Mate Paul Hann and Second Mate John Ellis. The most important seaman was the Bo'sun. Mr Rogers the sail maker, Mr Bennett the carpenter, and a cook called Maloney were referred to as 'idlers' as they did not take part in the ship's watch. Their work was however of high value, and they were paid well. However, Maloney seemed universally disliked by the hands for his laziness and meanness and was quite old. Similarly Edward Jones my Father's saloon steward was also an 'idler.' The Cap'n ran his ship very strictly. No alcohol was allowed on board with the crew and swearing was banned, although this was sometimes difficult to enforce!

My first order from the Cap'n was to spend a full week with Mr Rogers, the sail maker, a very quiet man, which I supposed resulted from his often solitary occupation. My initial task was to sew my own canvas 'ditty bag', which would hang on my bunk, and contain all my small tools, which would provide me with the means of repairing my own clothes and personal equipment. Whilst working with Mr Rogers I learned a tiny bit about the sail maker's art, gromets, basic stitches and ropework, with which as a working member of the crew I would need to develop expertise. Under Mr Roger's careful instruction, I learned the names and something of the usage, maintenance and storage of each sail - essential information, as I would be working practically, with each one. At the end of this first week I was transferred to Mr Bennett the carpenter, and taken over every inch of the Daphne, and learned the proper name for every wooden part and helped him with some of the maintenance and repairs. Again, as a sailor I would be involved in keeping the ship in good order. I reflected on the Captain's choice of Daphne, the wood nymph who turned into an olive tree as his name for the ship, which I now realized was undoubtedly linked to his great love of reading tales from Greek mythology, particularly Homer whilst on long sea passages. Together with the two junior apprentices, I reported every evening to the Cap'n at 'The Poop Deck' where we dined. Daphne's apprentices were treated far better than any others I met. Following our communal meal, served by Edward, we were given lessons in trigonometry, the use of six figure logarithms and other arcane delights, including the use of the sextant. The evening that stands out best in my memory is the first of July, when we looked at the stars in the night sky, and were tested on their names. The Cap'n, who turned out to be a most remarkable teacher, explained clearly how their positions were identical to a month ago, the difference being that they rise two hours earlier each month, so that the sky we were observing at ten pm would have been identical the previous month, at midnight.

Every day, for me, was now full. The Cap'n explained that a crew was a team, and none of us would ever be too high or too low to do any task aboard. Mr Tilsed, the Bo'sun therefore directed me to a whole range of duties, to be sure that I knew the names and places of everything aboard. Under his general supervision I also had to help with the unloading of the grain cargo, and the re-loading in preparation for our landing at Luanda. Mr Tilsed's powerful position included responsibility for the efficient work and discipline of the seamen, as well as rigging, cables, anchors, sails, boats and the command of the sail maker and the carpenter.

The Cap'n was everywhere, checking cargo stowage with Mr Tilsed, speaking with the grain merchants and shippers, teaching and supervising his apprentices, signing the crew and directing Mr Tilsed on re-provisioning the Daphne with everything that might be needed for the long voyage. I lay on my donkey's breakfast every night, exhausted. One Tuesday I was sent me up to the railway station to meet with Mr and Mrs Macdonald, our passengers, who were arriving from Alloa by train. John Paton and Son of the woollen mills in Alloa, had sent Mr McDonald to travel with us to Australia. Once there, he was empowered to select and purchase a cargo of the finest Australian wool for shipping back to the Kilncraigs mill in Alloa. The couple would set up home in Australia, with Mr Macdonald providing a direct connection between the Scottish company and the wool producers. The couple were quartered with the Cap'n at The Poop Deck until the final preparations had been made for sailing. I had never met Scotch people before, but they seemed pleasant enough.

On the final day before our departure, Miss Caroline arrived in the afternoon, driving her large delivery cart, complete with the Capn's order of the best fresh vittles available from Blake Hill Farm for which she said, smacking a massive leg of lamb on the kitchen table, she was expecting the best price from the Cap'n. 'That sheep was yourn' she said to me, as a loud, 'confidential' aside. 'I needs to recoup some 'a that there loan. For aught I know, you might not be cummen back, could be sunk, and would leave me a lone, lorn wumman.' There were tears in her blue eyes, and in mine too. She shoved an untidy string tied, brown papered parcel at me sharply. On exploring the contents I found a knitted watch cap and a balaclava helmet. 'Case you gets cold on that darned ship' she muttered, 'don't lose em, you know how I hates knitten worse'n torture.' There were two books, the Pilgrim's Progress and a large print Prayer Book. 'Got um big print case the light was bad', there was a spice box, 'specs the food'd be vile', a pocket knife, tobacco in a tin, a flint and two pipes. 'I know you aint smokin yet you little varmint, but you might need un.'

Miss Caroline was in the kitchen for the rest of the afternoon with Edward, and the leg of lamb was finally served, together with a marvellous selection of fresh vegetables. She didn't stay long after the meal, but said goodbye, muttering in a low tone to me 'Shassn't be seeing thee for a while. Must git homealong afore it gits dark', and in a louder voice to father, pointing at me, 'Thur's many a good cock comes out vrom a tattered bag' and departed to the back alley with Edward to help her put her horse back into harness. I could have cried. Well, I very nearly did. We were all aboard the heavily loaded ship that night. There were four pigs in a pen on deck, eighteen hens in a coop, six sheep and two goats and fresh vegetables hung around the place in nets, above and below decks.

The crew were paid once the Daphne docked, as the previous voyage for which they had signed up was ended. Some men were kept on to work whilst loading and unloading was taking place. A few of the previous crew, who did not have families in Poole, had signed on with other ships and masters. One of the local seamen John Fudge, who was a new member confided that he felt particularly glad to be on the Daphne, as he had sailed with her before, and found my father to be a fair and honest master. His previous Captain was generally drunk, a poor navigator, ill tempered and the crew were very badly fed. I should add here that my father had already discharged one potential 'sailor' for not knowing one rope from another, and a second sailor who 'knew his ropes' was discharged when found drunk on the lower deck. At long last a full crew was aboard. Before we left, the Cap'n, had to read out to all aboard the Crew Agreement, the contract between him and the crew. Penalties for misbehaviour were made clear, the quantities of food and water per man and the Daphne's permitted load line were made very clear to all.

We were fortunate to be able to sign Caleb Stone, a Poole man who had been employed not just for his seafaring experience, but because he was an excellent 'shanty man' who could lead the singing required to help crewmen work in rhythm on heavy jobs involving hauling sails or working the capstan. He began the first verse of 'Pay me my money down', and a team of men began winding the capstan to weigh anchor, singing as they worked. The two little steam tugboats, one on the headline and the other astern, pulled us out of the harbour on the first tide, with the crew now silent and the Cap'n on the bridge, reciting our morning prayer in his great voice:

'Oh eternal Lord God, who alone spreadest out the heavens, and rulest the raging of the sea, who compassed the waters with bounds until day and night came to an end; be pleased to receive into Thy almighty and most gracious protection the persons of thy servants on Daphne, in which we serve. Preserve us from the dangers of the sea, and from the violence of the storms. May we return in safety to enjoy the blessings of the land, with the fruits of our labours and with a thankful remembrance of Thy mercies to praise and glorify Thy holy name, through Jesus Christ our Lord. Amen'.

The Daphne was a beautiful ship, a wooden barque with four masts, rigged with fore and aft sails and square sails on the central masts. She could sail with a smaller crew, as she had less heavy, square sails to be managed by the seamen, but she could still attain speeds close to those attained by full rigged ships. The Cap'n maintained that she sailed 'better to windward'and to maximize her speed, Daphne's square sails were a little wider, to catch as much wind as possible.

I was terrified those first few days, and oftentimes later on, but then I suppose we all were, even the Cap'n sometimes, though he never showed it. It was all right at first, in harbour, I just did as I was told, and watched and learned a lot, but as soon as we cast off, I began to understand the truth of the expression 'all at sea'. I felt lost, completely out of control of my life. It was a very breezy day, and we went out of the harbour, past Brownsea Island and past The Haven with the pilot standing at the poop rail, beside the Cap'n. When the pilot was released, the lower topsails were set and the yards were trimmed as we approached Old Harry Rocks, and the wind began to freshen. I could feel the ship bouncing alarmingly relative to the horizon, and dreaded being seasick. It was very difficult, as I was fully occupied with deck duties. I had been permitted to practise 'going aloft' to stand on the spars whilst we were in harbour, but at sea only the 'top men' went up to manage the sails in bad weather. I was one of the 'lowest of the low' in the crew for the time being. The Cap'n came round and told me to keep my eye on the horizon as much as possible, and put young apprentice Le Lacheur who was already yawning and looking very queasy to take the wheel under Mr Ellis's supervision.

My first meal aboard ship that evening during 'the dog watch' was eaten in the tiny cabin I shared with the other apprentices. We ate the same as the men. As a novice sailor, I ate little, as Moloney's food was poor, and I felt queasy. As I was not on watch, I lay in my bunk with my eyes closed, as Mr Hardy, one of our senior apprentices said it tended to help with seasickness. On the Capn's instructions Edward visited our cabin, with a mixture of ginger wine, hot water, cocculus and nux vomica, which helped a little. I lay there, waiting for sleep, and reflected on the fact that my father was now my Master, my chief navigator, my physician and my clergyman.

Notes

The Paton's wool company actually sent their own man to Australia to obtain the best fleeces for them. He did not of course, sail on the Daphne...

All the prayers quoted in the following chapters as being used at sea were taken from 'Forms of Prayer to be used at Sea' in the Book of Common Prayer 1662 (this Prayer Book was in full use in Anglican churches until1980).

Glenlee, the Tall Ship in Glasgow harbour provided visual stimulus for the chapters set at sea.

Hogben R., Castle C., (undated). Five thousand days. The voyages of the Clydebuilt Barque Glenlee 1897-1919 pub. Clyde Maritime Trust was a helpful read.

Chapter Twelve

My life became governed by bells. The crew was divided into two 'watches,' the Port Watch and the Starboard Watch, with each watch working four hours on and four hours off, with the exception of the 'Dog Watch' from four pm to 8pm, which was split into two 2 hour watches to enable our two evening meal sittings and to alternate the watches so that we all worked a fair distribution of both nights and days. There was a system of ringing the ship's bell every half hour, so that if I were dozing in my bunk, I would know the exact time during the hours of darkness. You might think that this was somewhat unnecessary to make such a disturbing clatter, keeping people awake, but our deckhouse was very noisy anyway. As I gradually began to understand how closely navigation across the oceans was linked to knowing the exact time, I began to find the noise quite companionable. I was on the Port Watch, with the First Mate Paul Hann, junior Apprentice Bertie Snell and five hands. For the first time, I was able to 'take my turn' at the helm under Mr Hann's supervision. I experienced a feeling of great power, as I felt the vessel speeding through the waters, and the size of the wheel and the mechanics of it, made it heavy work, so one of the hands was also required to help, particularly in heavy seas. Paul was a kind and conscientious teacher, and showed me how to use the traverse board, and I inserted a peg every half hour to record the heading as shown on the ship's compass. Our speed, recorded in 'knots,' was calculated hourly by using a log line, and recorded at the bottom of the traverse board again, using wooden pegs on strings, with the hands usually supervised by young Bertie Snell. The 'log' used for recording our speed was actually a wooden quarter circle, held by a 'bridle' of three short lengths of rope, attached to a longer rope knotted at intervals of 47 feet three inches, on a reel at the stern of the ship. Three men were required for the job. One dropped the 'log' over the stern, one allowed the rope to unwind from the reel, and the third, Bertie, was responsible for timing using a 28 second time glass or pocket watch. The rope was hauled back onboard and the number of knots was counted. A speed of for example eight knots was then recorded on the traverse board.

On watch at night, I was fascinated to notice Edward our gentle, charming steward, often sneaking out of his quarters at about 11.30 each night, to disappear into the rope locker that lay on the forward part of the ship. He would usually be joined in this small dark space by one of the hands. I mentioned it to Paul Hann. 'The Cap'n is aware of it' he remarked. 'He doesn't think it does any harm, as the men will only be interested in women when they get ashore, and it keeps Edward amused. Each man and boy has his own peculiarities, just look at Mathew. His wife gave him that great bottle of holy water to keep sprinkling on himself, in the hopes that it'd keep him safe. It's best not to be too critical when we all have to live together.' And indeed, Mathew did anoint himself with Holy Water and cross himself before any major event. He was ribbed a lot about it, but was a cheerful fellow, and took the teasing with good humour.

Our passage through the English Channel had been relatively calm, and since that first short, unsettled sleep between watches, which I put down to my nervousness as much as anything, I felt better able to cope with the ship's movements and noises as the sails cracked on the masts, the timbers creaked and the bows rose and fell. Before long, we were out on the Atlantic, with our tiny ship like a cork on the terrible waters, where each dark wave was higher than our masts. When it was my turn to take the wheel, Paul Hann would stand beside me, checking that I kept the ship on course. From him I learned the primary lesson. If the helmsman ever allows the ship to get into a position where the waves are side on in heavy seas, there is an immediate risk of turning the ship over. This is referred to as broaching the ship. However, our many lessons with Mr Hann, Mr Ellis and the Cap'n made the complex dangers of wave power on a ship even more frightening. For example, simply steering the ship's course in a following sea (away from the waves) could result in a large wave overtaking the ship, and hitting it awkwardly on the stern, burying the bow and lifting the rudder from the sea, just at the very moment when it is most needed for steering. I had never understood all this before, and I realized that I hadn't even approached the extreme arts of sail management in heavy seas and how to manage in moderate and heavy winds.

I found the cold, the wet, the wind and the seas almost unendurable at times. We had some protection initially from our oilskins, long jackets and trousers made from rough sailcloth that had been soaked in linseed oil, but eventually the wet and cold wore us all down. I went to my bunk wet through, with no hope of drying before the next watch. The crew fared very badly in their fo'c's'le cabin at the front of the ship, with its door almost flush with the deck, which was extremely cold, often wet, and where bunk spaces were shared by the watches. We were little better off in our deckhouse. In heavy seas, we went day after day without hot food, but Edward, using a spirit stove and extreme skill managed hot cocoa for the passengers, officers as often as he could. Just occasionally he made enough for the rest of us as well.

I began to realize the importance of learning seamanship as fast as I could, if only for my own survival, and became conscientious in keeping my personal log, and the use of personal notebooks to assist my learning. When the sea was reasonably quiet, I also spent a lot of my 'spare' time in the chart room with the Cap'n, Mr Ellis and Mr Hann, trying to develop my knowledge of the complicated mathematics involved in plotting our daily course using 'dead reckoning.' The information recorded from the traverse board of speed and course were interpreted on to the charts, but further corrections needed to be made for the ship's 'leeway', as for example a northerly wind could cause a westwards moving vessel to make leeway to the south. Similarly, leeway could occur as a result of strong ocean currents. As you can imagine, the actual determination of our position could be quite inaccurate due to the limitations imposed by these factors. I quickly understood the importance of the recording of daily (or more frequent) observations in the ship's log. In addition to the recording of the above information, the sextant was used most frequently to measure the altitude of the sun against the horizon. The object used (sun, moon, planet or one of the 57 navigational stars), angle and time of the measurement could be used to calculate a position line on a nautical chart after consulting Bowditch's American Practical Navigator which specified for each *hour* of the year the position on the Earth's surface (in declination and Greenwich hour angle) at which the sun, moon, planets and the first point of Aries is directly overhead. I was absolutely fascinated with every facet of navigation, and gave myself many headaches trying to grasp the complexities of this art. The Cap'n told me he was very pleased with the fast progress I was making.

The navigation was only a part of the mass of information and experience of my life at sea. My work on deck was hard and even my rough, tough farming hands got split and chapped. When I was 'off watch' I rubbed tallow into them. The food for the Cap'n, passengers and officers was as good as it could be, given the fact that all aboard ate much the same rations. However, we believed that the officers' rations were more generous, and they had the comfort of the saloon and decent crockery to eat from. Food was therefore reasonably fair, except for the eggs. These were kept for the Cap'n and passengers. As a former farmer, I was personally acquainted with these Blake Hill Beauties. I guessed that the girls would quickly go 'off lay' and conspired with my fellow apprentices to *purloin* (not the same as stealing surely?) as many eggs as we could. It became quite a game. Edward and the officers kept careful watch. We competed with the crew to grab what we could. Eventually the hens ceased to lay. Our passage to Luanda was expected to take four to six weeks, and the fresh vegetables and fruit were quickly used and the Blake Hill Beauties were expertly slaughtered by Edward, one by one, as were the other beasts, in their turn. Eventually we had no fruit and vegetables left, and were reliant on dried peas and lentils. Although the Cap'n provided better food than most others for the crew, once the potatoes were used up, in favourable weather the crew were given bread baked aboard by Maloney. In poor weather they were often reduced to eating the big, coarse water biscuits purchased in Poole instead, that were made as hard as rock, commonly referred to as 'pantiles.' Maloney issued each man with a pound of these per day, and I watched how they managed them. The biscuits were put into a fold of canvas, and pounded with an iron bar. The crumbs were mixed with some of the water from their daily ration. Every Friday Maloney issued each man with either a pound of butter or a pound of jam or marmalade, which they often used to mix with the biscuit crumbs for their breakfast. This was washed down with a mug of coffee. For dinner each man had half a pound of corned beef or pork on alternate days. Maloney was frequently accused by the hands of giving them short measure, and nasty arguments often developed with him. Fresh vegetables and potatoes were served with the meat until they ran out. The dried peas or beans which Maloney served with the meat were often said to be inadequately soaked and boiled. Crew members also had a small daily allowance of tea, coffee or chocolate and sugar or molasses. The food was therefore better at the beginning than at the end. The Cap'n, officers, and passengers were however slightly more fortunate with their food, as Edward was an excellent cook, and also had the opportunity to use a small quantity of tinned food. Fellow apprentice Bertie Snell managed to purloin a tin of meat which was absolutely awful, just blobs of meat in congealed fat, but it did help to fill our stomachs a little. Our Cap'n strongly promoted fish as very nutritious, and often set one of the deck crew to fishing. He was particularly respected for his conscientious provision of as much fresh fruit and vegetables as he could to the hands. The hands however, got very irritated at being given no rum. The Captain was a great believer in mugs of cocoa, and thus rum was only issued on his specific orders on extraordinary occasions.

The Cap'n was also our medical man. He said to me early on, that if I was planning to take on the Daphne myself one day, I would need to build up experience in this task too. In my otherwise unacknowledged position as 'son of the owner' he taught me as much as he could. He was extremely thorough in questioning and examining the complainant, and for trivial matters, often issued Holloway's Pills or Holloway's ointment, which were supposed to effect amazing cures for an incredibly wide range of symptoms. He confided that he felt that these patent remedies were of little actual use, but if the patient believed in the remedy; his body would likely cure itself. Serious emergencies did however occur on board, and one was fatal.

One of the most popular of the hands was 'Squirrel' Oakes, a fine young man of about the same age as me who had earned the position of 'Able Seaman'(ABS) and was a highly capable 'top man'. He was named Squirrel by his shipmates because of his extreme agility and speed and because of his general cheerfulness and willingness at any task. Squirrel was a great favourite on our Port watch. To make more speed, Mr Hann ordered that a flying jiboom be rigged out to accommodate a flying jib sail. This would provide assistance to the helmsman as the lateral pressure on the jib sails helped counteract wave and swell action on the hull. It was quite a normal procedure, and ABS Squirrel Oakes and Sean Reilly were ordered to do it as they were the most nimble and speedy. While the two men were on the boom, the iron cap broke, and as the ship was speeding along under full sail, both men got entangled in the rigging and were dragged under the hull. The Cap'n immediately took charge, and Sean Reilly was dragged safely back on board. Our dear young shipmate Squirrel, who was eventually hauled aboard was dead. His neck had been broken. I have no shame to say I cried publicly, as did the Cap'n and most of the crew. Squirrel's body was taken below for the attentions of Mr Bennett the carpenter, who was to find some old iron with which to weight down the body, and for Mr Rogers to sew him into a canvas shroud. The following day, whilst the ship was lying-to, the Daphne's great brass bell was tolled and the whole ship's company were assembled on the deck. Squirrel's body, carried by members of the Port Watch was placed on a plank, covered with the Union Jack, and ABS Mathew O'Connor sprinkled a little of his precious holy water over the canvas bundle. The Cap'n read the burial service, and concluded with:

'We therefore commit Samuel Squirrel Oakes to the deep, to be turned into corruption, looking for the resurrection of the body, when the sea shall give up her dead, and the life of the world to come, through our Lord Jesus Christ, who at his coming shall change our vile body, that it may be like his glorious body, according to the mighty working, whereby he is able to subdue all things to himself.'

The slim canvas package was slid from under the flag, gently into the sea, and lost forever in our wake. I heard my father, in a breaking voice say as an aside to Mr Ellis and Mr Hann 'I would rather have cut off my own right arm than lose that lad.' I now truly understood that my father deeply loved me, and had protected rather than rejected me during all the years I'd spent on Blake Hill Farm. At the end of the day, all Squirrel's remaining kit and belongings were listed and put into the slop chest, to be sold to a hand that needed a coat, shirt or clasp knife. Father told me that the proceeds, plus Squirrel's pay would be delivered to Mrs Oakes when we returned to Poole.

Note
The Thirty Four Voyages of Joseph Price (from the internet) gave the idea for the tragic accident of Squirrel Oakes.
The two watch system:
http://boatsafe.com/nauticalknowhow/shipbee.com

Chapter Thirteen

Our voyage continued, with the waste of ten days in the doldrums. The Cap'n explained, using the globe he was so fond of as a teaching aid, that the equator, which we were expecting to cross soon, was the hottest area on the earth. Cold air from the North Pole and the South Pole sinks and moves as winds towards the Equator. However, he said, these winds do not move in straight lines to the Equator, but are affected by the earth's spinning motion, which creates the winds known to mariners for centuries as trade winds. The Doldrums are areas of low pressure where the trade winds meet the band of heat along the equator, and the breeze becomes milder, and a ship's progress slower.

We were absolutely fed up with daytime deck duties, which included swabbing the deck regularly with seawater to prevent the pitch from bubbling out of the seams in the deck planking in hot weather, chipping rust away from metal parts and re-painting. We took full advantage of the unusually calm seas for catching up with lost sleep when we were 'off watch'. Preparing to cross the Equator gave light relief in this otherwise boring time. As we crossed the Equator, we enjoyed an extremely jolly party, at which Isaac Gallop, the most experienced crew member dressed up as King Neptune presided over his court which included Edward, as Amphitrite, the sea goddess wife of Neptune, wearing ridiculous flouncy skirts strutting about in a terrible wig made of frayed rope. Various frolics were organized which involved being smeared with rotting rubbish, hair chopping and other horrors administered to all of us pollywogs who had never crossed the equator before. At the end of the ceremonies, certificates were presented to those of us who had previously been pollywogs, and who were now declared to be shellbacks, experienced sailors, by reason of having crossed the Equator. Work returned to the usual routine, and we reached Luanda after forty eight days at sea, a very long passage indeed, much affected by weather and delays in the Doldrums.

Prior to entering the port of Luanda, the Cap'n assembled the ship's company to prepare the Starboard watch for forty eight hours shore leave. (The Port watch would take their leave on the official return of their Starboard shipmates.)They were given small advances on their pay. He thanked all of us for our hard work and loyalty, and then went on to say 'I want to warn you all of the dangers of this, the first of many foreign ports, of the crime, brothels and gangs in the dock area. Be on your guard when enjoying the night life and music in the seafront shacks, which are in fact, brothels. These are highly delightful places for young men, where beautiful African women often choose their sexual partners for their dancing skills, and a man can expect to be judged on the way he moves against the woman's body, *a vertical expression of a horizontal desire,* dancing, rubbing male and female body parts together. These women are low, cunning snakes, tempting good sailors into all kinds of wanton and lewd behaviours. Fun at the time, but this may cause you to meet with the other cunning serpents in this and other ports, who hunt with greater subtlety. You will pay far more dearly for an encounter with one of these. As well as paying the woman of your dreams, you may be robbed. Worse still is the disease which you may easily catch in any port. You will lucky if you escape catching the syph or the clap, each event, the catching of syph or clap will represent a lifelong disaster for you and for your wife if you have one. Some unfortunate sailors actually suffer a double event on their very first time, through catching both. I'm not a spoilsport, go and enjoy yourselves, but if you get excited, save your money, stay well, use your hand and have a rub off instead.' Meantime, whilst I and the rest of the crew stayed aboard, the Cap'n and Mr and Mrs Macdonald stayed in a nearby hotel. The crew would all be continuing to live and work on the ship in the daytime, unless given shore leave. We were kept very busy helping to unload the cargo and we had to make any general repairs which had not been possible whilst at sea. I used some of my slightly increased spare time to write loving and descriptive letters to Liza, Miss Caroline and Mr and Mrs Teague.

Mr Hann and I were also required to spend a portion of each day working with my father. He needed Mr Hann as First Mate and me as 'owner's son' to learn as much as we could from him. On shore, Father was acting as Captain, owner and merchant. Luanda had what he described as 'a community of merchants' to whom we needed to be introduced, and he was looking to sell his cargo at a good profit and purchase another bound for Adelaide. He hoisted a big flag on to Daphne's mast, which said 'For Adelaide, Australia, taking on cargo.' He gave detailed instructions to Mr Ellis, Mr Tilsed the Bo'sun and Mr Downton (whose apprenticeship had been completed mid Atlantic and who was now an Able Seaman looking to become a mate) regarding maintenance and careful preparations of the ship to round the Cape of Good Hope.

I was astounded to hear from father, in private, that he had 'lost a packet' when the Weymouth Bank collapsed. He still owed the entire costs of provisioning the ship to Teague's grocers and Caroline Basket. He had also run up a heavy debt with Piplers on the quay for canvas, cordage and ships fittings and Mr Curtis had settled his debt with Lanning's boatyard on Poole quay. Father said reassuringly, that this long trip, carefully managed, would very likely begin to set his shipping business on its feet again. We took a short rent on a quayside warehouse for the current cargo, and began the process of unloading, stacking and gradually selling the various lots to local merchants whilst at the same time accumulating our next load. Messieurs Hardy, Tilsed, Downton, O'Connor and Stone supervised the crew and some local labour in the unloading and transporting of our goods to the warehouse. This group, working in twos, took turns to stay in the warehouse with the stock at all times. They had a pair of pistols between them. Mr Hann and Mr Ellis, also with pistols, together with the rest of the crew ensured the security of the ship. Father regularly took either me or Mr Hann with him to haggle with the local merchants in the sale of our own goods, and the purchase of consignments for our next cargo, or arrangements to ship small loads for other merchants. He eventually got good prices on coffee beans, sugar, raw cotton and hides.

In the evenings, the Cap'n often made Mr Hann, Mr Ellis, and me welcome at his hotel dinner table when we were not otherwise occupied at the warehouse, or the ship. He entertained us one evening with the legendary story of the Flying Dutchman, a mad sea captain. Apparently the Dutch Captain was sailing his ship around the Cape of Good Hope in the teeth of a violent storm, deaf to the pleas of his crew and passengers to turn back, save their lives and his ship. The mad captain still refusing to turn back, began singing filthy songs and challenging the Lord God Almighty to sink his ship if he dared! The crew and passengers mutinied and the captain shot their ringleader and tossed him overboard, at which point the storm clouds parted, and the voice of God was heard from the heavens, condemning the evil captain to sail the oceans of the world eternally, without peace. Most sailors believed that anyone who sighted the ghostly galleon would die. 'Is there any truth in this?' I asked.

'There have been many shipwrecks around the Cape' the Cap'n replied, pausing to draw on his pipe, and then taking another sip of his port, 'but the legend lacks credibility for intelligent men. Given that these stories are passed on, and many mariners *have* lived to tell the tale of sighting the Dutchman's ghostly galleon, I think it more likely that the story is based on some as yet ill understood phenomenon of the weather and lighting occurring around the Cape. We aren't scared of rainbows, are we, but the nature of the uneducated crewman is by upbringing and habits notoriously superstitious, and so these tales are repeated and embellished.'

A couple of days before our departure from Luanda, he took me and the other apprentices aboard the Daphne to show us, using the globe in his cabin, the route we would be sailing. He demonstrated how we would be following the natural winds and currents of the ocean, plying a south west course to the Trinidade and Martime Vas Archipelago, and then curving back south east past the small isle of Tristan de Cunha. The route seemed illogical on the one hand, but logical on the other, as we would be taking advantage of the winds and currents, rather than trying to sail against them. I was both glad and sorry to be going to sea again. I had got rid of some of my initial fears regarding such trivialities as seasickness, but these had been totally replaced by fears of extreme weather and the possible drowning of me and others.

Our passage went as planned. We picked up the favourable currents and light and variable winds as planned, and shortly after passing the south of Tristan de Cunha; we entered the fearsome Roaring Forties, and were making good time, in the most challenging weather conditions. As the Southern Ocean is the only ocean completely circling the earth, there are no land masses to absorb any part of its ferocity and strong westerly current. At all times in this ice zone, a sharp watch needed to be kept for the icebergs which were seen more and more frequently as the weather got colder from the Arctic weather. Two particularly unpleasant problems were encountered. During a violent storm, some of our water casks got loose and broke, and we were hard put to it to make our drinking water last out as far as Australia. The second problem was food, some of which was damaged when a hatch was torn away in the storm. I ended up smoking the tobacco so thoughtfully supplied by Mistress Caroline to calm some of my hunger. The thirst was probably worse, and some of the crew were finding little pieces of lead to suck, to try to keep some water in their mouths.

In the middle of this, tempers were apt to flare, and serious trouble erupted between Maloney and the crew over his management of the crew's water and vittles supplies. He was accused by a man called Farnon and others, of slopping and wasting drinking water and as usual, serving the men short with the rations. Farnon shoved him hard against the galley stove, and a large pot of precious hot water fell and severely burnt his right arm and shoulder. The Cap'n and I were summoned by his screams. On the Cap'n's orders, the men carried him up to the chart room, and laid him on the table, so that we could assess the damage in a good light. We dosed him with Laudanum, cut his clothes off, and dressed his burns as best we could. The Cap'n explained that most doctors used oils to cover burns and exclude the air in an attempt to encourage healing. He had observed that infection seemed the worse problem, and now preferred a weak solution of silver nitrate mixed with seawater, which he used to keep the dressings wet, and found the approach more useful. Given that most severely burned people died of infections rather than their burns, he felt that the silver nitrate offered a small chance of saving Maloney. His knowledge of, and experience of medicine was colossal, and I was grateful to have the chance to learn with him.

Once Maloney was more settled with the laudanum, and his burns were covered with the wet dressings, the Cap'n took the opportunity of looking at him more carefully. In particular, he looked at his eyes. 'Why man', he exclaimed, 'you're half blind! No wonder the crew has been complaining about your antics. You can't see clearly, can you?' He indicated to me a very red left eye. When we touched it, it felt as hard as a stone. I looked at the fellow eye, and could see a fine tracery of red blood vessels growing across Maloney's green iris. 'No, I can't see well at all sir. My eyes've been paining me awful for some months now, and worse these last few days.'

'Well, old friend, it's time for you to stay ashore in future' the Cap'n replied. 'We'll get you back to Poole. Meantime, I'll get Edward to make you a berth in one of the cabins.' As a form of poetic justice, the Cap'n appointed Farnon as cook for the crew in Maloney's stead, and he was less popular with the men than his predecessor. The crewmen were not slow to point out that even in heavy seas, Maloney was often skilled enough to at least make them the occasional hot drink.

References

http://www.occultopedia.com/f/flying Dutchman/htm
Wikipaedia - http://en.wikipedia.org/wiki/Clipper_routeClipper Route

Chapter 14

As we sailed into Adelaide, The Cap'n told us apprentices a little of the history of the port of Adelaide, which was the major port of the colony of South Australia, which had been founded in 1837. Due to its closeness to the mangrove swamps and the swarms of mosquitoes, it was formerly known to sailors as 'Port Misery.' Later improvements to the wharves meant that ships with deeper draughts could be accommodated, and the port was now known to seamen as either 'Dustholia' or 'Mudholia', according to the season. I wasn't impressed by it, and felt its name of 'Port Misery,' which related to melancholia, should be kept. Its location some distance out of town did not please any of us either. Clean water was scarce, and had to be transported to the ships in barrels, at a cost. I could see that Mr and Mrs Macdonald felt rather shocked at the size of their undertaking to become permanent residents in the area, but I know that the during our long voyage, the Cap'n had been at pains to point out the potential of living in such a rapidly developing province and the other possibilities that could be open to them. Mr Macdonald and his wife were clearly eager to leave behind the squalid port, and at least reach the town to enjoy fresh drinking water and food. Mr Macdonald already had the names and addresses of the major wool exporters and was seeking the best fleeces obtainable at the most reasonable prices.

We were allowed to stay aboard our ship whilst docked in Port Misery. This time it was the turn of Port watch to have shore leave first. The men made for the town as soon as they possibly could. I had quickly learned that most of them would all spend their money almost immediately on drink and women, and would be back on board as soon as their pockets and bellies were empty. Mr Ellis wanted to get home to his wife in Poole, who was expecting their first baby, and asked to be discharged. He signed on to a steamship bound for Liverpool. He had already told me that steam was 'the coming thing' that would revolutionize sea travel.

There was plenty of work to be done. The crew and dockers needed to be supervised in the unloading of the cargo. Paul Hann, Mr Downton and Mr Tilsed were overseeing the permanent repairs to the storm damage. Paul Hann was given leave to take his Board of Trade Ordinary Master's Examination and Mr Downton went with him to have his first try for his Second Mate's ticket. I was sometimes with the Cap'n meeting Elder Smith and Co and Fowler and Stilling, local merchants to sell the cargo, and sometimes I was with the ship. We needed extra crew as we had lost Mr Ellis, Farnon was finally dismissed for fighting again and Maloney was unable to work. It was bad enough in Poole to find good men, but we found it far worse in Adelaide. As a result of their poverty, most sailors were generally unhealthy men as a result of having rarely if ever, eaten decent food. They were illiterate, and some would thieve and would pick fights with one another on the smallest pretext. On some ships, men are signed who are so obviously ill that they died before they reach the next port. Fortunately Cap'n Lovejoy had a very good reputation for running a seaworthy vessel with a fairly paid and well disciplined crew. Eventually we made up the numbers with some 'half decent' men we found looking for work on the docks. We were fortunate to find an experienced sea cook who had been glad to leave his former ship as he said the Master was often drunk and the ship's crew generally disorderly and frankly violent. Mr Hann passed his Ordinary Masters' Certificate, but Mr Downton failed to pass his Board of Trade Examinations first time, so we also signed a new second mate, Mr George Thynne, a short, dark haired man in his middle twenties who had seemed very amiable. I was delighted to be appointed to the duties of 'Able Seaman', and officially sanctioned to help the 'topmen' who went 'aloft' in the rigging to handle sails. I would be working closely on the Port Watch with Sean Reilly and Mathew O'Connor. We said a sad goodbye to our Scotttish friends the Macdonalds, and with our cargo of fine fleeces, we were ready to sail again after a fairly unpleasant few weeks in Port Misery.

On our first day at sea, after Morning Prayers, the Cap'n made a little public ceremony, formally appointing Able Seaman (Senior Apprentice) Downton to work closely with Bo'sun Tilsed, and gave him special responsibility for helping to preparing both crew and ship for rounding the Horn. Mr Downton said he would be giving particular attention to re-checking all the ropes and sails, which had already been done in port, but it was essential that every member of the crew be familiar with every rope and knot, and well drilled for any emergency. The below deck security of the cargo was checked and re-checked, and nets were rigged above the bulwarks to provide added safety against any of the crew being washed overboard in heavy seas. Mr Thynne had seemed to be alright until we sailed. By our third day at sea however, his temper changed, he was very liable to hit crewmen on his starboard watch indiscriminately and he became frequently argumentative with Paul Hann, and silently surly with our well respected Cap'n. One night the Cap'n found him dead asleep on his watch, stinking of spirits which he must have smuggled aboard. I strongly suspected that Edward, who had suffered so much from Thynne's acid tongue, may have been making his way back from a nocturnal visit to the forward rope locker and had spotted the collapsed Thynne. Clearly the starboard men were not keen to report him. Edward alerted the Cap'n. Unsurprisingly, Thynne was dismissed immediately to his cabin, for a week on bread and water rations. He was relieved from all further duties as second mate for the duration of the voyage. He would be living with the crew and working as an able seaman. Mr Tilsed, with his many years experience at sea, had to temporarily take on the second mate's duties as we sailed across the largest ocean of the world – the Pacific, not that it was very pacific. Paul and I confided in each other how delighted we were that such a good man and excellent sailor should be temporarily promoted to cover for this emergency, but were sorry that Mr Downton did not have his second mate's ticket. We all missed Mr Ellis.

I began discussing with the Cap'n and Mr Hann the details of sailing around the Horn. I had found the Cape of Good Hope a great trial to my personal courage and physical reserves. The Horn promised to be far worse. I had already been exposed to the rages of the 'roaring forties', but the next challenge would take us into the 'furious fifties' and nigh to the Tierra del Fuego the 'screaming and shrieking sixties'. I knew I would meet for the first time, the greatest extremes in wind speed and wave height. These great winds of the southern ocean would blow us round Cape Horn and into the Pacific Ocean, the largest ocean in the world. The Cap'n warned us that these would be incredibly strong winds, producing terrifying waves. We would meet potent currents that were well nigh irresistible, at the same time as we were contending with massive icebergs, making the passage the greatest sailing challenge he knew.

The Cap'n said he had no expectations at all of our passage around the Horn as he was lacking in second sight. He explained that we would not be using the Magellan Straits, the fastest passage for a trading vessel, as he expected bad weather, and given the narrowness of this route, and the even greater difficulties of the Beagle Channel, we would be taking the Drake Passage. We would be doing this although it was acknowledged to be the roughest stretch of water in the world, being the area where the great circum polar current is squeezed through a relatively narrow gap. However, he felt that this passage would offer us greater sea room if we suffered a treacherous blast from the one of the dreaded williwaws, nasty parcels of compressed air which can be dumped over the high land of Tierra del Fuego and spill out across the ocean, causing blasts of well over 120 knots, whipping up the ocean into a white frenzy, causing havoc for mariners.

We made a brief stop at Dunedin, New Zealand, to replenish our water supplies and take on fresh fruit and vegetables, and I was fascinated to note the albatross breeding ground as we passed the Otago Peninsula. Some of them flew over the Daphne, and I estimated the wing spans of these birds to be nine feet or more. As we continued our voyage, we saw many more of these powerful, graceful birds, soaring, wheeling, diving, dropping, and skimming the waves. As we progressed through the ice, and drew nearer to

Tierra del Fuego, an albatross with black eyebrows landed on one of our spars. One of the crew generously offered some of his bread for the great creature. I was reminded of Coleridge's poem about the Ancient Mariner:

'The ice was here, the ice was there,
The ice was all around:
It cracked and growled, and roared and howled,
Like noises in a swound!

At length did cross an albatross,
Through the fog it came;
As it had been a Christian soul,
We hailed it in God's name.'

As we moved further south, in the freezing conditions our breath made great white clouds, both above and below decks. Snow blew around us, and the rigging became encrusted with ice, which needed to be cleared, lest we became top heavy, and the ship took a fatal roll. The Cap'n warned us – 'if you feel any sudden rise in temperature, sound the alarm - a williwaw is imminent.'

In the dying light of a December evening the Daphne entered that dread place where the waters of the Atlantic and Pacific collide. Acting Second Mate Tilsed and the starboard watch were in charge, but the Cap'n was on deck with them. As I lay on my bunk waiting to go on watch, the air in my cabin became subtly warmer, and more moisture laden and I had a deep sense of foreboding. As I sat up, suddenly alert I could feel the wind intensity change. The sails were snapping against the masts and ropes like whips, and I abruptly heard my father's great voice shout out 'all hands on deck', and the bell was being run furiously as we grabbed our oilskins and ran to help. Father had taken the wheel himself, assisted by one of the starboard hands, that great obelisk of a Poole man, with huge hands and arms, called so appropriately Caleb Stone.

We were in mortal danger. Sea was washing all over the decks, and was waist deep in the scuppers on the lee side and the Cap'n and Caleb were struggling with the wheel to try and keep Daphne's bow into the wind. Two of our male passengers joined them in their struggle with the wheel. Heavy seas broke on board over the forward part of the ship, carrying away the stanchions of the fo'c's'le, and the figurehead, and causing other serious damage. In the midst of this freezing, screaming hell of a wind, I was working as a 'top man' with a team of men struggling to reef the sails as heavy seas next carried away a section of Daphne's bulwarks and tore away one of our boats. At the same time Mr Downton, who was now acting Bo'sun, and four men struggled in the gale to throw our 'sea anchor' overboard. This was a large section of canvas, secured with ropes, containing bits of old anchor chain and other heavy weights to weigh it down.

I could just hear the Captain's voice below as he bellowed into the winds *'O most glorious and gracious Lord God, who dwellest in Heaven, but beholdest all things below; Look down, we beseech thee, and hear us calling out of the depth of misery, and out of the jaws of this death, which is ready now to swallow us up: Save us Lord, or else we perish. The living, the living shall praise thee. O send thy word of command to rebuke the raging winds, and this roaring sea; that we, being delivered from this distress, may live to serve thee, and to glorify thy name all the days of our life. Hear, Lord, and save us for the infinite merits of our blessed Saviour, thy son, our Lord Jesus Christ. Amen '*

References

Book of Common Prayer (1662)
Coleridge S.T. 1798. The Rime of the Ancient Mariner.

Background reading:

Castle C., MacDonald I., 2005. Glenlee: The life and times of a Clyde built Cape Horner. Pub. Brown, Son and Ferguson Ltd. Glasgow.
Mason C., (undated) Five Thousand Days - Voyages of the Clydebuilt Barque Glenlee. Pub. Clyde Maritime Trust

LIZA

Chapter Fifteen

My name is Liza Loader, and I'm the daughter of Jimmia Loader, who was in the Poole Union Workhouse on account of being a lunatic. I was born in the Workhouse, and never knew nothing else for the first thirteen years of my life. My ma was locked away, and I didn't get to see her very often. I never knowed anything about my father. I know now that life in the workhouse was fearsome hard, but I never knew no other way to live for the first years of my life. The other children who had a parent living very rarely got to see them. We were strictly separated, and just lived our lives out within the workhouse walls.

When I lived there, there was more than a hundred of us paupers, all ages we were. There were the newborn like I once was myself, generally fatherless, sometimes also motherless. Then there was the children of widow women, or orphans who had lost both parents to sickness or those who had been born idiots or something and weren't right. There were children who were just not wanted and there were children from huge families whose parents could not afford to feed them all. Those children who had known and loved their parents, whose parents were alive and present somewhere in the workhouse suffered most. Families was just allowed a little time together on Sundays. The men were separated from the women as well you see.

As far as adults was concerned, it was pure poverty and starvation, usually made worse by sickness that had stopped them from working that had caused them to come into the workhouse. Sometimes people were taken in who had gone blind or deaf and couldn't work no more. The skin and bones shapes that the old women had been shrivelled to was well hidden under their dresses, aprons and shawls. The epileptics was housed in with the rest of us, not locked up with the lunatics, as they were more easily manageable unless they had a fit of course, which we got quite used to. Some of the epileptics had long 'spells' too, when they just stared like strangers, and answered to nothing.

I started off in the infant school, and we were all kept together for our ages, and didn't mix with the junior children. We had quite a good schoolroom, with windows set high in the walls, and a high ceiling. We used our slates and did our reading, writing and rithmatic same as any other children. Our desks were arranged in lines, across the width of our classroom. The teacher, Miss Mathews had a high desk in front, and the line of cleverest scholars was in front of her right hand. Each group was set different work. She moved the blackboard and easel in front of each group. She was harsh with us, and no one dared to put their hand up to ask to go to the privy during a lesson. I remember wetting myself one day. I felt some relief when I was forced to let things go, but watched the wetness soak into the floorboards, smelt the smell and felt not only my sticky wet clothes, but the terror of being found out. Found out I was, too. She pulled me out of my desk by the hair, and shoved me hard into a corner. I was left facing the walls until my legs ached, my clothes had dried and the rest of the children had left the room. Then she pulled me out of the corner and smacked me across the back of my hand with a stick, before pushing me out into the yard. The result was that I learned how to hold my water.

Once we grew out of the junior house, we were expected to fully work for our livings. Some girls were sent to work for people in the town, generally doing laundry work, scrubbing and stuff like that, and some of the boys went out as labourers. Many of these eventually settled to live and work in the town. It wasn't easy to get a job, and because we were not used to being in a family. I can see now that most of us had developed our own little ways which didn't make us easy to live with. We weren't always as polite and thoughtful as those who lived on the outside neither, as we hadn't had mothers and fathers to tell us how to be about things. I'm not saying it was a completely *bad* bringing up that we had, just different. The women who looked after us had either come into the workhouse themselves because of poverty, or were still in the workhouse, having come, like myself, as a little child. These women could be quite kind and human, even generous with what little they had themselves. Mr and Mrs Cave, the Master and Mistress of the Workhouse worked hard, and done their best for us. The Overseers of the Poor, good men from the four parishes, came and checked regular that all was as it should be. The idea of the way the workhouse was run was that it should never be so easy, so comfortable that it would ever make an idle person want to come there. Just being very poor was often thought to mean that the person had somehow brought their troubles on their self, or was somehow a bad person. Our lives was expected to be hard, and so they were. The women were set to work scrubbing the great long, cold stone passages. Some of them were with child, but it made no difference, they scrubbed almost until their babies were born.

More than anything else, I remember the workhouse being a home to old people. There was every kind of old person in there. There were sensible old people, but I remember them all as a collection of ugly, sad, toothless old things. They munched on nothing, mumbled, and were runny eyed. They wiped their red eyes with dirty old pocket handkerchiefs, held in their skinny bony hands. They would go to sleep in the womens' refectory, sitting on their backless benches, sprawled across the tables. On good days you would see them slumped in the corners of the exercise yard, trying to keep warm in a patch of watery sunlight. Very unlucky old women ended up in the infirmary ward, nursed by other, younger paupers, bedridden, having their stinking sheets arranged to dry in front of the fire at the end of the ward as the laundry could not keep up with a supply of clean, dry sheets. There was just one nurse for the lot of them.

On the two times when I saw my mother, things were even worse for her. There was one, lonely sane attendant, the only attendant for lunatics in the whole workhouse, among about a dozen mad women, in a locked up ward. My mother was half dressed, untidy, leering at nothing and talking to herself, clutching a bit of dirty old cloth, her finger nails chewed down to the bleeding quick. Her hair was matted and filthy. Others were cuddling and rocking themselves, or sitting still, as if they were already dead. The smell and sight of human soil was unbearable. My own mother didn't know me. I have no memory of her ever knowing me.

Altogether the atmosphere in the workhouse was grey, depressed and subdued. We all had to work, and worked very, very hard. Few of us ever got sent out, and some of my friends became scrubbers of the dreaded stone floors. Others worked in the sweaty heat of the laundry. I was lucky, being put to work in the kitchens, where the very ingredients of the meals were grey. Grey porridge, bread, potatoes and an occasional bit of grey boiled meat was what we had, and it was served on grey tin plates. Vegetables didn't cheer things up much as they were boiled to death. The workhouse stank of generation after generation of boiled cabbage. There was never really enough to eat. The rations were weighed out in the kitchen, and we never felt like we'd had enough. The old women waited in the cold, stone paved refectory, waiting and waiting for their dinners.

I do remember that we all got treated one New Year by some kind ladies. Mrs Lane Shrubb sent us a stock of tea, sugar, tobacco, snuff, oranges and sweets which we was all most thankful for. In the evening we all sat down together in the chapel, men women and children for cakes and tea from Mrs St Barbe. The chapel looked lovely with all the Christmas decorations still up. The ladies and gentlemen played and sang for us, and there was a magic lantern show. Mr and Mrs Cave were very helpful in making it a wonderful treat for us all.

I was thirteen when Missis Teague came in one day. She swept in like liquid sunshine. She was dressed in bright purple, and we'd learned in school that purple was the colour of royalty. She walked so stately, and Mrs Cave was at her right hand. Missis Teague's face shone with good humour and kindness like I never seen in anyone before. She walked round and looked at all of us working paupers. Her eyes came on me, and she smiled. I heared Mrs Cave say something like 'You don't want that one. Her mother's a confirmed lunatic.'

'I'll be the judge of who I take' she said. Right haughty. 'Come and speak to me, my maid' she said, and asked me all about myself. There wasn't much to tell. I just said I work in the kitchen, and I like cooking. Missis Teague said 'Would you like to come along a'me, and get trained up to have a better life outside?' I cried, 'cause I was scared to think of leaving the workhouse. It was all I'd ever knowed. I cried because she was a kind lady who seemed to want to help, and I never remember anyone except a couple of the pauper women being that kind to me before.

Missis Teague told Mrs Cave to get me washed properly, and gave her fresh clothes for me, and said she'd be back tomorrow. In the morning she took me home along of her, riding in a wooden cart with a driver called Wesley. Wesley bounced us down the cobbled High Street to Teague's Grocery Store. Missis Teague took me in the front door, where a bell behind the door clattered loudly. We went through the back of the shop, to a big room she called 'My room' which had a big table, and chairs round it, all laid up for a meal. She took me into the kitchen where I met Ann, who was the Cook Housekeeper, and Lucy, the 'senior girl'. Suzie, who had been a couple of years ahead of me in the workhouse had, she said, been 'training' for a while. I was shown the privies in the back yard, and was told to hurry up and wash my face and hands at the pump as it was lunchtime.

I'll never forget that first, lovely meal at Teagues, with Mr and Missis Teague at the head of their table and all of us, the staff, clustered round, with them being kind, interested and polite with me. I was so unused to this that I cried, and Suzie fetched me a soft, clean rag to dry my eyes and wipe my nose. They was all trying to tell me that if I worked hard, and was a good girl, I would have a chance of 'a better life.' Lunch was a hashed cod pie and the biggest, brightest show of vegetables, boiled and roasted I'd ever seen on my life. There was sponge pudding and custard after.

Suzie was real nice to me, and said she'd been happy at Teagues. I was glad to have a friend there, though she was a bit older. There were two senior servants, Ann the Cook/Housekeeper was in charge of everything, and Lucy worked under her direction. Suzie and me just had to do whatever we were told by either of them, but they seemed to have a good system worked out between them so that there was never any confusion about who did what. My first job was to help Suzie with all the washing up of plates, cups dishes and things, and then the pots. It took us a long time, as though I wasn't slow, I had to learn where each thing lived, and I had to be really, really careful, as I wasn't used to handling china, and heard that Missis Teague got real iffy if it even got chipped a bit.

Eventually I could see that each day of the week had it's own work. Suzie and I shared the pull out bed in the kitchen. We agreed it was the best bed in the house, as we slept close to the range. If we were lucky, the fire in the range stayed 'in', and we only needed to riddle out the ash and put more coal on the fire in the morning. If we was unlucky, we needed to start from scratch, and relight it using newspaper, wood and small coal. Getting this going was important, as the Teague family needed hot water upstairs for washing. Then Suzy and me went upstairs with a cup of tea for each member of the family. We lit tiny fires in the bedrooms if it was very cold, and left a can of hot water in each room so's they could get washed. Then Lucy lit the fire in the upstairs dining room, laid the tablecloth and arranged the cutlery. Whilst the family were washing and dressing, Lucy, Wesley, Suzie and me went to the kitchen for a quick breakfast. As cook, Ann ate a bit later. When we had finished eating, whilst Mr and Missis Teague and any guests went into the upstairs dining room for breakfast Lucy ran up and downstairs with breakfast dishes. Wesley cleaned the boots and shoes, Suzie and I cleaned the doorstep outside the shop, polished the brass fittings on the doors and cleaned Missis Teague's downstairs room. When the family came downstairs, Suzie and I quickly opened the bedroom windows to let the stale night air out, emptied and cleaned any commodes used during the night, cleaned the wash basins and wash stands and stripped the beds. As Missis Teague often said to us 'There's no work like early work.'

Then shop staff began to arrive, were greeted, and we all sat round the table in Missis Teague's room ready for Mr Teague to read a few verses from the scriptures and say a prayer with us, before opening the shop. The days passed quickly, with each day having its major work to be done. Our work divided after breakfast. Missis Teague liked the new girl, which was me at the moment, to start working on the cleaning and laundry side with the guidance and help of Lucy. The 'improver' which was Suzie, worked on the cooking side with Ann. Each day's duties were slightly different, with every room in the house being thoroughly turned out and cleaned once a week.

Ann said that Missis Teague was a really good planner as she gave her instructions for meals twice a week. This gave Ann plenty of time to check her stocks and get the things she needed together in good time. It wasn't difficult in a grocery shop anyway, but Ann did have to arrange for any meats, fish and fresh vegetables with the delivery men. Ann said some of the other cooks she knew in the town only got told on the day what would have to be served for lunch or dinner! Those servants were mighty glad to have Wesley knocking on the door early to take their orders and come back quickly with the goods. Anyway, for the future, I was generally kept busy with household cleaning, washing and ironing. I began to settle into my new life happily. Suzie and I were pleased to have extra reading lessons one evening a week with Mr Teague and book keeping and arithmetic with Missis Teague once a week.

Missis Teague is a very smart woman. When I watched her, I thought, no wonder that shop is such a success. She always kept well in with the housekeepers of all the big houses. Wesley called on them every day for their orders, but sometimes they were preparing far ahead for special do's at their big houses, and wanted to discuss what would be available. They never had to wait in the front of the shop to have their business attended to. She took them into her back room, and sat them by the fire, very welcome on a cold day, ordered tea and biscuits and took their orders herself. She listened to all their troubles, and tried to be their friend as well as their grocer's wife. They was free any time to use our privy in the yard, even if they was only passing, not actually shopping. All women knew the value of that, if they wanted to be out of the house for a while. No other shop in the High Street tried as hard as she did to win and keep the good customers. It was said that Mr Teague was good in different ways. All the other traders and business people had a lot of respect for him, and folks said that he was very clever at choosing the best goods for his shop, particularly cheeses, the finest coffee, and his tea blends were said by many to be the best in Poole. Mr Teague was a Guardian of the Poor and an Alderman on the Council. They gave their family and us, the rest of their household, their own good examples of hard work, kindness and common sense to follow.

References

Charles Dickens, Walk in a Workhouse, Short story.
Fred Copeman Reason in Revolt, Internet.
Poole and Dorset Herald archived newspapers- Mrs Lane Shrubb and Mrs St Barbe
Mrs Beeton's Cookery Book. (Undated). New and Revised Edition, Ward Lock and Co. Ltd., London.

Chapter Sixteen

I look back on the years at Teagues, and they was like heaven.
I worked hard, I was treated kindly, learned a lot and I had no
worries. I grew up a lot. I got very fond of Wesley, who was a
naughty boy, full of fun. I had never had any experience of men
before, as we was kept so separate at the workhouse. Each of us
live in staff at Teagues got just an afternoon and evening every
month to ourselves. I had little idea of how to spend my time or
my wages at first. I went down to the quay on one of the afternoons,
and saw a nice young sailor who smiled at me. I went into the
sweetie shop and bought two ounces of mint humbugs. As I was
paying, the shop doorbell pinged, and the smiling sailor went to
the counter to buy a quarter of Army and Navy sweets. We come
out of the shop together, and he asked me if I'd like to come up to
Holmes's Refreshment Rooms with him. I said yes, because I knew
that it was part of the Temperance Hotel. He was real nice, clean,
and had lovely blond hair, tied at the back of his neck, sailor style.
He bought me a currant bun as well, and told me he was looking
to sign on another ship, having just come down from Newcastle,
with a load of coal. He was looking for a longer voyage.

My new friend's name was Joses, and he told me about his
family in Newcastle. He spoke very strange English, and so I found
him hard to understand. This was his first, short trip at sea, and
he'd left home to make his own way, as there were seven living
little brothers and sisters (two had died) that his parents had to feed.
He could have gone into the mines like his Da, which would have
meant bringing home a few shillings every week for his Ma, but
he wanted to stay outside in the air. It sounded so beautiful to my
ears to hear of his loving home, where his parents, though poor
could make him feel special. We walked round the new park that
was being made, together. We looked in the aviaries and I saw a
monkey on a chain, so that it didn't run away. At last, I judged it
time to go back to Teagues. Joses admitted that he had followed

me into the sweet shop, hoping to be able to talk to me. I never met him again. The world is a big place, he had told me.

Unfortunately, I'd been seen by Mr Teague in the Temperance Cafe, with a young man. He and Missis Teague spoke to me kindly that evening. They asked me about my half day, and I told them all about it. They both agreed that it was quite harmless, but warned me to be very careful with young men. Sitting in the Temperance Cafe talking, but not touching was nothing but good, but really I should have had a female friend with me. They said that walking in half deserted areas in the dusk 'put a young woman at moral danger.' Missis Teague went on to say not to hold hands with a young man unless I had known him and his family for a little while, and such hand holding should only occur when in mixed company of respectable family and friends. Touching of any sort could, she said 'lead to other things.' 'Keep yourself nice' she said, 'you're too young to be keeping company with young men yet.' I think my face went red, but she was kind, and understood I didn't want to spend my half day on my own, and arranged for Miss Jones's maid Beatty to come and call for me on my next half day off. Beatty was good company, but I liked the lads best, so I saw her for the afternoon, then told her I'd be going back to Teagues for my evening meal, so that I still had my evening 'free' to do what I wanted.

I got the chance to watch and learn a lot at Teagues. Mr and Missis Teague was very tender to each other, all the time, when they didn't think anyone was looking. It all fitted in. They was very serious about going to church and all that, and made sure that all their staff went too, but they were quite happy with different Christian beliefs, 'so long as we went', so Wesley, who had been at the workhouse too, was encouraged to follow the faith of his late parents, and be a Methodist. The rest of us were all Church of England, so we all went off to St James's of a Sunday morning. I started to get the hang of what the Teagues were about. God first, close family next, employees, and then the rest of the world. Taken in that order, that is what they did. They only had the one daughter,

Mary, and that's a pure surprise, as it was said they were married young. Very surprisingly for people their age, they had stayed very, very close. Missis Teague was a beautiful lady, and kept herself very well. She loved colours and patterns in her clothes, and had long brown hair, peppered with gray that she wore braided up in different ways every day. Her cheeks were pink, and her mouth well creased in smile and laughter lines. Her figure hadn't gone to fat, she worked too hard for that. She had a good girth, but it seemed to be mainly muscle, as she was very strong. Mr Teague was upright and slim, but strongly built. His hair was pure white, but he still had plenty of it. He wore a carefully waxed moustache and sharply trimmed beard. He was always busy boning and jointing sides of bacon. He cut the bacon on that great big slicer he was so fond of, that made a grating, singing noise to move the meat back and forth against the cutting wheel. He cut the great cheddar cheeses, and blended coffees and teas for specific customers. He wore no jacket in the shop, but was well wrapped in a big starched bright white apron, the top of which buttoned on to his shirt, below his black bow tie. He sang quietly to himself when he worked alone, all sorts, sea songs, hymns and what he told me were folk songs. He was in the church choir, and led us all to church, wearing his stovepipe hat, made of real beaver fur. The hat was carefully brushed to a fine shine by Missis Teague.

I don't know how the Teagues was so patient with that there daughter of theirs, Mary. They must have brought her up proper, and she was married to a lovely man, but she was wilful and rude. I wasn't in the household more than a couple of days before I met her daughter Lydia. What a little stunner she was, a real beauty. Even I could see that something had frightened her good and proper, and she'd run away. When I saw how Lydia's mother, Missis Curtis was with her later, I wasn't surprised. In her eyes, Lydia couldn't do right for doing wrong. The Curtises all came round for Sunday meals in the dining room upstairs once a fortnight, and Mr and Missis Teague went the alternate Sunday to them. However, Miss Lydia spent a lot of time with Missis Teague, learning all about everything. She was as sharp as anything with her reading and rithmatic, reading anything, and adding and figuring in her head as fast as ninepence.

I was with the Teagues for seven years, before Missis Teague kindly passed me over to Missis Curtis, to help with the new house and the children. I was really cut up to leave Poole, as I'd been seeing a young man regular on the evenings of me day off. Barry worked with the vegetable carter, as an assistant with loading, unloading and delivering. I was very fond of him, and we'd go up the Bunny, the path that runs alongside the railway line at the back of the park lake, at first just holding hands and walking, but with being so fond of each other, and having such rare chances to meet, it led to a fair bit of kissing and on from there. I saw nothing wrong with pleasuring each other, as it seemed so natural. I knew from my bible studies that it was wrong to lie with a man I wasn't married to, so we didn't lie down. We took what furtive pleasures we could accomplish standing up. It was very painful to me first off, but eventually it became like a drug to us, and I could scarce wait until we next met, as each time felt better than the last.

I was about twenty or more when Missis Teague said that I'd learned as much as she could teach me, and it was time to take on another girl. That was it. I was sent round to live at Missis Curtis's in Market Street. I had a week with Ellen showing me around, and then she went off to prepare the new house in Parkstone. There was a powerful lot to do, I can tell you, but Mrs Kitkat who did the rough work at the Market Street house was very kind, and Miss Lydia and Master Michael were very helpful. I was really glad when the move was over, as although the house in Parkstone was bigger, there were a lot of things to save us work, particularly them new lavatories, which made emptying the piss pots in the morning a piece of cake. There was an upstairs lavvie for the family, and one in the back yard for the rest of us. Once I got the hang of that geyser thing, morning hot water for the bedrooms was easy too. We didn't have Mrs KitKat when we left Poole, and more was expected by way of entertaining, evenings and afternoons, and Missis Curtis did get more than her fair share of sick headaches.

I couldn't see my Barry no more, as my half day had been changed, so I felt a bit lonely. Ellen was much younger and less strict than Ann, so we had more laughs between us. Miss Lydia was very funny in the things she said sometimes, particularly after she'd been in trouble with Missis Curtis, but she used such big words, I didn't always understand her jokes. However, nice though the Otterwood household was (if you left out Missis Curtis), I still craved the tenderness of being held by a man, and being kissed proper and really cuddled. I suppose this was because I never knowed this for all them years in the workhouse. Eventually I met up with Ken, who worked at the Post Office in Parkstone, and was free most evenings, and would sometimes lurk in the back gardens, and there was Arthur, the gardener, who was good for a go, when I felt frisky, but not that I liked him that much. Then Harry Lovejoy walked into my life, much younger than me, and very innocent, but knowing exactly what he wanted, and what I wanted to give him. I know what caused the baby. I done it with Harry, in a moment of great passion, actually lying on the ground. That was my undoing.

I first noticed that my monthlies stopped. My chest got heavy and sore, and my clothes tighter, so I wore a very big black cardigan over the top as a cover all. Then I felt something begin to move inside me, and began to guess what might be happening. I don't think Ellen noticed anything, but she kept noticing the master putting his hands over me where he oughtn't. I didn't care. I really liked everything the Master did. He was good for a go now and then as well. Maybe she noticed my condition and thought it was down to him. I was getting pretty desperate, wondering what would become of me, and then, in an instant, it was Missis Curtis what spotted it. I was sent immediately to the back kitchen. The routine of the house stopped completely. Missis Curtis was worked into a right state, and had to be dealt with immediately. I sat on a wooden chair at our table in the back kitchen, and waited and waited. Ellen come downstairs very white, and made a pot of tea for the family, which Miss Lydia fetched. Then she made a cup for both of us, never spoke to me. Mr Curtis came eventually, gave me two sovereigns in my hand, much more than the wages I was owed, and told me to collect my things from upstairs and leave immediately. I expected to be shouted at, but it was the silence of the two of them that was worse. I think they was both as shocked as me.

Chapter Seventeen

Where to go, what to do? I had no idea. It was a dark January evening, fortunately clear and dry, with only the moon and stars to light me. I went to the little wood at the bottom of the road, but it was so cold and frosty, that I couldn't sleep there, so I decided to go to Mistress Baskett at Blake Hill Farm, seeing that it was Harry what got me into this frightening condition. The child was leaping and moving about inside me something terrible, and I was wondering if it would be coming that night. I got to the farmhouse, and rapped the knocker against it's brass plate causing great echoing thuds inside the house.

'God almighty. Can't be doin wi callers this time of night' I heard her swearing and grumbling as she came to the door. It was wrenched open, and I nearly fell in. 'God in heaven. Bissent ee Liza vrom Zandringum?' She brought me into her kitchen, sat me down by the range, and poured me a cup of well stewed tea from the chipped brown enamel teapot that stood boiling on the hotplate of the range. 'Youm in zum state', she observed calmly. 'Stop bawlin yer eyes owt. Bide quiet.' After two cups of bitter tea and several lumps of soft bread from a fresh loaf, with dollops of butter, she allowed me to tell my tale, in full, with no interruptions at all except my own sobbing, for which she provided a big handkerchief.

'I be awl of a vlummox' she said when I'd run out of words. 'How janoo tiz 'arry's chile? I be no fool. You bin seed abowt with other men assnt?' 'He's the only one I ever _laid_ with' I answered defensively. She very neatly got the whole story of all my experiences with men from me, and made it very plain that all that I had been getting up to before and since Harry was sinful, and likely to get me with child. Most people, specially women, were feared of Mistress Baskett, but I must say, she done good by me. She fed me and warmed me before she questioned me. She made me understand I'd been a bad girl without being nasty about it, and was helpful. She give me a proper bed in the house for the night, fed me again in the morning, sent me away with a gold sovereign in my hand, and advised me to get myself back into the workhouse as quickly as possible, as 'the babby might come soon.'

I wandered around when I left Blake Hill, as I wasn't never wanting to go into the workhouse again. I knew from attending St Peter's church with the Curtis family that there was an orphanage, St Faith's in upper Parkstone. I wondered if they might be able to give me and the babby, when it came, a place. I went through their big green gates, and knocked the door, but they just sent me away with some bread, and told me to go to the workhouse. I felt lost and helpless, so I went down to the quay, and asked after Harry there. All I could find out was that he was at sea with his father in the Daphne. No one could say when they'd be back, but the best answer I could get from the shipping office was one to two years. I felt desperate, but still had some pride left, and had no wish to have my condition known by anyone in the Teague household. I felt that I'd let them down so bad.

The tide at the quayside was low, and there was a little boat at the bottom of the steps near the Custom House. I seen a woman being helped in, and seated with another passenger. I asked where it was going, and was told Wareham. The boatmen took my sixpence and helped me in, and we cast off, to sail up the river. The air was still, but the day was absolutely freezing, and I was terrified as I never been on the water before, and felt dizzy and sick. The woman give me a stripped clove ball sweet to suck on, and it helped a bit. She asked me when the babby was expected to come. I said I'd no idea. She looked at me pityingly with my little bundle of belongings, thin cloak and gloves. I asked her about Wareham, and she just said that it was a little town, much smaller than Poole. She sometimes took the boat into Poole to see her sister who lived in Fish Street. We got off the boat, at the place they called Wareham Quay, and exactly as the woman had said, the town was very small.

I went into the baker's and was able to get me a hot meat pie, and stood in the street eating it, as the gravy dripped down my fingers. I went back into the shop, and asked the woman 'for pity's sake, can you give me a hot drink?' She told me to go around the back, and come out with a pint mug of steaming hot tea. I tried to pay, but she wouldn't take no more money off me. I felt better after, and a bit warmer. Dusk and darkness was fast falling as I made my way up the town. I was feeling very uncomfortable in my belly, and felt my thighs very wet. All that was before me on the right side of the street was an old church. A bitter wind was starting up, blowing tiny bits of ice about as I entered the small church and lay on the floor between two pews. The pains in my belly was coming and going, and I clenched my teeth. I delivered my own child there in the darkness, and held her to me, and put her to my breast. I don't know how she lived, but in the morning the verger come and found us, in a dreadful sticky mess, and half frozen. An old woman was sent for, who sorted me out a bit, cut the cord that had bound me to my little girl, and wrapped her in a cloth. We was put in a cart and taken up to a great grey building, Wareham and Purbeck Union Workhouse it was. We was admitted together, my little girl who had no name, and me. I had the wits to conceal my three sovereigns in my mouth before they stripped and bathed me. 'You'm a silent one' said the woman who washed me roughly with carbolic soap and shaved my head to get rid of imagined insects.

We were admitted to the workhouse 'Lying in Ward' for mothers and babies, and I was asked for my child's name, so I called her Maria. After lunch, the usual grey workhouse food, I was woken from a sleep. Mrs Hallett, the Matron fetched another patient who she called 'Gates' from the Sick Ward, which she had sneaked into to visit a friend. She was very sharp with Gates, and told her to clean and dress her baby. I was by the door to the stairs, but took little notice of what was going on around me, until I heard a slight thud by the stair well and heard Gates shouting 'Missis, Missis'. Mrs Hallett and Miss Whittaker the nurse rushed to the top of the stairs, with me behind them. I saw Gates with her head between the banister rails looking down at her poor little babby lying in a heap on the stone floor below. The Matron and nurse went to the little child, which had been dropped on it's head, and was so hurt they didn't think it would live. They questioned Gates, who said she was going to carry the child downstairs in her arms, when she tripped on something, and the babby fell over the banisters. The babby died later that day.

If you think the story of Gates and her baby is bad, then sadly I can tell you worse. Miss Whittaker our nurse, read it aloud to us from the Poole and Dorset Herald. The story was about another, very weak patient in the Sick Ward opposite, called Emily Coakes. She had appeared in court on a charge of attempting to commit suicide on the 24th December. She was the cook for Mr Stokes the Bank Manager in Wareham. Early in the morning Mr Stokes was disturbed by a noise he thought was coming from his boys' bedroom. He and Mrs Stokes went to look, and found both children sleeping. Eventually they found the noise coming from the servant's room. Mrs Stokes went into the room, and he followed. He heard Emily Coakes say 'I have taken poison, send for the doctor'.

Mr Stokes thought she was dreaming, and said 'don't talk nonsense, what poison can you have taken?' She continued to say send for the doctor, so he fetched Doctor Hartford, who came and found Emily lying in bed, being sick.

The doctor asked her what kind of poison she had taken, and she said 'Vitriol'. She told the doctor that she had woken and found herself in labour, and took the bottle she had for cleaning the grates, and drank it. The bottle was half full. When the doctor asked her why she took it, she said 'you will find the cause here in the bed.' He turned down the bedclothes and found a dead boy child. She said the child had died shortly after she had taken the vitriol. When the doctor asked her if this was her first child, she replied she had had one before and that it was fifteen months old, and with her mother. She told him that the pain from the vitriol was so great that she did not feel the child being born. In the bed with her the doctor found a bible opened at the 23rd psalm and a framed picture of her parents. Mr and Mrs Stokes and the doctor looked after her for a week, and then she was committed to the workhouse, to stand trial at a later date.

I cried at the sheer awfulness that I and these others were suffering as a result of our ignorance, stupidity and desperate desire for affection. I saw all that the Teagues and all their wonderful servants had tried so hard to do for me as being wasted. I could feel no hope for myself or little Marie. However, it wasn't too long before I began to feel a little better. I knew Matron Hallett had to keep us mothers and babies together until the babies were at least weaned. They would then be taken off to the nursery, and looked after by other paupers. We, their mothers would probably only get to see them for a short while on Sundays. This gave me time to build my strength, and with the help of the three sovereigns and some change, to try to escape from the workhouse and make a life for myself and Marie in Poole, with the hope of meeting with Harry again.

Not only did workhouses make every attempt to keep poor people out, they strangely kept us quite safely inside, particularly at night. Everyone who came in or went out was noted in a book kept by a clerk in a building by the front gate. It is very unhealthy to stay inside all the time, and there were no baby carriages in either of the two workhouses I experienced. To get Marie into the sunshine and fresh air, I had to walk in the yard with her in my arms. I was able to bribe one of the girls who worked in a laundry in town to get her hands on a big old cloak for me, and one day Marie and I slipped out of the workhouse and made our way back to Poole.

Reference

The two stories, of the woman who dropped her baby down the stairwell, and the woman who took poison, were both found in the Poole and Dorset Herald archive, 1800's. The names have been changed.

Chapter Eighteen

I knew what I was going to do. I did the same as I done first off, and went down to Wareham Quay and took a boat back to Poole. I went looking for Mrs Kitkat in Boar Lane, a narrow alley with its washing strung across clothes lines across the street, slipping roof tiles and crumbling chimneys. I asked her if I could stay in her room with her and the family. She and her husband and two working boys lived there. The room felt very crowded after what I'd been used to at Otterwood. The Kitkats disapproved of me and what I'd done, but they was poor, and liked the colour of the gold sovereign that I offered up front. I was given a shakedown bed of straw in a bag. I had to go out and buy an old plate, dish, mug and knife and fork, and blankets as there was none to spare. Marie needed changing, so I also had to buy rags and a bucket. I had planned to take in sewing, but quickly realized that I'd need some more cottons and needles than I had in my pack. It was a bad idea, as no clean, respectable person would want to bring their mending to Boar Lane. Besides, the light was very poor through the dirty little window, especially with the houses opposite being so close.

I was too ashamed to go to Missis Teague and ask if she could find work for me. Her customers were always asking if she could put them in the way of a good servant. Her staff took a long time to 'train' to her exacting standards, but she sometimes knew of someone's daughter who could be useful. Mrs Kitkat said to go to the vicar of St James's church instead, which was a good idea. He knew me, and would likely give me a written character if I was truthful about my circumstances. The next morning, I left little Marie wrapped tightly in a bit of blanket on top of my shakedown, as no one else was at home, and I didn't fancy leaving her with any of the other hags in the street. It was only a short step to the vicarage, but I knew how bad I looked. I couldn't remember when I had last washed my hair. I was out of the workhouse uniform, and Mrs Kitkat had given me her own change of clothes to wear that day. Washing was difficult you see, with just a bucket of water from the pump and one bowl for everything between the five of us in the room.

I went round to the servants' door at the vicarage, which was answered by the vicar's clean and tidy cook. She went away, and spoke to Mr Lawson. I heard him say that he was busy, but would see me by and by. She sat me down, give me a cup of tea, and set me to work peeling and chopping vegetables while I waited. After a couple of hours, Mr Lawson rang, and asked her to 'bring me through' to his fine study. It was a dark room that smelled of old leather, ancient books and pipe smoke. He had a very lean, kind face that I'd always thought of as 'meek.' He never raised his voice, or was ever known to be unkind, but at the end of our 'talk' I felt like a filleted fish. I went in whole, but he carefully and quickly got the whole truth out of me, with his razor sharp mind and constant, careful questions, never being taken in for a second by any lies. He ended by wanting to write me a ticket, to gain me immediate re-admission to St Mary's workhouse. I cried, and pleaded that I could never give Marie up, so he shrugged his shoulders, and said that he knew of no immediate work. He gave me a florin, and said he'd ask around for work for me. I knew he would, but I was desperate now.

It was a fine day, and I went on down to the fish shambles, never thinking of Marie. A large catch was just being unloaded, and I offered to help gutting the fish. I got paid cash in hand, and went back to the room late, to find Marie screaming for a bit of titty, and the Kitkats furious that I'd gone off and left her for so many hours. That became my life. I'd get any casual work I possibly could. It never paid enough, and Marie was often left alone for long hours, but what could I do? They was nice people though, the Kitkats. They helped where they could, and never turned me out. The Vicar found me a scrubbing job at the Antelope Inn in the mornings. I tied the growing Marie to the leg of the table with a leather strap at home, so's I could go out to do it. I was no better nor worse than any of our neighbours.

One day, when Marie was two and more, I seed the Daphne unloading coal outside of Burdens' the coal merchants. Master Harry was supervising. He looked just like a prince. His hair was bleached gold in the sun, and his eyes, when I looked into them later, were like pale blue sea. The men seemed to have a lot of respect for him, and I could see that his body had filled out more. He had great muscular arms on him, and a big chest. I called him, 'Mister Harry, Mister Harry.' He come over to me and said 'Should I know you?' 'It's me' I said, 'Liza Loader.' He did remember, and I saw a shadow pass over his face. 'I must finish up here' he said. 'I will see you at Hibbard's Coffee House on the High Street at six.' Somehow, I didn't feel as if things were going as I expected they might.

I felt too poor even to be seen at the coffee house with him. He told me he'd been back in town three months, well before the Daphne. He said he'd written to me as often as he could whilst I was away, but of course, I'd never had the letters had I? He had been told by Mistress Baskett that I had left my job at Otterwood, and made further enquiries. I wasn't surprised to hear that Mistress Baskett'd told him the lot. He ordered us a large pot of chocolate and sat and listened while I told him everything that had happened to me, and patted my rough, dirty hands! Not what I'd expected at all. Apparently he had given up strong drink, amazing, and was thinking of joining the Catholic Church! It was like speaking to a completely different person than the one I'd knowed. Somehow I'd always had the hope inside me that he'd come back and save me from my miserable existence. He asked after my child, and liked the name I'd chosen. 'Will you be a father to her?' I asked bravely. 'I think not,' he said. 'I understand from Mistress Baskett that there were many others besides me?' 'Yes' I snivelled, and he passed me a fine white handkerchief, and told me to keep it. He'd went away a boy, and come back a man, no question about it. He walked me back down Market Street, and put two sovereigns in my hand and bid me goodbye.

I'd had enough. Something inside of me just snapped. It was a very cold day, I now had a little bit of money in my pocket, and I went straight into the Poole Arms, and ordered up a glass of gin as it was cheaper than beer. I liked that warm rush that you get with the first drink. I ordered and another and another. It was completely dark when I was ready to fumble myself home, crying drunk, and on the way, I went with a drunk sailor into a dark alley, and what we did for each other felt so very very good. He give me some money, and I shuffled back to Blue Boar Lane. The Kitkats were, as expected, furious with me, and old Pa Kitkat warned me that I was on a very, very short string as far as he and Mrs Kitkat were concerned. Well, I did harken to him. I had to. They were the roof over our heads for Marie and me.

I carried on working as hard as I could for another couple of years, but there was no end to the drudgery. Marie was about four, and I was still buckling a leather strap round her waist, and tying it to the table leg to keep the little mite safe when we was all out. I started to go out drinking again. I enjoyed the warmth and cheer in the Poole Arms. True enough, many of the sailors were violent men, but some were very good company. We had sing songs. The Kitkats were always on about me. I got to love my gin, and my little bits of firkytoodle out in the alleys by the quay. Many of the men were so drunk they were no good, didn't pay me anyway, and sometimes beat me up. This was balanced out, as others amongst the very drunk often overpaid me. I didn't care. After a while I was let go from the Antelope for being poor at my work, and not turning up when I should of. I kept it quiet from Ma Kitkat.

Then my monthly never come. Old Ma Kitkat knew right away what I'd been up to when I started being sick, and was so furious that she threw Marie and me out into the street with our belongings. I was lucky there. I wasn't that bothered. I went straight next door to Clara Fancy. She was a bit older than me, and rented two rooms, all to herself. She had a lot of male visitors, some dressed like real toffs. She told me that if I could give up the gin, I was sitting on a bank, right there between my legs. She'd been asking me to go into partnership with her for some time, suggesting that with my looks and learning, she and I could 'move up in the *fancy work* business.' She sat me down, and made us a cup of tea from the kettle boiling on the fire. 'Two things first' she said, looking at me seriously. 'One, dump the brat. Two, get rid of the one you're carrying.' 'Well,' I said, 'Marie's not going in the Workhouse, and that's flat.' 'You've got till tomorrow evening,' she replied, and if you don't get rid of her, you're both out on the streets.' 'And number two?' I asked. 'You deal with number one first, and I'll get something sorted out for number two.'

That was it. Clara had forced me into it. I'd been thinking about it myself already. Marie was simply a tie. Something would have to be done about her. I thought she looked more and more like Harry, with her little blue eyes and her fair hair. I remembered St Faith's, that nice looking house on the hill, behind the green gates, much better for children than the workhouse. They only took children, and the ones I'd seen looked well and happy. It would be no good me trying to hand her in, as they were probably busy and full up anyway, but I thought if they had to keep her for a few days, they might get to like her. Early the next afternoon, Clara had given me the eye, and said 'You'm going to do something about er ain't you?' 'All right, all right' I said, putting on my cloak and bonnet, and grabbing a little bundle of her things.

I walked and carried her all the way to Parkstone. We skulked around St Peter's churchyard a bit until dusk, and then I carried her up Constitution Hill. It was simple, she was a good girl, and kept quiet. We got in quietly through the big green gates, and I left her in the porch with a label saying 'my name is Marie' pinned on her clothes and said I was only going to be a few minutes, and to stay quiet and I would be back quick. I never saw her no more after that. It made me sad, but what could I do? I only prayed that they wouldn't send her to the workhouse after all.

Notes

St Faith's Orphanage – See Wheway E., 1984. Edna's story. Memories of life in a childrens' home and in service in Dorset and London. Pub Word and Action, Dorset.

LYDIA

Chapter Nineteen

My life changed the day that Liza was sent from our house. We were all absolutely horrified, and to make matters worse Mother was allowed to sink into a further, more acute stage of her embarrassing 'illness' by having such a self-indulgent outburst of pure bad temper. Instead of trying to reason with her during her attention demanding hysterics, Father and Doctor Stone colluded to silence her with the use of drugs yet again. What they did not foresee was her future intelligent use of poor behaviour to secure increased dosages again and again. Father, in spite of his general astuteness, also failed to predict the rapid escalation of medical costs for her 'care.'

Grandmother was summoned the following day, and appeared in an unusually petulant mood, fed up with having her busy week's work interrupted by yet another of our domestic crises. She went white when Father told her of Liza's summary dismissal, and refused to be deterred in her intent to 'have it out' with Mother and Father. 'You should have been acting like good foster parents for that girl, and kept her on the straight and narrow. Whatever were you doing? Does anyone even know or care where she has gone?' Not that I was particularly listening outside Mother's door, just dusting on the landing. Not only was Grandmother genuinely distressed that Liza had got herself into 'such a fix', but she was also very angry about the loss of a good and helpful servant to our needy household. Clearly Mother and Father were expecting that she would find them another. This was not the case, as good servants were so very hard to come by.

The net result was that following an in depth conversation with grandmother, I decided to give up going to school to run the household. I was sixteen anyway, and there was little point in my continuing, as I was probably better at learning for myself than Miss Squires was at teaching me. I had however, enjoyed the daily journeys to and from Poole with Father, and the escape from Mother's tantrums. The change in my situation sounds as if I was taking on a lot of drudgery in the absence of a second servant. However, Grandmother had pointed out that the change would mean that I had overall management of the house, and staff, which had been sorely lacking during Mother's decline. It was a notion that appealed to me at the time, and I felt ready to step into the shoes of 'The Lady of the House'. I would be dealing with the orders from all of the local tradespeople, and managing the housekeeping budget and any social engagements, if I dared to make any, with Mother lurking around the place.

I started by changing some of the household cleaning schedules as we were seriously understaffed. We sent as much laundry as possible to the Primrose Laundry on Mansfield Hill. I changed some of our regular menus to relieve some of the food preparation after consultation with the Misses Greenish who lived over the road at Trefloyne. These two elderly maiden ladies became surprisingly good friends and confidantes to me, despite our age differences, and often kindly lent me Joanna, their second maid when we were deep cleaning rooms, or attempting to be sociable with close friends. It was wonderful to have the extra pair of hands particularly when bedsteads needed to be taken apart and have their disjointed fragments turpentined. I was more directive with Mr Barnes, who had replaced Arthur as gardener, and stated that all root vegetables should be washed and scrubbed prior to delivery to the kitchen, to save us a little work and mess. There was a water tap outside, for goodness sake.

I re-instituted some afternoon teas to which I personally invited the most kind and discreet people amongst our neighbours. Mother was included, but sometimes appeared dressed inappropriately, and was generally either mildly belligerent to all around her, or dozed off and spilt her tea over her dress. Colonel and Mrs Fawkes from The White Lodge, just up the road, were with me, taking tea in the back garden one day. The tea things were beautifully arranged on the tea trolley and cake stand, and the copper kettle was sitting on its little spirit stove, gently steaming. Mother appeared from the conservatory, and walking like a string puppet, tripped over an empty garden chair and fell full length over the cake stand. Mrs Fawkes called for Ellen, who came rushing out to help me. Mother was not injured, but we had to accept the help of the solicitous Colonel to get her back inside the house, and into her own bedroom. 'What you need, my dear Miss Curtis, is a resident nurse,' he remarked. 'I will have a word with your father tonight.'

I thought that the Colonel's suggestion was excellent, and felt that taking on a nurse might enable us to give more attention to little Babs who was five, and already attending the infants' class at Sandecotes School. Poor little scrap. Ellen and I were substitute mothers to her, as Mother generally 'snapped' as soon as she saw or heard Babs, which had made her a very 'nervy child.' Grandmother's telephone advice was sympathetic but consistent. 'Don't let it get too much for you girl. Use your brains to manage your way out of the problems.' And so I did. Father agreed that a nurse would probably be helpful, and approached his friend Dr Philpotts at 'Moorcroft' for advice. I felt rather nervous, having recently read Nicholas Nickleby, that we might end up with a 'Mrs Gamp.' In the end, there was no choice, as Dr Philpotts was only able to suggest one lady.

Grandmother came up to Parkstone to help me with studying the lady's reference, and the interview. I had hoped for someone reasonably young, but Miss Hordle was in her mid forties. I was not greatly impressed with her. She had a sallow complexion, a lean, stringy body, loose false teeth and smiled little, possibly as a consequence of the teeth. She did agree that she would also be able to help a bit with overseeing Babs and would participate in other household duties when not required by mother. In our discussions, Grandmother suggested that Miss Hordle might possibly have the moral gravitas to manage mother rather well, so we agreed to engage her for a month's trial period. She was soon a member of our permanent staff.

The appointment of Miss Hordle improved family life almost immediately. Grandmother had been absolutely right about the gravitas. Miss Hordle was not someone to have an argument with. She explored situations very carefully before adopting a course of action, which she then pursued impassively. She spent a week observing Mother's behaviour, and watching the effects of the laudanum doses on her. She used her observations to construct a daily routine for her which resulted in fewer outbursts, simply because Mother was kept more active and involved with life at Otterwood again, and thus tended to forget herself and her own preoccupations a little. Miss Hordle took responsibility for all of Mother's clothes and linens and the cleaning of her room, and made Mother responsible for some of the tedious and routine household tasks like mending. They sat together on cold days, either side of the coal fire in Mother's bedroom, which Miss Hordle referred to as The Boudoir. They walked together to the shops in Lower Parkstone, where Miss Hordle introduced herself at Perrett's Grocery, Elfords the Bakers and Grocers and Roses the Butchers as 'Mrs Curtis's Companion.' On my behalf, they discussed the household requirements with these excellent tradespeople. Sometimes they sat together in the new Victoria Park, which had been made by culverting the little stream and landscaping the field. They watched the pretty little fountain, and sat companionably together, reading their books. Miss Hordle was even sufficiently brave to take Mother to church services and some of the church activities, confident that she had the power to curb Mother's extremes with one of her hard 'looks'. As a very young woman, I was less pleased at these public appearances by mother. I often heard the sneering voice of Mrs Beeney, remarking to her fat friend Miss Eyers, a woman oozing with eau de cologne that Mother would be 'better off locked up.'

Mother and Miss Hordle went on very long walks on fine days, and with Miss Hordle in her customary position close to her side, Mother's demeanour improved a little. She actually looked better, with some colour in her cheeks, particularly when they had made their regular walk to Blake Hill Farm to visit Mistress Baskett on Thursday afternoons. I was rather surprised that Mother would ever countenance visiting with Mistress Baskett, whom she had shunned like the plague during her 'better years.' The success of these visits, according to Miss Hordle was 'based on Mistress Baskett's great capacity for toleration of the different states in which persons find themselves.'

It sounds simple, but without Miss Hordle's immutable will and sheer persistence, such changes would never have been possible. Doctor Stone did not have to be sent for in any emergency, but continued to visit regularly. He insisted that Mother should continue with the Laudanum regularly, and take chloral hydrate at night. Against this background of unwonted peace, a second servant, Lily, was finally employed. She had come to us from St Faith's Orphanage, near Constitution Hill after Grandmother had approached Miss Langley personally. Grandmother had said to Ellen and me 'You must keep the sharpest eye on young Lily, and I'll show no mercy to either of you if this girl drifts off the straight and narrow.' I heard her making the same vehement warning to Father as well. Lily proved to be a mixed blessing, with a great capacity for strategic, quiet dusting outside any rooms where something significant might be going on, and an even worse tendency to knock at the door and offer tea at what she divined were significant moments.

Babs, as things turned out, did not get much attention at all from Miss Hordle, who was generally fully engaged with keeping Mother on the straight and narrow, but the development of a calmer, more orderly household had beneficial effects on us all. I had far more time to spend with Babs and Michael when he was home. He was just a few months away from leaving school at Winchester and going up to Oxford. However, things rarely run along predictable lines. Just ten months after joining us, Miss Hordle received a letter saying that her sister in Abbotsbury was very ill with consumption, and that she was urgently needed to help her brother-in-law with the six children. 'You must pack immediately' I told her, and went to telephone Parkstone Station to ascertain train times and routes so that she would be able to leave the following morning. We all cried when Miss Hordle left us, as we had lost a lady who had become a dear friend to each of us, and we were all aware that it was reasonably unlikely that she would ever be able to return to us. I cried because I was aware of the level of responsibilities that would once again fall upon my shoulders. Michael, who was home prior to going up to university put his arm around my shoulders, and said 'Dearest Sis, try not to take on so. I will help you all I can, until we can get another nurse.' He really did help too, taking over a big part of the timetable Miss Hordle had developed for Mother.

Father confided in me that he had become very concerned about our household economy. It would be very expensive sending Michael up to Oxford, but he felt that he had to do this for him. He was uncertain as to whether we could stretch to paying the salary of a replacement nurse. Privately, I had to admit to myself that I found Mother utterly repugnant to me, and didn't feel that I would ever be consistently able to keep an even temper with her foibles. I insisted that Father should ask Dr Philpotts immediately if he could find a temporary replacement for Miss Hordle until we ascertained whether or not she could come back. No suitable nurse was forthcoming. Dr Stone did send an inmate from the workhouse for interview, who had experience helping the nurse who managed the lunatics. Grandmother and I turned Mrs Wareham down as she was a big, beefy woman who was superficially deferent, and would probably manage Mother efficiently through bullying and constraint. She was totally lacking in manners and refinement, and I didn't want her under our roof.

I became frankly overworked as soon as Michael left for Oxford, and became almost immediately guilty of calling Doctor Stone in as soon and as often as Mother started to become difficult, and he not only injected her with more diamorphine, but left Veronal tablets with her, 'to take if you begin to feel distressed my dear.' I suspect he was getting heartily sick of the situation himself. The Veronal tablets marked the beginning of the end. I had never perceived Mother as being a person with an illness. I believed her to be immature and selfish, always wanting her own way, and always expecting to be the centre of attention. One morning, about five months after Miss Hordle's departure, Lily went into Mother's room with her cup of tea and a can of hot water for her to wash with, and found her looking very white and still. She fetched me, and I immediately concluded that my mother was dead. An empty bottle of Veronal was beside her.

Notes

Victoria Park. This was formerly Three Acre Field, and was bought for the council by Lord Wimborne for Queen Victoria's Jubilee. It was opened in 1888, so this chapter, set in 1884-6 ish is slightly inaccurate. It is now known as Parkstone Park or Parkstone Green.

Chapter Twenty

Well, it's true, I never liked my mother, but I never wished her dead. We lowered all the blinds in the house, as the first indication to the whole of our neighbourhood that someone had died. The blinds were left so until after the funeral. As soon as Doctor Stone had confirmed Mother's death, I sent a message down to Parkstone village, asking old Connie Coles from Parr Street to come up and do the necessary. Unfortunately she was also known in the village for being an inveterate gossip. She would attend the home of the bereaved, and wash and lay out the body. She generally began her stories with 'The whole family was there, all sobbing and carrying on.....' and then add her choice of unsavoury, and I'm sure, general untruths about the manner of death / state of the corpse / family. A week or so later, Lily reported that she'd heard old Connie in Perrett's Grocery, 'confidentially' whispering to another customer that Mother had bulging eyes and a rope mark around her neck when she had attended to see to the body.

Mother's funeral was delayed, as the Coroner's court made enquiries concerning her death, which of course further fuelled the imaginations of the gossipmongers in Parkstone. Father, who was required to attend the court to give evidence, told me that the conclusion reached was that Mother's death was an accident following years of ill health, and hastened by her absent minded ingestion of an overdose of Veronal tablets. Mr Negus attended our home to discuss the funeral, which was to be held at St Peter's church. The little man's sandy hair provided a sparser cover to his head than before, and I liked his gentle blue eyes as he followed me courteously into the morning room, to wait for father. He was very pleasant and kind with me. I wrote and sent out all the black bordered cards and envelopes to inform our family and friends.

On the day of the funeral all the family and our close friends were assembled at Otterwood. Mr Negus and his little team issued all the gentlemen with black hatbands, black gloves and black scarves. As a family, we walked in front of mother's glass funeral carriage. Behind her carriage followed all our more distant friends and relatives. At the back of the long procession were the empty carriages of those people who were unable to attend. The funeral service in St Peter's church was a very grand affair, conducted by Canon Dugmore assisted by young Father Caliphronas, with much swinging of incense and sprinkling of holy water. Many parishioners offered their kind condolences, but Mrs Beeney, her pale green cat's eyes seeming to glow in the dark of the porch, said in her clipped tones 'I hope your mother's illness of the mind will not prove to be hereditary.' It was like a smack in the face, but I held my ground, and kept my face bland, thanking her for her kind concern. I heard her saying to her atrocious friend Miss Ayres as they withdrew 'Jumped up grocer's daughter, that Mrs Curtis, gave herself such airs. Little wonder that she could never cope in society.'

Looking back, I can see that it must have been difficult for Mother growing up in the Teague's large establishment, never being given a great deal of attention, but knowing that a lot was expected of her. Her parents, my grandparents, certainly had great expectations of her. They themselves had, in spite of enormous odds, progressed from being semi literate struggling young people into respected members of the Poole business community. It would be no exaggeration to say that they were both very sorely grieved at the loss of their daughter at such a young age, and following such grave emotional difficulties. We all went into deep mourning. My own sorrow was exacerbated by the fact that I felt that I had never really known the woman Mother was, and could have been before what I now acknowledge was the development of her illness. We had a very kind letter from Miss Hordle, who was sadly unable to attend the funeral because of continuing family duties in Abbotsbury.

Years of worry and stress were apparently over for me, but I was left with the lingering thought that I had not done enough to help Mother, never been sufficiently patient. I should never have left the Veronal tablets beside her in the room. I was sure that the overdose had been deliberate, not accidental. Day after day, these thoughts returned to me, and combined with my general feeling of grief melted into a deep, cold blackness in my soul. Father and Michael were kind and helpful with me, and Ellen took firm charge of all domestic matters as far as she could, but I had the added stress of watching the household finances very carefully. Michael's education was indeed costing father 'a packet', and the funeral costs had been enormous. A lot was spent on the funeral, because I suppose that in our hearts we all felt that we just might have been able to do more to help Mother. Other feelings came to me such as 'good riddance', 'glad she's gone', and I was left in turmoil, unable to sleep, night after night.

Michael went up to Oxford. One morning, I got up, to carry on managing as best I could. The day was no better, no worse than the ones that preceded it. At 11.00 when Ellen brought me my coffee tray, I just felt paralysed, just couldn't carry on. You need help, Miss Lydia' she said gently. 'Shall I send for Mr Curtis?' I gritted my teeth, and tried to say 'Grandmother.' 'My poor lamb', said Ellen, making for the telephone instrument, which she had never used before, but had observed. She managed to get herself connected to the Parkstone exchange, and asked for father's number in Poole. He came straight home, bringing Dr Stone with him. I shrank from the Doctor, and was all tears, still trying to make myself understood, 'Grandmother, Grandmother.' I had developed a deep mistrust of medical men as a tribe, and hated this Doctor, blaming him for what I felt to be misguided treatment of Mother. I wanted none of his nostrums.

The result was that Ellen packed some bags for me and Grandmother came and collected me that very evening, leaving Ellen in charge. Grandmother was all tender smiles and affection towards me, and I felt better, having the mantle of responsibility removed completely from me. She assured me that Ellen and Lily would easily be able to manage such a small household without my help, and Ellen, having shown the ability to use the telephone instrument had been instructed to ring daily and more frequently if any domestic problem arose. Grandmother sent for her Doctor,

Dr Penney, who came to me that evening and prescribed complete rest, a very light diet and that the curtains should be kept closed at all times. He said, as if I wasn't in the room, 'This is a very severe nervous disorder Ma'am. Very severe indeed. We must protect Miss Lydia from any strain or worry. She must have positively no stimulation. The consequences of overtaxing her could be very dire Ma'am. Very dire indeed.' My brain was not so torpid that I didn't realize that he was already thinking that I would go the way of my Mother. I didn't care if I did. Anything would be better than feeling this awful. I was offered some Chloral Hydrate, and finally acquiesced in drinking the bitter mixture. Dr Penney assured me that I would sleep that night. I heard him telling Grandmother as she closed the door behind them, 'I know a splendid chap in London, absolutely first class in managing nervous disorders........'

I slept a little. The removal of any responsibility was a help, but I still kept breaking out into tears. Between the little naps I woke often to find fresh tears on my face. Grandmother clearly slept little herself. She left the bedroom door ajar, and several times in the night I was aware of her standing quietly in the room, looking at me. In the morning, I was able to drink a weak cup of tea and eat a plate of slack porridge. I was disconcerted to notice that my abdomen was very sore and distended, and I had some relief as I passed prodigious amounts of wind. Rightly or wrongly, I put it down to the Chloral Hydrate I'd taken the previous evening, refused to take any more, and had no further problems with my tummy. Grandmother didn't come and stand in my room during the night again. She was either very tired, which wouldn't be surprising, or had settled down to waiting for me to get better. I absolutely insisted on having the curtains opened in the daytime, but had to content myself with my incarceration. I did want to feel better, and wanted to be co operative. The days hung fearfully heavy, and without any form of stimulation, sleep remained difficult. I still couldn't speak even to Grandmother without bursting into floods of tears, and I began to grit my jaws together in an attempt to gain some control of my face. The left side of my face began to twitch, sleeping or waking, in my efforts not to sob noisily. I noticed that even the looking glass had been removed from my room, so I couldn't check if somehow my facial features had become permanently distorted.

Grandmother had decided not to accept Dr Penney's recommendation of the expensive London specialist in nervous disorders. She pleased me by allowing the looking glass to be repositioned, and gave in to my demands for something to read. She selected one of her prized Household Edition of the illustrated works of Charles Dickens for me. She adored reading Dickens. I found several large round tea stains in the book, from where she'd probably been surprised whilst reading in her downstairs room, and spilled her tea on the pages. I was given a very light, fairly monotonous diet, on the doctor's orders. The occasional biscuits were the best part of it. 'Morning Coffee' were boring, 'Petit Beurre' and 'Osbourne' nearly as bad, but the 'Digestives', particularly recommended for invalids and people with dyspepsia, which commonly appeared in the afternoon, with a cup of tea, were preferable. Father was eventually allowed in to see me, and seemed mightily concerned about me. Grandmother kept saying 'Lydia will mend. She just needs plenty of time.' I trusted that she was right, she generally was, but of course, this did not help me at all in the short term.

I was better pleased when Ann and Lucy were allowed to visit and help look after me. Ann asked whether there was anything special I'd like to eat? I did tell her that the evening egg flips with a drop of brandy in them were very helpful, and that I'd been sleeping a lot better. She knew how well I like my puddings, and suggested that a 'black cap pudding' with plenty of blackcurrant jam in its black cap might be 'good for putting some flesh back on your bones.' They were all so very kind, that it often made me cry anew that such good people should care so dearly for me. Grandmother sometimes said that she often wished that dear Captain Lovejoy would make haste to come home. 'He has to doctor all those men on that ship of his' she said. 'I feel certain sure that he would know what to do to help you get well again.'

I was trying as best I could to get well myself well again. Grandfather came and read me bits from the Poole and Dorset Herald, and told me any news from the town, including which ships were in. I know he scoured them carefully for any news of the Daphne, and asked regularly at the Shipping Office. I later discovered that uncharacteristically, Captain Lovejoy had received considerable financial backing for the voyage from his friends, as he had been heavily hit by the collapse of a local bank. My father and grandparents were amongst those who had made loans or allowed credit. The reasons for our family financial difficulties were becoming clear.

Finally, after two weeks in my room, Dr Penney allowed me to begin taking my evening meals with Grandmother and Grandfather again. This was only permitted for the evening meal. Lunchtimes downstairs with the staff, which I had always so enjoyed remained forbidden initially. One morning, Grandfather was particularly happy. 'The Daphne is in dock at Alloa, and young Mr Harry Lovejoy is in town, having travelled down from London, where he has been sitting a navigation examination, and will dine with us tonight' he announced. I did mention quietly that I would rather drink a vial of prussic acid than sit at table with that young man, but Grandfather insisted that I would find him greatly changed for the better.

It is hard to put my impressions of that meal into words. I have clear memories of the white table cloth with blue embroidery in the corners, and the blue of the crockery. Harry was dressed as a prosperous seafarer, with a new short cut, well fitting pea jacket for the warmer weather and a white, white shirt. He kissed my hand, and I felt strange and tight inside. I sat opposite him, and saw the strong outline of a man's body within his clothes, his beautiful blond, wavy hair, and those deep, deep blue eyes. I have no recollection at all of the conversation at table. When we had finished our meal, he followed me into the parlour and we sat down with Grandmother and Grandfather. I remembered seeing him in the bush as Otterwood with Liza, and suddenly felt that my stays were laced too tight, causing a squeezing sensation against my chest. I clasped my hand to my bosom. Grandmother, sharp eyed as a ferret, said 'I think you've done quite enough for this evening, Lydia' and ushered me across the hall to my bedroom.

I lay down quietly, and woke to hear Harry making his goodbyes to my grandparents. I distinctly remember hearing him say 'I can state with certainty my father's opinion on the treatment of Miss Lydia. What she needs is Dr Diet, Dr Quiet and Dr Merryman.' The rest of the conversation was muffled.

HARRY

Chapter Twenty One

By the grace of God, and with excellent seamanship on the part of the Cap'n, officers, apprentices, crew and passengers, the Daphne survived her extreme passage around the Horn. Two days later, whilst I was 'on top' I sighted a colossal mass of ice which as a farmer, I guessed had a sea level base of about a quarter of a mile. At each end of this iceberg there were mighty pinnacles, which I estimated to be about three hundred feet above the water level. It looked like the broadside view of a great ship. I shouted down to Paul Hann on the poop deck. What an exceptional sight! The next day, we saw another vast piece of ice, which Caleb Stone described as looking like the great Rock of Gibraltar. Paul steered us past it carefully on its leeward side, at a safe distance. Just as we were passing it, a great pillar of ice, the nearest part to us gave way, and about a hundred tons of ice dropped away from the mighty berg and fell off with a terrifying explosion of sound into the unfathomable depths of the ocean, causing massive waves. The mighty berg, losing its former balance, rocked and heaved terrifyingly downwards and finally turned upside down, revealing the hideous bulk which before was previously under the water. The lower parts of the ice seemed quite smooth and rounded by beating of the waves. I suspect we were all silently meditating on our good fortune. We had not met that monster either during the night or during the storm.

The storm damage was such that we needed to make a lengthy stop at Valparaiso for urgent repairs and fresh provisions. We did not arrive in Alloa until November, 1885. Our passage home from Adelaide had taken us 140 days. It was a calm day as the Daphne slipped into the Forth estuary, being tugged into Alloa on the rising tide and gently moving up to the mooring posts by the red harbour light. It was a rarity in early November, a reasonably warm, still day. The light was coming and going rapidly across the broad expanse of the Forth, now bright and now dull as I saw for the first time, the Ochil Hills on the horizon. I stood watching the light on the water for a long time, remarking the difference of the light up here in Scotland, allowing the water to be at one moment blue, and the next grey, the hills at one moment green and sunlit and the next almost invisible.

The Cap'n asked me almost immediately to go into town in search of medical supplies for two crewmen who had broken limbs in falls during a recent storm. He gave me a list of what was needed and asked me to hurry as we were completely out of laudanum, and I walked up from the shore, past the Mar Hotel, across the tramway and into Limetree Walk, right up into Broad Street, past the manse and into a place called Coalgate and asked for a pharmacy. It was getting quite dark, but eventually I reached the pharmacy of A. Ross in Drysdale Street, at the junction of Mill St and Shilling Hill. By this time, I had not taken any strong drink for more than two years, but somehow, being back in Britain, and passing the brightly lit bars, and hearing the noise, and smelling the smells became a great struggle to me. One half of me was saying 'You have been through so much; you deserve just a little drink.' The other half of me was saying 'You know it was only ever one drink intended, but you have no ability to stop.' After all this time, I was sweating with my desperate need for a drink, and the tearing struggle inside me not to give in as I made for the Pharmacy.

The Pharmacist was just about to turn the key to lock the shop door, when he saw me coming, and courteously invited me in, locking the door behind me, and saying 'Last customer of the day.' I gave him my list, and he motioned me to sit down on the chair by the counter. 'Mistress!' the man called, and a beautiful dark haired woman appeared. 'Your list is long, sir, and the requirements will take me some time to prepare. You have the look of a man who is suffering. My wife will take you to the back of the shop, and pour you a cup of tea while you wait.' Mrs Ross led me behind the counter, through the dispensary room to a cosy sitting area, where a kettle was singing on the hob at the fireplace. She made all three of us a cup of tea, and gave me a small cake of shortbread. I told her I'd never tasted shortbread before, and the delicious buttery, crummy, sugary texture was exquisite, and melted in my mouth. I told Mrs Ross about our journey all the way round the world to fetch a cargo for Patons. She was a lovely person. She asked me questions in such an encouraging way, that I found myself telling her about my early life, and my problems with strong drink, and even how I'd been feeling as I entered their shop. Eventually the Pharmacist, who seemed a nice chap, a little older than me, reappeared, and asked me if I was feeling better. He had been listening whilst he was doing the dispensing. He asked me very courteously if I would like to stay and share their evening meal with them.

I stayed, and I'm thankful to say that it was the beginning of a lasting friendship with them both. Sometimes in life, you sense that you have met someone absolutely exceptional, and Alec and I developed a bond that was almost instant. After we had eaten, he insisted on seeing me back to the Daphne, as the Alloa streets would be rather dark, and they were both concerned that I might lose my way. I kept company with them for a couple of weeks, during the evenings. They also entertained my father. Alec admitted to me previous problems that he'd had with drink himself, and he and Mrs Ross took me to the Greenbank Mission with them. Before I left Alloa for London, where I was to sit my examinations, I too had become a proud wearer of a blue ribbon on my coat. They both promised to support me as a lifetime abstainer from alcohol.

Both John Downton and I were nervous about the Board of Trade Examination to gain our Second Mate's tickets. It would test us in particular on our navigational skills, which required a high level of competence in plotting a ship's position using spherical trigonometry, six figure logarithms and the ability to measure angles in hours, minutes and seconds rather than degrees. I was extremely sorry to be leaving my father and the other officers and apprentices to manage all that needed to be done with the ship and cargo in Alloa without my help. My father had arranged the examinations for me, as a testament he said, to my professional and moral development during the time I had served with him. He had completed my apprenticeship papers early, and made me an Able Seaman in Adelaide, and in the event of my passing the examinations for the second mate's ticket at the first attempt, he promised to sign me on again with the Daphne and to repay my debts to Miss Caroline in full. In the privacy of his cabin, he embraced me and kissed me, and said 'My dear Harry, you have made me so proud of you. I confess that I had little hope of you redeeming yourself, but I perceive that you have done all things well. In particular you have steadfastly kept your promise to abstain from liquor, even when the temptations in Luanda, Montevideo and Adelaide were almost irresistible. The speed at which you have developed your navigational skills is breathtaking even to an old man like me! You lead men well by the strength of your example, and I am impressed that unlike other, weaker men, you have never resorted to physical violence against any crewman.' We both had tears in our eyes after he made his little speech. I had always loved and respected my father, but the bond between us had strengthened mightily during the time we had sailed together. Despite the fact that he was the master, and I was the apprentice, the opportunity to work together and support each other had been immensely satisfying to us both.

After sailing all the way round the world, Downton and I found negotiating the railway system to get ourselves down to London for our examinations was 'a breeze.' We started our journey in Stirling on the Caledonian Railway, and transferred to the London and North East Railway at Carlisle for the run to London. I both liked and disliked London. Our lodging house in King's Cross was run by a pleasant woman, Mrs Frodsham, a widow with a pair of rooms at the back of the house, stuffed with her children of various ages. The upstairs rooms were for paying guests. The entire premises were pervaded with the intense smell of brassica, both recent and dating back to ages past. It is certainly true that both the crew and apprentice cabins stank whilst at sea, but after the fresh air I was accustomed to on deck, I found the foetid air inside the house quite intolerable. It was of little use to open a window, as the London air was no better. We were ten days there, being examined, and both emerged successful, with our second mate's tickets. Father had already pointed out that he had no intention of appointing me second mate immediately, as I still needed to build up my practical experience, but I knew John Downton would receive his just reward.

Chapter Twenty Two

It was with thankfulness that I returned to Poole, to stay with Miss Caroline and find my dear Liza again. With my new found maturity, I was aware of how I had taken advantage of my dear girl, and hoped that she would accept my marriage proposal. When I said to Miss Caroline on my first morning home that I was going to find Liza, a sordid and shocking story unfolded. Apparently the girl was of very low moral character, and had been going with other men for years. Unsurprisingly under the circumstances, she had found herself to be with child, and had been dismissed by Mrs Curtis when her condition was far advanced. She had been looking for me, as she was sure that I was the father of her child. I was very shaken to hear all this, and spent two days walking about, and deciding whether it could be true or not. In the end, I felt that what I had been told was probably true. She had been over eager, and had shown no modesty with me. I had been in love with my idealized view of her, but did not want to tie myself in marriage to a person who was in fact a lowly maidservant with low morals, as I felt that I could not count on either her love or faithfulness over a lifetime. I felt very sad about her difficulties, and determined to search for her and finish with her formally, but kindly.

On my third morning home, I went to see Squirrel Oakes's mother, in Oak Alley, alongside the Lord Nelson Inn, to impart the sad news of the loss of her son and to give her the money my father had sent her, together with her son's cotton neckerchief and clasp knife. It was a very sorrowful errand. I walked down to Poole quay, and smelled all those familiar smells of turpentine, tar, hot train oil, burning coal and fresh fish turning into rancid fish. Near the fish shambles, fishermen were busying about, some of them wearing Guernsey smocks and loose trousers. Further along, customs officers and tidewaiters were pacing about, watching and taking notes on ships loading and unloading. Three feral dogs were running around, chasing each other, and anything that moved. All the quayside pubs, the Portsmouth Hoy, Poole Arms, Jolly Sailor,

Lord Nelson and the Eight Bells were doing a roaring trade. Dockers and sailors were singing capstan shanties as they worked on the ships. One cheeky shanty man spotted the rickety cart of the 'Ancient Mariner', an old man who regularly drove up and down the streets of Poole, selling fresh mackerel. He started a new song, and his crew, cheeky young louts hanging about the quay and the drinkers outside the Poole Arms joined the chorus:

Oh, poor old man, your horse will die,
And we say so, and we know so
Oh, poor old man, your horse will die,
And we say so, and we know so
We'll hoist him up to the main yardarm,
And we say so, and we know so
We'll drop him down to the depths of the sea
And we say so, and we know so
We'll drop him down with a long, long roll
And we say so, and we know so
Where the sharks'll have his body
And we say so, and we know so
And the devil will have his soul
And we say so, and we know so!

The Ancient Mariner man fluently rolled out a mass of obscenities sufficient to make the devil himself cringe and viciously whipped his poor old nag to within an inch of its sad life and disappeared into Thames Street.

I had simply no idea where to look for Liza, so I decided to approach the problem logically and go and ask in Teagues first, which I did, and enjoyed a lovely cup of tea with Mrs Teague in her back room. I was very surprised and sad to hear that her only child, Mary Curtis had been found dead one morning, nine months previously, following a long illness with a nervous disorder. Mrs Teague was aware of Liza's trouble, but said she had seen nothing of her and was surprised that Liza had never come back to her for help. She invited me back for an evening meal on Thursday.

Apparently Lydia who was coming up seventeen was staying at Teagues' for an indefinite period for a complete rest. My next call was the Union workhouse at Longfleet. Again, nothing had been heard of Liza Loader since Mrs Teague had taken her on, all those years ago. Mrs Cave, who looked after the female paupers was quite helpful, and said that Liza may have felt too ashamed to come back, and that it might be a forlorn hope, but the nearest other workhouse was in Wareham, and it was just possible that despite her condition, she could have managed to get herself over there to give birth to the baby in safety and shelter.

I felt very despondent about the whole sordid matter, especially my involvement in it. I went and sat on a seat in the new park that was being developed, near to the frozen freshwater pond, beside a very seriously dressed young man who was wearing a clerical collar. Despite the coldness of the January day, he was reading a thick leather book with thin paper leaves, like a bible. I must have sighed very heavily, as he looked at me and smiled. 'Do the cares of the world hang heavily upon you today my friend?' he asked. 'Would a cup of coffee in Holmes' Refreshment Rooms appeal to you at all?' In fact, a cup of coffee did appeal, very much. I was at that very moment having a serious battle with myself around the idea of going for an intoxicating drink at the Lord Nelson. We walked back into the town, to the Temperance Hotel, to which Holmes's Refreshment Room was attached, and I found him very easy company indeed, despite his being an assistant priest at the Roman Catholic church of St Mary and St Philomena in the town. He told me he was known as Father Michael, and we enjoyed our coffee, and I felt a lot better. He seemed simply fascinated with my travels, and I confided in him the struggle I still had to remain sober. 'I've met many drunken sailors' he said, 'but you are the first I've ever met who has developed the ambition to stay sober all his days!' His genuine care did not make me feel diminished following my shameful admissions.

The following morning was fine again, but remained cold, as I left Blake Hill Farm to set out for Wareham, in the knowledge that a boat supplied a regular service between the two towns. I described Liza to the boatman, and asked if he had taken such a passenger aboard. He replied that he had no memory of doing so, as the boat went to and fro daily, he had carried many passengers, and I was asking him to think over two years back. That was fair enough. I made my way through the busy little main street of Wareham, and asked a man for directions to the Union Workhouse. He looked a bit surprised, but directed me up Cow Lane, to begin the longish walk to the great gaunt building at the end of Christmas Close. The Porter in the little office sent a messenger to ask the Master to come down. The Master very kindly checked the records, and said that a woman called Liza Loader had been admitted, together with her new born baby girl. She had absconded from the womens' ward two weeks after giving birth. No one knew where she had gone. I thanked the man, and gave him a florin for his trouble.

I felt very shocked. They had told me that Liza had given birth alone, in the dark, in a cold church. I was fortunate to be able to catch the same boat back to Poole, and arrived in the fading January light. I went to the Poop Deck, and Vasistha my father's servant made me a cup of hot chocolate, which was my best alternative to calling at the Lord Nelson Tavern. I felt very restless being ashore, as the memories of old friends, old haunts and old habits taunted me. I was back in the cold sweat of temptation, and in a ferment of agitation, I went out walking the streets. The gas lamps were lit, and I found myself outside the Roman Catholic presbytery, and decided to see if Father Michael might be available for a chat. A chubby, rather tough looking old lady answered the door, and told me she was the priests' housekeeper. I was shown into a very spartan room at the front of the house, and Father Michael eventually appeared, apologizing profusely for keeping me waiting. He looked at me carefully, and suggested taking a walk together. I was in quite a bad state, and told my new friend all about my relationship with Liza, and my deep feelings of guilt, particularly around the possibility that I could have been the father of her child. He put his arm round my shoulders, and we walked round and round the dark park together, until I felt calmer. We went back into the town, and he took me into the little church, I knelt down and he laid his hands on my head and prayed for me and blessed me. I felt so sorry about taking up so much time from this dear, good man, and apologized profusely. I was late back at Miss Caroline's, but felt calmer and more comfortable with myself and the circumstances surrounding my former relationship with Liza.

My trip home to Poole, ahead of the Daphne, marked several important turning points in my life, providing firm foundations to my adulthood. My friendship with Father Michael, begun initially in his kind response to my weakness, became more equal. We met often, and he said that my friendship was refreshing in the honesty we offered to one another, untainted as it was by the stupid adulation of a young priest afforded by some in his congregation. I enjoyed disputing matters of Christian doctrine with him. He helped me with my Latin and Greek studies which I had begun with my father. The meal that I later shared with the Teagues on the Thursday was a revelation of the development of my own maturity in connection with matters of the heart. I had been told that the Teagues' pretty little granddaughter, Lydia would be there, and since 'an extended rest' had been mentioned, was expecting to meet with a pale little girl.

Notes

Legg R., 2005. The Book of Poole. Pub. Halsgrove House provided a detailed description of Poole harbour, which I have drawn from.
The sea shanty about the Dead Horse is based on the practice of some seamen being able to negotiate a month's pay in advance of a long voyage. Sailors saw this as a 'dead horse' to be paid for. On some ships, at the end of a month, a canvas stuffed bag, like a horse, was rigged up on a yardarm and then given a sea burial. The words of this popular shanty vary slightly.

Chapter Twenty Three

I sat opposite to Lydia at the dining table. Lydia's figure had filled out in a most charming manner, and her beautiful chestnut brown hair which I had last seen lying on her shoulders in curly tresses was dressed in an adult fashion, pinned to her head in delightful waves and curls with pretty tortoiseshell combs. I told her how very sorry I had been to hear of the sad loss of her mother, and she thanked me. I didn't know what exactly had been going on, but she had the air of a young lady who had suffered greatly.

Mr and Mrs Teague wanted to know how my sea trip had been. They were most impressed that I had already sailed all round the world. I remarked that Doctor Johnson's famous observation that 'going to sea was akin to being in prison, with the added danger of drowning' was generally true. I told them the sad story of how Squirrel Oakes had lost his young life, and saw tears sitting along Lydia's lower eyelids. I admitted how much going to sea had forced me to grow up, and to work not to please myself, but to feel more responsible, and consider the interests of the whole ship's company. I even admitted that I had given up strong drink, as it had caused me, and many of those I loved, such damage. Lydia was looking at me very hard. By the time the meal was finished, Lydia was looking very jaded, and Mrs Teague bustled her back to her room.

'Lydia has been very poorly for some weeks', explained Mrs Teague, when she rejoined us in the parlour. The subject was dropped, as the Teagues wanted to know all about my travels around the world. I told them the amusing bits, but kept the more serious parts to myself. They didn't need to know about how we had all been feared for our lives, or how vile the port of Adelaide had been in the dusty heat. They were interested to hear that I had been using the time at sea to start learning Greek and Latin to look at some of the classics with my father. After a very pleasant evening with these dear people, having enjoyed nothing stronger than a few good cups of tea, I prepared to return to the Poop Deck for the night. I was standing on the landing whilst the maid handed me my coat and hat, when Mrs Teague said 'How I wish your dear father was here Harry. Lydia is so very far from well. She hates the doctor, and I'm driven to my wit's end to think how to deal with her. I gave her my opinion of what father would have recommended, and walked home, turning the matter over in my mind.

In the morning I called into Teagues' to leave my new copy of The Poetical Works of Alfred, Lord Tennyson, in which I had enclosed a little card for Lydia, dedicating the gift to her and wishing her well soon. I also said to them that I was sure that father would have suggested that it might be a good idea for her to take up her music studies again gently. Mr Teague looked at me very suspiciously, and I strongly suspected that he knew rather a lot about my previous ne'er do well exploits, including those that had not been published in the Poole and Dorset Herald. I realized what a struggle I would have to engage in to persuade the good people of Poole that I had genuinely turned over a new leaf. I decided to confront their unspoken doubts regarding my character by explaining that I was in a bit of a hurry to get back to Blake Hill Farm, as Miss Baskett would probably be worried about me as I'd spent the night at the Poop Deck, which was close to so many ale houses. However, I remarked ruefully, I had resisted far worse temptations abroad, particularly in Luanda.

I was back at Blake Hill in time for lunch, and was delighted to find a letter for me on the table, from father. He was loading a cargo of coal, which he would shortly be bringing down to Poole, having already arranged to sell it to Burdens, on the quay. He had two even better items of news. He would be bringing Mr and Mrs Ross from the Pharmacy in Alloa down with him. They had decided to relocate their business in Poole, and wondered if I would be kind enough to see if there were any suitable premises available to them. Secondly, he had decided, after many years of being effectively married to the Daphne and the sea that he was going to ask Miss Baskett to be his wife. How did I feel about the matter? The letter went on to say that Daphne 'required her bottom seeing to properly' and that there would be a long layover in Poole. Our finances were now stable again, as a result of our trade so far, and the cargo of coal he expected to bring down from Alloa. He left it to me if I would like to sign on for any short haul trips in the meantime to gain further experience in navigation and seamanship.

'Hmmm....' I thought to myself regarding father's hope to marry Mistress Caroline. 'She may not agree as easily as he thinks.' I was aware that her name meant 'ruler, strong, and joy', and on the farm she was the Mistress of all she surveyed and a very strong person in many, many ways. I couldn't easily visualize this big, strong woman surrendering all to my father, even though it was a local legend that she had 'saved herself' for him. She was past her childbearing years, and being so well able to take care of herself, he would not need to worry about her whilst he was at sea. Since my father had always had an 'eye' for Caroline, but he had confided to me that he would never, ever want to lose another wife in childbirth, the situation looked hopeful. His letter showed a remarkable 'sea change' in his personal thinking regarding marriage. Meantime, I was doing a fair amount of thinking myself, around how to help Lydia feel better, and how to arrange to spend more time in her company. I spent the rest of the day around the farm, repairing a fence and helping with milking. I decided that I would invite Miss Lydia to take a walk with me around Poole Park. As I had an appointment the following morning with Father Michael to discuss taking some instruction on the Catholic faith, I would call in to Teagues. Miss Caroline wanted some Fry's Coffee essence and Keen's mustard anyway. When I had finished at the Catholic Church, I went into the shop, and was invited to join the Teague's 'Household Lunch' in Mrs Teague's room at the back of the shop. There were fourteen of us round the table that day, including Miss Lydia who was opposite me again. The Teagues had a peculiar, personalized morality that could be quite annoying at times, but I knew what they were trying to do. They were trying to train their staff who all came from very underprivileged backgrounds in the ways of the world according to Teagues' grocery morality. Talk over the lunch table varied from day to day around subjects such as religion, world events, politics and morality. Unbeknown to me, today's subject was going to be personal morality, and I would be the focus.

Somehow, Ethelred Teague veered the conversation round to me, and asked how my life had been since I had gone to sea as my father's apprentice, and actually referred very tactlessly to my previous dissipated behaviour and court appearances as a young man. The speedy travel of forks to hungry mouths was visibly arrested. I explained haltingly that thanks to other peoples' good examples, kindness and faith in me, I had made a new start in my life, was abstaining from strong drink and considering the place of God as the moral anchor in my life. I felt that I had gone very red. My neck was burning against my starched collar, and I could feel sweat beading on my brow. Mr Teague smiled benignly and progressed by reading a little from that blasted Samuel Smiles book he kept in his pocket. Apparently Smiles had written 'It is a mistake to suppose that men succeed through success; they much oftener succeed through failures. Precept, study, advice, and example could never have taught them as well as failure has done. The apprenticeship of difficulty is one which the greatest of men have had to serve.' I replied politely that I felt that Mr Smiles certainly had a remarkable insight into the human condition, and went on to say humbly 'life is a struggle for everyone in their own way. We all have to deal with our demons on a daily basis. I thank God for his help.'

I continued to feel deeply embarrassed throughout the whole meal, and this was obviously noticed by Lydia who tried her best to draw the attention away from me on two occasions by deliberately - I was watching- spilling her cup of tea, and later thinking to ask 'Is there any further news in the paper today of General Gordon in Khartoum?' This led to Mr Teague having to quickly inform the staff as to who General Gordon was, and having to fetch his globe to pinpoint the Sudan, as lunchtime was nearly over. Thank God! However, at least my discomfort had allowed me to put my cards on the table as it were, and to declare myself to be a changed man. Lydia had been very supportive, and the Teague grandparents had a better idea of where they stood with me too.

After lunch, I told the family that my father hoped to be back in town in a matter of days, and was intending to stay quite a while as major repairs were needed to the Daphne. Mrs Teague invited me to sit in the parlour upstairs whilst she did some accounts, and said that I would be welcome to read the newspaper. To our surprise, Lydia was looking through some music, and eventually sat down at the pianoforte and played and sang 'Come into the garden Maud'; causing me to remark 'I think you're telling me that you liked the book I gave you.' She said 'yes', smiled, and then quietly collected up the music and shut the pianoforte down. Mrs Teague stood up, and went with Lydia as she left the room, to spend some time on her own, having a rest. Before I left Teagues, I asked Mr Teague if he would have any objection to me accompanying the household to Divine Service on the following morning. He warmly agreed, and suggested that since I would be on my own in town, I might care to lunch with them again. I accepted the invitation. I had always loved this dear, kind family and admired the standards they set themselves and others. I was also hoping to see Lydia's father, and meet her young sister, Barbara.

As it turned out, I was able to walk beside and sit beside Lydia at church. On the way back, we each took one of Babs's little hands. She had been such a good girl throughout the service, which was very demanding on the patience of a little child of five. Sunday lunch was served in the upstairs dining room for family only, no staff or large helpings of morality, thank goodness. Mr Curtis was very pleasant to me. He had aged a lot since I last saw him, and above each ear, there were grey wings in his once brown hair. After the meal, I got down on the floor, and played lions and tigers with little Babs, with lots of chasing and growling and Mrs Teague, doubtless thinking this was rather unsuitable for a Sunday, fetched out the Noah's Ark, which was a special family toy, for Babs to play with instead. I was utterly enjoying being in the same room with Lydia, but was at the same time sensitive to the fact that she was only sixteen, and had been very poorly.

Note

Delius did not actually compose the music for Tennyson's poem Maud until 1891

Chapter Twenty Four

I was very excited the day that the Daphne tied up again in Poole. That good old boat had carried most of us safely around the world and restored the Lovejoys' fortunes so that father would be able to redeem all his debts to his friends. He had enough cash left to repair the ship well and take her on her next voyage. Father didn't much like carrying coal, but had been unable to get a cleaner cargo. The filthy stuff took some unloading, as it was packed loose, and the stevedores had to shovel it into baskets to hoist it out. Mr Downton was made Second Mate, Mr Tilsed reverted to his position as Bo'sun, and I became his direct underling. My new responsibility was to ensure that the hold was thoroughly cleaned.

Daphne had been unloading for nearly a week when a woman came over to me, who seemed to know me. It took me quite a few seconds to recognize Liza. She was, frankly filthy, and had aged very considerably. She still had her teeth, but her once lovely hair was matted and dirty, and her eyes looked quite wild. I think our meeting again was a shattering of dreams for both of us. Whilst away, I had entertained romantic thoughts about her, and intended marrying her, but all such ideas had fled when Mistress Caroline had exposed to me exactly what had been going on. I had determined to deal kindly with her, which I tried to do, but given her history, I'd little suspicion that her child might be mine. I was taken aback when she asked me straight out, to be a father to her daughter. I felt that she was lying like a flatfish. I could clearly see how hard I would have to work to repair my bad reputation with Mistress Caroline, the Teagues and young Miss Curtis, so I rejected the idea of supporting Liza and her daughter immediately. Obviously, I wished well for both of them, but didn't see myself as being in any way the cause of her present sad state, besides which, a man in my position had to think very carefully indeed before tying himself up in a scandalous situation like this one. I had no doubts at all that I had made the right decision in the circumstances.

Father had finally plucked up the courage to ask Miss Caroline to be his wife. As I had predicted to myself, the path of true love did not run smoothly. He described her to me as 'lively and changeable, like a flaming gorse bush in the wind at times.' Apparently she was taking a very long time to make up her mind about his proposal. Of course, Miss Caroline confided in me too, and had commented 'I be betwattled. Ee's an ansom man, and luv is lik measles. Kand say when I ketched it. Tidden easy to decide. I'm shammed ter say I'm feared I shassn't be Mistress O'Blake Hill no more.' Besides her obvious reluctance to give over control of the farm, she expressed the concern that 'ee might leave I a lone, lorn wumman.'

After Miss Caroline had been going about the place like a sow with a sore belly for a week, I made an act of charity -for the good of the three of us- and broke her confidence, and told father exactly what her worries were. I then made sure that I was very busy on the quay all day whilst he went to see her. He was able to finally resolve her doubts by promising her that his next voyage would be his last. He also explained to her that the Married Womens' Property Act, recently passed by the Liberal Government provided her with full legal control of Blake Hill Farm for the rest of her life.

Preparations began for a wedding. Miss Caroline consulted Mrs Teague about a suitable dressmaker, who ordered a whole bolt of cloth for the dress and was doubtless praying that this would be enough to clothe such a large person. Father arranged for a new pea jacket and some smartly cut wool trousers. The wedding was at 9.30 on a Monday morning in March. Mr Teague gave away the bride and Mrs Teague was Matron of Honour. I had the great pleasure of escorting Miss Lydia Curtis. The service in St James's church was a small, quiet affair, and to the great surprise of us all, Miss Caroline enunciated her vows in clear, classic English, as she was in fact, a very shrewd, highly educated person. She enjoyed speaking her broad 'Darzet' as it was the common tongue of those she dealt with on a daily basis. The small gathering of family and friends at the church to support the happy couple was very pleasant.

Mr and Mrs Ross formerly of Alloa were there too. Smiling broadly, Miss Caroline confessed, again in her perfect English, that for the past two years and more, she had felt as lonesome as a bell buoy clattering to itself in the harbour, waiting for father to come home. Father was smiling and smiling, and kissing everyone completely indiscriminately, men, women and children. He announced that he felt as important as the Doge in Venice, who marries the Adriatic Sea, not knowing what may be found in that sea, treasures, pearls, monsters or even storms.....' Miss Caroline smiled indulgently, as did I. None of us present, knowing the passionate nature of the individuals, doubted that this had the makings of a happy but stormy coupling. St James's full peal of eight bells rang out as the happy couple, with father driving, departed in the new Mrs Lovejoy's delivery cart to stay at Blake Hill Farm. I had fully moved into the Poop Deck the day before.

Since my return to the town, I had in fact been in and out of Poole a fair amount, working on short trips where I could, in order to obtain a broader understanding of seamanship. I had been on short runs to the Channel Isles, and taken stone barges into the perilous waters around Seacombe and Dancing Ledge to load stone blocks. I even went on a run as mate on a very small boat to Le Havre to pick up a cargo of brandy, but was upset when we pulled up to Seacombe at dusk on the return journey, and off loaded a considerable amount of the goods. I had no desire at all to compromise the good reputation that I had been trying so hard to build up, so I avoided further work if I felt there might be anything underhand going on.

In the little time that was left to me, whilst Daphne's considerable refurbishment was progressing, I spent as much time as I could at Teagues, and managed to obtain the permission of Mr Curtis and Mr and Mrs Teague, to walk out with Miss Lydia. I had to promise that my liaison with her would 'be free of any romantic attachment' and had to agree that as she was very young, only approaching seventeen, I would be very careful not to compromise her reputation in any way. Of course, I agreed to everything, stating that I merely wanted to 'assist her recovery.' We went for morning walks together by the salt lake in the developing Poole Park, but we were rather disconcerted at times to note that we were being followed by Mr Teague! Anyway, my efforts to get Lydia better were working, as she seemed much brighter, and her cheeks had a little colour in them again. I was very surprised to hear from Lydia that her father intended to marry a Miss Dacombe who had been working for him for several years as an amanuesis in his office. The wedding date was set for the week following Easter. Since his announcement, he hadn't shown any interest in Lydia's recovery or possible move back home. Apparently Miss Dacombe was already spending a lot of time at Otterwood, hosting dinners on Mr Curtis's behalf and making what Lydia described as 'a nauseating fuss over Babs, who was getting quite spoiled.' Michael was described as 'unimpressed', but it didn't really matter too much to him, as he was mostly away in Oxford.

Evenings spent at Teagues became increasingly pleasant. Typical male activities that I escaped from by being there were smoking, gambling, clubs, drinking and going to 'dubious places of entertainment'. It was acceptable for Lydia and I to sit in the less well lit area of the parlour, as Mr and Mrs Teague wanted to be in the best light for their evening activities, which were generally devoted to going through their accounts and ordering. They got quite wrapped up in this, and were often in serious discussion regarding customers with large unpaid bills, and how to deal with this tactfully. This meant that they didn't see, or chose to ignore me discreetly holding Lydia's hand and talking to her in a quiet voice. Sometimes they were both out of the room together, and we ventured a little kiss.

To provide some positive, health giving distraction for Lydia, and because father and I would soon be away again, I suggested that we went on a picnic with father and my new stepmother in the sailing boat that father kept in Hamworthy. The project was agreed, and on a bright Tuesday March morning, we set off from the quay.

On their arrival at Teagues, there had been considerable bickering between Father and Mistress Caroline, as she didn't like Father's driving at all. Apparently they had nearly been involved in quite a severe accident caused by the many large horse-drawn carts and carriages rushing in and out of the station yard and on to the busy High Street. A pedestrian, quite a young man, had been killed near the same spot only last week.

'Stick to what you know', Caroline grumbled, 'you sail the boats, I'll drive any carts. I don't want you damaging my only means of transport.'

'Ah,' said Father, 'from the sweetest wine, the tartest vinegar.'

'Hmmm. She's continuing to speak clear English' Lydia remarked. 'They must be having a considerable effect on each other.' Father put a fishing line and lure over the edge of the boat, as the fishing between the quay and Brownsea was reckoned to be good. In no time at all, he had a small pile of mackerel lying by his feet. I just sailed us as far as Shell Bay, and we used the large, wheeled platform on the beach to put the women and all our picnic apparatus ashore, then anchored in the shallow water and waded back to the women. I announced to father and Mistress Caroline that Lydia and I were away to visit the Agglestone, and we were off, finally free, unchaperoned!

The Agglestone was about a mile away, on Godlingstone Heath. Some people said it was the Devil's nightcap, which he had taken off his head whilst sitting on the Isle of Wight, and had thrown at Corfe Castle and missed. Fortunately Lydia, being well warned, was wearing her most comfortable walking shoes. I had the opportunity to tell her yet again, how very fond I was of her, as we walked across the heath, and she blushed. I mentioned that, as before, father and I would be away again soon, probably for about two years at least.

We reached the Agglestone, and stood at the foot of it, in the soft surrounding red sand. I pulled Lydia gently towards me. 'I love you very much' I said.

'I love you too', she said into my neck.

'Will you marry me?' I asked. '

Yes' she replied. We kissed deeply and tenderly.

'You do know, I said, 'and 'that local legend also says that those who plight their troth beneath the Agglestone shall never be parted asunder?' I looked at her beautiful, smiling face, as she laughed at me, accused me of being an old romantic and said we'd better hurry back to the beach, as if we didn't, the picnic and all the mackerel would be cooked and eaten. The memories of that day remained bright in my mind through my long months away at sea, providing clear pictures of my dearest love in the darkest days.

LYDIA

Chapter Twenty Five

Illnesses have a habit of going around, and staying their course and then going away again. It didn't seem to me initially that there was anything I could do at the time to force the progress of my depressive illness for the better, but I was really glad of all the help I received from those around me. Apparently the Doctor had suggested to grandmother a specialist in London who massaged his patients, male or female (naked) all over, on a daily or twice daily basis to speed their recovery, and the results were very good. I wouldn't wonder at it either. She was thinking of sending me to him, but he was rather expensive...... Just hearing about such a monstrous treatment immediately stimulated me into enormous efforts to get back to normal. Cynically, I believe Grandmother told me this to have just that effect. To my relief, she still seemed to have placed great trust in Harry's quotation from his father regarding the effectiveness of 'Dr Diet, Dr Quiet and Dr Merryman.'

Anyway, I think that Harry re-appeared at just the right time for all of us. He brought good news of his father and the Daphne, which offered considerable relief to the businesses which had supported the voyage. I was absolutely amazed at the change in Harry from that obnoxious, truculent young man he had been, into a strong, decisive, capable man, who had sufficient insight to be genuinely sorry for all of the awful things he'd done in his recent past. I could have died a thousand deaths at what Grandfather put him through, in front of the staff at the lunch table, but Harry had the self possession to handle the situation well. I particularly remember too what he did for Mr Maloney, formerly the Daphne's cook. Harry told me that there had been quite a serious accident aboard, and he had helped his father manage some very serious burns Mr Maloney had sustained from an accident in the galley. Amazingly, he had survived, but later became quite blind, although Harry said this further misfortune was not as a result of his burns.

Apparently the day after the Daphne had tied up at the quay for unloading, Harry had fetched Mr Maloney over to the Poop

Deck to board temporarily, as Edward and Vavisthar would be there to give Maloney a lot of help. As his father was very concerned with matters around arranging for a cargo and ship repairs, and of course, Miss Caroline, Harry had undertaken to 'sort Maloney out.' He took Mr Maloney to St James's vicarage to enquire if the vicar would arrange an admission ticket for him at the workhouse. Obviously it couldn't be organized immediately, as such 'cases' were only admitted on Fridays, and Harry suggested a week's delay, fixed Mr Maloney up with a stick, and when he could find time, he took him out, the poor man with his left hand on Harry's shoulder, and in the right hand his stick. They were seen in the evenings, going up and down the quay and sometimes up and down the High Street together during the following week. Harry never took him into an alehouse, but was apparently quite happy if others did so. The gossip was that Harry went quite white, sweaty and shaky if he went near the door of an alehouse, but obviously people were exaggerating. Anyway, the day before Mr Maloney was finally due to be admitted to Union Workhouse, Harry came by and asked if my grandparents would have the pair of them to Friday lunch with the shop staff, as he felt that this might be a pleasant social event for Mr Maloney, and would prevent his former shipmates from taking him into the Poole Arms.

Extra places were laid at table, making fifteen in total, with Harry to sit at Mr Maloney's right hand. He was tender and kind with the old man, making sure he could feel the sides of his plate, checking the fish for bones and cutting the potatoes and vegetables. He allowed the old chap to use his hands to eat with as obviously Maloney knew no better. Harry then told a few exaggerated tales about dining at sea, making the point that in very stormy weather, in a wildly lurching ship the important thing to do was to get some food into one's stomach, cramming it in by hand if necessary. This was to divert everyone's attention away from watching Mr Maloney constantly, and to suggest that his behaviour was not abnormal, given his background. Harry continued his sea stories by praising Mr Maloney's skills in the galley, producing hot food for the freezing crew under nightmare conditions, and when all else failed, with the ship pitching too wildly for cooking, still managing somehow to produce occasional hot drinks of cocoa. Harry made sure that Mr Maloney was clean and tidy after leaving the table, as frankly, he had the most atrocious manner of eating I've ever seen in my life. Grandmother had by comparison faced much smaller challenges when training new shop staff in use of cutlery and appropriate table manners. Mr Maloney was encouraged to shake the hand of each member of staff and to thank the host and hostess for their kindness. He was then walked by Harry, using shoulder and stick as guides, to the workhouse. I know that every Sunday that he was in Poole, Harry went to visit him.

Harry was unfailingly kind and attentive to me too. He had broken the ice by leaving the book of poems for me, and my respect for him grew. He packed a great deal into his days 'in port.' He was kept very busy during and after the Daphne's repairs, as he had big responsibilities helping the Bo'sun. In the evenings, he went to the Catholic Church for services and instructions and still found plenty of time to help me to feel better. It was very clear from the way that he looked at me that he found me attractive. Our eyes would meet often, and he would allow the skin around his eyes to crinkle subtly in unspent, secret smiles. We were not able to meet alone, as that would have compromised my respectability, and in any case, I still had haunting memories of what he had been getting up to with Liza at Otterwood. Could he be the father of the child, I asked myself? No one but I knew that he was implicated in that scandal. I began to ask myself whether I could truly love him, even if he had fathered that child.

Further cause for stimulation around that time, was the arrival of Mr and Mrs Alec Ross all the way from Alloa in Scotland. They were staying at the Poop Deck on the quay, as guests of Harry. My grandparents invited them for dinner one evening, together with Harry. Mr Ross, a very withdrawn, quiet man, spoke clearly in a fine, educated scotch accent, but his wife at times seemed to be speaking a different language entirely. She was absolutely lovely anyway. They explained that Mr Ross was intending to set up a pharmaceutical chemist's shop in the lower part of the town, and with Harry's help had identified possible premises beside the Minerva print works on the High Street. Mrs Ross was expecting a child, whom she kept referring to as 'the wean', and I acquired my first scotch word. Mr Ross who was very pleasant, explained that scotch described a very strong drink, and that they were actually Scots, from Scotland. 'Wean is a Scottish word', he explained 'wee is the Scots word for small, and a wean or wee yin is a small child. I'm sure we'll all get to understand one another properly soon.'

Well, Mr Ross was right, our families did all begin to draw together, the Lovejoys, Teagues, Rosses and I began building yet a further healthy business and personal relationship, which all began, as did so many good things, over my grandparents' dinner table. As for my father, I now saw him regularly, as he often called into Teagues before going home to see how I was getting along. He looked well, and far less strained than he had in mother's latter days, and assured me that all was going well in my absence. Miss Dacombe had been installed as a paying guest at Dr Stone's house at the bottom of Sandringham Road, and spent most of her time managing Otterwood and its occupants. Babs was now reading everything fluently, taking after me in that respect. I began to feel that I would like to visit Otterwood, but not yet.

Ann, our cook told me that some of the gossips in town were suggesting that there was a little fly in the ointment at Otterwood. Miss Dacombe and Ellen were not getting along too well, as Miss Dacombe had 'different ways' of wanting the house run. Bessie, in the shop elaborated on 'the Dacombe matters' by telling me that there had been gossip in the town for years regarding possible 'carryings on' between father and Miss Dacombe. Frankly, I had always been aware of father's liking for women, and couldn't have cared less, just as long as he was happy and the household was in decent order in my absence. Actually, I had no intention at all of returning home to live, and was hoping to continue to stay at

Teagues. For one thing, it meant that I was closer to Harry whilst he was staying at the Poop Deck. I found myself craving for his visits.

Mr and Mrs Ross, Harry and I were all most excited to be invited to a ball at Dr Ellis's mansion, Beechcroft, in the High Street, which was being held in honour of his daughter's twenty first birthday. Only the 'right sort' of people were invited, the parameters noted by Harry were that invitations had only been issued to people aged between twenty and thirty, who were either 'professionals' or persons who owned their own businesses. Harry admitted to being staggered to receive an invitation himself, as his police record was a matter of public knowledge throughout the town. 'Perhaps', he laughed, 'even at this early stage in my seafaring career, they have noted my penitence and desire to reform.' He gave a rueful grin, and reminded me, not for the first time, of his namesake, Harry Paye, a privateer. Harry Paye was famous for sacking the Spanish town of Compostela, which brought disaster to the very doorsteps of Poole, as it resulted in an armed, retaliatory raid by the Spanish on the harbour and lower town. This was a good opportunity for me to say candidly how awful I had thought him to be in his younger years. I went on to ask him why on this earth, he had decided to become a Roman Catholic? He said 'like Harry Paye, I have sinned a great deal already as a young man, and only the Catholic faith holds out to me the possibility of absolution for all these sins. I hope that with God's help that I can begin to live a better life'. He continued ruefully, 'even old Harry Paye took the precaution of having a Latin inscription on his tombstone which meant Lord, wash away my iniquities and cleanse me from my sins!'

Anyway, to return to the ball at Beechcroft, Mr and Mrs Ross declined their invitations. Phemie, as I now knew her confided that there were several reasons for them not being able to attend. The most obvious was her 'condition', Alec himself was not always too well, and couldn't manage too much company, and neither of them touched alcohol as they had signed a 'pledge' never to do so.

I was well acquainted, via Harry of the problems of being a total abstainer, as the water in Poole was unfit to drink, and the small beer which most people drank throughout the day contained a little alcohol. He drank endless cups of tea, and was referred to by his friends as teetotal, but I know he often felt as if he was being a nuisance to his hosts.

I was feeling so much better, that I was very keen to attend the ball, if Harry would escort me. Grandmother had Madam Ford the milliner and costumier from Thames Street call up to Teagues to measure me for a gown in apricot satin. When the date for the ball came, Harry called for me, and we departed for Beechcroft in a fly he had hired from the station. The evening was wonderful. Harry was well fortified with cups of tea before we went, and led me into Beechcroft on his arm. He signed my dance card to book a polka and a waltz with me, as sadly it was bad manners for couples to have more than two dances together. I danced with a variety of the town's rich, personable and well-connected young men, and I particularly enjoyed a Mazurka, which involved much stamping of the feet, and the gentlemen had to click their heels together. It was a shame that my partner, an excellent dancer, was so odorously sweaty. The buffet was excellent. I already knew a lot about the menu, as Mrs Ellis's cook had spent ages in the room behind the shop, with grandmother, poring over the recipes they had spread over the large table to calculate all the ingredients required.

I thoroughly enjoyed the polka with Harry, and found it quite literally breathtaking, from both the energy required for the dance, and his proximity to me. However, I felt quite tremulous towards the latter part of the evening, particularly as the strict etiquette required that Harry could spend so little time with me. Eventually, thank God, the music for the last waltz was played, and I was transported into delight with Harry's strong arms around me. However, the magic didn't last, and by the end of the dance, I disgraced myself by crying openly, and being the subject of kind attentions from two other ladies. Harry and I were thus the first to leave, and the blasted etiquette meant that he couldn't even put his arm around me in public.

Chapter Twenty Six

We reached the last week before Harry would board the Daphne for another around the world voyage. Harry had told me that he had been very sad when his father's old dog Cerebus, had died in an accident during heavy seas around the Horn. He was very busy on the ship during daylight hours, supervising the crew working the windlass to lower the cargo into the hold and making sure that everything was safely lashed in place ready for stormy seas. I was really, really surprised on the Monday morning, when he appeared at the back door of Teagues' establishment with a beautiful young parti-coloured chocolate and white dog. 'He's a springer spaniel, which the new Mrs Lovejoy gave me as a present on my return home. She has him well trained already as a house dog, and suggested to me that you might like to look after him for me whilst I am away from you' My eyes filled with tears, which I tried to hide by kneeling down to caress and stroke the darling creature, who licked my hand with his moist, velvet tongue. 'He already has a name', went on Harry, dropping to his knees beside me, 'as in my absence at sea, my step mother had to call him something, and so he answers to Zephyr or Zeph. She chose the name because of the way I always blow into animals' noses to make friends with them. A Zephyr is a warm westerly wind' he went on. 'She felt that it gave the little chap a connection with me away at sea. I think you might miss me whilst I am away, and thought Zephyr might be good company, would help you to stay well, and could even take you out socially. Besides, I wouldn't feel jealous of him!' Harry held Zephyr's head gently, to allow me to breath into his nose. I caressed the beautiful silken haired little animal, and admired his bright clean white dicky front.

Suddenly, Grandmother appeared, and looked transfixed with horror at the sight of an animal standing on her back kitchen floor. 'I've told your father, and now I'm telling you, young Harry, that I won't have a dog here in a food store. Even if it was clean and tidy in its habits, and I'm not saying it isn't, I admit I've no experience with em. It might encourage customers to start bringing their own animals into the front of the shop.'

Harry gallantly stepped into action, pointing out the obvious advantages that Zephyr would bring me, and she grumblingly agreed to take him on trial, provided he never ever came into the shop or preparation areas. Mrs Lovejoy would have to take him back immediately if he misbehaved. 'There is no chance that Zephyr will lower the tone of your esteemed establishment' Harry concluded. 'He is fully housetrained, gentle, alert, intelligent, sensitive and loving.' She seemed slightly mollified, and went back into the shop huffing more quietly.

We found Zephyr a bowl of water and some meat scraps. Harry said that Zephyr had slept at the Poop Deck overnight, and was raring for a good walk and the chance to run about, and commented that I, as his foster parent would need to learn how to look after him properly. I arranged with Grandfather that I could walk to the park with Harry, to give Zephyr an outing, and off we went. Harry told me to say 'heel', and Zephyr obligingly trotted along, slightly behind me. His lead seemed almost superfluous. Harry went into great detail about thinking things through from a dog's point of view, establishing good patterns of care, and consistent routines. Zephyr was taken off his lead in the park, and was really good until he tried to jump on the back of a fat dachshund, much to the chagrin of its lady owner. Harry quickly retrieved the situation, explaining to me quietly later that the other dog was a female 'in season' and therefore deliciously attractive to young Zephyr. I rather foolishly asked Harry to explain, which he tried to. At the mention of blood, I felt as if I'd gone rather pink, but he just laughed, squeezed my hand, and started talking to me about my music instead.

'You know, Lydia, you really are rather good at the pianoforte. Have you thought about developing this talent with a view to giving music lessons to other young ladies?' I was thunderstruck. Yes, I'd always loved playing and had been well taught by the music master Miss Squires employed at her school. Learning more about music, and teaching my own private pupils would give me the possibility of an independent income. He even went so far as to suggest that before he left Poole, he could have a word with Mr Short, the organ and choir master at St James's Church about possible supplementary music theory lessons. I began to feel rather excited, and hoped that father would be prepared to finance the scheme.

On the way back to Teagues for lunch, Harry took me down to Snooks the stationers where he bought me paper and envelopes. He had already explained that the great oceans of the world were criss crossed by ships making their individual trading voyages, and thus letters could be carried around the world using the international Paquebot system which allowed mail to be passed between ships for posting in Britain or Europe. Royal Mail Steam Packet vessels operated throughout the British Empire. He gave me a list of ports and approximate dates where Daphne was expected to dock. He did of course stress that the oceans of the world were so vast, that it did not necessarily mean bad news if there were very long intervals between letters received.

After lunch, Harry excused himself, as he had many matters to attend to in the afternoon aboard Daphne, but accepted a dinner invitation, commenting that he would need to call back to check on his dog! The cheek. I departed to my room, with Zephyr, to relax and read Elizabeth Barrett Browning's 'To Flush, my dog'. I was certain that Zephyr would be an even better companion than Flush. Afterwards Zephyr and I went for another little walk along the High Street, and I really did feel more confident now that I had my new 'friend' with me.

Father and Miss Olive Dacombe joined us for dinner, and I began to revise my opinion of her. Father was looking better than he had in years, and was much more relaxed. Miss Dacombe, whilst not obviously well read, seemed to have a very neat, organized approach to everything that she did. Apparently Babs, far from being spoiled, was really being quite difficult to get settled down into a decent routine. Ellen and Suzy had been magnificent with her over the years, but I could see her point, it was not really a good plan to have the servants raising one's child. Speaking quietly to me at the table, Miss Dacombe said that as far as she was concerned, disaster management at Otterwood was over, and new and better ways would have to be found in the future. She commended me sincerely for all the wondrous things I'd done under such difficult circumstances, and suggested that now was my opportunity, for the first time in my life, to make some decisions about what I would like. She said, smiling lovingly and confidentially at father, that he would be having a word with me after our meal.

I stayed in the dining room with father after the table had been cleared. I wasn't worried. Miss Dacombe had left me with a warm feeling regarding the conversation that was about to take place. 'My dear Lydia', father said. 'Harry has been talking with me at some length this afternoon. Principally, he has asked for your hand in marriage. I have refused permission for a formal engagement between the two of you. However, the depths of your feelings for each other are clear. As he will be going away again tomorrow for at least a further two years, I want you to concentrate on making good your recovery, and I thoroughly endorse Harry's excellent suggestion that you further your musical studies with Mr Short. I will meet with Mr Short and make some arrangements for you, as he will be particularly helpful with the theoretical side of your musical education. Additionally I would also suggest sessions with Mr Aldridge at Inglewood in Parkstone, as he is a concert pianist, and plays regularly in London.' He went on to say that obviously I should have no aspirations to be a concert pianist myself, as this was of course, both unsuitable and impossible for women. Perhaps when I was in Parkstone for these lessons he suggested, I might care to spend some time at Otterwood, provided that this did not upset me in any way. At the end of our conversation, I kissed father very fondly, and wished him great happiness with Miss Dacombe.

I had just an hour or two to spend with Harry. No one lifted an eyebrow when he took me downstairs where we sat opposite each other at the table in Grandmother's room. I could see that he was feeling nervous about sailing out of Poole on the afternoon tide the following day. 'Why are ships always described as she? I can't think of any other object which has a gendered pronoun.' I asked.

'Well,' he said, stroking his chin and considering. 'I regard Daphne as female because at sea, she looks after us all, like a mother. We completely dependent on her at sea, and she provides for our needs to the best of her abilities. In part, we relate to her like lovers. As part of her feminine allure, Daphne wears stays, those heavy ropes and wires that support her masts. Her waist is between her foremast and her main mast. If you look at Daphne, her body is rounded, with beautiful, sensuous, symmetrical curves. To be truly beautiful she has to put on all her clothes, her glorious billowing sails. We help her to change her dress frequently, as we exchange, raise and lower her sails. Helped by our strong, capable hands, she is proud and graceful in her movements.'

'And why do you have that naughty figurehead on her?' I asked.

'Ancient people really believed that the ships they had created were living things, and needed eyes to see' he answered.

'But why does she have to have those exposed um....hmm..?

'Because sailors believed that the sight of a woman's ah......mmm calmed the sea. On this subject, any damage to the figurehead is regarded by sailors as a very bad omen for a ship. As you know, Daphne has had to have a new figurehead as a result of the storm damage on our last trip. This is giving the Cap'n some worries at the moment, as we have had difficulty signing a full crew. Sailors can be ridiculously superstitious about something as silly as that. Before you ask me, yes Lydia, I am also in love with Daphne.' We both laughed. 'I do understand my father's obsession with the beautiful Daphne', he continued, 'but I applaud his decision – at long last – to marry Caroline.' He held my eyes with his. 'I have a little present for you' he said, producing a small round, blue leather box from his jacket pocket. He passed it to me. I opened it, and found a beautiful little round gold locket and chain. The locket had a tiny shield engraved on the front, with the letters H and L entwined. 'This is not an engagement ring', he said, laughing. 'We're not allowed one, so do wear this secretly, under your clothing, and think of me often.' He showed me how to open the locket, and inside was a tiny photograph of him.

The following day, Zephyr and I went down to the quay to watch the final loading of Daphne and to see Harry and Captain Lovejoy prepare to sail on the afternoon tide. Mrs Lovejoy was there, speaking in broad dialect again, and shouting and getting really cross with everybody in order to keep from crying. Harry, who was very busy and sweaty, gave me a big hug and a very long kiss, which was totally unseemly behaviour on both our parts, it being such a public place. Captain Lovejoy as usual, had no qualms about hugging and kissing everyone around him, man, woman or child (but not dogs). Mrs Lovejoy and I stood on the quay, alone at last, watching Harry supervising the crew who were busying about on the ship. When a group of men moved to the windlass to raise the anchor, I heard Harry suggesting to Caleb Stone 'Singin 'a bell bottom trousers.' It was so rude- probably deliberate- that as ladies, we felt compelled to leave. We withdrew to 'The Poop-Deck', to stand looking out of the magnificent bow window, watching Daphne gently slipping away from the quay, and into the channel in front of Brownsea Island. I sobbed on Mrs Lovejoy's ample bosom, and Vasistha made us a pot of tea.

Chapter Twenty Seven

Zephyr and I walked home together to Teagues Grocery. I felt very sad, and it was good to have his amiable company as he gently pulled me along the High Street. I took the back entrance into the kitchen, and Ann told me that Grandmother was ensconced in her room with one of her special customers. I was at a loose end, with nothing constructive to do, so I ate some cold meat and vegetables as I'd missed lunch, and went with Zephyr to Ross's Pharmacy as I needed some hand lotion. I was the only customer, as the shop had only recently opened and the Rosses were trying to build up a clientele. There was the noise of Scottish voices from the back room behind the dispensary, and Mr Ross appeared behind the counter, beaming. This was very unusual for him, as he seemed very subdued normally, and generally stayed behind a stained glass screen in the dispensary with Mr Bennett, his young spotty apprentice, leaving the serving to his wife.

'Come away into the back, and bring your dog' he said, 'Mrs Ross's mother, Mrs Maude, finally arrived yesterday, from Scotland.' I found Mrs Maude was a tall, well built woman, whose speech was beautifully enunciated, but full of so many dialect words that I found her to be delightful, but largely incomprehensible. Both the women were full of smiles, and most welcoming. I was able to understand that Mrs Maude had come for 'the birthing of the wean.' She said that she had considered travelling by sea with Alec and Phemie, but as they left at very short notice, she had no time to prepare. She told me that she was a 'Howdie Wife'. When I asked what on earth this was, she explained 'birthing weans.' Mrs Maude expressed that she was glad that she had missed the journey on 'Daphne' as she was rather afraid of getting sea sick.

Alec interrupted 'I assured her that we parsimonious Scots have a perfect cure for sea-sickness. If you find yoursel hinging oot over the side of the ship feeling wabbit, clench a silver shilling between your teeth. It always works for us Scots.'

Mrs Maude smacked him on the head with her newspaper, and kept telling some hilarious stories about her peregrination from Alloa to Poole, referring to me as 'hen'. I tried to look keenly interested, rather than simply bemused. Fortunately Phemie's spoken English was improving, and she did some translating! When her mother had calmed a little, Phemie took the opportunity to say 'It's as well you came by Lydia. Alec and I have been minded to have a wee word with you about possible employment here with us in the pharmacy. It is very important to us to build a good staff, as I will be able to do less once the wean is born.'

I felt very perplexed. Here was I, in loco parentis to a darling dog, just about to begin my musical career, possibly being offered work in a pharmacy! I felt myself going pink with pleasure and confusion. I really, really liked Alec and Phemie, but just didn't see how I would find time to fit in shop hours and my other activities.

'It would just be mornings Lydia', Phemie said, having seen my face. 'Alec will be taking on a second apprentice, and I think that between them three men might be able to handle the shop for me in the afternoons.'

'Ahhhh, yes. Hmmm. I see', I said. 'Of course, I will have to consult my family first'.

'It really is a most suitable position for a lady,' Phemie continued. 'Only the most intelligent and discreet folk can work in a pharmacy, given the confidential nature of many of our customers' affairs, and there may be opportunities to help with the scientific work that goes on behind the scenes to prepare the stock items that we will be selling.'

I stayed for what Alec described as 'a Scottish High Tea.' Phemie and her kitchen girl Jane produced fried egg, bacon and what Phemie described as fried pudding, eaten with fried potato cakes. The table groaned with things I had neither seen nor eaten before: oatcakes which Phemie called Bannocks, tiny little sweet pancakes, 'dropped scones', 'snowballs' and great big Abernethy biscuits. I also noticed that my Scots friends had some very quaint habits. They had no tea cosy, and kept putting the pot back on the range to keep boiling. They poured tea into the teacups first and added the milk last. Fascinating. I enjoyed myself so much. However, I had to leave eventually, as Zephyr still needed a bit of a walk. I promised to let them know about the proposed job as soon as possible.

Zephyr and I were very late back to Teagues. Grandmother was slightly annoyed, so I guessed that she had been worrying about me. She said 'If it wasn't for the fact that Ann said you'd been home for something to eat after lunch, I would be suspecting that you'd stowed away on the Daphne.' (How I wish I had!) I told my grandparents all about my interesting afternoon at the Rosses' Pharmacy, and the mention of a possible job for me.

'Would you like to have the job Lydia?' asked Grandfather, fingering his beard pensively.

'I should say so!' I replied enthusiastically.

'I see the need that Mr and Mrs Ross are in', he agreed. 'It is so difficult to get good staff. Even one of our most experienced shop assistants would be entirely unsuitable for them. We are in trade. Mr Ross is a professional man. Most difficult. You should think it through very carefully Lydia.'

'We don't want you poorly again dearest' said Grandmother. 'The decision will of course, rest with your Father, but before he is approached, you must carefully consider your music teaching plans, and decide whether you could cope with the very considerable additional load this would place upon you.'

Well, as you've guessed, I'm one of God's most impulsive creatures. I decided overnight that, although all my responsibilities would keep me very busy, I could handle the pharmacy work, my musical development and some pupils if I organized my time carefully. I'd seen far too many single women having no control at all over their own lives, as they were financially dependent on fathers or husbands. Developing these skills would assure my future if anything happened to Harry. I had to face up to the knowledge that the sea and everything to do with it is hazardous. Mrs Oakes could never have expected to lose 'Squirrel' at such a young age.

After breakfast, Zephyr and I went to see Mr and Mrs Ross at the pharmacy again. I went round to the back door, as the shop was not yet open, and was escorted into the comfortable 'back room' where Phemie and Alec spent time between their shop activities. Alec carefully showed me around the shop, which was magnificent. The window had a great high shelf for giant onion shaped display carboys, filled with different bright colours of blue, red and yellow. Alec said he had plans to put a gas lamp behind each of these, so that the window display would be more attractive to customers on dull days, particularly in the winter. Empty, brightly coloured jars and bottles were displayed beneath them in the window, adorned with attractive labels such as Milk of Magnesia, Liver Pills, Witch Hazel.

Within the shop itself the mahogany shelves held a profusion of what Alec called 'proprietary medicines', items he had 'bought in' for re-sale. There were some items that had been produced by Alec and Phemie in the dispensary. I felt quite panicky. I was well able to help out in my grandparents shop in an emergency, but this was much more demanding than weighing out two ounces of tea and cutting four slices of bacon for a customer. 'We really need you Lydia', they said. 'We promise to be very patient with you, and will help you to learn as much as you can.' Alec got quite excited, and started telling me of his plans to make and sell his own brand of soda water. Phemie cut him off, being more practical with me. 'I'd love you to start on Monday,' she said, 'as my condition is advancing, and it isn't seemly for me to be serving in the shop as I get bigger. I might be indisposed for a while after the wean comes, and then I will have less time anyway, as I'll be feeding as well.' She told me what my weekly pay would be, as Father was bound to ask that when I went to see him.

Zephyr and I made our next call to Mr Inkpen's offices. I asked one of the men standing writing into ledgers at the high desks in the outer office whether I might see Mr Curtis, my father. Father and Mr Inkpen each had a separate office, behind glass screens, which reached to head height in the lofty office. I was called in by my father's secretary, who returned to her desk on the other side of the office. I could well understand how working so very closely with Miss Dacombe in the seclusion of this office, intimacy had grown between them over the years. Her successor was a lady with grey hair and a long, rather lined face, who seemed very pleasant. I explained carefully how much I would like to work at the pharmacy. Father looked very perplexed, and suggested that as I would be in Parkstone on the following afternoon for my first music lesson with Mr Aldridge at Inglewood, I could take my evening meal at Otterwood. Miss Dacombe would be there, and the three of us could have a lengthy discussion. I readily agreed, feeling that it would be a good plan to revisit the place that had caused me so much unhappiness. It was strange to think that father and Miss Dacombe were now happily planning to use the marital bedroom that had caused our family such sorrow.

Zephyr and I walked up to Parkstone for our music lesson as it was a chilly, but fine day. Inglewood was a pleasant, large, gentleman's residence, situated just outside the village, in impressive, sloping, landscaped grounds. Mr Aldridge was a tall, lean man in his late thirties, with an abundance of black curly hair and the largest, fluffiest eyebrows I have ever seen. He was very flamboyantly dressed in a purple velvet jacket, with a red cravat. He introduced me to his friend Mr Bristo, who lodged with him, as they were both bachelors. 'Bristo is a violinist. We're old friends,' Mr Aldridge explained, 'and rub along well together, so we decided to share expenses, until we find the right women to get hitched to.' They both seemed very cheerful and informal with each other. I was given some music to sight read and play. I was very nervous, playing in front of two strange men, but apparently they were pleased with my initial effort, and Mr Bristo clapped and smiled and blew me a kiss before leaving the room with Zephyr to have a walk around the gardens. I felt as if I was going very red. Mr Aldridge sat beside me on the wide piano stool, and spent a very demanding hour with me. 'I have two things to say to you my dear' he said at the close of the lesson. 'Firstly, you have talent, and I wish you had been sent to me at a younger age. Secondly, it is a great pity that you are a young woman. A young man with your aptitude might well have the possibility of a musical career before him. However if you study your music theory well with Mr Short and practise the techniques which I will coach you in, you will become an excellent piano teacher. You have every possibility of being able to earn your keep.'

I felt delighted, as this was just what I had been hoping to hear. I was aware, from being at Teagues, how many genteel ladies on very slender means struggled to maintain themselves if they did not possess the means of making a respectable living. It was therefore with a very warm feeling that I ascended Sandringham hill. Doubtless this information would be reported back to Father.

Father, Miss Dacombe and I enjoyed a very pleasant early supper together. When the table was cleared, we continued to sit round together ready for our discussion. I noticed Father's hand surreptitiously caressing her knee under the table, and I remembered how very familiar that he had been with Liza. He really had taken ridiculous liberties with her, a servant, having her at the table, reading and writing his letters. I sincerely hoped that was the only liberty he had taken. 'To business' said Father. He carefully elicited from me the details that I had been able to gather regarding my proposed work at Mr Ross's Pharmacy. Miss Dacombe asked helpful supplementary questions. 'I have no objection to this proposal in principle' Father said cautiously. 'Both your grandparents and I have had to make our own opportunities from scratch. As the successful people we now perceive ourselves to be, there is a feeling of pride that we would prefer you not to have to work. However, the knowledge that you would, if the need arose, be able to provide for yourself means that none of us need have any undue anxiety about your future. Go to see Mr and Mrs Ross in the morning, and tell them that you have my blessing.'

I slept in my old room that night. The house felt better with another, much surer female hand at the helm, and although I felt that Miss Dacombe was too young to be my stepmother, I did feel that in just over another week, I would be gaining a very kind and supportive 'elder sister.'

Chapter Twenty Eight

My weeks suddenly became very busy following Father's wedding. With music lessons, piano practice, dog walking and work at the Pharmacy, many of my hours were filled. Harry had been wise in suggesting the music studies. I found the dumpy choleric Mr Short to be a hard taskmaster, but a good teacher. We met in the vestry at St James's church for my theory lessons, with the occasional opportunity to play the church organ. He stated that this was a privilege, as women could not be church organists. With his recommendation, I was allowed to play the harmonium -Grandfather hated them and called them 'pandemoniums'- at various evening meetings which generally involved ladies, children or both, but this all built up my musical confidence and competence.

At the Pharmacy I was learning some hair raising things about medicines. Seemingly there were preparations to insert or pour into every orifice of the body. I was never previously aware of this. At the back of the shop Phemie, Mrs Maude and sometimes Mr Ross himself were teaching me what Mr Ross, with a wry smile called 'the ins and outs of the human body.' I at last found out what the monthly 'curse' was all about. Mrs Maude and Phemie also tried to explain to me how babies were made. I was so shocked that Mrs Maude had to make me a cup of tea and I sat down until as Phemie said, my cheeks had some colour in them. It certainly made a lot of the odd physical feelings I had experienced when at close quarters with Harry more understandable. I also had a clear understanding of exactly what Liza had been getting up to. That explained the baby and Mother's anger.

'Why are you telling me all this?' I asked eventually.

'Well,' said Phemie, 'It does have a bearing on some of the preparations you will be selling, particularly to female customers, as they wouldn't want to ask the pharmacist's advice directly, him being a man and a'that. This is one of the reasons why we really need you to be in the shop regularly every forenoon, particularly if I'm no able to be there myself. Women often come in to buy items that will help them to avoid conceiving a child. They will often ask for 'feminine hygiene apparatus' she said, showing me a douche bag, tubing and metal nozzle. 'We mix up a special preparation, which can be sold from the stock kept under the counter, ready wrapped, so that there need be no embarrassment. Many women prefer to use this douche bag method. I always suggest the more efficient alternative, one of these little sea sponges soaked in a little oily preparation we prepare and placed inside the woman at bedtime. Of course', she went on, 'the church's view is that marriage is for the creation of children. You will however meet customers who already have children, and don't need any more. Sometimes women are in poor health and having a further child could lead to death. Given the position of the churches, we must act very discreetly. The doctors do direct needy women to us.'

'There is something that men can use to be helpful to their wives. It's called a 'French Letter' said Alec, producing a small cardboard box. It was labelled 'The Reliable' and small letters assured the reader 'will last a year.' It was priced at two shillings and threepence.

Alec continued, 'If more men used these, they would save themselves many times more than the initial outlay, but embarrassment and ignorance stands in the way of many people getting the help they need.'

Well, I really, really began to grow up as a result of my work in the pharmacy. Face cream, soap, soda water, witch hazel, calamine, cough mixtures, gripe water, and lozenges were the simplest side of the work. I often felt seriously embarrassed when confronted by people's little problems. It is a strange thing how when you are really, really embarrassed, you want to laugh. At least, I do. I feel myself getting very hot, think I must have gone frightfully red, and then my lips begin to twitch. Inside my head I am shouting to myself, 'I work in a respected pharmacy, I am a trusted assistant, I must not laugh, I must not laugh.' I confided this to Mr Ross, Phemie and the apprentice pharmacists over a cup of tea at the back of the shop one quiet wet afternoon, and we all laughed. They assured me that they still had their 'moments' with customers.

Zephyr came to work with me every day, and was a great favourite with Mrs Maude and the Rosses. Generally I had lunch with the family at the pharmacy before going out with Zephyr on my other work to study music and play the piano at meetings. I already had two pupils for piano lessons on Monday afternoons, Robert Spraklin and Isabella Spinney, and was very pleased to have the work.

Life at Teagues continued at its gentle, considerate pace. As an Alderman on Poole Council, Grandfather was very busy, attending to Council business and going to meetings. This brought him into frequent contact with Mr Negus the Undertaker, a much younger man, and as a Tory his views were frequently diametrically opposed to Grandfather's Liberal politics. In spite of their differences, they became very good friends, and worked together as Guardians of the Poor, which entailed going to the Board Meetings at the Union Workhouse and making periodic inspections. One of the small things that they had done for the comfort of the inmates was to insist on the provision of benches with backs to them as Grandfather put it 'for the easement of the inmates.'

Likewise, Grandmother continued being charitable. On one of my 'free' afternoons, we were sitting together at the table in Grandmother's room at the back of the shop, catching up on some letter writing. Ann came in from the kitchen, and said 'If you please M'm, there is a female person outside asking for you.'

'Is she respectable?' asked grandmother, removing her spectacles and sticking some wayward hairs behind a hairpin.

'I think so M'm,' said Ann. 'She has a lad with her.'

Grandmother looked quizzically at me.

'Bring them in then' she said to Ann.

Ann ushered in a very dusty looking woman and an odd looking little boy of about five. The child had most attractive almond shaped eyes with lids slightly drooping, a very round face, a slightly flattened nose and a rather small mouth and pokey tongue. His hands were like starfishes. He wasn't ugly, but different from other lads. His mother was in her middle years, dressed in worn navy clothes, with a great pinned navy hat above her brown, lined face.

'Thank you for seeing me Mistress' said the woman. 'The Parson at St James's said you might be able to help.'

'Hmmmm', said Grandmother. 'You'd better tell me your name, where you come from, and your business. You may speak with complete freedom in front of my granddaughter. She is utterly discreet. '

'My name is Elizabeth Cox, and this is my son Colton, but he answers to the name Cotton.'

'Married?' asked Grandmother sharply.

'No' she replied, 'but for general purposes, I call myself Mrs Cox. I will explain why. I was born in Hinton, in the New Forest, and as a younger woman, I went to work for an older, widowed gentleman who lived at Mudeford. Over a number of years we grew very close as you might say. Cotton was the result. There was never any question of marriage, as he had a son in London, who was going to inherit everything. We called our son Colton for the gentleman's middle name. He loved our boy dearly. Sadly, my dear old gentleman died suddenly one day when we were out in the garden together. He said he didn't feel well, put his hand up to his chest, and crumpled in front of our eyes. He must have been dead as he hit the ground. I contacted his son, who came home, paid up my wages for the year and sent us off without a character. We have been walking around for weeks, looking for domestic work, haven't we my darling' she said, looking fondly at Cotton.

'Oh dear, oh dear oh dearie me,' said Grandmother. 'At the present time, I have no idea of how to help you. I could probably find you a place in a decent household, but with the boy...........-smiling at Cotton- I shall have to pray for inspiration. I can quite see why the Vicar pointed you in my direction. At the moment I can offer you nothing except the chance to clean yourselves up, meals and the chance to sleep together in the basement on a palliasse.'

'Mistress, we would be so very grateful just for that' said Mrs Cox.

When Grandfather came home, he and Grandmother put their heads together during our evening meal upstairs. Grandfather agreed that the pair couldn't possibly go into the Union Workhouse, as they would be split up. They agreed 'a boy like that will always need his mother'. He mentioned Mr Negus's recent marriage to a young lady from Devon. She had just a young girl coming in daily to help her, and a nine roomed house to keep. Finding Mrs Cox and Cotton work was urgent, as Grandfather needed the basement for storage and preparation work. He decided to go and visit his friend that very evening.

Before I left for my work the following morning, Grandmother was inspecting Mrs Cox's tidier appearance, as she had brushed the travel dust off her clothes. She was briefing her on her forthcoming visit to young Mrs Negus. I saw her passing her wedding ring, which she rarely wore, to Mrs Cox. 'Take it' she hissed firmly. 'Everyone around knows I'm well and truly wed. Just wear it, and say you're in mourning. Folks will probably not ask any more if you look very sad. Don't tell lies, but learn to be economical with the truth.'

Back at the Pharmacy, Mr Ross was getting worse. I had noticed over the previous couple of weeks that he seemed to be full of ideas for developing the pharmacy, some of them quite ludicrous. He was springing around, concentrating on nothing but these strange ideas, and seemed to have little control of these random thoughts. I had noticed Phemie tipping large doses of Laudanum into his tea and trying to get him to keep still for long enough to drink it. He had such difficulty focussing on his dispensing tasks, often breaking off what he was doing, walking about and talking to himself that Phemie and the apprentices were doing all of the preparation for him. He wasn't difficult with us, as such, but was very tiresome around Phemie, touching her immodestly in public, making her blush and kissing her. Mrs Maude got cross with him many a time. I commented to Grandfather later that he was riding so high, he reminded me of Pegasus. 'Icarus more like,' Grandfather commented darkly.

On this particular morning, Mr Ross was talking to himself, his speech was fast and making little sense, but I did get the impression that he thought that he was getting very, very rich as a result of the sale of Ross's Patent Soda Water. None of us were sorry as he vanished at speed up the High Street. Phemie looked pale and tired, and said she had a back ache. Mrs Maude gave her a questioning look. 'I'm perfectly all right Ma' she said, and started organizing the apprentices to mix up the prescriptions ready for Mr Ross to check when he got back. Halfway through the morning Phemie went upstairs to lie down, and Mrs Maude went with her. The morning passed and Jane started making our lunch. Mrs Maude called me upstairs to speak to Phemie, who she said 'has started her pains.' Labour they called it properly. Phemie was surprisingly well in control of herself, but kept having to stop speaking as the pains grasped at her. 'Shut the shop immediately. Send the junior lad, James to look for Alec. Tell Alfred to go to Hayman's Pharmacy and ask if he can help us out in this emergency by checking and finishing Alec's prescriptions. When he has done that, ask him to let Dr Mullins know that the wean is coming. Can you stay to help?'

I stayed, and was glad I did, as everything happened fairly quickly over the next hour. Alfred reported back that Dr Mullins was out on another call and so was Dr Griggs. Mrs Maude smiled at me and said 'so its jist the three of us lassies. We'll cope.' The baby came in exactly the way they'd already explained to me. Phemie lay on her back. Mrs Maude arranged herself at the bottom end 'to catch the wean' and I just followed her orders of 'get me this, pass me that.' The pains must have been awful, as they were coming almost continuously at the end, but Phemie made little fuss apart from grunting loudly as her mother shouted 'Push, push!' Finally I saw a mat of dark hair from the baby's head, then a dear little squashed up red blue face as first one shoulder and then the other emerged. Finally the whole babe slipped out in a mess of blood and liquor, still connected to his mother by a quite substantial cord. 'We'll call him Hugh' said Phemie, as her mother handed the baby to her, wrapped in a bloody white towel. At that moment Dr Mullins appeared. 'Tae jist cut the cord and collect his fee' said Mrs Maude loudly. 'They're aye the same, these Doctor bodies.'

Mrs Cox

Chapter Twenty Nine

I was ever so grateful to old Missis Teague for finding me a place with Mr and Mrs Negus. I was nearly running out of hope of ever finding a place for Cotton and me. Mr and Mrs Negus were pure gold. She was from Devon. They hadn't been married long. Seems he had gone on the train to High Hampton to pick up the body of a Poole man, who had died on a visit there. He took the coffin with him, and stayed overnight in the town, where he met his love. It was unusual that, marrying someone who lived so far away, but that is what he did anyway. They had only been married five months, and were proper lovebirds.

Mrs Negus gave me the use of two attic rooms upstairs, but impressed on me that she was already with child, which didn't surprise me, the way they were with each other. She made me understand that as her family started to grow, I would have to find a room locally. She was a lovely lady, kind and full of smiles, speaking in broad Devonshire. Cotton and me fitted in happily and gratefully with the two of them and the daily girl, Betty who was twelve, and not the smartest. I was never made to feel that Cotton might be a problem. He is and always has been, a lovely, good tempered boy. Straight away, Mr Negus began to teach Cotton some jobs which he could do around the house. His most important job was to keep all our shoes highly polished. He was allowed to do little jobs in the carpenter's shop like brushing up the floors and tidying up. It took him a long time to learn, and he worked slowly, but he enjoyed being busy, and Mr Negus made clear that he would be paid a little. I already knew that Cotton was very different, and looked and was, slower than other children his age. Mr and Mrs Negus really appreciated his beautiful calm temperament and wanting to be helpful. By helping me to keep him busy, it stopped me worrying about him constantly.

I'd only been with Mrs Negus for a week when Mrs Ross at the pharmacy was labouring for her first child. Mrs Teague told Mrs Negus, and it was Mrs Negus's idea to send me straight round to help out with the washing and whatnot. Perhaps Mrs Negus wanted me to learn a thing or two so that I would be more help when her little ones started to come. Any rate, the baby came really quickly. Jane and me were sluicing out the bloody sheets and rags late that afternoon when there was a fearful commotion in the back yard. Mr Ross, who I was told had been missing all day arrived. Such a din there was, that Jane and me went outside. He was sitting in a splendid four wheel dog cart, painted in blue and burgundy with red velour seats. It was clear that 'Sir' had no more notion than the man in the moon as to how to drive it. The two fine black horses harnessed to it were foaming at the mouth, and had flared nostrils and were lathered with soapy sweat. I told Jane to fetch two buckets of tepid water immediately. So lucky that I'm a Forest woman born and bred! She ran off, for the water, and I unbuckled the harness of the first one, and gave the bridle to Sir to hold, whilst I undid the harness from the second. I'm not a woman to swear, never ever, but I was cussing the stupid man very loudly. Those poor horses were that distressed, I was feared they might die. I couldn't manage the two of them, so we gave them a drink, and I sent Jane off to Teagues to fetch their Wesley. Nice young man. We'd already engaged in horse talk in my brief stay there. The scotch woman came out, mother of Mrs Ross, very sensible body, and I sent her in to get rags to rub the poor things down. Clearly she knew nothing about horses, but was very calm, took the bridle from Sir and sent him in to see to Mrs Ross, and then young Miss Lydia came out. By the time Wesley came, we'd rubbed them down a bit, and Miss Lydia had a couple of light blankets ready. Wesley and I put the blankets on and we walked the two horses gently up and down the lane at the back of the shop, talked to them and stroked their faces as they slowly cooled down.

Wesley told me that Mr Ross had never had a carriage before. It was a complete mystery to both of us as to what had been going on. Wesley very kindly took the two horses down to Teagues, as he said he could get permission from Mr Teague to get the delivery cart out of the shed, and keep them overnight. When I finally got back into the house, Mrs Maude the scotch woman, Jane and Miss Lydia were sitting in the kitchen, in a state of shock, drinking tea, and there was a commotion going on upstairs between Mr and Mrs Ross. Mrs Maude was going 'He's no a wee bit interested in the wean', and Jane and Miss Lydia were stunned that he had bought the carriage and pair and so upset his wife.

Clearly serious help was needed, so I put my cloak on, as I was mightily chilled having been outside with the horses for so long. I ran back to Mr and Mrs Negus, who were just sitting down to their supper. They allowed me to interrupt them and tell my tale. 'Dear God', said Mr Negus, 'I always thought that young man was a bit unstable,' grabbed his table napkin and threw it down on the floor, and went off at a dash. I don't know what time he got back. I sorted out the supper things as Mrs N. was tired and peaky looking. Cotton and me had a bite to eat together, and retired to our attic.

Of course, Mr and Mrs Negus would never have discussed the well respected pharmacist with a servant like me, but next morning they both told me that they were glad I'd been at the pharmacy at such a critical time, that I had done very well, and that they were proud of me. I was very pleased to be so well appreciated! It wasn't long before Wesley appeared at the back door with his horse and cart, to ask if we had any orders for the day. We did need more flour and dried fruit, and as he kept some provisions on the cart for immediate supply, I walked out of the back gate with him. 'Such excitement last night!' he said. 'You did well it seems, to send Mr Negus over, as when I'd explained it all to Mr old Teague, he also went off up the street to the pharmacy like a hound dog. I have been able to gather that Mr Ross has been declared very unwell. Dr Mullins and Dr Griggs were both there most of the night with him. He should never have bought that fancy gig and horses. He has no money to pay for it. Mr Teague said Mrs Ross and Mrs Maude are beside themselves with distress. Mrs Ross has cried and cried. I've got to rush my round this morning, as Mr Negus is going to drive the gig and horses back to the man in

Bournemouth this afternoon, and has asked me to help to harness the horses. He and Mr Teague are going to persuade the man that sold it that he has little choice but to agree with them and accept it back. Mr Ross will not be able to pay. I'll have to give the horses a good check over before they go. I only hope there is no serious hurt to their mouths. Mr Ross hadn't a clue. You did well though,' he said, smiling broadly at me.

After I'd made Mrs Negus a bite of lunch, and Betty was clearing up, I sat her down in an armchair, and she asked if Cotton could stay with her, and help her wind some knitting wool. I could have cried at her kindness to the two of us. She was sending me back to the Pharmacy, to see if there was anything that needed to be done. 'I'm sure Cotton and I can manage to make supper between us' she said, 'so stay for as long as you can be useful.'

Curiosity is in each one of us! I hurried back to the shop, and tapped on the kitchen door. Jane looked relieved to see me. 'Mrs Ross has re-opened the shop' she said. 'She's had hardly any sleep and is in the dispensary, supervising and helping the apprentices in their work. Miss Lydia was here as usual this morning, but had to leave after lunch. Mrs Maude is upstairs looking after Mr Ross who is heavily asleep. The doctors gave him goodness knows what last night apparently. Thank God Mrs Maude is here to look after the baby too, but Mrs Ross still has to put him to the breast regularly.'

I just set to work methodically. I went upstairs to sort the bedrooms out, empty the slops and clean. Mrs Maude said it was alright to clean out the grate in the big bedroom, as it was unlikely to disturb Mr Ross. He was as white as a sheet, and he and the room stank really queer. The smell reminded me of acid drops. He was quite literally breathing it out with every breath, and his body smelled as if he had been soaked in it. Mrs Maude said the doctors had tried some new stuff on him, paraldy something or other. They only tried it after everything else had failed, so he was absolutely full of medicines. 'It's the puir wee wean ah feel si sorry for' she kept muttering. 'Alec's aye been aw over the place. It's only

Phemie keeps him straight. Some new beginning for the two of them eh? And there's my puir lassie down the stair trying to keep things going.'

'And what is the baby's name to be?' I asked, trying to keep the conversation on a more normal footing.

'Hugh, for Alec's father. Alec still misses his father, although he was cut off by his family for marrying Phemie. Thought he was too good for my lass. Between you and me, she's the only thing stands between him and the madhouse. Alec's family should be grateful.'

I worked my way downstairs. Jane had cleaned the shop early on, and I couldn't get into the dispensary as Mrs Ross was working in there with the apprentices. Mr Hayman was expected late in the afternoon to check the prescriptions with them before the junior apprentice, James, delivered them. I heard the baby crying, and Mrs Maude came down the stairs with young Hugh in her arms. 'The wean's wakened hungry', she said. 'Fetch Phemie frae the dispensary.'

I put my head round the dispensary door. 'Mrs Maude says the baby is hungry' I said.

Poor woman. To have had her first baby is one thing. To be up all night trying to calm her husband is another. To leave her baby and to have to get straight back to work is quite desperate. My heart went out to her. Her face was white and drawn, but it was not the face of defeat. I was looking into the face of a woman who had herself under control and was calm and coping well. Her eyes met mine, and she smiled and said 'I'm so very grateful for all your help, Mrs Cox. I don't know how we would have managed without you yesterday. Please thank Mrs Negus for her great kindness in sharing you with us. I hope to thank her personally next time she calls to the shop. All is well here now. Tell your mistress that there is no need for you to return.'

HARRY

Chapter Thirty

How I miss my dearest Lydia ! I am writing a small part of a letter every day, so that I can take the first opportunity to send her news by the paquebot system when we meet a suitable ship, and can get close enough to exchange mail. In this, my journal, she will also be able to read something more of my time at sea. This second voyage is not proving to be very easy. I felt very emotional as the Daphne slid out of the harbour. We were carrying five passengers who were going to make new lives in Australia. I could see the tears on their faces as we slipped carefully through the narrow channel at Sandbanks and past the cluster of coastguards' cottages. My own feelings were more mixed. I had the prospect of spending more valuable time learning my sailing profession aboard my dear father's ship. On the other hand, my brief time ashore had changed my life forever. I had left my dear Lydia, and was again facing a life of menacing uncertainty as our little ship and crew faced the unpredictable powers of the seas and the winds. I understood then why my father had steadfastly refused to re-marry for so long. His wife, who was with child, was dead and buried on his return. Of course, some masters take their wives to sea with them, to look after them, and deliver their own children! On the other hand, many, many ships never return. When I am back, Lydia and I will have to consider our future together, and how we might deal with these long separations. Father is deter-mined that this long voyage will be his last, and that he will appoint Paul Hann as captain in his stead.

As an able seaman on the crew, and a man who also holds a second mate's ticket, I have increased responsibilities on this voyage. Acting as Mr Tilsed's first assistant in supervising the loading and stowage of the cargo was my first experience of serious responsibility. Under Mr Tilsed's critically sharp eye, I was majorly responsible for the safe stowage in terms of weight distribution of all these tons of pottery drainage pipes throughout the hold. Mr Tilsed carries the final responsibility of making sure that it is all carefully stowed and lashed. If any part of the cargo shifts in heavy seas, it could affect the handling of the ship so severely that we will all drown. All is well so far, so hopefully I will be more confident next time we load a cargo. I see the Capn's wisdom in giving me my present responsibilities. I had been so very glad to be working throughout the loading with such experienced and good men as Caleb Stone, Mathew O'Connor and Sean Reilly again. I am sure we have done the loading well.

The Daphne has been re-rigged during her lengthy time in dock. We are all used to working with ropes on the rigging and are highly skilled in what is called marlinspike seamanship which entails splicing ropes, knotting and lashings for sails, ship's boats and deck work. Some slight changes have been made to our current rig, so our Daphne feels a little different now! We are again planning to make our first stop at Luanda again in the expectation of selling our cargo of drain pipes. As we may well be there at the same time as any post is likely to come from Lydia, I'm not particularly expecting mail, although I will post to her. I'm hoping that she will have written to me via our friend Mr Macdonald, the Paton's Wool Agent in Adelaide. We are hoping to re-load with suitable goods to sell in Adelaide, to turn a handsome profit again.

Over the last few days Daphne has became a very eerie Siren, as her new rigging sometimes makes little wild primitive shrieks, which vary in notes and volume. The crew keep complaining about the bad luck that they fear will attend us as a result of the new figurehead on Daphne, and simply hate the eerie noises from the rigging. So do I, but only because it has been upsetting the crew. The situation with the men was made worse today when St Elmo's fire appeared on the topmast as a faint blue, glowing cloud. Two of new crew members were very, very frightened.

The Cap'n having sensed the dis-ease of the crew over the creepy noise and this ghostly appearance, got very excited, and said 'If you see just the one light, it's called Helena, after the Greek goddess, whose name means a torch of light. Obviously this is very lucky, and even luckier if we see three at the same time, with the other two masts being lit up. We seafarers call the other two Castor and Pollux. They were Helen's brothers, you know, and are great friends to sailors.'

This brightened us up a bit. The Cap'n does love his Greek! I wonder what Caroline will make of it all when she has him to herself at Blake Hill.

I am still overawed at times with the responsibilities I have. Mr Tilsed is getting me to supervise all the deck work for the crew, making sure that everything is maintained to the highest standard. I will never forget, as long as I live, that very stormy passage around the Horn on my last voyage, and I want to make sure that the Daphne and her seamen are always ready, whatever the weather! The weather has been very quiet today, and this morning I have been up on the foremast with Mathew, checking the stays. At noon, as all was plain sailing, I was able to help the apprentice Snell and LeLacheur taking a sighting with the sextant. The Cap'n was explaining to them why he always sails to Australia via the West African Coast. It is of course, in order to make the best time between Poole and Adelaide, with the wind and currents. On the return, we will take advantage of the stronger winds found by going around Cape Horn.

The sea is reasonably calm today. We were 'spoken' by the brig 'Harlech' this morning. They are bound for Queenstown in Ireland, with a cargo of wheat, and have taken our post. Mr Tilsed has told me to use the calm weather to train the ship's company in fire fighting and emergency procedures. They are typical sailors, and think that I am driving them too hard during a reasonably favourable period of weather. They don't understand my desire to think ahead, as I told them, it's no good waiting for an emergency to happen, then wondering what to do about it! We should all know our duties and responsibilities before trouble strikes. If misfortune occurs, we shall be prepared.

Perhaps my previous words were prophetic. We encountered very stormy weather for some days. We lost some of our bulwarks, the head board and most of our livestock, but were able to save the three pigs my step mother had reared. The most terrifying occurrence was that I, and three of our crew were nearly washed overboard. One of the men was afterwards observed to have shit himself in terror. None of his normally crude shipmates remarked upon it. Our deliverance from this near disaster reaffirmed my faith in God. I am also less inclined to feel annoyed at the ridiculous superstitions of many of the crew.

Today, still in moderate seas but reasonable visibility, Luke, a new but clever lad, fell overboard and was lost. The ship was travelling fast, but fortunately the Cap'n was on the poop deck, and immediately brought her to the wind and ordered me and two crewmen to be lowered in a boat. The boat filled with water and capsized. The three of us and the boat were brought in safe, after a great struggle, but fourteen years old Luke Miles was lost. The Cap'n had expressly forbidden him to climb the rigging, but he had been up there, hanging out some washing. We were told later by Alf who called out the alarm that he had struck the end of a spar on the way down. Perhaps he was unconscious as he struck the water. Later in the day we observed that the foremast was sprung due to hauling the ship to the wind under such heavy sail in our desperate attempt to pick up the poor lad.

We are making slow headway due to the damage to the mast. Mr Rogers our carpenter has 'fished it' by organizing the lashing of spars tightly around the damaged area to brace it. I am feeling very low indeed. I cannot sleep. Every time I shut my eyes, and begin to drift off to sleep, I am back in the cold, cold sea, struggling to save the little boat and to help my ship mates in the water. I am not helped by having taken in a great deal of water myself, and am fevered and coughing. I trust that my strong constitution will make me well again soon.

Father keeps saying he is 'not right in his head' and is missing my stepmother greatly. He keeps saying 'may it please God that I will meet my dear Caroline again. There is something sadly wrong with me.' I think he is still haunted by the memory of my mother's death. Perhaps he should have stayed at home with my stepmother, but I feel that he believes that we cannot manage without him yet. He is such a wise captain, devoted teacher and kind man.

Our voyage to Luanda took us 90 days, the longest time ever, according to the Cap'n. In port, the Cap'n kept Paul Hann and myself close to him again, in all his duties, obligations and in the way of selling the cargo and choosing another. Managing the finances is a heavy responsibility on him. Trying to keep together a reasonable crew at the end of every leg of our journeying is another sore trial. The crew, with only a few exceptions, are always inclined to settle arguments with their fists. The Cap'n always deals severely with trouble makers, and never re-signs them. Some men can be so contentious, and adept at stirring up their shipmates that desertions ensue as a result of bullying. If the Bo'sun does not deal effectively with the men serious problems in terms of disputes with their officers and Captain occur. The Cap'n with his long experience and the information secured from other masters vetoed two of our proposed signings in Poole. At the worst, an agitator aboard can cause a near mutiny. As a result of a careful choice of crew, no-one 'jumped ship' in Luanda. We will however, be looking for more apprentices.

Today Mr Downton, our Second Mate, formally requested the Cap'n for an early discharge, in order to sign on with a steamer, the Hydra, to widen his experience. Apprentice Mr Hardy was already an Able Seaman as was Bertie Snell, who had completed his indentures on our return to Poole. I was promoted to Second Mate today. Words fail to describe my great pleasure in my promotion. I can feel myself smiling a lot, but at the same time, I am very aware of the weight of my new responsibilities. The prospect of a second trip around the Horn to get home makes my heart race.

I am already working hard for my First Mate's Ticket, and will be taking my examinations in Adelaide. The move out of the deckhouse and into the Second Mate's cabin is really helpful for study, given that we have Edward to steward us, a proper table to sit at and the company of the passengers at the table. Paul Hann is studying very hard to obtain his Extra Master's Certificate. A pass at first attempt is a complete rarity. We sailed out of Luanda today, having made a reasonably speedy turnaround allowing for the work on the mast. We took on mainly coffee and sugar again, as the Cap'n is hoping to trade these in Adelaide with the same merchants as before. Our cargo of wool will be already baled and waiting for us, and with the mast problem now fixed, he foresees another speedy turnaround.

Notes

'St Elmo's fire is a fascinating weather event. It is a bright blue or violet glow appearing on an upright structure such as a ship's mast.

Chapter Thirty One

The wind is still blowing very hard from South, and the ship is rolling fiercely. Mrs Way, one of our passengers is expecting a child, and her pains have begun, possibly as a result of the violent weather. All five of our passengers are being very sick and some of the crew too. The Cap'n has ordered the ship to lie to. We have had no hot food for over a week now, and are just eating tinned meat and biscuits.

We are still laying to. The wind continues very hard from the south and we are shipping a good deal of water. All the hatches are battened down very securely to try to keep the water out below decks. Today, Mrs Way gave birth to her child, a baby girl. She was helped in the birthing by her husband and her mother, Mrs Yates. It was Mrs Way's first child, and her travail was lengthy, spread over about thirty hours. In a ship full of men, there was no one else to help them. Men who already had their own children were much moved by her loud screams in the final stages. I was moved too, at the thought of my dearest Lydia having to go through this in the future. I felt very guilty too, in case it was I who had fathered Liza's child. The thought that Liza had given birth in an empty, cold church filled me with self reproach. Edward had scarcely seemed to sleep over the period of the birth, constantly providing the little family with every comfort that he could think of in these extreme conditions.

We are making headway again through sunshine and quieter seas. The ship, particularly below decks, has been cleaned up, and there is only a light wind. We are enjoying better food. The passengers are delighted with the shoals of porpoises around the ship. This afternoon, Mr Tilsed piped Bo'sun's 'general call' to indicate that an important announcement was to be made. As the weather was staying good, the Cap'n had decided to baptize the baby on deck. Following the announcement, a small company of the five passengers and most of the crew gathered. Reading the service from the Prayer Book, he baptised the little girl with great ceremony, using seawater in a blue spode bowl, which he poured over her little head with a pink scallop shell. Mr and Mrs Way had decided to call her Daphne Aquina, and we sang a modern hymn:

There is a green hill far away,
Outside a city wall,
Where the dear Lord was crucified,
Who died to save us all.
O dearly, dearly, has He loved,
And we must love Him, too,
And trust in His redeeming blood,
And try His works to do.

I thought the hymn was well chosen for a child in its simplicity, and it linked well with Mrs Way's own recent bloody and painful experiences. I was very, very surprised that she had decided to travel in that condition. Father had confided that it was essential to baptize the infant sooner rather than later, as so many babies and young children died at sea, particularly on the immigrant ships, where the conditions were generally terrible.

Mr Pearce, another of our passengers, caught a shark yesterday. This morning Edward prepared shark for our breakfast, fried in butter and toast. We are expecting a change for dinner, shark cooked in vinegar, served with peas. Early this morning, we saw some porpoises swimming alongside of us. Mr Draper, an idiot passenger, wounded one of them with a shot, and then they all took off. The rest of us are still very angry with him. Porpoises are a big part of our diet at sea, and their red flesh makes excellent 'steak' when served with onions. The Cap'n is very partial to the liver. The normal thing to do is to to harpoon them and haul them aboard. The crew were thus disgusted to be cheated of a good dinner of what they call 'puffing pig'. The night is clear and beautiful.

Today the Daphne is still running at 7 knots an hour. The weather is very dark. This morning we sighted a vessel at a distance, which had no canvas up except the fore top sail all torn to pieces with the wind. The Cap'n inspected her in his glass and steered towards her to come within about a quarter of a mile of her. Her davits were swung out and her boats were gone. The vessel was waterlogged. The waves were washing over her and every time she rose with the swell, water poured out of her cabin windows. The Dutch colours were still flying, and we could just see her name, Hollandsche Tuin. The Cap'n thought she must have been abandoned ten to fourteen days previously and believed another crew must have already boarded and stripped her. Hopefully after they had rescued the crew! He hailed her, inspected her very carefully again with his glass, found no trace of anyone alive, and then told me to hold the Daphne's course. He would report the information and position when he reached Adelaide.

The weather is very fair today. Edward appeared on deck with a bundle of Daphne Aquina's napkins and little clothes, tied in a sheet, which he handed to Caleb. These will be trawled behind the ship for a few hours, to clean them. Later on, a couple of 'flying fish' landed on the deck. They were each only about the size of a teacup, so I gave them both to Edward for the Captain's supper. Several albatrosses were flying about.

We steered south to give the Cape of Good Hope and Cape Agulhas a wide berth. As we sail further south, the weather is becoming colder and wetter. We are rarely out of our oilskin suits. I am wearing an extra shirt, but Paul Hann and my father seldom seem to feel the cold. The Cap'n warned us to look out for occasional icebergs heading north. We are in the 'Albatross Latitudes' now, where the wind is hardly ever still. Clearly the birds need the wind to keep their large, heavy bodies airborne. Surprisingly, the seas are moderate. We had reduced sail in anticipation of storms. This afternoon, we were becalmed. An albatross perched on a spar. Mr Draper, the idiot, suddenly appeared with his gun and shot it. Since sailors believe that the albatross carries the soul of a sailor, if an albatross follows a ship, it brings good luck.The Cap'n ran out of his cabin, and was so furious when he saw what had occurred that he came as near as I've ever seen him, to hitting the wretched man. He confiscated the firearm.

The rest of us discussed what to do with the carcass. In the end, the Cap'n gave the carcass to Edward to stew. Edward wasn't at all pleased, as the meat was very greasy, and produced a lot of what he called 'slurry.' However, he produced a tasty, fresh stew which was quite palatable. Mr Draper, at the Cap'n's order was excluded from dining at the table with the rest of us for a week. He must exist on hard tack and jam in his cabin until the period of his exclusion is over.

Today, in quiet seas, we 'spoke' a ship from London, the Royal Norfolk, with a cargo of case oil and engineering parts, bound for Sydney. Mr Urquhart, the first mate, shouted over that his Captain was very ill, and asked if we had a doctor aboard. As we had no doctor, the Cap'n offered to go across himself. We drew alongside, and Bo'sun Tilsed shot a line across, so that the Cap'n could go across on the Breeches Buoy. It was just a sort of large canvas bucket, with holes for his legs to go through. Mr Hann and I were to follow in turn, to as the Cap'n put it 'widen our medical experience.' In fact, Captain Rogers was in a very poor condition indeed. He was able to keep down very little food or fluid, was emaciated, seemed to be in pain, and was barely conscious. Our Cap'n opined that it was some malignant condition, which would very soon lead to death. He advised regular doses of laudanum, and suggested that at most, Captain Rogers had a few days, possibly only hours left. He took out his Prayer Book and putting his hand on the man's shoulder, prayed in a loud voice, firmly and in a tone of great compassion 'Captain Rogers, unto God's gracious mercy and protection we commit thee. The Lord bless thee and keep thee. The Lord make his face to shine upon thee, and be gracious unto thee. The Lord lift up his countenance upon thee, and give thee peace, both now and evermore. Amen'. We stayed with the dying man for a while, the Cap'n holding his hand. As we made to leave, Mr Urquhart was very upset, and said that he doubted his own ability and that of the Second Mate, Mr Holland to manage the ship without help. He asked if Captain Lovejoy would be able to spare an officer.

We returned to the Daphne, and I, who had been very moved by Mr Urquhart's appeal, privately offered to my father that I would help them. He turned me down flat. I was quite glad really, as he put into words what I had already observed. 'We cannot spare you Harry. Anyway, the crew look like a sack full of lazy, undisciplined, malignant men, who would cut your throat as soon as look at you if you displeased them. The disordered state of that ship indicates serious the serious problems which exist unconnected with the illness of the Master. Mr Urquhart is more dubious and frightened of his ability to manage these men than he is of his own seamanship. I am not prepared to risk your safety, my boy. The relative calm that we experience on the Daphne is as a result of choosing our men very carefully and having an excellent Bo'sun to enforce discipline. In addition, men like Caleb Stone, Mathew O'Connor and Sean Reilly lead their fellow seamen by example which tends to further encourage order in the fo'c's'le. Because others are less careful or greedier for their own profits, I see no indication for bailing them out. If I was to grant your request, your very life could be in danger.' He was right of course. In the morning, the Royal Norfolk hailed us again. Captain Rogers had died during the night. The Cap'n confirmed that he was unable to spare an officer, and wished them Godspeed to Sydney.

On arrival at Port Adelaide, I found the situation less difficult than on our previous visit. With less building work going on, and the magnificent government buildings shown to advantage by the clean, well ordered streets, the port was consolidating its position as the significant commercial community of South Australia. The Cap'n was looking very tired and drawn, and Paul Hann and I, together with the senior members of the crew did everything we could to help him. Mr and Mrs Macdonald invited the three of us to stay in their new home when our duties allowed. It was in Gawler Place, close to the Scots Church at North Terrace. We were made very comfortable.

I called at the post office almost immediately, and the three of us were delighted to receive several long letters which had been delivered by our loved ones poste restante. Father continues to look too tired, and is again occasionally muttering that he is 'not right in his head'. Paul and I persuaded him to see a doctor, who looked at his tongue, felt his neck, sounded his chest and palpated his abdomen but said –expensively- that he could find nothing the matter with him, and that he was probably just tired. He supplied father with a disgusting tonic containing nux vomica to stimulate his appetite. I concluded that he was missing Mistress Caroline very much, and that possibly the letters from her had made him feel worse rather than better. Mr Macdonald insisted that father rest more, and gave us much useful practical help with the sale of our cargo. Paul and I were occupied for a week with our Board of Trade examinations, and were particularly grateful for the work done in our absence by Bo'sun Tilsed, Bertie Snell, Caleb Stone, Mathew O'Connor and Sean Reilly who supervised the unloading and re-loading of the ship. As Paul had been successful in his Extra Master's examination, a truly amazing feat at first try, and I was now possessor of a First Mate's Certificate, we were jointly entrusted by Father with the task of 'swinging the ship's compass.' This is a complicated and time consuming scientific process to check the deviation of the compass, which enables the construction of a 'compass deviation card', enabling the navigator to calculate for the difference between the compass reading and known magnetic bearings. Of course, further adjustments have to be made regularly at sea too, due to variations in the earth's magnetic fields at different latitudes. With all our tasks accomplished that we were ready to leave port after just forty days. Just before our departure, more post arrived from home, and I learned that Lydia was, with her father's permission, -amazing- taking instruction to join the Catholic Church. At her request he had taken her to see Father Michael about beginning the instruction and the possibility of a wedding on my return, if we were both still of the same mind. Her father was being extremely radical about the change of religion. My father said he could remember catholic priests being stoned as they walked down the streets when he was a lad. They were still not allowed to appear on English streets in clerical dress. He did comment that Mr Curtis was no fool when it came to money, and the financial advantage of our two families being connected by marriage would mean that he would not have to provide for Lydia in the future. I commented that Lydia had every appearance of being a young woman who was capable of making her own way in life, with or without me.

Chapter Thirty Two

We were fortunate that no member of our crew 'jumped ship', or went missing. It was touch and go with Bert Cox. In fact, Bert did not actually report aboard. His shipmates dragged him aboard with permission from the Cap'n. In port, Bert was rarely sober, and preferred to sail on the Daphne as it had such a strict alcohol policy. Small beer was available, which had only a tiny amount of alcohol, and we preferred to drink it as it stayed fresher than the water from casks. When 'dried out' Bert was an efficient and likeable crewman, but because of his addiction, at least a week of each passage was required to dry him out. He was put in a locker below decks, and his crew mates, Sean and Caleb attended to him in his squalor and degradation. The Cap'n sent me down regularly to administer small doses of laudanum, as apparently he has seen many men die of this dreadful condition if they have received no help. I can still remember waking up from drink, trembling, sweating, sicking and shitting. I think he wanted to remind me of the pledge I had signed.

We have five passengers aboard for this voyage. Mr Jones and Mr Petrie have successful businesses in Australia and are returning to visit their families in Scotland after many years absence. Of the other three, Mr Hayward has retired from his work as a bank manager, and one of the younger two, Mr Lord is an engineer returning home and Mr Marsden has made money working in publishing and hopes to open his own small publishing house in London. Mr Lord and Mr Marsden are taking a particular interest in the workings of the ship, and enjoy being on deck and giving a little unskilled help here and there.

It is a long and wearisome journey through the Southern Ocean. The Cap'n is suffering greatly from indigestion, no matter how carefully Edward prepares light meals for him. Some days he looks very grey with the pain. I was dosing him regularly with Aqua Mentha Piperitae, but it gave him little relief. I am now giving him small doses of Phillips' Milk of Magnesia, which he asserts is more helpful, but I suspect that he is just trying to please me and to stop me worrying. He rarely comes on deck these days, except to do the morning prayers. He seems content to let Paul Captain the ship for him. I have stepped very prematurely into Paul's shoes and we have Mr Tilsed to again take on the responsibilities of Second Mate. Cap'n Lovejoy's absence is a sore loss to us both, as a lot of time needs to be spent with the four remaining apprentices of various ages and experience, teaching and supervising them. Fortunately Able Seaman Hardy, who has temporarily taken the bo'sun's position and AS Snell are both excellent teachers of the new juniors. We have a strong team. I am glad of this, as all too soon we will be facing the roiling seas and tempests of the Horn. Just the thought of going through this again makes me feel sick, particularly given my unexpected promotion. I haven't actually said this to father, but I think he senses it. He is frequently heard to say 'The last turn around the Horn was the worst ever. It cannot be as bad again.'

We are now heading towards 56 degrees south, into the teeth of the fiercest winds to take the Drake Passage again. We are becalmed with very little wind, but a following current is permitting us to progress an average two knots an hour. This is enabling us all to get some rest, but the cold is beyond belief. I am wearing as many of my clothes as I can fasten around myself, and the crew are presenting an even more motley appearance, with wrappings of bits of old canvas and old socks pulled down over their heads and ears. Hot food and drinks are very welcome. After morning prayers today, the Cap'n issued a tot of rum to each of us. I even accepted mine. Mr Lord has busied himself organizing 'team games' for the ship's company and Mr Marsden is taking a turn as an instructor for 'keep fit' exercises, with such delights as 'running on the spot' and various arm and leg exercises. We are cheerful, but in the mind of each of us, lurks the fear of the dreadful seas and winds we are about to face.

This evening Father became very ill, with terrible burning pain in the left side of his chest, which spread right down into his left arm and up into his neck. My worst fears, which had been building inside me since we left Melbourne were confirmed. It was his heart all the time. I think he had known all along. The concern for his digestion had been a charade played out by us both. At least we were enjoying some calm from the ocean. Both he and I knew he was unlikely to survive.

'Tell Caroline she is the most beautiful woman in the world, and I love her' he murmured.

I called Paul Hann, and together, we helped him to drink a very large dose of Laudanum for his pain. This was all we could do for his body. I summoned Edward, and he and Paul held his hands whilst I read the prayer for the dying as Father slipped into a deep sleep. Edward and I stayed with him. From the decks came the firm voice of Caleb Stone, soon joined by his shipmates singing for us:

Abide with me; fast falls the eventide;
The darkness deepens; Lord with me abide.
When other helpers fail and comforts flee,
Help of the helpless, O abide with me.

Swift to its close ebbs out life's little day;
Earth's joys grow dim, it's glories pass away;
Change and decay in all around I see;
O Thou who changest not, abide with me.

I had been so distracted with concern and grief, that I had not been conscious of the sudden, greater cold, the increase in the ship's movement, the creaking of her timbers and snapping of the sails. I heard the Bo'sun pipe 'all hands', and within a couple of minutes the bell was clanging furiously, to call each man of us onto the deck, including the passengers.

'Stay with him, Edward' I ordered, and went on to the deck, to find Caleb and Paul already at the wheel, together with passengers Jones and Petrie and Sean Reilly. Passengers Hayward, Lord and Marsden were at the pumps and hauling ropes and being generally helpful. Father had been quite right, although my second traverse around the Horn was terrifying, it did not measure up to the horror of my first experience.

Paul Hann had assumed full command of the ship and acted throughout with confidence and skill. After about six hours, when the immediate peril had passed, he ordered a tot of rum for every man. We were soaked, frozen, exhausted and grateful for the warm flush of the rum into our chilled systems. I took the next watch, and most of my men had been awake for twenty four hours already. I looked in on Father every couple of hours, and he was grey, making shallow breaths. Mr Marsden had relieved Edward in watching over him. When I finished my turn of duty, I found Caleb with Father. He promised to inform me of any change and I went to my bunk and collapsed into the dreamless sleep of exhaustion. Suddenly, Sean was shaking me awake. I fought my way back to consciousness. 'Nearly time to be on watch Sir', he said. 'The Cap'n has just woken and is asking for you.'

I shot off my bunk and along to his cabin. Edward, who had been helping Father with a mug of tea passed it over to me, and sashayed out of the cabin to fetch me porridge and coffee. Father was very tired, and still looked grey with pain. 'Either I'm taking a long time to die, or Almighty God has heard my prayer to get home to Caroline' he muttered. He finished his tea, and went back to sleep. Edward returned to find me crying like a baby. I felt foolish and weak, but knew I could rely on his discretion not to gossip about this. I ate, drank, and went to relieve Paul on watch. He looked into my eyes, squeezed the top of my arm and punched my chest gently. I had a lot to think about.

By the time Paul came up to relieve me, I had a plan to put to him. Our cargo of fleeces was urgently required at Paton's Mill in Alloa. Putting in to Poole first, on our return was not possible given the growing threat to sailing vessels posed by the steamer companies, who were faster. Assuming that father continued to recover, we could make a short stop at Buenos Aires, and send a message via the developing telegraph system to Poole, advising Mistress Caroline of Father's illness. She could be given the best estimate of our arrival in Alloa. Perhaps Phemie's mother could give her lodgings? Paul readily agreed, as putting into port on the coast of South America was indicated anyway, to replenish our water supplies and take on fresh food. Buenos Aires was further than we wanted to sail prior to this, but we were unsure whether the new telegraph system had reached further down the continent.

I went straight into Father's cabin, and found him very weak and sweating with pain. Edward was feeding him some slack porridge with a spoon, which was difficult, given the motion of the ship. Fortunately, it was a soup spoon with a very deep bowl. When he had finished the porridge, I poured him another very large dose of Laudanum. Before he drank it down, he murmured to me very quietly 'No need to worry about finding a penny to pay Charon to ferry me across the Styx to the land of the dead. I feel that I shall be with you a while yet, dear boy.' I kissed him, and held his hand until he went to sleep.

The days passed. The five gentlemen passengers all took turns reading to the Cap'n, and all our long serving crewmen came and spent time with him. His condition improved day by day. Not only a kind and loving father, but a gracious master, he took to referring to Paul respectfully as Captain Hann. When he started getting out of bed, he delighted in seeing the apprentices for an hour or two most afternoons, and used the time to teach them their mathematics and trigonometry with great patience. He also talked them through the little day to day squabbles and problems they had experienced with some of the rougher members of the crew.

We docked in Buenos Aires and sent our telegram. It would need to be re-transmitted many times until it reached its final destination. We hoped and prayed that it would safely reach Mistress Caroline. We made all speed to get back to Alloa. Unfortunately the weather we met crossing the North Atlantic was ferocious. In freshening winds, we quickly reduced canvas to half. Soon after, all the sails had to be reefed. We were in violent storm force south westerly winds, which Paul and I estimated were travelling at around sixty knots. We believed the waves to be at least sixty feet. We threw out a large sheet anchor, to drift with the current rather than be propelled by the cyclonic wind. It was difficult to fix our position, but after five days we believed that we had drifted in a large circle. Eventually, as the winds abated, we hauled the sheet anchor back in, having loosened the shrouds to break its shape first. We had deployed it in good time, and all things considered, the ship had sustained minimal damage. The crew however, did not come off so lightly. Two men were lost. A huge wall of water had knocked Bert Cox and Amos Knight off the deck. Many of the crew had sore, skinned hands from rope injuries, and I had seriously injured the first and second fingers on my left hand with a rope. Mr Hayward had a severely broken lower leg, having been flung off a ladder below decks. Though the seas were calmer, the ship had a grossly depleted crew of exhausted, battered and bruised seamen. We could only pray for safe passage back to Alloa.

My hand injury was a serious nuisance to my duties. When Paul had assumed the captaincy of the Daphne, all our responsibilities had increased. I had taken the greatest interest, under the tutelage of father in any medical matters arising. I was now only able to advise Paul with the straightening and splinting of Mr Hayward's leg. After two days, Father insisted at looking at my bandaged hand. He saw my broken, swollen black fingers, and said what I already knew 'These are gangrenous, and will have to come off at the knuckle now my boy, if you value your arm, and ultimately your life.' He did the job himself, helped by Mr Bennett the carpenter and Edward. I was glad he had been able to do it, in spite of his breathlessness, as at least he was quick and sure about what he was doing. The loss of two such vital fingers was painful both physically and mentally, as it was likely to change my whole future. For a long time I had been feeling unsure about my future as a married man, going on further long voyages around the world. As result, I had been turning different ideas over in my head around becoming a medical man or getting my own fishing boat or setting up a business and getting elected for Poole Town Council as a Liberal. The last, and least favourite began to look like my only option.

Caroline

Chapter Thirty Three

Well, I told that old varmint, my husband, not to go off round the world again at his age. To be truthful, I had waited for him so long, that I was frightened I might lose him at sea. The sea is a cruel master. Give me the land under my two feet any day. Strikes me, men are like untrained stallions altogether, get ideas in their heads and just go galloping off and doing their own thing all the time anyway. Me, I like a challenge, and he certainly was a challenge. He would have his way. I don't suppose I'd have wanted him if he was any different.

He sent me some lovely letters mind, very tender. Fairly heated me up reading them. Made me feel I could hardly wait to get me hands on him again. But yes, I knowed he was an excellent mariner and looked after his ship and his men well. Very highly thought of in the town. Then I got the telegrapher thing. Postman came all the way over to Blake Hill, on one of them new bicycle things I think they call them, sweating like my old pig by the time he got here. I made him a cup of tea, though I was near crying when I read the message. Jeremiah, my farmhand harnessed the horses into the delivery cart, and I went off into Poole at speed. I had to get advice and check up you see. Clearly that telegrapher thing had taken a time to reach me, across the world.

I needed to talk to my friends Ethelred and Lottie Teague. I needed sailing advice. How long would it take the Daphne to sail to Scotland? They would know who to ask. I needed to give the news to young Miss Lydia. I needed to go and ask Mr and Mrs Ross at the Pharmacy how long it would take me to get to Alloa on the railway line and ask them where I could find good clean lodgings up there in case I was there waiting a long time. Truly I was all of a vlummox. Well, things got a little bit sorted out fairly quickly. The man at the Shipping Office thought it would be a few weeks afore they were back, depending on winds and currents. Sounded very complicated. I had plenty of time to ask Mr Curtis and Ethelred and Lottie if young Lydia would be able to come with me. They said yes, but only if we had a 'male escort'! Of course, I have been perfectly well able to preserve my own virtue over all these years, and no varmint would tangle with me, but they insisted. Old Vasistha, my husband's steward was the right person to ask, as he wouldn't be likely to be a nuisance. I didn't like that hair oil that he uses. Oh dear, no, but he was quite good looking still, if you don't mind that sort of oil I suppose.

Mrs Ross was good enough to write to her mother, Mrs Maude for me, and had a letter back in two days. The old woman she shared her house with had recently died. She and her daughter Isa were certain that they could find space for the three of us. She recommended the train journey rather than the sea passage, but warned that we would need to be 'brave souls.' We left matters for two worrying weeks. Lydia and me took a trunk between us, plus hand baggage. We went Second Class on the train, and I bought old Vasistha a Third Class ticket.

Mrs Maude was right. The travelling was a nightmare. First off, I got an attack of 'the vapours', my age you see. Put the window down with that leather strap thing, and stuck my head out to get some air but all I got was a blast of smoke and black stuff in my eyes. That learned me. The privies at the stations was filthy. Lydia and me were each wearing a pair of drawers, you know, you put one leg into each one, draw them together with the string round the waist, so they was actually split in the vital area. We were able to stand with our legs spread in the street, and our skirts slightly hitched above our ankles and have a piss that way. As I said to Lydia, 'tis no good getting older if thee cassn't get crafty!'

Anyway, we took it easy, and stayed overnight at York and again at Edinburgh, before reaching Alloa on our third day. I'd never travelled outside of the Poole area in my life before. No more had Lydia. Old Vasistha never bothered nothing about any difficulties with travel, food or other people. I spose he was bold from travelling around the world with my husband all those years. He was very polite, called me mistress and Lydia missy. He took good care of us, our hand baggage and trunks. He was very firm with the cab drivers in York and Edinburgh. It felt very strange to me to be out with a dark, skinny heathen in white pyjamas. I heared it said that Queen Victoria had black servants too. He was cheap to keep as well, as he ate vegetables, saying 'to eat vegetables brings me greater rewards.' He explained that it was to do with being a Hindu. The poor man had some strange notion that killing poor helpless animals and eating them as food would bring him a bad karma, whatever that is. He was so pitifully convinced that meat would be bad for him that he admitted that he had never even tried it!

I just like food myself, and eat only the things I've raised for myself up at Blake Hill. Except for bread. I do buy in good flour to make my bread, but everything else, it's just there on the farm isn't it? By the time we finally got to Alloa in the late afternoon, my belly was fairly giving me hell, eating all that town and city food. I couldn't be doing with it, and was just waiting to get to Mrs Maude's house in Bank Street for a decent meal. Vasistha found a man with a handcart to take our luggage to Mrs Maude's house in Bank Street. Lydia and I walked. I thought it wasn't too bad as a town, not very much dirtier than Poole. Of course, I couldn't understand a word people was saying. They talked loudly, in deep voices, using words I'd never heared before. Vasistha didn't seem to care at all, as he'd had a lifetime of meeting queer foreigns all around the world. It was very much colder up there, and he was very shivery, in his --now very dirty- white pyjamas. We finally reached the house in Bank Street. In fact, to my mind, it wasn't a house at all, just two rooms upstairs, but it was in a very nice looking building. The stairs was very clean, and Mrs Maude come to the top of the stairs to greet us, and bring us into her kitchen, where she sat me by her lovely kitchen range. She had it well black leaded, with the steel bits looking like they'd been very recently polished with emery paper. She greeted me like an old friend, though I'd only met her just a couple of times before in Ross's Pharmacy. We had a battle to understand each other, as I think we were both broad in our local speech. I was thankful to have Lydia with me, as she was used to the way Mr and Mrs Ross spoke together. Anyway, we got along fine, and were very grateful to get a hot cup of tea and hot buttered girdle scones. As we ate, Mrs Maude told me how she'd planned for Vasistha to stay with her friends Mr and Mrs Lennox across the stair.

Lydia and me tried to be as helpful as possible to our friends. Mrs Maude had decided that we would share the kitchen bed, which was built into a kitchen alcove, behind a curtain. She said it would be warmer for us with the heat from the range. She and her elder daughter Isa would be staying in what she referred to as 'the room.' She proudly showed me a lovely parlour, which had a double built in bed in a cupboard at one end. She said that she did a 'fair bit' of what she called 'in and out' at all hours of the day and night, helping Dr Christie with expectant and nursing mothers. Her daughter Isa was hard at work in Paton's Mills, and when she wasn't at her work, she went out to the Greenbank Mission a lot. She seemed a bit worried as to what Isa would think when she met Vasistha. Isa was hoping one day to become a missionary in a heathen country. I was worried too. Vasistha had his ways, but I take no issue with folks that are different. I've had a lifetime of people in Parkstone village, and down in Poole calling me a 'one off' just because I've stuck in there, a woman in a man's world.

When Isa finally came home from Paton's mill where she worked as a fully trained carder, she was all smiles and welcome, just like her mother and younger sister. Clearly dead beat, she hurried into 'the room' to brush off the whisps of creamy wool that was sticking to her hair and clothes. Then she came into the kitchen to scrub the oily sweat and deposits from her hands and face.

'Mother says we could stuff pillows with the odds and ends that come home with me', she said cheerily, plonking herself down in a chair and accepting a cup of tea gratefully. Not just tired, she had rather a cough. She said the cough was because of all 'the flyings' in the factory air, in spite of the fan to keep the air moving out of the carding room. She smiled at Vasistha, and started telling us about a new young girl, Elspeth, who had just started in the carding room that week, and was working with her. Isa's responsibility was to feed the cleaned wool into one of the carding machines. The other end of the machine then sends thick slivers of wool into drums which fill quickly. Elspeth has to change the drums every few minutes. Isa said it is very tiring work for Elspeth, who is small and weak. This afternoon, the lass nearly fell onto the teeth of the huge machine, probably out of pure exhaustion. Mr Strachan the taskmaster for the carding room was just behind her at the time, and barely managed to snatch her from danger. The Forrester Patons were, Isa said, one of the best local employers, but the fact remained that those who put in a lifetime of work at the mill are likely to suffer. Most older workers end up looking bent at the shoulders and hollow chested from a lifetime of bending to their machines. Many older people in the town are deafened from hours and hours in the noisy factory, and have bad coughs and weak chests from constantly breathing in wool fibres.

Isa went on about how God was calling her to become a missionary like Mary Slessor. Mary had started out working in a jute mill in Dundee, but was now a missionary in the Calabar, converting black heathens to Christianity she explained, smiling at Vasistha. Miss Forrester Paton was starting a women's missionary home in Glasgow, and she hoped to be able to go there herself to get training. She ate her tea quickly, apologised and left, as she had work to do at the Greenbank Mission. We were all glad to get to bed early.

In the morning, having taken directions from Mrs Maude, I took Lydia and Vasistha with me down to the Shipping Office. I left a silver sixpence with the man in charge, asking him to pay a young man to run up to Bank Street as soon as Daphne was sighted, and we walked down to look at the docks. There seemed that there was a lot more going on at these docks than we was used to at Poole. We were told that there were many coal mines about, and that was powering the Glass Works and the local breweries and mills. Plenty of goods were being shipped out to other British towns and cities and overseas. There was plenty of work about, which was a real difference with Poole.

Reference

Reid S., 2002. Mill Girl. Pub. Scholastic Ltd.

Chapter Thirty Four

We settled into Mrs Maude's home fairly quickly. Mr and Mrs Lennox, an older couple who seemed fairly short of money were delighted to have Vasistha staying. Mrs Lennox offered to do the washing for the three of us as well. It was better that way. It was quickly clear to me that people in Alloa needed to have different ways of doing things, and washing and drying in their scotch weather was one of them. It gave Mrs Lennox a bit more money anyway. She said that Vasistha was very cheap to keep, and she'd never met a man with such an amazing liking for vegetables before. She tutted fondly about him walking around the place in pyjamas, and had already started knitting him a sweater in plain, undyed wool as he was finding the Scottish air cold. She was surprised to hear that I didn't knit normally -I think she meant like other women! So, we all got along well, but Vasistha ate and stayed most of his time across the stair, away from Isa's evangelical talk, which was luckily only coming in small doses.

We were in Alloa for nine days before a red, breathless young man come to Mrs Maude's door early on the Friday morning to tell us that the Daphne had slipped in on the high tide and was mooring. I couldn't help myself. Something snapped, and I cried, as I still had no means of knowing if my dear husband was still alive. This isn't like me at all. Lydia and Vasistha hurried me into my outdoor clothes, and went one on either side of me, down to the docks. The Daphne was made fast, and we shouted to get one of the crew to put a board over, so that we ladies could get on board. Vasistha had hopped over and left us standing. Harry ran down from the poop deck and managed to hand us over without a board. He hugged us together. 'You have come in time, he is still with us, though God alone knows how he found the strength' he said. We made our way aft, to my husband's cabin.

'Oh, you silly man!' I shouted when I got over to the poor old darling, who was lying in his bunk. 'Why ever couldn't you bide with me at Blake Hill?' He was breathing with difficulty, propped up on pillows. His face was gone awfully lean and grey, and his hair and beard were all over the place, tangled and long. I bent down to kiss him.

'You know there was always another woman, Daphne, and I am her Apollo' he said, 'but we finally agreed to go our separate ways somewhere in the middle of the Atlantic. The affair is finished. I'm all yours now.' He put his hand in my hair, and pulled me to him. We both cried.

When I looked round, Harry, Lydia and Vasistha had vanished, to plan what to do next. Harry and Lydia went back to Mrs Maude's, and fortunately she was back home from a local delivery.

Everything was arranged at Bank Street for my husband to be brought back to the house. He would be put in the recessed kitchen bed, and Lydia and I were to sleep on what was called a hurley bed, which rolled out from under the kitchen bed. I rather think Mrs Maude had planned for this already. Vasistha had called on Mrs Lennox, to ask where they might borrow a large handcart to bring my husband over from the ship, and he and Harry had managed to borrow one from the Co-Operative food store, where Mr Lennox worked. Lydia stayed back to help with the bed making and preparations in the kitchen.

My poor dear husband was carried out of his bunk on a piece of sailcloth by some of his crew, and arranged on the cart. Caleb Stone, Sean Reilly, Mathew O'Connor and Mr Hann came with us, as he would have to be carried two floors into the house. Although he must have needed Harry dearly, Mr Hann immediately discharged him of all his duties and set off back to the quay without even taking a cup of tea himself. They looked tired out and scrawny, all of those men. As we sat round the range with Mrs Maude, Harry gave us a brief account of all that had happened at sea. His hand was heavily bandaged with old rags that were none too clean, and Mrs Maude and I persuaded him to let us look to it. It was no pretty sight. The two fingers had been taken away at the knuckle. Lydia nearly fainted at the look of it, and had to be sent away off with Vasistha to Alec's old pharmacy for some special ointment.

Things began to come to an end. My dear James was able to have some of Mrs Maude's homemade lentil soup spooned into him during the evening, but even propped up, his breathing was very rough. Dr Christie came, and listened to his chest, and showed me James's swollen legs and stomach. 'His heart is just giving up,' he said. I could give him morphia to make him more comfortable, but it will speed his departure.' I asked James what we should do, and he grunted 'no', and held my hand a little tighter. Mrs Maude suggested that the Minister from the West Kirk should be sent for, and he squeezed my hand again, so that is what we did. Mrs Maude and the doctor didn't think he had long left. Vasistha, old, lean and strikingly fit, ran down to the docks again, and fetched Paul Hann, Edward, Sean, Mathew and Caleb back up to the house. They arrived slightly before Mr Brown, the Minister. I sat close to the bed, holding my dear James's hand. He was very distressed in his breathing.

The Minister was a very skinny, shy looking man, and I must confess, I didn't think nothing to him. He stood beside me, put his right hand firmly on my shoulder, and held James's shoulder firmly with his left hand, and then started off, from memory, saying loudly and firmly some verses from the bible, Romans, I think these were:

'The spirit bears witness with our spirit that we are the children of God.

We are heirs of God and joint heirs with Christ. If we suffer with him we shall also be glorified with him.

Who shall separate us from the love of Christ? Shall tribulation, or distress, or persecution, or famine, or nakedness, or peril, or sword?

No, in all these things we are more than conquerors through him who loved us.

For I am persuaded that neither death, nor life, nor angels, nor principalities, nor powers, nor things present nor things to come,

Nor height nor depth, nor any other creature, shall be able to separate us from the love of God, which is in Christ Jesus our Lord.'

As the minister spoke, I could see my husband's face relaxing slowly, and his breathing was easy, slow and shallow, until the last verse. He was dead. I kissed him, and remembered all those many kisses this dear man had given to all of us throughout his life. He was gentle and kind in all his ways. From the little I'd heard from Harry, James had clung on to life against all odds, just to be able to say he loved me, and kiss me for one last time. They left me with him, holding his hand. He was so peaceful now. I thanked God for the short time of my marriage, and the knowledge that I had Blake Hill Farm to go back to. I knew that I was going to spend a lot of time standing on my hill and thinking of him, as I watched the boats go in and out of Poole harbour.

We arranged the funeral in Alloa. The Reverend Brown was very kind, and helped us with all the arrangements. Some people found me rather hard to understand, allowing him to be buried in the Greenbank cemetery, and not taking him back to Poole, but when you're dead, you're dead, that's what I think. I knew his spirit will be hanging around with me everywhere I go, back at home. I was so grateful; James's crew, Mrs Maude and some of the neighbours from the stair in Bank Street were all there for the funeral. The crew especially wanted to sing something seafaring at the graveside. Isa helpfully suggested two hymns, which Caleb thought the Cap'n would really have liked. He and Harry went and borrowed hymnbooks from the Greenbank Mission, and practised with the mission's harmonium player. This was because the men, if they read at all, were very poor at it. Caleb, Harry and Isa, who sang well, were going to have to rehearse them. Vasistha decided that he wanted to join in, which Isa misinterpreted as a footstep on the road of salvation for him. The Reverend Brown was rather perplexed about all these strange hymns for the graveside, but felt better when I asked him if we could sing 'Be thou my vision' at the church. When I said we'd also like to have 'O love that will not let me go', he was delighted, as seemingly it had been written by a Scottish Minister.

My dear James was buried in his best seagoing clothes, stitched into a canvas by Mr Rogers, Daphne's sail maker. The Alloa weather, as usual, couldn't make up its mind, and on the day we had rain, wind, cloud and sunshine. The sun shone at the graveside, and everything went well. When James was lowered into the grave, the crew started singing

'Oh the deep, deep love of Jesus,
Vast, unmeasured, boundless, free
Rolling like a mighty ocean
In its fullness over me
Underneath me, all around me
Is the current of your love
Leading onward, leading homeward
To your glorious rest above.

Harry and Caleb never left my side, and their lovely singing voices never faltered. I bawled my eyes out, throughout all those beautiful verses, but I felt much better after. He had come back to me. We had said our goodbyes, and his precious Daphne had brought most of her crew home safe.

Mrs Maude had arranged for everyone to go back to her house for what she called 'a wee swally whisky to warm ourselves,' or tea for the abstainers. I kept a very hard eye on young Harry, who was very upset, but Lydia dealt with him, and he had umpteen cups of tea and ate up a stack of crumpets, buns and sandwiches that the neighbours had provided. Later, when the other guests had left, Paul and Harry had a serious word with Lydia and me. It was going to take a while for Daphne to be unloaded, have some essential repairs done and to be re-loaded with suitable cargo for Poole. We would be welcome to stay and wait for a passage back to Poole, or alternatively we could return by train. Paul was James's choice as Captain for the Daphne, and would retain the command he had taken when James became ill. Harry told us about his reconsideration of his role as a sailor, and that he was looking at other ideas. He put his arm around Lydia, and smiling at her, said that he hoped that their marriage would not be delayed and that he hoped never to be too far away from her ever again. He and Paul had talked things over, and Paul would be looking to sign a new first mate. Paul punched Harry playfully, saying 'They'll never be as good as you, mate!' Harry said he would be travelling back to Poole with us, to make his home at the Poop Deck with Vasistha, and he and Lydia were planning, all being well, for a marriage at St Mary and St Philomena's church in Poole as soon as possible. Frankly, Catholics aren't popular at all, oh no! I can remember seeing people throwing stones at a catholic priest as he walked down the High Street. I was happy enough to go along with what the young couple wanted. I couldn't give horse's dingle-dangle what they did as long as it was legal. I could see their path wouldn't be easy though, as I didn't think that the other members of the family would care to attend a wedding in Latin.

LYDIA

Chapter Thirty Five

Poor, poor Mrs Lovejoy. She was married for such a short time, and only actually shared a home and bed with her husband for an even shorter period. I was so glad that I had been allowed to go with her up to Alloa to meet the ship. The pair of us had made a journey of a length and complexity that few women would ever have the opportunity to do in our lifetime. She is such a brave, strong woman, and made such a splendid consort for our dear Captain. We were all, Mrs Lovejoy, Harry, Vasistha and I, very quiet on our journey home to Poole.

For my part, sorrow was partly mitigated by the hope that Harry and I would soon be married. My family had been utterly against me joining the Roman Church, and the divisions that it would mean between us. However my father had already allowed me to take this step once it was clear that I was very determined, without any further spoken criticism. At Teagues, I know my grandparents dearly wished that I would change my mind. My attendance at St Mary and St Philomena's Church was tolerated and finally accepted, just as Wesley's commitment to Methodism was acknowledged. I could already see further pain for my family in the future regarding the actual ceremony. I slotted quickly back into my normal routines. Wesley had looked after Zephyr well, and it was a delight to caress his furry coat and silky ears again. I was delighted to hear that at some stage in the future, dear Wesley would be promoted from deliveries to take a position in the shop second to Mr Belben, the 'Senior Man'. I think that Grandmother and Grandfather were making a public admission that they 'were not getting any younger'. They were taking Wesley with them to an appointment at the Union Workhouse to see if there was a suitable lad for Wesley to 'train up' to fill his current duties.

I started back at Ross's Pharmacy almost immediately, and things seemed to be running fine. Alec seemed fairly calm again, and the business was continuing to build up slowly. At lunchtime, we sat in the room behind the shop, eating our lunch, Phemie with young Hugh clasped to her breast. They wanted to know every detail of the sad events in Alloa, and although the telling of it was a tearful experience for me, the tears were slowly easing the pain of my grief.

'I was so glad that you were able to stay with Ma and Isa', Phemie commented, wiping her eyes.

'Mrs Maude, Isa and the neighbours round about couldn't have been kinder' I assured her.

Alec laid his hand on top of mine and said 'The more we see of you, the more you feel like a member of our very own family, Lydia.' I shed a few more gentle tears then. My childhood had not been good in many respects, but it certainly made me really appreciate my good friends and my family.

Phemie passed on good news from the town. Mrs Negus had produced a little daughter, who would be christened Esther on Sunday. I felt really sad that I wouldn't be able to go to the christening, as my change of faith made it impossible for me to associate on a spiritual level any more with the rest of my friends and family in terms of attending their church services and ceremonies. Even taking part in daily prayers at Teagues was really forbidden. However this was a piece of advice that I forgot as soon as it was given! Things were getting very serious indeed on the church front, as Harry and I were to be accepted into the Catholic Church at Easter, on Sunday 17th April, which was just two weeks away. We would have to be conditionally re-baptized and re-confirmed at the ceremony, as the Catholic Church did not recognize our previous Anglican sacraments. A week after this, our wedding was planned.

I was eagerly anticipating this. Unlike other young women, I already knew rather a lot about the actual 'marriage act' through my friendship with Phemie and the discussions about matters surrounding this at the back of the shop. Grandmother was particularly sweet with me. One quiet afternoon, she took me upstairs to the parlour, and asked me if I knew what to expect of my husband. I said 'Thank you. Phemie has already told me a lot.' She smiled, and suggested that as the time was now getting short before the wedding, Harry and I should seek opportunities to be alone in each others' company. 'There is no harm at all in feeling each other, even inside one's clothes at this stage, as it will make everything much easier later', she suggested. 'Ethelred and I did. What you do together in your marriage is not shameful, and should give pleasure to both of you.' I was really surprised when she told me that my Mother's birth had been so very difficult, and that she had been told by the doctor that another child could be the death of her. 'It was very, very hard for both of us, but Ethelred did nothing with me to cause another child for many years' she said, her eyes looking watery. 'It was only when I reached a certain age that we were able to come together again.' I was glad that she had told me, as it explained a lot about their very close relationship. We shared a lengthy hug.

Harry and I spent as much time as we could together in the parlour, confident that Grandmother and Grandfather would make a lot of noise coming up the stairs, and probably bang their bedroom door unnecessarily before entering the parlour. If they could hear me playing the piano, they entered the room with confidence! In my developing love for Harry I felt increasingly defenceless, disordered, exhilarated, and intoxicated with the intimacy of our physical feelings and emotional closeness.

One of the first calls that Harry and I made together after our return was to Mrs Lovejoy at Blake Hill Farm. He hired a fly from the station. I became aware just how much the loss of his fingers was affecting him when I saw him with the reins in his hands as we drove out during the afternoon. The farm seemed almost deserted. Jeremiah the live in farmhand and a small man who was known to everybody in Parkstone village as 'Piglet' appea396 eventually when we had been searching and shouting for a while. Mrs Lovejoy was nowhere to be seen, and the kitchen didn't look as if anything much had been done in terms of bread making or any other form of cookery since her return. I asked Jeremiah exactly what was happening and where his mistress was. 'We jus cassn't get er to come into the 'ouse' he said. 'She's been up on that there hill ever since 'er come back. I've taken er a chair to sit on an' a rug.'

'You should have sent word before. Leave this with us now', Harry said, giving Jeremiah a look of dismissal. At least Jeremiah had kept the range going to feed himself and Piglet. Harry took the kettle from the hob, made a jug of tea and wrapped it in a clean towel. The afternoon was warm, but breezy. It was a fair step from the farmhouse to get to the hill, and I was quite out of breath by the time we had scrambled through the gorse bushes and over the gravelly soil up to the top. Caroline was up there in a wooden armchair, with just three scrawny windblown pine trees to keep her company. Her blue eyes looked quite wild, and she didn't take them off the harbour entrance. It was a wonderful clear view. I think she was watching the narrow entrance to the harbour, and the place where the navigation channel passes in front of Brownsea Island. The wind was gently blowing through her long, white, unbraided hair. She looked at us as if we were strangers. 'I'm looking and looking for 'im to come ome,' she said. I was quite shocked to see her utter devastation, as Mistress Caroline had always seemed the epitome of female strength.

Harry put his arms round her, and said 'My dear mother, you know we will none of us see him again in this lifetime, but he still lives in our hearts.'

She was very cold and weak from sitting up there without food or drink, for such a long time. We made her drink most of the warm tea, and then, one on either side of her we helped her down the hill and into the farmhouse. As there was no bread, I found some oats and made her some slack porridge, which she ate, and started to look a little better. Harry and I made a plan. We were both very, very concerned about her, but Harry felt that we would be better to return to Poole. We would buy some bread to keep her going until she was well enough to bake again, and send Vasistha to deliver it and to stay and care for her in the meantime. If matters did not improve, he could send a message back to us for further help. Harry felt that she would be better to try and get back into her familiar routines as soon as possible. She had taken a real shine to Vasistha, and he had an uncanny knack when it came to getting her to accept his help. Harry gave Jeremiah a severe talking to for not sending us a message, and telling him not to leave her alone to grieve any more, but to keep asking for her help with the animals and other matters on the farm, and at least keep her moving around. Harry dropped me off at Inglewood for my music lesson, and returned to Poole alone.

The days flew past, and the day of our wedding grew nearer. Mrs Lovejoy and Vasistha moved into the Poop Deck two days before the event, to 'get everything shipshape.' The Capn's berth was moved out of the room on the first floor, and a double bed installed for us by the two of them. She shouted at poor Vasistha quite a lot, but he seemed to take it in good part. It was marvellous to see her so much better.

Monday morning, 25th April finally dawned. The day began as usual at Teagues, with morning prayers. At 10.30 my grandparents and I went upstairs to change. I put on my chemise but then had to ask Lucy, our senior house servant to help me into my new, long corset. It was a splendid thing, all shell pink with great long laces, and I ended up with an S shaped figure. I was unrelentingly kept in shape, and felt like Queen Boadicea, encased in battle armour. It was quite a cold day, so I put my drawers and four petticoats on under my blue wedding dress. The dress was going to be very suitable for 'best' wear later. Father and Mr Eeles, a catholic friend of his who was going to 'give me away' arrived in a carriage at about 11.30. Grandfather, Grandmother, Michael, 'Babs' and Wesley left the shop on foot, slightly earlier, for the church. I couldn't help noticing that Wesley had turned into a devastatingly handsome and charming young man.

As I entered the church, I noted that despite all her loud grumbling about Papists, Mrs Lovejoy was present, with, even more surprisingly, Vasistha at her side, wearing some very new white pyjamas that she had made for him. I could see my darling Harry at the front of the church, with his back to me. He was wearing a new, slightly shorter pea jacket. I walked confidently to the front of the church with Mr Eels's arm to rest on. The marriage service was very brief, the Parish Priest officiated, and I received my wedding ring and the ceremonial gifts of gold and silver from my darling in the form of a golden sovereign and a silver half crown. A nuptial mass followed, and the few Catholics present participated, then the wedding party adjourned to the Council Chamber on the upper floor of the Guildhall, where lunch was served.

Chapter Thirty Six

Our lives as young Mr and Mrs Lovejoy began to settle down. The Daphne returned to Poole, and surprisingly, after everything that they had been through in her together, Harry and Paul decided to take her to London and sell her. She had developed a slow leak, and Paul and the shipwrights in Alloa had been unable to detect the problem. They suspected that deep in her hull, there were rotten boards. Harry split the sum they eventually raised equally between them. He also split the profits from Daphne's last trip with Paul, in the hope that Paul might someday be able to buy a share in a ship of his own. Paul came to stay with us for a while at the Poop Deck, whilst they decided their separate futures. Paul chose eventually to transfer to steamships, and went to Southampton where he initially accepted a second mate's position. This was because he had a lot to learn, as obviously a steamship is entirely different.

Harry decided to use some of his money to purchase a fishing boat. He asked his friends Sean Reilly, Mathew O'Connor and Caleb Stone, who were looking for shore work, to dinner with us. He enquired if they were interested in fishing from Poole? They were, and agreed to go to Newlyn in Cornwall with him that week to look at some boats that he had heard about. Those three men were rough, but I loved them too. It was lovely to see them so filled with enthusiasm. Caleb's wife and family had long been hoping that one day he could spend more time with them. Mathew and Sean were dreading the prospect of needing to sign with another ship. From what Harry had told me, some Masters and crews could be diabolical and the conditions for the seamen really dreadful. As soon as they had finished their dinner, the four of them went up to the railway station to check the trains. Harry came back and told me that it would be a long day travelling, and that they would be going on Wednesday. They would have to go to Newquay and hope that a fishing boat would take them down to Newlyn.

We were so newly married that we could hardly bear to part with each other. I packed two big baskets with food for the four of them. They were hoping to find a suitable boat and sail it back together. I was really quite worried since Harry now had only one good hand, but I now fully understood that they all knew their ropes! I completely lost my appetite whilst he was away, and got quite thin. As things turned out, they were actually away for two weeks. Harry wrote every day and let me know how things were going along. He had bought a new boat, and needed to try it out first. It had to be rigged and fitted with sails, so they did amazingly well to do so much in the time. I missed him so much.

They arrived back late on a Sunday, and were full of stories about the great time they'd had together. They'd bought a new fifty foot Newlyn style lugger, which sailed so fast that they'd had to tie ropes to two buckets and tow them at the stern of the boat as 'brakes' as she was coming into the Poole harbour channel so fast. Over an improvised meal, discussion was had about naming the new vessel, as the men all wanted a suitable successor to Cap'n Lovejoy's Daphne, so another Greek goddess was considered appropriate. As the only person who knew about such a subject, Harry was asked to make some suggestions. He first of all suggested as Hera as she was 'the protector of marriage.' However he then remembered that she was very jealous of other women, and wasn't very nice to anyone, including her children. The discussions, only fuelled by cups of tea became quite raucous. In the end, we all agreed on Artemis, the goddess of hunting as being suitable for a fishing boat. Artemis was also reputed to be exquisite in appearance, and, Harry said, looking at me 'she is the goddess of the moonlight and of childbirth, and the protector of young suckling animals.' I felt myself flushing deeply.

The days passed in a whirl of energy for both Harry and me. He was registering and insuring the Artemis and with the help of fishing friends was getting her equipped for her fishing career. He had also hired a medium sized warehouse on the quay front for the business he intended to set up as a 'general dealer.' That is to say, he planned to buy and sell whole cargoes and make use of all the careful teaching he had received from his father. I breathed a great sigh of relief at this, as I understood then that the Artemis was really for Caleb Stone to skipper, with Sean and Mathew as his mates. Harry, recognizing the problems with his hand, would not sail with her on every trip once all three were fully competent in all conditions and the criteria of the Sea Fisheries Act would need to be met. His friends should be able to earn themselves a very good living locally and Mathew and Sean could put down some permanent roots in the town. Doubtless our household would be regularly supplied with superb fish.

I remained busy too. Harry had also given Edward a job as 'house steward and cook' assisted by Vasistha who was back home with us. This had always been the arrangement when the old Cap'n was in port. I was thus given the opportunity to continue at the pharmacy, despite being a married lady who had no worries about money. I was also continuing with my musical theory training from Mr Short, but was given no further opportunities to play the church organ. I had been obliged to stop playing the piano at protestant church meetings. I still went to my piano sessions with Mr Aldridge at Inglewood, and taught my private pupils two afternoons a week on the piano in Teagues' parlour. There was just one little fly in the ointment domestically. I was not yet pregnant. Harry and I were having great times together, and often, but there was no sign of a child yet. Phemie was saying not to fuss, things happen in their own time, but I knew how much it meant to Harry. Every month, when I saw the first few spots of blood, I had a little cry, and Phemie who was very sensitive, could always tell by the look on my face when I came to work, and gave me a special little cuddle. She was already expecting her second, but said to me that it was good that Harry and I should be having a little time on our own, before our own family came.

Harry and I enjoyed some wonderful days out that summer. One Saturday we went on the paddle steamer from Poole to Swanage, and walked up to Durlston Head and saw Mr Mowlem's great globe. He gave me sailing lessons in Cap'n Lovejoy's little old dinghy, we sailed round Old Harry and his wife and watched the boats being loaded with stone at Seacombe. On another day we went to Tyneham, anchored the boat and walked up the track into the tiny village. I felt so happy and alive.

By September, Harry announced that he was planning a little break for the pair of us away from the sea. He was very mysterious, and said that it could only be done if the weather was set fair and the moon was in the ascendant. We packed old, warm clothes, and he said we needed to be prepared to spend a few days away. The adventure started at Poole railway station, and we chuffed through some beautiful countryside to Dorchester. We then caught a train from the West Station to Maiden Newton, where we alighted at a beautiful little station on the edge of a tiny village. Having found a clean cottage where a widow was willing to take us in for bed and board, Harry spent most of the afternoon trying to find a carrier to take us on to Cerne Abbas the following day. As we bounced about on the cart, I felt silent indignation as the carter who had few teeth and was extremely ugly kept smirking at me. We took a room at the New Inn, which looked distinctly old, and Mr and Mrs Buck, our hosts kept giving us sideways glances. Perhaps they were wondering why Harry had brought me to such a tiny village with such an enormous rude man pictured on the hillside. I had heard that there was a far more respectable chalk picture of King George the Third on a hillside outside Weymouth that was particularly handsome. At the time, I would have preferred to see that.

We had an excellent meal of roast lamb before retiring to our room. I was feeling quite woozy and relaxed after two glasses of port. Harry then suggested a walk, and advised me to wrap up very warmly, although it was a very balmy night. He had a very quiet chat with Mr Buck before we went out, and I saw him pocket a key. We went on a very long walk, which took us right up on to the giant. He took me right up to the giant's rudest part, sat me down, and began to make languorous love to me. We fell asleep in each others' arms. We didn't wake until dawn was nearly on us, and made haste back to the New Inn, where Harry produced a key from his pocket, and let us back in quietly. 'What is the meaning of this strange trip?' I asked him when we were safely in our little bed.

'There's a superstition locally that if a couple sleep with the Giant, the woman will very soon become pregnant' he replied.

'Oh, you and your superstitions!' I said. 'You're as bad as your father!'

Perhaps there was some truth in the old myth, because the expected never came that month. I started to have a complete aversion to tea and coffee and wanted nothing to drink except soda water from the Pharmacy. Phemie and Alec were delighted. 'Will I have to stop work?' I asked Alec.

'Well, my dear,' he said, 'Folks seem to get embarrassed about seeing a lady about who is obviously in a certain condition. When it begins to show, you can work with Phemie and me behind the dispensary screen. That way no one can be offended, you will have the chance to sit down and the apprentices and I will have to take turns at the front of the shop. Ladies who need something in particular generally call to the back door to see Phemie anyway.'

I did stop my music lessons with Mr Short and Mr Aldridge in the afternoons. Harry bought me a beautiful piano and installed it in the ground floor room at the Poop Deck, so I was able to get plenty of practice in the afternoons without leaving the house. I still taught my pupils on Monday afternoons at Teagues. Their parents probably wouldn't have liked them coming down to the quay, as it was so dirty, noisy and dangerous. My surroundings didn't bother me at all, as I loved the Poop Deck and its male residents!

Chapter Thirty Seven

It wasn't very long at all before Phemie had a further visit from Mrs Maude to attend her second birth. She confessed to me that she was more worried about Alec 'losing the head' as she put it, than the birth itself. It was pure delight to see Mrs Maude again, and Mrs Lovejoy came into town a couple of days later to see her, bearing edible gifts. She immediately invited Mrs Maude to spend a night or two at Blake Hill, if she and Phemie thought it would be all right. The two of them left within the hour, sitting beside each other on the cart. Mrs Maude returned a couple of days later, waxing lyrical about the view from Mrs Lovejoy's hill.

It was well that Mrs Maude had arrived in good time, as Phemie went into labour two weeks before the date she had calculated for herself. It had been made clear to me from the beginning that I was not to be in the house or shop once labour began. Mrs Maude explained, putting her arm protectively around my shoulders that this was no place for an expectant mother. Things sometimes did not go according to plan, with either the mother or child, and she didn't want me to be 'feared' unnecessarily as each birth should as far as possible be approached by the mother with an open mind. The Ross's second son, Jock was born at 10pm one Thursday night, after a short labour, so as things turned out, I did not miss any work. Alec had been present, and helped out. When I saw him on the Friday morning he was highly emotional, his eyes pouring tears readily. 'I'm just so, so sorry that I wasn't able to be with her for Hugh', he kept saying.

It didn't seem very long before my turn came round. Phemie said that she would not be able to help for two reasons. One was that I was such a close friend that it would not be right, and the second was that she had not delivered a babe herself for several years. Harry had insisted on booking Dr Mullins for the delivery. Under the circumstances it seemed best, as the Parish Midwife had a very poor record. Two of the recent babies that she delivered had died at birth, and one local mother had died of childbed fever within ten days of giving birth to a beautiful little girl. I asked Harry about getting a woman to help us in the house during my lying in. He laughed, and said that he would help with anything personal that I needed, and that Edward was very highly experienced in all of the other matters, particularly the washing. 'How on earth do you think we managed the birth on the ship,' he said laughing.

Grandmother thought that our arrangements were all highly unusual, and said that she had heard people talking about us in the town. I didn't really care. Most people thought that we had a very odd household anyway. In the end, Mrs Lovejoy said that she would leave Jeremiah and Piglet 'on trust' at the farm, and would come over immediately anything started, so Grandmother was satisfied. I didn't have an easy time of it in some respects. My labour started so subtly, that it wasn't until I had very obvious pains at three minute intervals that I realized anything was happening. Fortunately Harry was in his warehouse and Vasistha was able to fetch him home quickly. Edward ran for the doctor, who was nowhere to be found. Harry and I were getting desperate as the pains were continual, so Harry sent Edward back out to see if Phemie would agree to come. Thank goodness she did. Apparently the cord joining my baby to me was wrapped round his neck, he wasn't getting pushed out and was in danger of strangulation. After the birth, Phemie said it was fortunate that she had brought her 'instruments' with her, and that she had once dealt with a similar problem when she was working in Alloa. Doctor Mullins finally turned up after young Victor and I had been washed, and he was having his first feed. The doctor started getting very angry with Phemie, accusing her of costing him his fee. Harry just turned him round and pushed him out of the door, saying 'Without the help of this dear lady, I would have lost my son.' Mrs Lovejoy was as pleased with Victor as if he had been her very own child. She was only able to stay for two days after his birth, and left the house saying 'Juss like his father. Coulda bin peas in a pod.'

It was Harry who decided to call our son Victor. We had already agreed that he could name our boys, and I would name the girls. He was still feeling silently upset that year about the loss of his fingers, and had in the Summer come up with the idea that he, Caleb and 'the crew' would take some time off and try to see Nelson's ship 'The Victory' which was moored at Portsmouth. They disappeared in the Artemis for three days, and had a fine old time. How on earth they were able to bribe their way into the dockyard, I don't know, but Harry was very taken with the old ship. He'd even bought a picture, which he had framed. I think he took the view that Victor's name would give him a connection with the sea.

It was quickly clear to me that Harry had been wrong in suggesting that we could do without further help in the house. I couldn't really send Edward out pushing the perambulator for me, although he frequently offered. It just wasn't done, and I very much wanted to get back to my work. Victor was always welcome at Phemie's, where she had Jane to help her with the boys. I was very aware of how bad the air was outside our house on the quay, and its close proximity to the gas works. I needed someone to help me look after Victor when I was busy, and push him around the park to get some clean air. Eventually I was able to find an older woman, Mrs Green, to help me from Monday to Saturday, and so I was able to go back to the Pharmacy when Victor was six months old. I went to work in the morning, and if Victor needed a feed, Mrs Green brought him to me. I know that people said horrid things about me along the lines of 'It's not done, you know, to go to work and leave such a young baby.' However, at least I wasn't leaving him alone in some frightful room, alone, like the poor had to. Neither was I abandoning him to a permanent nanny for weeks on end like the rich. Victor was both wanted and loved, not just by me, but my family and friends too. He wasn't easy to rear. Obviously I fed him myself. No wet nurse was involved. He cried a lot, particularly at night, drawing his little legs up in pain. Phemie said he was a very colicky baby, and advised a patent medicine,

Dinnefords gripe water, which seemed to ease him a bit. Alec said he couldn't advise anything better.

The nappies from young Victor were something else. Well, not just the nappies, his clothes as well. When he moved his bowels, which he did frequently, it went everywhere, often reaching the hair at the back of his head. Dr Mullins was no use at all with this problem. We just had to deal with it. Mrs Green said that townspeople, putting their faces up to the hood of the perambulator to see the baby were frequently repelled by the sulphurous fumes! I couldn't care about that. I was glad they had reason to keep their snivelling noses away from my little darling. I just wished I could find a way to make his little tummy easier. When it came to weaning him from my breast, he quickly took to vegetables, but seemed to have a huge dislike for meat. Dr Mullins had no useful suggestions for dealing with this further problem with the little mite. Phemie and Alec encouraged me, saying 'At least he's not ailing.' Indeed he wasn't. He was a sturdy little chap, and Harry and I were so proud of him.

It wasn't very long before I was expecting again, but with no help from the Cerne Giant this time! I hadn't done anything to avoid this happy situation, and Harry and I were delighted. Jason came just eighteen months after Victor, in late 1891. I was very much more uncomfortable by the end of my second pregnancy. Dr Mullins, who examined me through a sheet spread over me, said that I could expect to produce a very large baby indeed. I had an awful time in labour. Dr Mullins eventually gave me Chloroform, and hauled my baby out with a pair of instruments. Harry had gone out that afternoon for a few hours fishing, and I was so glad that Edward sent Vasistha out to fetch Phemie to help the Doctor. Grandmother came round as soon as she could, and arrived tired and breathless. She was beginning to show her age.

She was very upset to learn that I was 'so beat about down below'. When Harry finally showed up, having missed everything, she was quite cross with him, and told him 'No more my lad!' He promised.

I smiled secretly at Phemie. We had yet to find out for ourselves, from practical experience whether all the bits and pieces we were selling at the pharmacy with such confidence would actually work for us. Harry called our second son Jason, after the Greek hero of mythology, who sailed the ship Argo, and had exciting adventures. He was easier to rear than Victor, growing up very big and strong, with a huge appetite, unlike his older brother who was very picky with his food, and still tended to eat only vegetables, and occasional fish. I would have worried more about Victor, if I hadn't known that Vasistha had for all his life only ever eaten vegetables, because of his faith. Mrs Lovejoy kept saying that the air on the quay must be bad for the boys growing up, and pointing out that Harry had been reared at Blake Hill. There was nothing much we could do about that, but the four of us went over to Blake Hill to stay every other weekend.

Harry seemed to get busier and busier building up his business on the quay. He was elected to the town council, which pleased Grandfather no end. He was particularly pleased that Harry was a Liberal too. We had been married for three years when we were invited to a 'business discussion' over a dinner at Teagues. We had been sensing for a while that there was something on their minds. Wesley was unsurprisingly excelling in his new position in the shop. He was now occupying my former room on the first floor, and normally dined upstairs in the evenings with my grandparents. On this particular evening, he was out, visiting his young lady and her parents.

'I won't beat about the bush with this matter' began Grandfather with an air of determination. 'Lottie and I are in our fifties now, and won't last forever. We have considered the future of Teagues' Grocery business very carefully. Wesley is now giving us valuable help that we need in the day to day management of the store, and we need to know that when we are gone, it will continue to exist, not just as a good grocery, but as a social project. We are proposing to make him our heir apparent so as to speak.'

Harry put his right hand over mine, and we smiled at each other. 'I think I speak for both of us,' he said. 'We hope you both live forever. However, we would be delighted if Wesley inherited the business.'

'There is precious little money to leave to anyone' said Grandmother smiling back. 'You both know that we live reasonably well day to day, but our main object is to re-invest what we have in the others around us.'

'What about Michael, since he is your grandson, and possibly should inherit?'

'Michael has benefitted from a fine education, will do well for himself, and should inherit substantial funds from his father when the time comes. More than leaving the business to one of our family in due course, we need the help with the shop and it's management now, and are likely to need the help a lot more in the future,' answered Grandfather. 'Besides,' he continued, smiling 'It would be good to see Wesley married and with a secure future.'

Harry and I smiled at each other again. On the way up to Teagues, we had already been discussing the problems with the business. In my opinion, Mr Belben the senior man must already be over seventy, and was not wearing well at all, being noticeably shaky. They were giving him less and less to do. We supposed that they didn't want to retire him, as they didn't know how he could live without his wages. We had already suggested to each other that Wesley could manage the shop wonderfully well, as we had no desire to perpetuate the little world of Teagues ourselves.

Chapter Thirty Eight

I continued to enjoy life. Besides my little routines of working at Ross's Pharmacy six mornings a week and teaching the piano two afternoons a week in the parlour at Teagues, I became very friendly with Mrs Negus. Both our husbands worked very hard, shared an interest in politics, and were friendly, although their politics were diametrically opposed. This additional friendship was quite helpful for both of us. Our children often played together, and we regularly visited each others' homes. In fact, without making any fuss about it, Mary Negus produced a total of six children, Esther, John, Ellen, Little Mary, Grace and Cecil, and reared them well with Mrs Cox's help.

Mrs Cox and Cotton continued to 'live in', as Mr Negus had divided one of the attic rooms for them to release space for his growing family. Cotton was a darling. We all loved him, and Mary would often say that she blessed the day the two of them came to her door. Mary tried to keep him busy with little jobs he could manage so that she and Mrs Cox could 'get on with things' as otherwise he would be fidgeting about looking for something to do all the time. She told all her children not to worry about getting their shoes and boots dirty, as Cotton would clean them. Young Esther, or Essie as her family called her, said that Cotton had once cleaned her shoes and boots seven times in one day! It was just as well that they had taken him in. The dear boy was a very slow learner, and as he grew, looked increasingly blue in the face and poorly. He liked the shoe cleaning, and it didn't tax him beyond his limited energies.

Mr Negus was a very funny man in his own home. I had only ever seen him being terribly stiff and serious around the town, but his younger wife and growing family were really bringing him out of himself. He was not at all the stiff sober undertaker with his family. He carried the sunshine of good humour around with him. The whole family understood exactly how he gained his main income. Victor and Jason came in from the garden one day, enthusiastically describing the funeral of the Negus cat which had been carried out by Mr Negus, with full pomp. Essie had read a little eulogy regarding Pussy's many attributes. When the grave had time to settle, a tiny marble stone was erected to

'Pussy, our beloved cat. Requiascat in pace. 1891-1899'.

You never knew what Mr Negus was going to do or say next when he was at home. Victor, Jason and I were sitting round their table one Winter lunchtime, when the frost still lay hard on the ground. He came in and said brightly 'things are getting so bad down at the cemetery that the grave digger says he hasn't buried a living soul for weeks. What's for lunch?' When he noticed that young Cecil had a cough, he smiled and said 'It wasn't the cough that carried him off', and his children shouted 'it was the coffin they carried him off in!' He followed this with 'Why is the graveyard such a noisy place?' The children chorused 'Because of all the coffin!!'

I found my own Victor and Jason quite hard work to manage, with all their energy and questions, but the Negus's eldest, Essie proved to be a worse handful to her frequently harassed mother. She had, like her father, an irrepressible sense of humour, which was always getting her in trouble at Miss Biles's school. She had a dreadful reputation for 'cheek', and was forever suffering from small punishments such as getting her comb confiscated. This was a disaster for Essie, who was inordinately proud of her honey fair hair. Notes regarding her poor behaviour were frequently sent home from the school. She did quite dreadful things like dipping the fair plaits of the girl sitting in front of her into her inkwell, and on one awful occasion actually tied this poor child's plaits to her chair. Mary reached complete exasperation on the day that Essie, who had a fine singing voice was reported for singing her own version of 'Linden Lea' at a parents' afternoon. Miss Biles attended personally to tell Mary that Essie had sung the first verse thus:

'Within the woodland flow'ry gladed
By the oak tree's mossy root,

The shining grass blades, timber shaded
Now do quiver underfoot.
And birds do whistle overhead
And water's bubbling in its bed
And there for me the apple tree
Do lean down low in Linda's wee!'

At this juncture, Mr Negus came in from his workshops at the side of the house for a cup of tea, leaving a trail of fine, curly wood shavings all over the floorboards. He nodded at Miss Biles and myself, and said 'My dear wife, I am craving for a cup of tea. I am utterly exhausted from my work ensuring that my dear customers lie comfortably in their graves.'

I looked at Miss Biles's bitter, yellowed face and saw her give him a look which would have curdled milk instantly, and hastily got up to say that it was time for Victor, Jason and I to go home, and would Jack, their eldest son care to come with us to play?

Anyway, the result of Essie's latest misdemeanour was that her parents moved her to another school, where the mistress recognised her low boredom threshold. She was clearly a highly intelligent child and needed to be kept busier. I was asked to give her weekly lessons on the pianoforte, which I happily agreed to do. She would be the first person in her family to learn to play a musical instrument and her parents were quite excited. She was my favourite pupil, brimming over with life, enthusiasm and humour, with a natural talent for the pianoforte. It wasn't very long before she was taking lessons on the mandolin too. She had a marvellous singing voice, sang a lot under my tutelage, and as she grew up was in great demand as a soloist at womens' church meetings. This was despite not getting along at all well with Mr Short the organist at St James's. She studied a vast collection of music, and I was told she was fond of impromptu singing of very loud, beautiful soprano descants at Christmas, Easter and other high days and holidays from her position in the congregation. I heard that the choleric Mr Short went an even deeper shade of puce than usual, and the men of the choir tittered. The Minister never reproved her, which made Mr Short madder.

My own family was as problematic as Mary's, but in different ways. Victor remained strongly built, but continued to have frequent agonizing digestive problems. He often lay racked with pain, doubled up on his bed. Alec and Phemie at the pharmacy were still of more help to him than the doctor. They regularly made him a special black walnut leaf tincture and recommended chamomile tea. Mrs Lovejoy helped with producing plenty of the herbs. On Alec's advice, she also cultivated aloe vera and occasionally when Victor was in a lot of pain, we gave him a few drops of the juice. He simply adored being with his step-grandmother at Blake Hill, and was already saying things like 'When I grow up, I want to be a farmer like Nanna'. Although he had no blood ties to Mrs Lovejoy, he seemed to have a lot of the same qualities. Even as a little boy, he seemed to have no fear of the farm animals, and from the age of about seven, showed the ability to ride nearly any beast on the farm bareback. He had trained himself initially on the sheep. He still had a great aversion to meat, and wouldn't learn such farm tasks as wringing a chicken's neck and plucking and drawing it, or preparing game. On the occasions when one of his beloved pigs had to die, he had to be kept completely away from Blake Hill, and grieved for the animal's loss.

Jason was very different. He loved the sea. As a family we often went out, particularly on summer evenings, in our little family sailing boat, and the boys pretended to be pirates sailing the seven seas. Both learned to swim in the warm, shallow waters of the inner harbour. Jason was always very protective of his older brother. At school, Victor tended to be picked on by the other lads. He was very strong as a result of all his farming interests, but would never bother to defend himself if the other boys involved him in a scrap in the yard. Jason however, often came home very beat up, having engaged in fights on Victor's behalf. Harry began to get very worried about the growing Jason, who seemed to be developing a very aggressive streak in him, and confided that he hoped that Jason never took to drink. In an effort to find Jason some more suitable outlets for his energies he encouraged him to attend the gymnasium regularly, and play football and rugby. As he grew older, he was allowed to go on fishing trips with his father and the crew in the Artemis.

Socially, our lives weren't simple. The move into Roman Catholicism had not been easy for our friends to understand. Many people in the town saw the Catholic Church as idolatrous. Phemie and Alec were never critical of our decision, but they had recently decided to become Quakers, and said they found it difficult to understand the Catholic reliance on sacraments and images. Their own faiths had, in different ways to ours, become deeper. Phemie said the peaceful Quaker way of worship and simpler approach to life had been of great benefit to Alec, and he said he 'felt that the Quakers are very accepting of my difficulties, and positively helpful.' He was particularly fond of Mrs Cox's son, Cotton, of whom he often said 'God himself shows respect to each one of us, in all our differences and difficulties.'

Phemie and Alec just loved having children. After Hugh and Jock, Agnes, Morag, Andrew (Sandy) and Douglas followed in quick succession. Sadly, little Sandy had club feet. No amount of binding and splinting cured the problem, and he walked slowly, with great difficulty. His parents were hard put to it to keep him in shoe leather.

In 1912 a serious tragedy occurred. It cemented the close relationships between the Ross, Negus and Lovejoy families. It was the school summer holidays. Cecil, Charles and Mary Negus's eleven year old son had been out playing with Douglas Ross at Longfleet Farm, when Cecil fell off the gate that he had been swinging on, cut his knee deeply on a piece of rusty wire, and landed in a pile of horse manure. Sensibly, Douglas bound his pal's knee with a pocket handkerchief, and brought him straight back to the pharmacy for his father to attend to. Alec took him into the dispensing area, lifted him onto the bench top, and cleaned the gash carefully, first with water, and then put an excruciating slug of iodine into it. I remember seeing the tears falling silently out of Cecil's eyes, and onto his sailor suit. 'This is quite seriously cut laddie, 'said Alec. 'I doot yer Mammie will need to let the Doctor look to this.' He sent Sandy, now an apprentice in the pharmacy, hobbling home with Cecil, to make sure that Mrs Negus got Doctor Lawton to have a look at the leg right away.

Within just two days, Cecil became very ill. It started with a high temperature and sweating. He was too ill to be left, and Phemie and I took turns with Charles, Mary, Essie and Mrs Cox, to attend Cecil around the clock, sponging him down and spooning glucose water into his mouth. On the fifth day he developed a stiff neck which was quickly followed by facial spasms and great difficulty with swallowing. Doctor Lawton confirmed our worst fears when he said 'Cecil has Lockjaw.' The nursing of this beautiful boy was excruciating for his family and friends, as we watched the muscle spasms which often pulled his body into the shape of a bow string. We were all there, when at 2.00am Mr Negus went to fetch Dr Lawton out again. The Doctor said quietly, 'There is nothing more that I can do for Cecil except to give him another larger dose of morphia. Unquestionably, I can give him enough to relieve his spasms, but such a dose will shorten the very short time he has left.'

Charles said simply 'Give it.'

We left Charles and Mary holding their lad in their arms. The simple accident had caused their beautiful son to be dead within just nine days. We were all, especially Charles, very aware of the frailty of human life, particularly of children, but until that moment, it was something that happened to 'other people.'

Notes

Cecil Negus was a member of the author's family. He died in 1911, of Lockjaw.

of iodine into it. I remember seeing the tears falling silently out of Cecil's eyes, and onto his sailor suit. 'This is quite seriously cut laddie, 'said Alec. 'I doot yer Mammie will need to let the Doctor look to this.' He sent Sandy, now an apprentice in the pharmacy, hobbling home with Cecil, to make sure that Mrs Negus got Doctor Lawton to have a look at the leg right away.

Within just two days, Cecil became very ill. It started with a high temperature and sweating. He was too ill to be left, and Phemie and I took turns with Charles, Mary, Essie and Mrs Cox, to attend Cecil around the clock, sponging him down and spooning glucose water into his mouth. On the fifth day he developed a stiff neck which was quickly followed by facial spasms and great difficulty with swallowing. Doctor Lawton confirmed our worst fears when he said 'Cecil has Lockjaw.' The nursing of this beautiful boy was excruciating for his family and friends, as we watched the muscle spasms which often pulled his body into the shape of a bow string. We were all there, when at 2.00am Mr Negus went to fetch Dr Lawton out again. The Doctor said quietly, 'There is nothing more that I can do for Cecil except to give him another larger dose of morphia. Unquestionably, I can give him enough to relieve his spasms, but such a dose will shorten the very short time he has left.'

Charles said simply 'Give it.'

We left Charles and Mary holding their lad in their arms. The simple accident had caused their beautiful son to be dead within just nine days. We were all, especially Charles, very aware of the frailty of human life, particularly of children, but until that moment, it was something that happened to 'other people.'

Notes
Cecil Negus was a member of the author's family. He died in 1911, of Lockjaw.

JASON

Chapter Thirty Nine

I make no pretence of the fact that I was often in trouble for fighting. I couldn't tell my parents that my older brother Victor was always, always at the bottom of it, could I? He is my older brother, but out of the two of us, I was always physically the strongest. He had a rotten time of things with all the problems with his digestion. I used to call him Veg too, the taunting name the bullies gave him. When I was younger, I probably wasn't the only person who felt he might have been better if he'd at least eaten some meat. To be fair, he did try. Our grandmothers tried. Grandma Lovejoy cooked him meat, but as he was personally acquainted with the animals involved, it wasn't helpful. Great Grandma Teague minced meat up for him, and made shepherds' pies and cottage pies which he ate to try to please her, but generally he sicked it up again. Some days he went out to the privy time and time again, troubled with wind and diarrhoea. 'Hardly worth pulling my trousers back up', he'd comment to me. 'I'll only be back out there in another few minutes.'

However, as he grew up, left to himself to manage his 'ins and outs' he did appear to be a bit better. Eggs, cream and cheese did seem to suit him well, and he did fill out a bit, but it was not enough to appease the bullies, Peter Duffett, Will Hayden, Henry Godfrey and Theo May. Peter Duffett was always the ringleader. They would isolate us from our school friends, or lie in wait to catch just the two of us. They would begin by pushing and shoving Victor and then start hitting him. Hugh, Jock and I always stood up for him. We could always manage without fighting if Hugh and Jock were there. Strength is in numbers and fitness and all that. One day, it was just Veg and me. Peter, Will, Henry and Theo plus two of their cronies had stalked us. We were cornered in Bowling Green Alley. We just had to fight. Once again, they punched Victor a bit in order to get me going. It was me they wanted to fight with, as I was strong and fearless. I fought well, and to be honest, I enjoyed it. I gave one of them a split lip, and another a nosebleed. Edward was very sympathetic when we got back to the Poop Deck, and he helped us to clean ourselves up before our parents got home.

After that fight, I became even more of a target. Finally, I appeared home with a black eye one day and our father got very, very cross, shouting so hard that he was spitting. 'Don't you realize my son, just what fighting like this can lead to? Why can't you act like a civilized person? You could land up in court. Believe me, I know. I was a complete idiot when I was young. You simply cannot believe the troubles I got myself into. Sort yourself out.'

The bullying of Victor and my fighting to protect him increased after Hugh and Jock went to Dollar Academy in Scotland. I had no strong, close allies watching my back any more. One evening, when I was set on again, I was too frightened to go home, for fear of my father. I tapped on the back door of Mr Ross's Pharmacy. I was filthy and dripping blood from grazes and small cuts. Mrs Ross fetched me in, sat me by the fire and poured me a cup of tea from the teapot stewing on the hob. When she and Mr Ross asked what was wrong, I told the truth 'a gang of older boys set on me. I'm worried about going back home in such a mess, as my mother will take a fright, and my father will get angry with me for fighting again. It's really not my fault.'

Mrs Ross got me to strip off my outer clothes, and set to work sponging and brushing them off with a moistened cloth and a nailbrush. Mr Ross took me into the dispensary, and sat me up on the work bench, so that he could clean my grazes, and put some Witch Hazel compresses on my bruises. He spoke to me so kindly.

'I have watched your difficulties laddie, and I understand how these boys are using Victor to taunt you. Your parents just love you. There is no need to fear them. As my friend, your father has often discussed his own early difficulties with me, and it is because he cares, that he is so severe with you. Shall we walk back to the Poop Deck together? If I am with you, doubtless your father will be calmer, and listen more carefully to what you have to say.'

We walked home together. Mr Ross's gentle influence enabled my father finally to speak to me as if I was a grown man.

We agreed that I would 'train' at the gymnasium in Mount Road two evenings a week so that my healthy body would become even fitter, and my muscles better developed. Additionally, I would spend another two sessions a week with John Scutt, a well regarded local boxer who had his own training gym at the back of Hill and Malden's granary on the quay. Hopefully, the troublemakers would leave me alone then. I would certainly be off the streets, doing so much exercise. I would learn to keep my temper, and fight well only under controlled conditions, within a framework of rules.

The plan worked well, in time. Mr Scutt liked me, and we were seen together every morning about the town, running, and the same again most evenings. I learned to box well, and by the time I was sixteen, I was an experienced amateur boxer, and had done well in locally staged contests. The gymnasium improved my personal strength, and I was eating well and growing stronger by the day. When I left the Technical and Commercial School, rather than going into business with my father at this stage, I chose to work in our fishing boat, the Artemis. Caleb was getting old, and Mathew and Sean were in their middle years, and I felt that my physical strength could be developed and used to the good in the boat. However, I did continue to box as an amateur, often travelling around the county and into Hampshire and Wiltshire for bouts.

Regarding Victor, as Grandma Lovejoy was now in her seventies, he had moved into Blake Hill farm with her, and was helping her to run the place. Jeremiah had died, and on his own, Piglet was little use. Victor and Grandma Lovejoy had decided to employ a married couple to help them out with all the work. Thus my defence of Victor was no longer required. We had both relegated the memories of these troubles to the dim and distant past. Victor worked very hard physically, and grew well and strong. He and Grandma Lovejoy had a few cows, and were building up the dairy business. Blake Hill seemed to bring out the reflective side of his nature, and he read a lot, and started writing poetry.

1911 was an appalling year for our friends, the Negus family. It started with the loss of Cecil in January, Mr and Mrs Negus's youngest son. Mrs Negus cried a real lot, and my mother and Mrs Ross spent a lot of time with her, listening, and passing clean handkerchiefs over. After a few weeks, most of the crying was out of her, and they took her out walking, and encouraged her to visit them at home. They became an even closer trio. Mrs Ross's mother, Mrs Maude wrote and invited her to Scotland, for a break, and she surprised us all by accepting. Mrs Cox, despite Cotton's increasing breathlessness and ill health took charge in her absence. I think Mr Negus suffered differently. The gossips in the town said that he had grown cold and hard, but to my mind, he was merely sad. Regarding his council responsibilities, he became so obsessed with his duties that I heard my mother saying that he had become positively Aldermanic.

I spent any spare time that I could at the Negus's home, as I had become infatuated with Essie (Esther), who was close to my own age. It's true to say that I had never met a more beautiful person in all my life thus far. Her looks were breathtaking. We had grown up together and played together, but it was during the Negus family bereavement that I really noticed her as a young woman. From the nets of the Artemis, I extracted the choicest fish to bring to them, and I happily fulfilled any little tasks around the Negus home or workshop. In time, Mr Negus's sense of humour began to slowly return. One day he came in for his evening meal, reporting the death of Gabriel Paddock, who was well known in the town to be a professed atheist. Over the dining table, he suggested a suitable epitaph:

'Here lies Gabriel Paddock
Atheist, all dressed up with nowhere to go'.

We were so glad that he was feeling better. This was further evident a couple of weeks later when he announced with undisguised relish the death of Bernard Biles, elder brother of Essie's detested former teacher, Amelia Biles. Mr Biles was in fact a competitor in the joinery and undertaking business. Of Mr Biles, he said 'The excellent Mr Biles died and went to Heaven early this morning. When he got there, he saw thousands of people ahead of him waiting to get through the pearly gates. Apparently there had been a long delay, which stretched into the afternoon. Saint Peter was heavily occupied with some paperwork. All the people in front of him in the queue were astounded when Saint Peter left the gates and walked down the queue to greet Mr Biles personally. 'What makes me so special?' asked Mr Biles. 'Well', said Saint Peter, 'I've looked at all the funeral bills you've ever sent out. I've added up all the hours of your time that you've spent caring for the bodies of our dear departed, and by my calculations, you must be 185 years old! You deserve a special greeting.'

Caleb often took the Artemis fishing in the region of St Aldhelm's Head. On top of the cliff they call St Aldhelm's there is an old, neglected ruin. Caleb and I climbed up there one fine day. The headland commands a spectacular view, and on the sea, you can see the Portland tidal race. Apart from the coastguard station nearby, it is a wild and desolate place. It is no wonder that on these rocky shores many sailors have been washed up dead, their bones lying bleaching on the rocks below. Caleb told me that in early times a lone priest lived in the chapel, whose work was to pray for the seamen distressed and tossed in the terrible storms from the south west that prevail in this region. He got quite carried away, as he said' many a midnight prayer has been offered up in this lonely chapel, with only it's glimmering lamp to tell the storm tossed seamen that there was sympathy for them in one human breast at least. They would know that one holy man was pleading for them at the footstool of divine mercy.' Well, those days are long past. Inside the chapel there was nothing but tools used by the coastguard. After a short reflection, Caleb remembered an old poem about the place:

'High on the top of bluff St Aldhelm's Head,
Round which the seaman oft delights to soar
At once a landmark and the sailor's dread
For at its base the foaming breakers roar,
Where many souls have sunk to rise no more,
A ruin stands- lonely and bleak and bare.

Upreared 'tis said by holy hands of yore,
For oft times, in the cold dark midnight there,
A solitary man was seen engaged in prayer.'

Caleb was a confident sailor, renowned locally for taking our boat out in questionable weather. We fishermen always looked out for other local boats, and gave help as needed. On the day of the Artemis's most dramatic rescue, we were out in quite bad weather, just off St Aldhelm's Head. Visibility was becoming poor, the tide was turning, and we were hurrying to pull up our nets. We had obtained a reasonable catch in difficult conditions. There was a crash of thunder, a flash, and we saw a ball of lightening explode on the small herring trawler, the Jolliffe, behind us. The tide was racing, pulling us away from the Jolliffe. Two of our men got the sails down, whilst Caleb and I, quickly helped by the others, took up our oars, to try to pull back to the Jolliffe, which was blazing. I put a line round my waist and jumped into the water to save two of Jolliffe's men who were in the water. We were able to get them all back to the quay alive. It was a good day's work, all the men were saved, but sadly the Jolliffe and her catch were lost.

In the October of 1911, I was invited by the Cox, Richard Wills, to join the crew of the Poole Lifeboat, the Hamar. My father said he was very proud. Up until then I had been a reserve member. The crew were all experienced fishermen like me. I think they fancied having me aboard because of my physical strength as an oarsman and my swimming abilities. I had gained a little local fame by twice diving off the quay to rescue men who had toppled into the water. There was nothing brave about the rescue of course. The brave part was entering the stinking, filthy water. I survived, as did one of the men I rescued.

References

The description and poem on St Aldhelm's Chapel were taken from The East Dorset Herald, April 1911.

Chapter Forty

On the night of November the eleventh 1911, I went out for my first rescue with the Hamar and her crew in a heavy gale. Distress signals had been heard by the coastguard station at the Haven, coming from the direction of Studland Bay. The Norwegian brig Solertia with a cargo of Russian timber headed for Poole was stranded, and was bumping heavily on the bottom. Her main mast, jerked out of its 'partners' was lying over the side. The seas were breaking over her, and her decks were underwater. It took us five hours to rescue the crew of eight and the Customs Officer who had been aboard when the emergency occurred. The rescued and the rescuers were finally back on Poole Quay at 9.00am.

I was out on the Hamar again on January 12th, 1912. Both the Swanage and Poole lifeboats were called out. The wind was blowing against the tides, and we would have been hard put to it to row out from the lifeboat station in the harbour. Fortunately, the local paddle steamer tug Telegraph, was able to tow us out of the harbour to the bar on the Hook sands. Meantime, unknown to us, the Swanage lifeboat, caught on the Old Harry Ledge in monstrous seas was swept over and broached to. She righted herself, and most of her crew, clinging to their lifelines were able to avoid being swept out of her. The Swanage coxswain William Brown and Thomas Marsh a crewman were left in the sea. Marsh was close to the boat and his mates quickly seized and hauled him aboard, but despite a frantic struggle, the Swanage crew were unable to reach their Cox, as in the struggle, some of their gear and oars had been lost. They raised sail to search for Cox Brown, but discovered that the mainmast had been sprung and they could not risk sailing. Using the few oars they had left, the boat could make no headway, so the search and rescue were abandoned, and they made their way back to Swanage with great difficulty.

Meanwhile, the Hamar was approaching the Hook sandbar and Cox Wills asked for the rope to the Telegraph to be slipped so that we could row close to the barque 'Brilliant.' The conditions were too bad for us to tie the lifeboat alongside, and each man had to be taken off during many perilous fresh approaches. The ship's boy broke a leg whilst entangled in a rope, but one of our men, Jonney Mathews, quickly cut the rope and prevented the lad's leg from being torn off. Captain Bjercke the Norwegian skipper (who had broken a rib earlier on, when he was thrown down on the deck in the violence of the storm), lost his grip on the rescue rope and fell into the sea but was quickly recovered and pulled into the Hamar. Eventually the whole crew of ten men were back in the Hamar, and the Telegraph tug passed a line to tow us into Poole. We were all totally exhausted. There was such a blinding snowstorm that in the lifeboat, we took what comfort we could under sails folded over to make a temporary shelter.

I started to see more of Victor in the later part of 1911, as he had taken up singing in Poole town with some friends of his, John Barringer, who was blind, and played the piano exceedingly well and William Rose a ladies' and gentlemen's hairdresser, Frank Travers the photographer and Claude Wareham who worked at a drapers'. They played and sang together at a lot of small evening parties. As Victor explained, it helped John Barringer to make a little income for himself. However, Caleb remarked to me one day 'I don't like the cut of that Frank Travers' jib.' I began to take more notice of what my brother was getting up to in the evenings. He had developed a very fanciful way of dressing, allowing his hair to flow in long fair ringlets. One night a street urchin was following him, shouting 'Oh my golly, Miss Molly!

By early 1912, concerns had clearly reached my father's ears, and he arranged for us to go out fishing together one evening, as a trio. We were sitting in our little bobbing craft, just off Brownsea Island, catching plaice and mullet on our lines. 'I'm very worried about Edward' he said.

'How so?' we asked.

There was a pause. 'Weeell', he continued, 'You must have noticed he likes to keep company with other men?'

'Yees,' we said, wondering what would follow.

'My father, old Captain James Lovejoy knew what some men got up to together at sea.'

'Yees'.

'So long as they were very discreet, he never interfered, and when I had charge of the Watch, I ignored it too. As far as Edward is concerned, I still ignore it. I've often thought to myself, that if he hadn't been such an unusually soft person, he would never have made such an excellent steward both at sea and on shore. However, on shore he runs the risk of arrest and prison if he is caught in the arms of another man. Do you think he understands that,' he asked, looking straight at Victor, who looked away quickly.

Trouble for our family followed almost immediately after this conversation. Peter Duffett, Will Hayden, Henry Godfrey and Theo May turned up in our lives again. They were well known local varmints, who had progressively drifted into local petty crime. It was well known that they had been at the Poole Police Court on numerous occasions for such offences as theft of fowls, drunk and disorderly and breaking and entering. George Brown, the Police Superintendant had told Father that they were all on the 'Black List' kept at the Police Station. Unfortunately, Peter Duffett had a bit of a brain on him, and was beginning to use it. He was known to be involved in a lot of illegal gambling activities in the town, but so far had not been caught. He and his cronies had taken to knocking Victor and his friends about a bit. It was all low level nuisance as far as Victor was concerned, and he said that neither he nor his rather 'soft' friends wished me to be involved.

Unfortunately, I was quickly and seriously involved. One evening, I was seized by the criminal quartet in Ball Lane, just off the quay, and very close to the Poop Deck. A filthy sack was put over my head, and I was roped. I guessed it was them, but there was nothing I could do. I was hustled over to Baiter. When they took the sack off my head, a large crowd was assembled around me, consisting of some of the worst type of men you can imagine. There were sailors of many nationalities, habitual drunkards probably from all the local towns and villages around and gamblers.

There were men with fighting dogs on leads, and fixers of illegal fights who had made unfruitful approaches to me in the past.

Duffett pointed to Victor, who had clearly been seriously beaten, being held by two large men. I was taken to a rough, roped area where I was expected to fight. If I refused, it was clear that Victor was going to suffer some more. I didn't fancy my chances either. If by some fluke I won, my only prize would be staying alive. My opponent was brought into the ring. Evidently this was going to be a bare knuckled fight, with no rules at all. I considered myself to be an exceptionally well built, strong man. I boxed at around twelve stones. However, my opponent, who it seems, was known as 'Cruncher', was only a tiny bit smaller than Caleb Stone, the biggest, strongest man I have ever met in my life. My father always described Caleb as an obelisk. I was terrified. If I got into any clinches with this tall, strong man, I knew he could throw me around until he broke me, or he could overpower me and pound my liver and kidneys to jelly. I was seriously afraid. I tried to remember the excellent training John Scutt had given me. I tried to pull together a few ideas for a strategy. It was clear that I would be faster on my feet, and could dodge and weave my way around this 'Cruncher', but this would not be enough. I was a boxer, but this man knew no rules, and was probably more of a wrestler. I stripped to the waist and rolled the top of my trousers down a bit. I tried to make it obvious how very, very frightened I was. A bell clattered, and I was shoved into the makeshift ring, almost losing my balance. The crowds were roaring. I danced round this 'Cruncher' on my toes. He looked bemused, and shouted 'You can't hit me in twenty years!' and kept trying to catch me with his huge hands, bent on throwing me around a bit to please the crowd. I got a few small jabs on to his chin with my right hand, and noticed that he was not rolling with the punches, but absorbing them fully. The man was no boxer. Quick as a flash, I landed a massive upper cut on his jaw with my left hand. I thought I must have broken my hand in several places. He tottered, and lost his balance completely, crashing to the ground heavily. It was such a blow that I thought his brain must have been shaken from its moorings and crashed against the top of his skull. He seemed to be out cold. Peter Duffett jumped into the ring, and tried to wake him up. I thought immediately 'I have killed him.' I was not wrong. The crowd were angry, as not only was money at stake; they had not had any of the entertainment they were expecting to get.

A police whistle was heard close by, and two policemen from the Market Street station ran up, truncheons drawn and arrested me. I was handcuffed. Someone had clouted Victor before dashing off and he was lying on the ground, semiconscious. A doctor was fetched quickly, and 'Cruncher' whoever he really was, confirmed dead at the scene. I vomited on the spot. Victor was taken back to the Poop Deck on a stretcher, to be cared for at home. I was taken to the Police Station in Market Street and locked up. I was very, very cold and couldn't stop shaking. Peter Duffett had been arrested too, and was in the cell next door. I lay sleepless on the plank bed in that brown tiled cell all night, thinking of how I had broken God's holy commandment 'Thou shalt not kill.' I was a murderer. I expected the full might of the law to crash down on me. I was certain that I would be made to pay for this with my life.

In the morning, my father visited with the Superintendant's permission. He brought with him Samuel Foster, a youngish, slightly balding man, thin and with a pronounced stoop, whom I knew to be an Elder in the High Street Methodist Church. I did not know until then that he was a solicitor. I was to appear in the Police Court shortly, where I would be charged with Manslaughter.

At the Police Court, Constable 46H stated 'I apprehended the prisoner last night. I told him that I was arresting him under suspicion of killing Frank Joy, known as 'Cruncher.'

I replied 'Poor man. I am sorry.'

I was remanded in custody for a week, pending the results of the post-mortem.

On the Wednesday Samuel Foster and Father visited again. Apparently the Coroner's findings were that 'the deceased had suffered a fractured jaw and brain haemorrhage. Death had quickly followed from pressure of blood on the brain causing heart failure.'

On the Thursday I was summoned back to the Police Court. I was formally charged with manslaughter. Bail was refused as I was 'well known in the town for fighting' and there was concern that I might threaten the witnesses. Mr Foster had entered a plea of 'not guilty'. My case was to be adjourned until my appearance at the County Assize court in Dorchester. Mr Foster told me that it was believed that one of Peter Duffett's associates, Theo May, had already made a complete statement to Sergeant Waterman regarding the circumstances surrounding my arrest. Mr Foster and my father were hoping to engage a good 'Silk' to represent me at the Assizes. He advised me to keep as calm as I could, and to keep my strength up. For such a weedy man, he had a discreetly powerful presence. Taking my father's hand, and mine in his own, he made a short extempory prayer to Almighty God, committing the three of us to His charge. He left me with my father.

References

The rescues described in this section of the book (apart from the St Aldhelm's Head rescue) were taken directly from Hawkes A., 1995. Lifeboat men never turn back. Poole Historical Trust, P.24. The dates of the rescues and the name of the lifeboat have been changed to place both incidents in 1911/12.

Chapter Forty One

I passed through a very sad and bitter time. I supposed that all prisons are evil places, and that consequently Dorchester was no different from other prisons. I came from a family of reasonable means and in good standing in Poole, and found myself among the poorest and meanest of society. The food, which appeared regularly, and was thus a blessing to many of my fellow inmates, was grey and dreary in texture, taste and smell. I grew thinner. The prison and the society it housed stank. I had no choice but to bear it. No overt aggression was shown to me by my fellow prisoners or warders. My reputation for having killed a man with a single punch went before me. There were people in there who knew Frank Joy (what a misnomer!), my victim, and were determined to make me suffer for what I had done to their friend. I started to get very suspicious of the contents of my meals and the mugs of tea served to me. I felt completely desperate about my future.

On the other hand, I was blessed to have letters from my dear mother, brother, Mr and Mrs Ross and Hugh and Jock. Cox Wills appeared one visiting day, to my great surprise. He told me that he brought with him the very best wishes of all the lifeboat crew and from the Artemis. I was so touched, that I broke down in tears. He told me that he was doing all that he could for me. Prior to my appearance before the Assize Court, my father came to visit me twice with Mr Foster. They had carefully pieced together the sequence of events that had led to the fight. Mr Foster promised that he would make sure that my counsel brought out all the circumstances of my case in court. On the second visit they were accompanied by Mr York QC, who was to represent me the following week.

I was charged at Dorchester Court with causing grievous bodily harm and death to Frank Joy. The Prosecution Counsel laid out a simple case for the charge, mentioning my previous 'bad character.'

When he took his turn, Mr York called two witnesses to the fight who had seen Victor being held captive and being beaten in front of me to goad me into the fight. He called two character witnesses. Cox Wills from the Poole Lifeboat cited the occasions when he had seen me fully commit myself to saving the lives of others. The other witness was John Scutt, who on questioning was able to relate the circumstances of my father engaging him to teach me to box. He described me as good tempered, and a 'gentleman in the boxing ring.' It took only four days for the evidence for the prosecution and defence to be heard. I could see my family sitting white faced in the gallery. The crew of the Artemis was there too. My mother looked frankly ill, and often held a handkerchief to her mouth as if she was nauseated.

In his summing up for the jury, Judge Bentley stated 'it is clear from the evidence offered, that the defendant and his brother have suffered for years at the hands of openly aggressive elements in the town of Poole. The defendant is from a reputable family, and has devoted himself to the preservation of life. There is an enormous partition between a glove fight under rules and a prize fight for money when the opponents are ill matched and the smaller one under intolerable duress'. He went on to say that 'On the night in question, two lives were obviously at stake, those of Victor and Jason Lovejoy. Frank Joy was the tool of gambling men, who were prepared to profit by the prize fight. Regrettably it was Mr Joy who lost his life. It is unfortunate that those persons responsible for arranging the fight are not in the dock today.' The Jury departed, and I was taken down to the cells to await my fate.

I was found 'Not Guilty', and released to my family and friends. I had been locked up for five months. I had no strength left in me. I had killed a man. I knew that I would never put on my boxing gloves again. I went home with my family so that we could begin to repair our lives together. I took a month, not really doing anything much. The tasty fish from the nets of the Artemis helped to rebuild my strength. Victor, who had made a quick and complete recovery, regularly appeared with the tastiest treats from Blake Hill.

No demands were made upon me. By the end of the month, having gained some weight and appetite for life, I was back on the Artemis again regularly. Cox Wills said he was anxious to get me back on the lifeboat crew as soon as possible, but suggested another couple of months 'rest', to build myself up with plenty of work on the oars. It was a good decision on his part. My left hand had recovered from its killer blow to Frank Joy's chin, but remained stiff and ached a lot. I went to the gymnasium regularly and exercised that hand in every way I could. Indian club exercises and press ups were particularly helpful. I ran around town and up to Blake Hill and back when I had time.

Just after I had gone back on to the lifeboat crew again, Victor got into trouble. He had been continuing to socialize with Barringer, Wareham, Rose and Travers. Victor's long, fair ringlets were frequently washed and dressed in William Rose's hairdressing establishment. Victor did not appear to have any female attachments, and his confidante was Claude Wareham, a very personable young man. Mother and Mrs Negus kept encouraging him to meet Helen (Nellie) Negus, but it was wasted effort. My brother had a busy work and social life, and this did not include Nellie. We loved Victor and liked his friends who were very pleasant, and often called at the Poop Deck. Indeed, William Rose cut all our hair, and mother was exceptionally impressed with him. It was just that we could all see that Victor was sailing against the tide.

I did not think that anything could be worse than 1911, when the Neguses lost Cecil, and I killed Frank Joy. 1912 came a close second. Peter Duffett and Will Hayden were back in town, having served short sentences for falsely imprisoning and assaulting Victor. They obviously felt that they had a score to settle with Victor. They left me alone. I had killed a man with a punch. They were very afraid of me. They didn't do anything overt to Victor. I just had a horrible feeling that they were watching, waiting for an opportunity.

The chance to cause trouble fell into their hands in the October. It was a Friday, and Victor had been drinking at the Angel

Inn, Market Street, with Claude. They were observed by Duffett, Hayden and their detestable friends to be heading into Hunger Hill Graveyard. One of their number, Sidney Davis, ran to the nearby Police Station to inform the sergeant that a crime was about to take place in Hunger Hill graveyard. Constable Barnes ran with Sid Davis to the graveyard. There he saw Claude Wareham with the fly front of his trousers open 'and his member in his hand' and my brother with his trousers round his ankles, half lying, face down across a raised tomb. Both were instantly arrested on a charge of gross indecency. On receiving the news, my parents and I were distraught. Father immediately contacted Mr Foster to appear for Victor in the Police Court the following morning.

Evidence was presented against Victor and Claude by Police Constable 12 Herbert Barnes who said he had apprehended the pair for an act of gross indecency in a public place. They were represented by Mr Foster who entered pleas of 'not guilty' for them both. They were remanded in custody to appear at the Quarter Sessions in Dorchester. Bail was refused because of the gravity of the charge.

I took my parents home, and Mr Negus came and sat with us during the afternoon. He was rather used to being with distraught people I suppose. He was very supportive. We poured out our fears into his sympathetic ears. Both men would be at serious risk from the general prison population due to their gentle temperaments. Victor's health was likely to be very seriously compromised by the prison conditions and food. I feared for his life. My physical strength had carried me through my ordeal. I had doubts about his. My poor, poor mother would have to go through the ordeal of having a second son in prison. In the evening, Edward who was looking extremely pale and shaky himself, showed Mr Foster in. Mr Foster was, surprisingly under the circumstances, quite positive. Victor and Claude would appear before the Circuit Judge in Dorchester in a month's time. Meantime, he would do a personal investigation into the circumstances around the case to see if he could find some evidence for the defence. I did not feel particularly cheery as I couldn't see what kind of a defence could be presented.

I went with my parents to the trial at Dorchester. Mr Foster had revealed none of his possible strategies for the defence. Once again, a 'Silk' had been brought in from London, a Mr Lindley. Mr Foster and Mr Lindley had only spoken to Victor privately, as they wished no details of the defence strategy to leak out to the prosecution prior to the trial. We visited Victor before the trial, and although he had suffered bodily from the lack of fresh air and the appalling food, he showed neither fear nor depression. On the day, Victor and Claude were put up together in the dock. Both men looked physically frail. Victor's curls had been shaven away on his admission to prison, and his head, close shaved looked bony.

The charges were read out. The prosecution presented their case as given. It looked 'open and shut.' Mr Lindley, a stooped elderly gentleman summoned his witness for cross examination. It was Poole Police Constable 12 Herbert Barnes. He was asked how the constable was able to judge that an act of gross indecency was about to take place. He repeated exactly what he had seen on the night.

Mr Lindley called old Doctor Mullins. He had brought Victor's medical notes with him to show the jury, and on questioning stated that since he was a tiny baby Victor had suffered from a disorder of the bowels. This was often accompanied by extreme abdominal pain and diarrhoea. The condition had not fully resolved itself in adulthood. He was asked 'might the pain be suddenly be so intense that a spasm could cause Mr Lovejoy to lean across a tombstone, seeking relief for his abdominal muscles?' Doctor Mullins gave a firm 'yes.' The final witness was quite a surprise. It was Mr Alec Ross from the Pharmacy. He was sworn in: 'I **Albert Ross** do solemnly swear....' There was uproar in the court from Peter Duffet, Will Hayden and their cronies. '**Albatross!** They brought an albatross for their defence!!!' The Judge pounded with his gavel. 'Silence in court, silence in court! Take care or I will have you in custody for contempt.' Mr Ross gave corroborating evidence in terms of supplying Victor with medicines for his digestion regularly throughout the years. In his summing up, the Judge made some very acid remarks about the desecration of the graveyard in terms of its use as a privy, which constituted extremely poor behaviour by the defendants. However, Victor and Claude were found 'not guilty' as charged, and were released.

Victor told me later, that Father had been very angry with him about his 'degenerate behaviour', and there being no possibilities of getting off 'Scott free' ever again in the event of being caught with his pants down in the company of another man. Mr Gulliver the Draper had immediately dismissed Claude on his arrest. Nellie Negus was happy to step into the vacant situation. On Claude's return to Poole, he was obliged to lodge with his sister, as he was without an income. He immediately sought work out of town, and found himself a position in Mr Joy's shopping arcade in Westbourne, at a gentleman's outfitters. He and Victor went about their lives chastened. My brother was very fortunate in being able to return home to the relative obscurity of Blake Hill Farm.

Chapter Forty Two

On his return home to Poole, it was evident that Mr Alec Ross had felt very embarrassed about the revelation of his true Christian name in public, particularly in front of the handful of the ne'er do wells of the town who had been present in the court. He was preparing for a lot of unpleasant name calling. In our absence in Dorchester, a magnificent new signboard had been erected above his pharmacy windows. He had ordered it as soon as he knew that he would be appearing as a witness for the defence. The timberwork had been constructed in Mr Negus's workshop, and the sign writer had worked there in privacy during the evenings. The previous signboard had said 'A.Ross Pharmacist'. The new board had gold letters set on a black background, and read 'The Albatross Pharmacy.' His friend next door at the Minerva Printworks had printed new labels for all the pharmacy products and for the medicines and pill boxes. As he laughed with everyone in the town about his name, his popularity increased as did the number of his regular customers. The pharmacy became known in the town simply as 'The Albatross.'

1913 wore on. Internationally militarism was increasing. As early as 1906 our government were building 'Dreadnaught' battleships to ensure Britain's mastery of the seas. The Germans were retaliating by building their own mighty battleships. Already, a quarter of British taxation was being spent on building up the navy. There were troubles between the Austro-Hungarian Empire and Serbia, but fortunately these problems were far away, and did not concern us. A great European war was being seriously discussed, and it was generally thought that the flash point would occur between Germany and Russia. Domestically, the campaign for women's suffrage was gaining strength. The Church of England was supporting the women's cause through the Church League for Women's Suffrage, although they deplored the violence of some of the methods used by the militant wing of the women's suffrage movement. In June Emily-Wilding Davison had thrown herself under the King's horse Anmer, and was killed. Other militant suffragettes were attacking private property by arson. Apparently illuminated addresses and medals for valour were being awarded to women by the militant organization for enduring a long periods of starvation and privation in prison for the cause of votes for women. The government of the day launched a legal attack against 'The Suffragette' journal. The emerging Labour Party contended that no government had the right to interfere with the press. Of course, the forces of law and order can seize papers containing offensive material and punish the publisher. However, no government has the right to suppress a newspaper just because it advocates politically unpleasant opinions. In the end, Ramsay Macdonald took over as editor of 'The Suffragette', stating that the Labour party had no sympathy for militant action, so no further incitements to violence or condoning of crime would be printed. In Poole, my mother, Essie Negus, Phemie Ross (now the first woman Guardian of the Poor for the Poole Union Workhouse) and her daughters Agnes and Morag were generally dressed in purple, white and green, the colours of the Suffrage movement.

Nationally the Labour movement was also gaining strength. In the small area of Poole, families were often living crammed into tiny rooms, down alleys so narrow that two people could hardly pass each other. Our skilled workmen were fortunate if they could take home between fifteen shillings and a pound a week. Health amongst the poorest working men, particularly those who worked in the foundry and the potteries was particularly bad. Many of them suffered from chest diseases. Five miles away in happy, pleasure loving Bournemouth, hundreds of people whiled away their time on its glorious beaches. There was no thought for the poor workmen sweating to make the ornamental tiles to decorate the fire places of their middle class homes or those who sacrificed their own health to make the health saving drain pipes for the big cities. The working class wanted change, and the Labour movement was growing.

The year was drawing to a close when at The Albatross, news was received by Phemie Ross that her mother, Mrs Maude had 'taken a slight shock' which in English translates to a slight stroke. Letters were being exchanged rapidly between Mrs Ross and her sister Isa. Isa had enrolled a few years earlier at Miss Catherine Forrester-Paton's non-denominational Missionary Training Home in Glasgow to become a missionary nurse. Isa was in fact now working in the East End of Glasgow, having 'gone out in faith' to do what she could for the desperately poor. She was massively overworked, and lived a plain life of service and prayer. She was not in a position to take her mother in. Hugh and Jock Ross had both settled in Scotland following their education at Dollar Academy and Edinburgh University at Mr Ross's mother's expense. As Christmas drew near, Victor and I were looking forward to meeting these old friends again. They were bringing Mrs Maude with them on the train, to spend her remaining years in the milder climate of Poole with her family at the Albatross.

Poole was getting ready for Christmas. Chickens, rabbits and pigeons were all hanging from hooks outside the butchers' shops to keep cool and grow tender, dripping blood spots onto the pavement. Young lads on butchers', grocers' and greengrocers' bicycles were racing around the town making household deliveries. Hawkers were selling holly and mistletoe. Women were putting the final stitches into new shirts for their men, finishing off the toes of new socks and pressing the new dresses they had made for their children. Children laboured over fine stitches for needle cases and nightdress cases. Unprepared people like me were buying pipe tobacco for father, Black Cat cigarettes for my brother and Parkstone Perfume for mother. Fathers were waiting for their children to go to bed so that they could make the final bits of the promised doll's house or wooden engine.

The day before Christmas, Victor and Agnes, Morag, Hugh, Jock I were lounging about in the upstairs parlour at the Albatross Pharmacy. Jock, now twenty six, was telling us about Alloa, where he worked as an English teacher at the local academy. Hugh was twenty eight, and having just finished his engagement with the Lovat Scouts was staying temporarily at the same 'digs' as Jock.

He was hoping to sign up with the Fourth Division of the Seaforth Highlanders in the New Year. His twin passions were the outdoors and playing the bagpipes. He had brought the pipes with him. Jock's main enthusiasm was painting, which he funded from his teaching. On their way back to Poole he, Hugh and Mrs Maude had overnighted in London to give Mrs Maude a rest and him the opportunity to visit the Omega Workshops in Bloomsbury. He had met with Roger Fry, Omega's founder, the British artist who had coined the term 'Post Impressionism' to describe the work of more recent French artists.

The conversation finally moved to the recent horrible experiences Victor and I had suffered. We told them the story of the Pharmacy's new name, and we all fell about with hearty laughter. The bad times seemed long gone. Hugh said there'd always been something strange about his father. We all started telling tales about Mr Ross's eccentricities, and laughed about some of the particularly entertaining ones. We were all impressed at how Mrs Ross always covered up for him so efficiently, and agreed that during recent years he had calmed down a lot. Trying to make light of my own recent personal problems, I concluded by saying that sadly that Essie Negus had lost interest in me. She was frustrated that her father was not allowing her to train for a 'proper profession.' He was going around the town saying that she was giving him 'earache' by asking day and night if she could train to be a nurse. We all laughed. 'She should get married' I said. I felt rather hurt. Obviously my fishy gifts had meant little to her.

Victor and I told our friends the rest of the news in town. Grandfather Teague had died recently, following a prolonged illness which had turned out to be cancer of the stomach. Mrs Teague was lightly supervising Wesley Taylor who now ran the business, much as it had always been. He and 'Mrs Wesley' and their new baby lived upstairs with Mrs Teague, 'as family'. Always a cheerful man, Wesley was now positively euphoric in his changed circumstances. Caleb rarely went out with the Artemis now, as his eyesight was getting poor, but his shipmates were making sure that he lacked for nothing. Our own dear Mistress Caroline remained strong and healthy for her age, but was leaving a lot of the management of Blake Hill to Victor.

We were interrupted in our boisterous story telling by Mrs Ross, who came upstairs with an invitation to the Ross and Lovejoy Families which had been hand delivered by Mr Negus. Victor had to read it out, as living with Mistress Caroline, he could manage the dialect:

> Come down tomorrow night; and mind
> Don't leave thy fiddle bag behind;
> We'll sheake a lag, an' drink a cup
> O'eale (or tea), to keep wold Chris'mas up.
>
> We got a back-bran, dree girt logs
> So much as dree ov us can car;
> We'll put 'em up athirt the dogs
> An meake a vier to the bar.
>
> An' ev'ry woone shall tell his teale,
> An' ev'ry wone shall zing his zong,
> An' ev'ry woone wull drink his eale (or tea)
> To love an' frien'ship all night long.
>
> We'll snap the tongs, we'll have a ball,
> We'll shake the house, we'll lift the ruf,
> We'll romp an' meake the maidens squall,
> A' catchen o'm at blind-man's buff.
>
> Zoo come to-morrow night; an' mind,
> Don't leave thy fiddle-bag behind;
> We'll sheake a lag, an' drink a cup
> O'eale (or tea), to keep wold Chris'mas up.

We enjoyed a wonderful Christmas celebration together. Mr Negus had cleared out his workshop as far as possible to accommodate his many guests. A couple of old threadbare and moth-eaten carpets had been spread across the floor. With the help of his men, he had moved the piano in, and we had music and singing from all the guests. The bagpipe and fiddle playing by Hugh and Jock was impressive. Some really stupid jokes were cracked. Jock, who rather fancied Essie asked her 'Why is a young lady like a violin?' When he gave her the answer 'because she is often touched by her beau' she went scarlet, and looked as if she would like to hit him. Of course, we all laughed. She stalked off, but a little later returned, and asked Victor and me 'Why are fishermen and shepherds like beggars?' We hadn't a clue of course. The answer was 'Because they live by hook or by crook.'

There were some very good parlour games. Essie obtained the best and final laugh of the evening over Jock. She persuaded Mr Ross to introduce a new parlour game called 'The Queen of Sheba.' One of the girls present would sit on Mr Negus's special chair as The Queen. The young men, all blindfolded, would be allowed one at a time, to kiss her. The Queen would submit to this, they were told, provided that the gentlemen were blindfolded. Jock took first go, having been unreliably informed by a 'friend' that the first Queen would be Essie. He was led up to The Queen. To his surprise, he felt under his lips the bushy moustache and whiskers of Mr Ross, who had silently changed places with The Queen! His expression of disgust as he tore off his mask was a sight to behold. We all fell about the place laughing. It was a raucous end to a very fine Christmas party. Victor and I walked back to the Poop Deck together, wondering what 1914 would bring for us, our families and our town.

References

Poole and Dorset Herald, Christmas 1913